☑ **W9-CNW-289**

Praise for *Good Boys and Dead Girls*

"A first-rate mind grappling in intriguing ways with important issues . . . [Gordon's] forte is to pinpoint precisely what it is that gives a book or a body of work its particular strength."
— Dan Cryer, *Newsday*

"She has the kind of lively, scrupulous, yet unpredictable mind whose reaction you want to get as soon as possible on virtually any topic. . . . Gordon is an impressive moral and ethical thinker . . . funny, contentious, and moving."
— *Chicago Tribune*

"Mary Gordon is so curious and honest that one almost wants to protect her from saying such outrageous things because they are true."
— Garry Wills

"Illuminating . . . Gordon is an important writer. . . . [her] personal voice is always audible, speaking assuredly and revealingly, without sacrificing her critical facility or her intellectual authority."
— *San Francisco Chronicle*

"A book of clear thinking and expression by a very fine writer."
— *Newark Star-Ledger*

"To meet Gordon through this book is to recognize the true depths of her subversiveness. . . . Her intelligence is so pervasive . . . that if you are interested in feminism, Catholicism, [or] literature, you're bound to find gems here."
— *Chicago Sun-Times*

PENGUIN BOOKS

GOOD BOYS AND DEAD GIRLS

Known for her bestselling and highly acclaimed novels, *Final Payments*, *The Company of Women*, *Men and Angels*, *The Other Side*, and a collection of stories, *Temporary Shelter*, Mary Gordon is the McIntosh Professor of English at Barnard College.

Mary Gordon

GOOD
BOYS

AND

DEAD
GIRLS

and Other Essays

PENGUIN BOOKS

PENGUIN BOOKS
Published by the Penguin Group
Viking Penguin, a division of Penguin Books USA Inc.,
375 Hudson Street, New York, New York 10014, U.S.A.
Penguin Books Ltd, 27 Wrights Lane,
London W8 5TZ, England
Penguin Books Australia Ltd, Ringwood,
Victoria, Australia
Penguin Books Canada Ltd, 10 Alcorn Avenue, Suite 300,
Toronto, Ontario, Canada M4V 3B2
Penguin Books (N.Z.) Ltd, 182–190 Wairau Road,
Auckland 10, New Zealand

Penguin Books Ltd, Registered Offices:
Harmondsworth, Middlesex, England

First published in the United States of America by Viking Penguin,
a division of Penguin Books USA Inc., 1991
Published in Penguin Books 1992

1 3 5 7 9 10 8 6 4 2

THE LIBRARY OF CONGRESS HAS CATALOGUED THE HARDCOVER AS FOLLOWS:
Gordon, Mary, 1949–
Good boys and dead girls:and other essays / Mary Gordon.
p.   cm.
I. Title.
ISBN 0-670-82567-0 (hc.)
ISBN 0 14 01.1693 1 (pbk.)
PS3557.0669G66   1991
814'.54—dc20   90–50467

Printed in the United States of America
Set in Garamond #3

To Philip Hamburger

Contents

I

ON WRITERS AND WRITING

Good Boys and Dead Girls   3

Edith Wharton: *Ethan Frome* and the Shorter Fiction   24

Flannery O'Connor: *The Habit of Being*   37

William Trevor's *Fools of Fortune*   45

Christa Wolf: *Accident/A Day's News*   52

Mary McCarthy: *Occasional Prose*   57

Mary McCarthy: *Cannibals and Missionaries*   61

Stevie Smith: *Novel on Yellow Paper*   67

Adam Hochschild: *Half the Way Home*   72

Virginia Woolf: *A Room of One's Own*   77

Edna O'Brien: *A Fanatic Heart*   84

The Priestly Comedy of J. F. Powers   89

Ingeborg Bachmann: Children Were Only Allowed to Whisper   103

David Plante: A World of Baffled Love   108

Ford Madox Ford: A Man Who Loved Women, a
Womanly Man   112

II

THE WORLD, THE CHURCH,
THE LIVES OF WOMEN

More Than Just a Shrine: Paying Homage to the Ghosts
of Ellis Island   123

Abortion: How Do We Think About It?   128

Abortion: How Do We Really Choose?   138

The Parable of the Cave; or, In Praise of Watercolors   148

Offenses of the Pope   153

Mary Cassatt   156

Getting Here from There: A Writer's Reflections on a
Religious Past   160

More Catholic than the Pope   176

"I Can't Stand Your Books": A Writer Goes Home   199

III

PARTS OF A JOURNAL

Notes from California   211

Having a Baby, Finishing a Book   215

Some Things I Saw   222

The Gospel According to Saint Mark   240

GOOD
BOYS

AND

DEAD
GIRLS

I

ON WRITERS
AND WRITING

Good Boys and
Dead Girls

I tell you they were not men after spoils and glory; they were
boys riding the sheer, tremendous tidal wave of desperate
living. Boys. Because this. This is beautiful. Listen. Try to see
it. Here is that fine shape of eternal youth and virginal desire
which makes heroes. That makes the doings of heroes border
so close upon the unbelievable that it is no wonder that their
doings must emerge now and then like gunflashes in the
smoke, and that their very physical passing becomes rumor
with a thousand faces before breath is out of them, lest par-
adoxical truth outrage itself.

Light in August

The truth, beauty, and heroism that Faulkner invokes in this description have inflamed the hearts of generations of male American
writers. Faulkner is in fact describing the rash attempt of a group
of boy soldiers to destroy Grant's stores in a small Southern town.
The raid ends in a series of unnecessary and foolish deaths, whose
effects reverberate through three generations. It is a member of a
third wounded generation, Hightower, who calls up the image of
the beautiful marauding boys as he broods on the castration of Joe
Christmas by the fanatical frustrated soldier Grimm. The blood of
one boy is on the hands of another, but the blood has been shed
to avenge the honor of a murdered woman. Beauty. Truth. Heroism. Civilization is no place for a boy.

The image of the moving boy has been central in American
writing. Motion is the boy's genius. He *must* be able to *move*. Move
freely. Quickly. The boy on his strong legs cuts through the world,
through time, constricting space, the accidents of birth, class, lim-

itation, law. He wriggles out from under the crushing burden of fate. And fate's agent, the embodiment of unmoving weight, is female. She who does not move, who will not move, who cannot move. Who won't allow the boy to move.

The innocent boy killers. Let us concentrate for the moment on the first word: innocent. In poetry, the word, or its nominal, made its mark indelibly twice. First in Donne's "A Valediction Forbidding Mourning": "Movement of earth brings harms and fears / Men reckon what it did and meant. / But trepidation of the spheres / Though Greater far, is innocent." And then there is Yeats's famous passage from "A Prayer for My Daughter": "How but in custom and ceremony can innocence and beauty be born?" Is innocence a passive state, as Donne's lines would suggest, a natural freedom from something, a marvelous lack, the adorable minus that makes possible the immaculate whole? Or is it, as Yeats would suggest, a product of a willed isolation, willed by someone (possibly not the innocent himself or herself), a conscious holding back or being held back from the world?

The ambiguities involved in the idea of innocence create problems when we try to define the word. The OED defines it as "doing no evil; free from moral sin or guilt, pure, unpolluted, usually (in modern use always) implying unacquainted with evil, sinless, holy." These definitions skirt, of course, the difficulties about innocence, the problem of consciousness or volition. The OED allows the possibility that innocence is almost a physical state: pure, unpolluted, a state almost like virginity, a state whose terms are bodily. A passive state. But if we define innocence using words like "doing no evil" and include the terms "moral" and "sin," consciousness and volition are implied; the body and the mind are in some communion.

In the depiction of innocence in fiction, there seems to be a real split between Americans and Europeans. For English and European writers, the emphasis is placed on the innocent as "doing no evil"; as "free from moral sin." For Americans—and this is not surprising given our Puritan past—innocence seems to be a state of nonpollution, which can endure even through behavior that ought, in ordinary contexts, to be polluting.

I am thinking of four European innocents: Félicie in Flaubert's *Un Coeur Simple*, Prince Mishkin in *The Idiot*, the Country Priest in Bernanos's *Diary*, and Portia in Elizabeth Bowen's *The Death of the Heart.* Two of these characters are women and two are saints, so it should not be surprising that they are removed from the center of power. All of these characters lack ambition—that so American virtue—which may be a way of saying that they lack the belief in change. And all of them suffer more than they cause suffering. They keep trying to do good in the world; their sorrow is disproportionate, unearned, and unjust.

Writers of American fiction have a habit of describing innocence as if it were a state of election removed from behavior, impervious to the state of defilement resulting from bad acts. When the American innocent is punished for what he has done, the punishment is seen as metaphysically incorrect, the inevitable result of the pressures of civilization. This kind of American innocent, typically a young boy, first appeared in Melville's *Billy Budd.*

Billy Budd, the handsome sailor, epitomizes life, youth, health, and unselfconscious, broad, instinctual behavior. His world is the world of free movement, skilled, deft action; he is at home with the elemental, the natural. In the world of language, however, he is clumsy and mute: he is entrapped by words, the coin of civilized and settled life. Melville says of him: "to deal in double meaning and insinuations was quite foreign to his nature." Double meanings and insinuations are intrusions by language into the world of action. Billy is the victim of language. Claggart's accusation, that Billy tried to mutiny, has no basis in the actual world, in the world of action: it is simply a fabric of language. At the moment of his accusation, Billy both realizes the inadequacy of language and is paralyzed by it. His tongue stops and will not serve him. But his arm is ready. His arm can *move.* He strikes and kills Claggart. The movement of his arm is the medium of justice. He is destroyed by law, a product of language. The law requires that Billy be punished for the murder of the one who plotted against him. But the plot was motivated by the frustration of instinct, the stoppage of male physical desire. (The homosexuality at the center of *Billy Budd* makes Billy a complicated figure in terms of gender relations. Desire is all male in *Billy Budd*, and in this way it serves as only a partial paradigm for later American fiction, which is, of course, primarily heterosexual.) Billy is hanged because of the civilized notion that the good of the individual cannot take precedence over the good of the group.

In his book *The American Adam*, R. W. B. Lewis talks about the distance between the innocent hero and the world he must cope with, a strategic gap he cannot bridge. Billy Budd bridges the gap by an act of irrational, heroic forgiveness. He forgives his accusers, particularly the reluctant, Pilate-like captain, and in his utter submission to his own death, he rises above fate. But Billy lives in the nineteenth century; his twentieth-century brothers will not be, as Melville says of Billy, "like the animals, without knowing it, practically a fatalist."

The story of America is the story of the escape from fate. Europeans crossed the ocean in order to be free of it; the movement from the small town to the city is a move out of the grip of fate. The freedom and autonomy that America is meant to stand for is the attempt to define the self outside of the bruising authority of fate. In the language of American mythology, fate is that over which the self has no control; the ultimate limiter of individual freedom. It is the villain in the American dream. This dream is overwhelmingly male in its tone, and romantic—as Leslie Fiedler noted thirty years ago—about the pure relation between males in contrast to the muddled, corrupt relation between males and females. The female is the counterpart of fate in that her condition is fatalistic in the natural weakness that makes her susceptible to rape and vulnerable to death in childbirth. This natural weakness means that she requires protection, shelter, assistance. The boy on the run cannot stop to shelter a woman from violation or to assist her in the pangs of childbirth. In speaking of Cooper, Leslie Fiedler said that, in American literature, the only good woman is a dead woman. The habit didn't end with the *Leather Stocking Tales*.

It is more likely that a woman, at least a lady, can be kept healthy and alive in civilization than in nature. She is safest in the center of the world. But if we agree with R. W. B. Lewis that the "American hero must take his stand outside the world, remote or on the verges," the woman is the centripetal force pulling him not only from natural happiness but from heroism as well.

In earlier American literature, where the alternatives are a constricting civilization presided over by the schoolmarm or a limitless frontier graced by the noble savage, the pull of the woman is always decidedly weaker than the call of the wild. But as the frontier becomes a less real possibility—both in reality and in the imagination of writers—the pull of the woman, the woman pulling the man into the world, becomes a much more difficult force for the hero to resist.

Clyde Griffiths of Theodore Dreiser's *An American Tragedy* is a boy who cannot master his fate. He is never on top of the rules of the world's game; his heroism is in longing, his inchoate desire for movement in a life where there is none. Dreiser describes Clyde's character as "fluid and unstable as water." He is tender; he can be impressed. In contrast to the cold, rocklike religiosity of his parents' life, his very motility is a kind of life force—they are living death. One of the terrific achievements of this novel consists in Dreiser's ability to convey the small dreariness of Clyde's childhood—he is the son of itinerant evangelists of the least flamboyant sort—and to contrast it with the bustle and shine of prosperous life. The *things* that money can buy—cigars, garters, furs, dresses that swish and glitter—are conveyed by Dreiser with a voluptuous excitement to which the reader is as susceptible as Clyde. The "good things in life"—as defined by upper-class American businessmen—take on a sexual charge in this novel, and sex for Clyde is never unconnected with class and social mobility.

Clyde is an attractive boy, but the first girl he desires uses him, manipulates her sexuality, doling it out in small pieces in return for presents of jewelry, perfume, and clothes. Clyde is so overmastered by this girl, however, that he refuses to help his desperate pregnant sister because he has promised Hortense a fur coat. At this point in the novel, Dreiser's moral position in relation to Clyde is masterful and subtle. He in no way softens his description of the sister's wretchedness to let Clyde off the hook; at the same time we are carried up by the sexual fever Clyde seems to have caught. The moral position is not rejected, it is merely seen to be out of the question, weak and tepid compared to the tremendous, vital allure of the world of things, movement, and sex that Hortense represents.

One night, while Clyde is still working as a bellboy at the "good" hotel where he learned about the "good" things in life, one of his friends steals his employer's car. In the course of this joyride, Clyde and his friends run over and kill a little (and, it might be noted, upper-class) girl. The first of the book's female corpses! Clyde and most of his friends run away. In starting a new life in Kansas City,

Clyde meets up with his wealthy uncle, who offers him a job in his collar factory. The factory is located in a prosperous little town in western New York, with a cohort of "good" families in large houses, families whose wealth is earned by the workers of whom Clyde is both one and not one. This placement locates him exactly at the painful center of the unstable plane that is American social reality in the early twentieth century. Clyde becomes foreman in the factory—he oversees girls stamping collars—but he cannot mix socially with any of the girls he oversees, because he is his uncle's nephew. At the same time, he isn't supposed even to dream of mixing with his cousins and their friends. His anomalousness would immobilize him if he obeyed its dictates, but he doesn't. He rebels both up and down. He has a love affair with Roberta, one of the girls who works for him, and in the midst of this he is taken up by Sondra Finchley, a shining dream girl of his cousins' social set.

Dreiser makes both Roberta's attractiveness and her virtue real. She is a genuinely loving young woman who is sexually awakened by her feelings for Clyde. Hollywood's casting Shelley Winters, the perennial slut, to play her in the second movie version of this novel, A Place in the Sun, was a serious violation of the spirit of Dreiser's book. The confusion is an important indication of our culture's difficulty in embodying female sexuality as it connects to male violence. Dreiser's Roberta is a genuine innocent, forced by poverty to leave the "reduced grimness" of her decaying farm (in the marvelously named town of Biltz) in order to take up factory work, which is really beneath her. Dreiser makes the point that, like Clyde, she has an innate finesse, which makes mixing with rougher (read immigrant) girls in the factory difficult for her. Hollywood couldn't have Montgomery Clift kill a nice girl, but Dreiser faces the problem: in order to achieve his dream of social mobility with Sondra, Clyde must murder Roberta, who is morally and emotionally Sondra's superior. We can think of Shelley Winters as one of those girls who "asked for it," since we all understand that any woman who consents to sex and enjoys it is automatically deserving of murder or rape.

Sondra, on the other hand, is a dreadful girl who happens to be irresistibly beautiful and marvelously rich. Her clothes, her cars, her sports equipment, at least as much as her body, are the locus of her sexual allure. In a superb scene in Sondra's kitchen, Dreiser brings before our eyes all that Sondra represents for Clyde. Sondra has brought Clyde home after a dance, to make some cocoa. She is playing cook in her palace kitchen, and when Clyde admires the room she says, "Oh, I don't know. Aren't all kitchens as big as this?"—a thrillingly arrogant thrust of top-down sadism.

> Clyde, thinking of the poverty he knew, and assuming from this that she was scarcely aware of anything less than this, was all the more overawed by the plethora of the world to which she belonged. What means! Only to think of being married to such a girl, when all such as this would become an everyday state. One would have a cook and servants, a great house and car, no one to work for, and only orders to give. . . . It made her various self-conscious gestures and posings all the more entrancing. . . .
>
> Having prepared the chocolate in a commonplace aluminum pan, to further impress him she sought out a heavily chased silver service which was in another room. She poured the chocolate into a highly ornamented urn and then carried it to the table and put it down before him. Then swinging herself up beside him, she said, "Now isn't this chummy? I just love to get out in the kitchen like this, but I can only do it when the cook's out. He won't let anyone near the place when he's here."
>
> At the sight of her in her white satin and crystal evening gown, her slippered feet swinging so intimately near, a faint perfume radiating to his nostrils, he was stirred. In fact, his imagination in regard to her was really inflamed. Youth, beauty, wealth, such as this—what could it not mean?

Clearly, Dreiser wants us at once to realize Sondra's ridiculousness and the allure of all she has. Nothing about her is still; even her clothes glimmer and catch light. She is a moving girl. She is not slowed down by either poverty or desire. Power and freedom create motion, and in having more money than Clyde, being in charge of the sexual vector, and being far from any suggestion of maternity, she takes on the properties of mobility usually reserved for boys. Compare her kitchen to Roberta's house in Biltz:

So lonely and bare, even in the bright spring weather! The decayed and sagging roof. The broken chimney to the north— rough lumps of cemented field stones lying at its base; the sagging and semi-toppling chimney to the south, sustained in place by a log chain. The unkempt path from the road below . . . the broken and displaced stones which served as steps before the front door. And the unpainted, dilapidated out- buildings, all the more dreary because of these others.

Just as we begin to believe that Clyde has a chance with the glittering Sondra, we learn that Roberta is pregnant. If Clyde mar- ries her, he will lose everything: his job in his uncle's factory, and, most important, his trip upward on the social ladder atop which Sondra sits, swinging her tiny, satin-shod foot. Astonishingly, we are on Clyde's side in his conviction that marrying Roberta, with whom he was quite happy until Sondra appeared, is impossible. We hope that something will happen: an abortion, an accident. We hope that Roberta will be a good sport and go away—or die. We are at one with Clyde in his plans to murder this encumbered woman, this encumbrance, heavy with child and the limitations of her poverty, as heavy as the uneven stones in her dull, unpainted house. We follow Clyde through detailed plans to kill Roberta at a deserted lake. But in the end, Dreiser doesn't have the toughness to follow through with the moral vision he has so skillfully created. He doesn't allow Clyde to be the cold-blooded murderer he had planned to be. Having described Clyde's life before the scene of the murder in perfectly realistic terms, Dreiser suddenly goes limp and expressionist.

This still dark water seems to grip Clyde as nothing here or anywhere before this ever had. For once here he seemed to be fairly pulled or lured along into it, and having encircled its quiet banks to be drifting, drifting—in endless space where there was no end of anything. The insidious beauty of this place! Truly, it seemed to mock him—this strangeness—this dark pool, surrounded on all sides by those wonderful soft fir trees. And the water itself looking like a huge, black pearl cast by some mighty hand, in anger possibly, in sport, or phantasy maybe, into this bosom of its valley of dark green plush, and which seemed bottomless as he gazed into it. And yet what did it all suggest so strongly? Death! Death!

Something—the craftsman, perhaps—in Dreiser is uncomfortable with the psychological falseness of the situation: his lapse into melodrama betrays him.

For this melodrama, he uses imagery that is unmistakably female. The lake itself, a great vagina, hypnotizes Clyde so that he can't feel responsible for his conduct. The wet, dark circle surrounded by firs suggests nothing but death to him. Hypnotized by the weirdness of the lake, Clyde experiences something strange. At the moment he is about to kill Roberta, he is "struck by a sudden palsy of the will." Roberta approaches him, thinking he is in some sort of dangerous trance and attempting to save him from falling into the water. "Instantly yielding to a tide of submerged hate, not only for himself, but Roberta—her power, or that of life to restrain him in this way," Clyde strikes her with his camera, in a simple gesture of self-preserving recoil. It is important that the murder weapon is a camera. Walter Benjamin has noted that the camera diminishes the notion of the authenticity of any particular object by rendering it infinitely reproducible. Because of this, it is the ultimate agent of the modern, the ultimate distancer of the human being from the unique act. For Dreiser, as for many writers, women represent, alternately and interchangeably, the encumbering aspects of both nature and culture; in Clyde's murdering Roberta with a camera, modern culture is striking out against nature, to the destruction of both.

In the end, Dreiser wants us to believe that Clyde didn't mean to kill Roberta. His pupils dilated, hypnotized by the dark lake, he only meant to push her away. So that he could get on with life. The trouble is that Dreiser has just spent a hundred pages showing Clyde plotting the perfect murder. Clyde goes to his death believing himself innocent, and we are sympathetic to him because in the context of the corruption around him everywhere, he is the most pure. The D.A. wants to make political hay out of the case; Clyde's lawyer wants to block the D.A.'s ambitions; the newspapermen suck Clyde's blood to get their daily bread. His fellow prisoners are horrifyingly brutal compared to him. Even his mother succumbs to the pressures of modern corruption; to earn money for Clyde's appeal, she agrees to write up her experiences as the mother of a condemned man; she goes on the church lecture circuit to raise money for her son. She is the first media disaster-mom. Clyde is appalled even as he is touched by her mixing in the company of his tormentors, by her going public with a lack of dignity of which he would never be capable. In the end, we see Clyde as simpler than the environment in which he has been put, clearer than the events by which he is entrapped; we mourn his death as we don't mourn Roberta's. She was the heavy, dull, cling-ing object. He might have moved, hitching his wagon to Sondra's shooting star.

Like *An American Tragedy*, *Jude the Obscure* is about an ambitious young man in sexual thralldom to women. Both young men have plans and dreams that we know will never be realized. Both are the victims of what their authors perceive as monstrous systems—cruel amalgams created by the distorting pressures of nature and society—which must blight the flowering of the imaginative young. Yet Jude suffers and is touched by suffering, and perhaps more important, he loses his youth. At the novel's end, Jude is in no way a boy. Clyde dies one, complaining that after all this time his mother still doesn't understand him. The maturing process is not one that deeply interests a certain kind of American writer. Sher-wood Anderson, for example, always ends his tales before the boy has to be tested. This kind of writer tells us we have to love the boy, not because he is good, or talented, or perceptive, but simply because he is full of life.

Hardy, being English, allows Jude to mature. But who is to say that Jude's maturity does anyone around him any good? Jude's wanderings around Wessex with Sue and their tribe of children, his hopeless search for work and prosperity, is a protracted living death that ends only with the horror of the oldest child, little Father Time, hanging himself and his siblings in the closet, leaving the note "Done because we are too menny." By comparison, the quick, modern deaths of Roberta and Clyde—both induced by mechanical agents (the camera, the electric chair)—are a blessing and a mercy. Hardy's is a tragic vision, and the problem of the sexes may be a tragic one; perhaps we are doomed to want different and oppos-ing things from life. But it is tempting to guess that had Hardy been American, Jude would have been unable to say no to the impulse to get both Sue and Arabella, his first love, out of his way by force.

In *Light in August*, Faulkner adds Joe Christmas to the list of American boy killers. Leslie Fiedler has spoken of Faulkner's comic antifeminism, but the definition of the comic has always depended upon who is doing the laughing. Miles apart from Dreiser's syntax of pulsing realism, Faulkner's language has its source in myth and dream. At the center of his mythology is his idea of the innate and inherent corruption of women.

Like Billy Budd, Joe Christmas is at home in the world of elemental, deft action. His naturalness is due in part to his Negro blood—another part of Faulkner's mythology: women (except in their moments of purest maternity) are corrupt, blacks are close to nature. We often see Joe running: running for sex to the prostitute Bobbie, running away from his executioners after he has killed his lover, Joanna Burden. The significance of her name is obvious—Burden, the woman, the heavy one, the one who slows down. One of the ways Joanna Burden slows Joe down is by her insistence upon language. You can't run and talk at the same time. Joe says of her, "She is like all the rest of them. . . . Whether they are seventeen or forty seven, when they finally come to surrender completely, it's going to be in words."

Joe encounters Joanna living by herself in the woods, in an aristocratic house, the sole survivor of a family of liberals who tried to bring justice and education to blacks. Joe and Joanna become lovers, and eventually he kills her when she insists upon praying over him: prayer is, after all, the conjunction of the supernatural and language. As in *An American Tragedy*, the circumstances of the murder are ambiguous, and, like Clyde's, Joe's mental state at the time of the murder is extreme and outside the realm of rational control. Christmas describes himself as the "volitionless servant of the fatality in which he believed that he did not believe. He was saying to himself . . . I had to do it . . . I had to do it . . . already in the past tense; I had to do it . . . she said so herself."

And in fact, Joanna is concealing in her bosom a loaded gun, a Civil War relic (how's that for symbolism), in whose practical, rather than metaphoric, efficacy it is hard to believe. As in *An American Tragedy*, it is difficult to determine the guilt of the boy murderer. Joanna may indeed be asking to be killed, but someone's asking to be killed does not confer an obligation on another to kill her or him. One of the truths of relations between men and women is that most men are physically stronger than most women. Certainly Joe is stronger than Joanna; he could easily have disarmed her. But by both praying over Joe and suggesting that he go to law school and take his place alongside Peebles, her black lawyer, Joanna is bringing into Joe's life the physical, the nonconcrete, the symbolic: God, money, the future. And in connecting him only with his blackness, in denying his half-whiteness, she is, in his terms, lowering him racially. Most important, Joe must kill Joanna because her existence threatens his: her presence in his life endangers his identity, already fragile because of his mixed blood. When Joe considers marrying her, he says to himself: "Why not. It would mean ease, security for the rest of your life. You would never have to *move* [italics mine] again. And you might as well be married to her as this thinking. No. If I give in now, I will deny all the thirty years that I have lived to make me what I chose to be."

Joanna's life jeopardizes Christmas's grueling struggle to be himself: "With the corruption which she seemed to gather from the air itself, she began to corrupt him. He began to be afraid. He could not have said of what. But he began to see himself as from a distance, like a man being sucked down into a bottomless morass." These words could be expressing simple sexual terror, but there is more at stake than that; everything is complicated because of race, age, and class. Joe is a young, half-black, poor male; Joanna is a middle-aged, aristocratic white female. He can't figure out whether he is a nigger stud to Joanna, or a cherished husband, or a future business partner. He can't figure out whether she is nurse or whore. Her combination of power and submission maddens him.

She had an avidity for the forbidden words . . . an insatiable appetite for the sound of them on his tongue and on her own. She revealed the terrible and impersonal curiosity of a child about forbidden subjects and objects; that rapt and tireless and detached interest of a surgeon in the physical body and in its possibilities. And by day he would see the calm, cold-faced, almost manlike, almost middle aged woman who had lived for twenty years alone, without any feminine fears at all, in a lonely house in a neighborhood populated, when at all, by negroes, who spent a certain portion of each day sitting tranquilly at a desk and writing tranquilly for the eyes of both youth and age the practical advice of a combined priest and banker and trained nurse.

We see a confusion of gender to which Faulkner returns again and again. The woman's name is gender mixed: Jo (as in Christmas) Anna; the areas in which she operates are both male and female—she controls money and access to the larger, certainly the professional, world. But she retreats into conventional femaleness (the world of prayers and talk of marriage and babies), and when she does this, she is abhorrent to Joe and worthy of death.

For Faulkner, Joanna is the product of the neurosis of her abolitionist forebears who moved South. She is meant to stand in part for the doomed attempts of white liberals to weaken the magic power of the curse between the races. Nevertheless, Faulkner's attempt to portray this spinster discovering sex in middle age is the novel's great failure. When Faulkner tries to render rapt abandon, he is merely risible. "Now and then she appointed trysts beneath certain shrubs about the grounds, where he would find her naked, or with her clothing half torn to ribbons upon her, in the wild throes of nymphomania, her body gleaming in the slow shifting from one to another of such formally erotic attitudes and gestures as a Beardsley in the time of Petronius might have drawn . . . breathing 'Negro! Negro! Negro!' " If you try and picture the scene, you understand that Faulkner didn't get the Nobel for this kind of writing. As in the murder scene in *An American Tragedy*, there is a kind of uneasy relationship between author, subject, and language that the language betrays. Dreiser puts Vaseline on the distorting lens; Faulkner has to invoke Beardsley in the time of Petronius. Both tactics are an attempt to distance the author from his error; the tactics don't work.

Perhaps Faulkner writes badly about sex because for him it is the complication that makes the free life impossible. Joe, for example, first gets into trouble when the dietician in the white orphanage where he lives as a child comes upon him hidden in her bedroom, the unwilling spy of her tryst with a young doctor. He is punished by her for a sexual crime he never committed: he wasn't in her room as a voyeur; he was sucking the paste out of the nurse's toothpaste tube, a literal search for sweetness that expresses itself in a metaphorically gender-ambiguous act. He leaves the orphanage for the house of the hyper-Calvinist farmer Calhoun, whom he will kill when Calhoun tries to separate him from his prostitute lover. This murder leads him to the town where he will perform his second killing and be killed himself. Joe is linked to death by sex, by the frustration of what Faulkner sees as his natural sexuality. But only when Joe is by himself in nature is he intact, and safe; what pulls him out of nature is women.

He is the only character in the novel who has a life that partakes in any kind of freedom or autonomy. Working in the mill, laboring at a job that is entirely physical, or moving through the woods, he is portrayed heroically. He is tender as the lover of the prostitute and impressive in the bushes with the wild Joanna. Like Clyde Griffiths, Joe, in comparison with the people who surround him, represents life, and like Dreiser, Faulkner wishes his reader to believe that Joe's consuming desire to preserve him*self,* a self that is physical as well as spiritual, is a life force that should excuse him from the charge of murder. The corpse of Joanna Burden is a cipher; we do not regret her passing; our attention is taken up with our concern that Joe escape. That he does not, and dies horribly at the hands of another boy, who kills in the name of religion, race, and history, is the brilliant paradox of Faulkner's book. We mourn Joe's passing, but we never call him a murderer. Rather he had to clear away brush, as the pioneers did, to create a space large enough for him to live, breathe, be himself. Faulkner beautifully describes Joe's running away from his pursuers:

> It is just dawn, daylight: that gray and lonely suspension filled with the peaceful and tentative waking of birds. The air, inbreathed, is like spring water. He breathes deep and slow, feeling with each breath himself diffuse in the neutral greyness becoming one with loneliness and quiet that has never known fury or despair. "That was all I wanted," he thinks, in a quiet and slow amazement. "That was all, for thirty years. That didn't seem to be a whole lot to ask in thirty years."

The two sexy men in *Light in August*—Joe and Lucas Burch, who fathers the earth mother Lena's child—run away from women as if they are running away from death. Faulkner is clear in his linking of women and death. He describes the female witnesses to Joe's capture and prospective hanging: "And the women came too, the idle ones in bright and sometimes hurried garments, with secret and passionate and glittering looks and with secret frustrated breasts (who have always loved death better than peace)." Bunch and Hightower, who care for Lena in her pregnancy and early days of maternity, are ruins or jokes as males. To murder is sexy, to nurture is a sign of softness, the *last-ditch* virtue of a man who has no place in nature. Life goes on with Lena, Bunch, and the baby, but there is no place in it for the healthy male animal, the running boy.

The pile of female corpses in American literature grows higher through the thirties and forties and includes diverse ethnic and economic groups. In Farrell's *Studs Lonigan*, Studs's girlfriend, who is standing in his way, dies in a fire that takes place at an orgy he has taken her to. There are the double murder of the white and black women in Richard Wright's *Native Son* and the triple killings in Mailer's *An American Dream*. But it took an Eastern white Protestant like John Updike to put a new spin on the ball with *Rabbit, Run*. Consider the title. *Rabbit, Run*. The innocent is urged to move.

Updike takes from Faulkner, Dreiser—or the American air—a habit of association that connects females with stasis and death; males with movement and life. The pattern of moving boys killing females who get in their way expresses itself in the Rabbit books in a new way: carelessness causes the death of at least two females. The literal acts of murder committed by Clyde and Joe don't find a place in Rabbit's Pennsylvania; America changed radically between the composition of *An American Tragedy* and that of *Rabbit, Run*, and the change is reflected in the casual relations between the boys and the deaths that occur in connection with them. By the time of Rabbit's appearance, the possibilities for physical and social movement in America had greatly diminished. Dreiser's Clyde had the city and the world of upper-middle-class luxury to move to; Faulkner's Joe had the wilderness and an endless series of small Southern towns to which he could flee. But Updike's Rabbit continues to live where he was born—and he was born into suburbia. Similarly, the arenas in which the three boys—Clyde Griffiths, Joe Christmas, and Harry (Rabbit) Angstrom—are able to be successful as healthy young animals demonstrate the difference in the stakes for each writer. Clyde can turn his ability to be personally ingratiating into a way of making a living; Joe turns his physical dexterity into an employable asset at the mill. But Rabbit's métier is the local basketball court, where no one pays you a salary and where there is no percentage at all in growing up.

The first dead female in the Rabbit books is the child Rebecca, who is killed by her mother, Rabbit's wife. On the most obvious level, it is Janice who kills the baby and not Rabbit—indeed the death can be read as proof of the murderous carelessness of a mother in relation to her child. But the death of the baby occurs after one of Rabbit's runs. Rabbit walks out on Janice while she is still pregnant, returns to her for the birth of the child. But he can't stay long. He takes off again after Janice, still feeling the effects of her episiotomy, refuses to have anal sex. Depressed and hopeless because of her husband's second leavetaking, Janice gets drunk and allows her baby to drown in the bathtub. This death can be read any number of ways that are conducive to negative mythologizing about women. If we say that Janice was suffering from postpartum depression and therefore not fully responsible for her act, we can seem to be buying into the raging-hormones school of psychology. But it is at least possible to say that a responsible father does not leave his children in the hands of a woman who is clearly depressed. This is a possibility that never occurs to Rabbit or to Updike. Updike has a real gift for describing the claustrophobia of depression as it hits the domestic life of the working class; in his hands, the impossible collection of dirty glasses and filled ashtrays serves as a justification for Rabbit's flight: being who he is, he has to *move*.

He moves not only into middle age but into a second volume, *Rabbit Redux*, where the second female death occurs. Rabbit has been (temporarily) abandoned by Janice, who moves in with a lover. Rabbit takes up with Jill, a girl of rather loose sexual standards, a hippie arrived in Pennsylvania by way of a good family in Stonington, Connecticut. She brings a black man into the ménage—

a pimp and drug dealer—who reduces her to a state of helpless drug dependence. In a dramatic collision of cultures, Rabbit's neighbors burn his house down, punishing him for allowing a black into the neighborhood. Jill dies in the fire; the black man is killed years later in a shootout with the Philadelphia police.

The third volume of the Rabbit series moves Rabbit into later middle age and a Toyota dealership. In this book, we don't see a woman die; she merely moves her diseased body closer to death in order to have sex with Rabbit. Rabbit and his wife travel to the Bahamas with two other couples, a friend of Rabbit's and his young, desirable wife, Cindy, and Rabbit's old enemy and his tired school-teacher wife, Thelma. Thelma is dying of lupus; a week in the sun is the opposite of what the doctor ordered. The couples decide to swap, but Rabbit doesn't get his coveted Cindy; he is chosen instead by Thelma. Thelma is menstruating; she tells Rabbit that this makes her so disgusting that he shouldn't have to come near her genitals. He is too wonderful, too beautiful for that. She performs oral sex on him, and he sodomizes her at her urging. And they talk. They really talk. In the three novels, she is the only one who understands him. (She's also the only one who willingly takes it up the ass.) She gives him wonderful, loving advice. She has always loved him. After he has sodomized her, Rabbit asks, "What does it do for you?"

"Makes me feel full of you. Makes me feel fucked up the ass, by lovely Harry Angstrom."

"What have I done to deserve it?" he asks.

"Just existed. Just shed your light. . . ."

He then asks, "What is it about me that turns you on?"

"Oh darling. Everything. Your height and the way you move, as if you were still a skinny twenty-five. The way you never sit down anywhere without making sure there's a way out. Your little pro-visional smile, like a little boy at some party where the bullies might get him the next minute. Your good humor. You believe in people so. Janice, you're so proud of her it's pathetic. It's not as if she can do anything. . . . You're just terribly generous. You're so grateful to be anywhere, you think that tacky club and that hideous house of Cindy's are heaven. It's wonderful. You're so glad to be alive. . . . I love you so much for it. And your hands. I've always loved your hands. And now your prick, with its little bonnet. Oh Harry, *I don't care if this kills me* [italics mine], coming down here, tonight is worth it."

When Rabbit, grateful Rabbit, asks Thelma what he can do for her (obviously, genital sex in her degraded menstrual condition is out of the question: too disgusting), she asks him to get into the tub so they can urinate on each other. The scene concludes with a staggering display of unearned lyricism. "Having tried together to shower the ammoniac scent of urine off their skins, Thelma and Harry fall asleep among the stripes of dawn now welling through the louvers as if not a few stolen hours but an entire married life of sanctioned intimacy stretches unto death before them."

There we have it. Rabbit is, indeed, lovable to the ideal woman, demanding nothing, disappearing the next day, dying—who loves him just for that little light of his that shines, shines, shines.

For Updike, women are messy; they are slow; and they get in a boy's way. Rabbit's glory days ended because he got a girl pregnant. He moved from the free world of the basketball court into the horrifying constrictions of domesticity. Of course he had to leave. He had to be able to move. "I just felt like the whole business was fetching and hauling, all the time trying to hold this mess together she was making . . . It seemed like I was glued in with a lot of busted toys and empty glasses and television going and meals late and no way of getting out. Then all of a sudden it hit me how easy it was to get out, just walk out, and by damn it was easy."

Women prevent movement; they are also, for Updike, inexorably caught up in a process of decay. He is almost unable to describe a woman—however attractive she may seem at first—without pointing out some defect that is attached to her through sheer living. Janice has varicose veins. Ruth in *Rabbit, Run* is fat and has scaly yellow heels. Peggy Fosnacht in *Rabbit Redux* has nipples like wet gumdrops. But that's better than Janice, who by *Rabbit Is Rich* has breasts that "hang down so her nipples, bumply [*sic*] in texture like hamburger, swam an inch above her belly." Even Cindy, the young wife of Rabbit's friend in *Rabbit Is Rich*, turns out, in her nude photographs, to have breasts that are disappointingly unfirm.

In each book, someone accuses Rabbit of being a bringer of death, and the end of *Rabbit Is Rich* seems written to prove that Rabbit's creator is onto his "woman problem." When Rabbit is handed his baby granddaughter, named Rebecca after the baby who died, he feels "Another nail in the coffin. His." But the aura that Updike works hard and consistently to create around Rabbit is an aura of blessed innocence, and none of his bluff-calling diminishes the force of his overriding impulse, which becomes particularly overpowering when sex or paternity is involved. Like Dreiser and Faulkner, Updike's hand starts to shake when he approaches the land of female habitation. And like Dreiser and Faulkner, he jettisons the question of moral responsibility for the boy on the move.

But he goes further than Dreiser and Faulkner would have dreamed. He keeps trying to characterize Rabbit in pseudotheological categories, to turn him into an unselfconscious saint. He elevates what is essentially a physical characteristic—Rabbit's ability to enjoy life as long as no one asks anything of him, as if life were a meal, or a swim in a hospitable sea—into a spiritual virtue. Instead of settling for portraying Rabbit as a lovable forked thing, Updike insists that we see him as a kind of suburban John of the Cross. He is consistently described in images of light and holiness. Janice praises her husband for "trying to keep himself pure." Thelma, his lover in *Rabbit Is Rich*, calls him "a source of light." *Rabbit, Run* is full of observations about how close Rabbit is to God. "His feeling that there is an unseen world is instinctive and more of his actions than anyone suspects constitute transactions within it." When playing basketball, Rabbit is said to be "gliding on a blessing." In *Rabbit Is Rich*, when the specter of the dead females—Rebecca and Jill—does momentarily intrude on Rabbit's consciousness, he excuses himself by comparing himself favorably with God: "The years have piled on, the surviving have patched things up, and so many more have joined the dead, undone by diseases for which only God is to blame, that it no longer seems so bad, it seems more as if Jill just moved to another town, where the population is growing. . . . Think of all the blame God has to shoulder." Sodomy inspires Rabbit to say that "in the shadows he trusts himself as if speaking in prayer."

Rabbit's feelings for his baby son in *Rabbit, Run* are also pitched in terms that are both overly transcendent and metaphorically unsatisfying—as if the suggestion of the eternal in the tenor obviates the need for an acutely observed vehicle. "As the child hungrily roots for the bottle in his mouth, Rabbit hovers, seeking what you never find, the expression with which to communicate, to transfer those fleeting burdens, ominous and affectionate, that are placed upon us and as quickly lifted, like the touch of a brush." Even that Big Painter in the Sky is on the move—certainly Rabbit's occasional impulses of tenderness don't last long enough to result in any corresponding behavior.

But behavior is not the point for the American innocent. All that matters is that his heart must be pure, and he must move forward to the quest which for so many male American writers is the most crucial one: the search for the unfettered self.

The self must live in the world, though, and this is the problem. In seeing Other People as antithetical to heroic fulfillment, many male American writers have locked themselves into an adolescent solipsism that often blames women for the frustration of the boy's solitary dreams. In the end there is something unsatisfying in this and something more than disappointing in having to read American literature as a boy's own story, in having to watch the dominant storytellers falling through the hole, the blind spot, in their vision.

How, then, do we read these dominant storytellers after we have acquired a certain kind of vision? Or do we simply give them up, saying, "Life's too short and I still haven't read *La Princesse de Clèves*." To renounce them in this way would be a mistake; we deprive ourselves of the pleasures of these writers' aesthetic mastery, we keep ourselves from important information, and we grant both the books and the writers more power than they ought to have over us. As if even proximity to the books were dangerous. Our decision to read or not to read should include a decision as to whether the pleasure we get from the book is worth the displeasure of its distortions. And this will vary, of course, from reader to reader and from book to book. If, as an experiment, we replace misogyny with anti-Semitism, we immediately know that it is harder for us to give up some books than others: we may find it easy to give up the *Pisan Cantos* but feel the loss of Céline, or vice versa. In the case of the three writers of whom I have spoken, I would be sorry never again to experience Dreiser's vibrant descriptions, or Faulkner's dreamy poetry, whereas it will be no loss for me to contemplate not reading the final installment of the Rabbit tetralogy, *Rabbit at Rest* (did the ever gallant John Updike entitle the book just to help me out?), because Updike's style, with its fake poetic otiosity, provides me with insufficient compensations.

Perhaps when we consider reading gifted but distorting writers we should keep in mind two metaphors. We can think of this kind of reading as a journey made in the company of an arresting but undependable guide. He can show us a hidden waterfall, a stunning glimpse of the river, but he may also take us to a fetid swamp and call it exotic wetlands. We may have waded into the swamp, and then been puzzled at the stench that seemed to linger on our hair and skin. Now, knowing better, we can say to our guide: "I'll go with you to the waterfall, to see the view of the river, but the exotic wetlands are a stinking swamp, and I won't go with you there. I will stand at the edge of the swamp, but I won't hesitate to describe the smell."

Or perhaps we can think of this kind of reading as a process of unveiling. Before, we were afraid of what we would see, expecting that we would encounter the august patriarch, bearded and implacable, fixing us with his authoritative eye. We girded ourselves like Antigone before Creon. Now we have learned that the face beneath the veil is not the bearded father's but the pimply boy's. Absorbing in his power to tell a tale. Nevertheless a boy.

Edith Wharton:
Ethan Frome and the
Shorter Fiction

Edith Wharton was a lady. Every aspect of her life, from her birth on Fifth Avenue to her death on the Riviera, was touched by the enlivening hand of privilege, a sure and firm hand that could readily constrict. An astonishing number of critics, seemingly almost against their will, think of her in terms of her class and wealth; even the most admiring commentators adopt a punitive tone. An upper-class woman was an absurd figure as a writer, particularly as a writer of fiction. The novel, we have been told, grew up with the middle class, and by and large its creators have come from that temperate zone. Few of the genuinely poor have written novels, nor have the unimaginably wealthy kept up their end. It takes a long time to write a novel; more than any other literary genre, it partakes of toil. The novelist as laborer is an idea that fulfills something important in the readerly imagination; to imagine a fashionable woman writing on a lapboard in her bed, as Edith Wharton did, offends our sense of what should be. Is it because we feel somewhat ashamed of devoting so much time to reading what has not happened and is not true? For most of its history, the novel has had to defend itself against the charge that it is read by indolent ladies alternating pages with chocolates, killing time while waiting for their rakish lovers, or their fittings at the dressmaker's, or the shampooing of their little dogs. We want to believe that such a reader of novels could never have written one.

Edith Wharton wrote in bed, her secretary sitting across the room patiently waiting to pick up the pages as they fell, like petals, to the floor. Wharton never wrote in a mean room, or an ugly one. The look of things, the rightness of them, was important to her. She could afford to make distinctions. She was the daughter of one of the oldest families of Old New York—the kind of family that resented the Astors and the Vanderbilts as parvenus. The love of beauty, but not only of "beautiful objects," seems to have been one of her earliest driving forces. She spent eight years of her childhood in Europe, and the return to New York shocked her: she would always, even in her most charitable moments, find New York to be a horror aesthetically. It seems odd to think of her as having been born during the Civil War, but 1862 was the year of her birth; and she lived to decry Mussolini. She came of age during that acutely felt and self-reflective historical time that was the transition to modernity.

But what was it a transition from? Our image of the nineteenth century as a time of solid and predictable probity is mere fantasy; Europe was regularly convulsed by political events, and by 1860 economic life was radically different from what it had been fifty years before. But the conventions of private life, it would seem, held. How they held and at what cost is the subject of most of the fiction we associate with Edith Wharton.

Her most successful and most fully realized novels, *The House of Mirth* and *The Age of Innocence*, concern themselves with the collision between the free spirit and the restraints of conventional society. But Edith Wharton was no simpleminded romantic; if she was aware of the price that society exacted, she was appalled by what would happen if society's foundations were pulled away. Her heart was with the sensitive, the impetuous, the sexually responsive souls, but her reason concluded it was better that they be sacrificed individually than bring down those who stood in their way. We find her caution sometimes hateful: why keep the structure up, we moderns ask ourselves, when it is only a shelter for rotting corpses, who steal oxygen from those who still draw breath?

But none of the great novelists was optimistic about the outcome if the human heart followed its course. Tolstoy's Anna and Vronsky end up quarreling and disillusioned; Emma Bovary poisons herself, and not a day too soon. Oddly, for the texture of their fiction is so different, Wharton invites comparison with Hardy. For Hardy, the universe and its ambassador, Cruel Nature, are strong, implacable, ill-wishing forces. The weak human spirit has no chance. For Wharton, the universe is not natural but social; no less than the heaths or the unloving storms, the world of men waits to devour the responsive flesh. But unlike Hardy's natural forces, which destroy heedlessly and to no benefit, the society that Wharton presents feeds on its young for its survival. And the alternative is— what? An anarchy she shrank from and condemned. We do not go to Edith Wharton to find a problem solver. Her view of life is tragic; her gods sit not on Olympus but on upholstered furniture in perfectly appointed rooms. And unlike the Greek gods, they have Reason and reasons on their side, which they can summon by the silent raising of a gloved hand.

The biographical roots for Wharton's preoccupation with the sensitive, generous soul thwarted by society are obvious. She was the daughter of a stiff, judging mother and a kind but ineffectual and distant father. She had no reason to believe her parents understood her. They inhabited a world of social duty and social pleasure; her father's dilatory interest in his library—and in his daughter's increasingly frequent presence in it—was the closest anyone in the family came to an artistic or an intellectual life. Edith "scribbled"— poetry mostly—but no one took much notice of it. This, perhaps, was fortunate, for if they'd noticed they'd have discouraged it in no uncertain terms; ladies did not write. Edith came out, was proposed to, but the marriage was thwarted by the groom's mother, who resented the Joneses and their kind for having treated her with the cold indifference they reserved for the nouveaux riches. A man named Walter Berry then courted her but inexplicably failed to propose, although he became her lifelong friend.

These two rejections left her humiliated, and at twenty-four she married Teddy Wharton, a genial, simplehearted man who loved the outdoors and shared her affection for dogs. The dogs were almost all they had in common. Sexually, the marriage was a disaster, and after a short time there was no physical union between husband and wife. Nor did he understand her work. He seems not to have read her books, and once, while walking behind her, he remarked to a guest: "Look at that small waist. You'd never think she wrote a line of poetry."

When she was in her forties, her strong erotic nature was awakened by an affair with a journalist named Morton Fullerton. But as their relationship was reaching its maturity, Teddy Wharton had a kind of breakdown and revealed to his wife that he had squandered part (though by no means all) of her fortune and had kept a mistress in a Boston house—renting some of the house's other rooms to chorus girls. To Edith this must have seemed a grotesque, distorting mirror held up to her own life with Fullerton; their sexual relationship dissolved soon thereafter, though they remained always on good terms.

Long before the Fullerton affair, Edith Wharton had transformed herself from lady scribbler to *femme de lettres*. More than that: she had begun to earn money by her writing. It is impossible to trace this transformation; the pressure of some thrusting assurance—without which no one goes on writing—must have inexorably made itself felt. She never gave up her interest in society, her position as a hostess, her luxurious and indefatigable traveling. But every morning she wrote, and her production is staggering: a score of novels and collections of stories, poems and travel writing. Her great friends were Henry James and Bernard Berenson, but she was on easy terms with the nobility of several countries and entertained the artistic luminaries who passed through or lived in Paris (although, notably, not the circle whose center was Gertrude Stein). How odd, then, that she should write a book like *Ethan Frome*.

The source of the novel was a sledding accident that took place near Wharton's American home, in Lenox, Massachusetts. The incident resulted in the death of one eighteen-year-old girl and the maiming and permanent disfigurement of two others. Wharton kept this incident in her mind for four years before she began writing *Ethan Frome*; one can imagine it cropping up, crowding out other, more intellectual or fashionable, images. The preface that Wharton attached to *Ethan Frome* betrays her insecurity about her subject. She is almost defensive, as if she feels it necessary to assert her right to cross the class boundaries she so fervently believed in. Yet, she assures us, in a sentence odd if only for its rather humble straightforwardness: "It was the first subject I had ever approached with full confidence in its value, for my own purpose, and a relative faith in my power to render at least part of what I saw in it."

What can she possibly have meant by this? That other subjects, closer to her immediate experience, failed to grip her with the immediate rightness of this one? Perhaps what took hold of her as a writer of fiction was the possibility of portraying a life shaped almost exclusively by necessity. For, as Cynthia Ozick has pointed out, Wharton's life never felt the impress of necessity. The double chance of her being free from any economic constraint and any familial emotional tie meant she could live anywhere, see anyone, do anything. For Wharton and the people she chiefly wrote about, anguish came as a result of the soul's wrong choices. But the limits of Ethan Frome's life had their roots in the physical. The poverty of the land and the ill health of his parents prematurely turned Ethan from a promising young man studying engineering in Worcester—shyly taking pleasure in being referred to by his fellow students as "old Ethe" and "old Stiff" and worrying about his awkwardness with local girls—into the embodiment of the Suffering Servant. Scarcity is a character in the novel, the dark side of the Puritan austerity that was part, Wharton felt, of the New England landscape itself. As the novel progresses, the grip of winter is more and more surely felt. Interestingly, the French translation of *Ethan Frome* is titled *Hiver*.

Ethan Frome is a masterpiece of evocation, and it is remarkable that in this tale about rural life written by a woman, some of the strongest images are not natural but mechanical and metallic, two categories that we associate with the urban male worker. Consider this description of a winter night:

The night was perfectly still, and the air so dry and pure that it gave little sensation of cold. The effect produced on Frome was rather of a complete absence of atmosphere, as though nothing less tenuous than ether intervened between the white earth under his feet and the metallic dome overhead. "It's like being in an exhausted receiver," he thought. Four or five years earlier he had taken a year's course at a technological college at Worcester, and dabbled in the laboratory with a friendly professor of physics.

And here is Edith Wharton describing the excluded Ethan looking in at the dance from which he must fetch Mattie:

> Seen thus, from the pure and frosty darkness in which he stood, it seemed to be seething in a mist of heat. The metal reflectors of the gas-jets sent crude waves of light against the white-washed walls, and the iron flanks of the stove at the end of the hall looked as though they were heaving with volcanic fires. The floor was thronged with girls and young men. Down the side wall facing the window stood a row of kitchen chairs from which the older women had just risen. By this time the music had stopped, and the musicians—a fiddler, and the young lady who played the harmonium on Sundays—were hastily refreshing themselves at one corner of the supper table which aligned its devastated pie dishes and ice cream saucers at the end of the hall. The guests were preparing to leave, and the tide had already set toward the passage where coats and wraps were hung, when a young man with a sprightly foot and a shock of black hair shot into the middle of the floor and clapped his hands.

These images are astonishing on several levels. Like metaphysical conceits, they bring together surprising combinations: the winter night and the ether; the country dance and volcanic fires. In the case of both passages, some larger spiritual realm is suggested with a telegraphic spareness. In Ethan's mind there is room both for the whole world of scientific knowledge and for the sensual over-richness of hell. The young man with a shock of black hair is a diabolic figure; the pie dishes are "devastated." In contrast to this, the emptiness of the winter night in which all traces of the body have been eliminated seems infinitely desirable. Yet these are the thoughts of a young man in love with a young woman—and how appropriate. Ethan imagines that fate has destined that he will be forever the frozen child staring in at the warm room where his beloved stands before the fire of ordinary happiness. What happens, of course, is incalculably worse.

The second extraordinary aspect of these images is that they were written by Edith Wharton. One of the problems for *Ethan Frome* is that, perhaps because of its brevity, perhaps because of its emotional accessibility, it has become a standard high school text, and much of Wharton's extraordinary imaginative achievement is lost to its first readers. But it might not be a bad thing if all readers could be taught before they are of voting age that it is possible for a writer to write far outside the experiential range of his or her own life, well, that could only be a good thing for the body politic. The reader should marvel—and I mean marvel literally, as in a response to a genuine mystery—at the fact that a woman who spent all her life among the rich and powerful knew to the marrow of her writerly bones how a young man who had had one year at a technical college felt when he was cold, and what it was like at a country dance for New England farmers. She could not possibly have attended one; she could not possibly even have looked, like Ethan, through the window: her self-regard would not have permitted it. Yet in a paragraph we know everything about those dances just as, in a few words, every unreal winter night in our personal histories comes back to us, its inorganic beauty heightened in our memories by the breathtaking power of Wharton's language.

The power of the language—spare, passionate, and durable—is one of the factors that contribute to this highly dramatic story's utter lack of melodrama. Another factor is the story's relentless insistence on the impossibility of happiness in the lives it describes. Melodrama is a palliative; it allows for release, even if the release is death. The death in melodrama is a beautiful one, eminently illustratable. The circle is inevitably closed; if the young mother dies, she has not failed her child; the lovers, if temporarily parted, will meet in eternity. Had Wharton allowed Ethan and Mattie to succeed in their original plan, she would have written melodrama. And she would have failed us, for what she has portrayed is far worse than the violent, untimely, self-willed death of two lovers. It is the horrible reversal of love that she shows us, the change of the beautiful love object into the disfigured, petty tormentor. *Ethan Frome* has elements of romance in it, but Wharton radically refused the Romantic's romance with time. Time here is not the swift devastator—like the consumers of the pie and ice cream at the dance. It is rather the gradual, relentless poisoner; each day a bit more of life is soured, hardened, and the crust, unpalatable, must nevertheless be consumed.

The end of *Ethan Frome* is, in fact, the triumph of the realistic mode over the Romantic one. Our penultimate vision of Mattie is of an ardent young woman about to face her death for love, suicidally sledding down the hill with Ethan. She doesn't die, though; she is crippled. Our last encounter with her—we are spared the visual details of her impairment—is our hearing her complain about the insufficiency of Zeena's tending the fire: "It's only just been made up this very minute. Zeena fell asleep and slep' ever so long, and I thought I'd be frozen stiff before I could wake her up and get her to 'tend to it."

The character of Zeena is a brilliant portrayal of the kind of woman whose métier is illness and whose strength comes from the certainty invented by the invalid's unlimited free time and the innocence born of the truth that most wrongdoing requires a physical capacity the invalid lacks or chooses to stifle. Ethan married her because he was both grateful to her for nursing his mother and fearful of losing his mind, as his mother did, if he stayed by himself on the desolate farmstead. But marriage turns Zeena from nurse to invalid. She becomes expert at her own symptoms, a connoisseur of the latest medical knowledge as it applies to her own case. She makes trips to consult doctors—her last one is the occasion of Ethan and Mattie's only night alone together—and comes back "laden with expensive remedies . . . her last visit to Springfield had been commemorated by her paying twenty dollars for an electric battery which she had never learned to use." But in fact, Zeena does not travel only to consult a doctor; her trip's real purpose is both to get medical justification and to lay plans for Mattie's being replaced by a hired girl. The efficiency and speed with which she achieves her goal are thrilling to watch: she is the consummate destroyer, all the more horrifying because her destruction brings her no pleasure. Her only prosperity will accrue from nursing her symptoms, from her satisfaction at having destroyed the lives of two people whose capacity for happiness is greater than her own, and from the triumphs of having pressed the claims of her legitimacy and having kept her man.

But fate is not even kind to the twisted desires of the legitimate wife. Zeena must nurse the woman who stole her husband from her; Mattie and Ethan's physical incapacity restores her strength. Nonetheless, the suggestion is that however unbearable the conditions of Mattie and Zeena's life, Ethan's is worse. The women afford each other a kind of dreadful company, carping at each other with the freedom of equals. It is Ethan who has been utterly destroyed. The worst aspect of his survival is the Frome longevity. "Ethan'll likely touch a hundred," says a Starkfield observer. We recall that the wife of one of the Ethan Fromes in the graveyard was named Endurance. Endurance is both the stone that crushes Ethan's life and the dark god in whose service he is raised up. Silent, maimed, he is heroic in his very bending to the Necessity that Edith Wharton lived so far removed from.

It is with a jolt that we turn from Starkfield to the world of Edith Wharton's short stories. The characters in these stories are typical of the people Wharton lived among, and if the stories lack the austere perfections of *Ethan Frome*—which Wharton referred to as her "granite outcroppings"—they provide a worldly massiveness that satisfies another kind of readerly desire. If *Ethan Frome* is a Shaker pie safe, these stories are a Louis XV armoire; if Scarcity is a character in *Ethan Frome*, then Artifice lives in the stories. Concealment is an important activity for people whose lives are radically divorced from the natural. Spontaneity is no virtue in a world whose center is the drawing room; under the gaze of ancestral portraits in heavy frames, one does not act directly from the heart. Or one does at one's peril and most probably to one's loss. Yet under all the well-tailored clothes are hearts and bodies whose demands press. These people must live their lives and move among their kind; their employment is the work of human relations, and the enforced constrictions of that field create demands and sorrows almost as impossible as the situation of Ethan and Mattie.

"The Other Two" is one of Wharton's most curiously modern stories. Alice Haskett Varick Waythorn is the survivor of two divorces; the story begins at the inception of her third marriage. It is told from the point of view of her new husband, who looks upon the prospect of marriage with Alice with a comfortable and quiet optimism. Alice so embodies the domestic harmony he has always prized and so easily fits into his notions of private felicity that he congratulates himself on his liberality in not balking at her past failures. He understands that she has triumphed over her victimization with a quiet heroism of a particularly feminine kind. In the end, however, he discovers that what he thought was heroism was really a species of ambitiousness. She does possess strength, but it is the strength of being able to invent herself in the image of whatever man is the next step on her steady upward climb. In a brilliantly realized scene, Waythorn takes tea in his library with the other two husbands and realizes that he will never genuinely possess his wife, because if there is an essentially true Alice, she will never give it to a man. Mysteriously, ineffably, this consummate wife will nourish the self that will present itself to no husband.

The theme of divorce recurs frequently in Wharton's fiction, and this is not surprising, either in biographical or in aesthetic terms. If marriage is the perfect metaphor for the conjunction of public and private life, divorce is the ideal one for that life's dissolution. Wharton must have often contemplated divorcing Teddy, but she shrank from the implications of divorce that she suggests in "Autres Temps." The theme of this subtle, wistful story is that "the success or failure of the deepest human experiences may hang on a matter of chronology." "Autres Temps" is the story of a Mrs. Lidcote, who left her husband and was divorced in an age when this meant being cast out by society. Her daughter, Leila, does the same thing at a time when it means only a new note in a hostess's engagement book.

Mrs. Lidcote has an admirer, Franklin Ide, who tries to reassure her that her belief that she is still being punished by society is only her paranoia. But it turns out that she is right. Leila must uneasily hide her mother upstairs—with protestations that she is merely securing her mother's rest—while she entertains an ambassador's wife below. It is understood that Mrs. Lidcote's presence at the table would scotch Leila's new husband's chances for a diplomatic post. Changes in mores have come too late for Mrs. Lidcote; she has lost everything, including her lover. "She had had to pay the last bitterest price of learning that love has a price: that it is worth so much and no more. She had known the anguish of watching the man she loved discover this first, and of reading the discovery in his eyes." She cannot accept the kind offer of Mr. Ide because she knows that for women like her there are no second chances.

It is interesting to compare the treatment of attractive, traditionally feminine women in the works of Edith Wharton and George Eliot. For Eliot, they are destructive parasites, manipulative, acquisitive, a symptom of all that is harmful in human life.

But Wharton grants these women their strengths; she sees that prettiness need not be a veneer covering up corruption, that underneath a charming facade there may be a valuable repository of virtue. This idea is treated comically in "Zingu," in which Mrs. Roby, the beautiful supposed flibbertigibbet, shows up the pseudointellectual women of the reading circle, thereby saving them from social disaster but being ostracized by them (it can only have been a relief) for her pains.

The question of female beauty and its powers forms the center of the novella "The Touchstone." "Genius is of small use to a woman who does not know how to do her hair," Wharton tells us. But does she speak from the secure perspective of a woman who believes she does know how to do her hair, or the anxious one of the woman who fears that she does not? The matter of "The Touchstone" concerns the love of a distinguished woman writer, Mrs. Aubyn, for a young man, Glennard, who cannot reciprocate her passion because he does not find her beautiful. After Mrs. Aubyn's death, he falls in love with a young woman as poor as himself and as lovely as his dreams. In order to have enough money to marry her, he offers Mrs. Aubyn's love letters for publication. The book is a wild success—but Glennard is torn apart by self-revulsion. He deliberately arranges that his wife will find him out, and her response—to stay with him—is the triumph of one of those Wharton women, cool, harmonious, seemingly impassive, who are the source and the embodiment—the "touchstone"—of the only genuine virtue in a world steeped in corruption, self-service, and self-deceit.

The great strength of her stories comes from the beautifully sculpted sentences that are the foundation of Wharton's formal genius. I mean *formal* in its two senses: pertaining to form, and the opposite of informal. Wharton, like her friend Henry James, writes always from a distance. The observer, never dispassionate, is at the aristocrat's remove. This position allows Wharton the opportunity for the grand, patrician generalization, impossible in a less wrought prose. It may no longer be open to writers in the new democracy of fictional language to write sentences like these: "The desire to propitiate a divinity is generally in inverse ratio to its responsiveness" ("Zingu"). "If man is at times indirectly flattered by the moral superiority of women, her mental ascendency is extenuated by no such oblique tribute to his powers" ("The Touchstone"). And it would be difficult to imagine a contemporary feeling free to describe Rome as Wharton does in another story, "Roman Fever":

> The clear heaven overhead was emptied of all its gold. Dusk spread over it, abruptly darkening the Seven Hills. Here and there lights began to twinkle through the foliage at their feet. Steps were coming and going on the deserted terrace—waiters looking out of the doorway at the head of the stairs, then reappearing with trays and napkins and flasks of wine. Tables were moved, chairs straightened. A feeble string of electric lights flickered out. Some vases of faded flowers were carried away, and brought back replenished. A stout lady in a dust-coat suddenly appeared, asking in broken Italian if anyone had seen the elastic band which held together her tattered Bae-deker. She poked with her stick under the table at which she had lunched, the waiters assisting.

The genius, then, is formal, it is distant, but it is never cold. For all her sophistication, Wharton believed in innocence (Ethan is an innocent), and her sympathy is with the innocents who are shredded in the teeth of the machinery of the world. Perhaps the truest reflection of her sense of life occurs in her story "The Last Asset," which has at its center two innocents: Samuel and Hermione Newell, a father and daughter whose lives have been shaped and disfigured by the shrewd and desperate calculations of the woman who is wife to one, mother to the other. Newell offers his philosophy to a fellow American whom he meets in a Paris restaurant: "If you make up your mind not to be happy there's no reason why you shouldn't have a pretty good time."

Newell has been estranged from his wife and daughter because his wife has, in some way that Wharton does not specify, emotionally assassinated him. But Mrs. Newell has made a brilliant match for her unpromising daughter, with a member of one of the oldest French families, and the marriage cannot take place unless Mr. Newell appears at the wedding. At first he refuses; he has asked only to be left in peace, to his life of small activities. But in the end the goodness and courage of Hermione triumph. "It was one more testimony to life's indefatigable renewals, to nature's secret of drawing fragrance from corruption; and as his eyes turned from the girl's illuminated presence to the resigned and stoical figure sunk in the adjoining chair, it occurred to him that he had perhaps worked better than he knew in placing them, if only for a moment, side by side."

It is possible that only a woman born of privilege could have written those sentences; but what is necessary is that the woman who created them was first and most passionately from her birth a writer, and a writer with a heart.

Flannery O'Connor:
The Habit of Being

After Flannery O'Connor's death, Katherine Anne Porter wrote to a mutual friend: "I am always astonished at Flannery's pictures, which show nothing of her grace. She was very slender with beautiful, smooth feet and ankles: she had a fine, clear, rosy skin and beautiful eyes."

O'Connor's face was a peculiar one for a writer, even allowing for the effects of the disease she contracted at twenty-five. Not all writers are beauties, but usually there is something in the face to suggest distinction—a habit, if not of fashion, then of style. No face could appear less fashionable or stylish than Flannery O'Connor's; it is accepted rather than invented; it is a face from the provinces. In her early photographs, her expression is sour; a fearful, pure intelligence presents itself, unqualified by deep affections. There is no humor in the face here; she is sullen, judging; she is Mary Grace in "Revelation," she is Hulga in "Good Country People."

Later, after years of illness, she is oddly more attractive. Prematurely aged, she has grown graceful; the sourness is gone, the humor enters. Still, it does not seem a writer's face; rather that of an aunt more educated than the rest of the family, full of good sense and works of mercy, sharp-tongued but practical in a crisis. It is a face untouched by sexual experience or curiosity, which is why, perhaps, it seems not one of our own.

She was born in Milledgeville, Georgia, in 1925, attended the local women's college there, and went north for the first time at twenty-two to become part of the School for Writers at the State University of Iowa. At twenty-five, when she was living with Sally and Robert Fitzgerald in Connecticut, she discovered that she had lupus erythematosus, the disease that had killed her father. She knew she was dying, and she knew that her physical disintegration would take years. She returned to Milledgeville, where she lived on the family farm with her mother until her death fourteen years later.

She seems to belong to another age, but then in what age could one place her? Certainly she is a kind of Puritan, but of a very particular variety. Her interest lay not in the damnation of her characters but in their redemption. She has the formality and the reasonableness of a neoclassicist, the social acuity of a Victorian. But the darkness of her conclusions about the world, a darkness illuminated only by her belief in mystery and in mysterious salvation, personally expressed in a passionate, traditional Catholicism, creates both her appeal for modern readers and their problems with her.

Always revered by a small world of critics and serious readers, she has only recently achieved popular reputation. For many years, she was less well known than her fellow Southerners Katherine Anne Porter and Eudora Welty. Perhaps this is because her greatest genius is expressed in short stories, and the form of the short story has always attracted a smaller, if fiercer, audience than the novel. This, in addition to the quirkiness and difficulty of her themes, assured her a limited, passionate audience. In her lifetime she published two novels, *Wise Blood* (1952) and *The Violent Bear It Away* (1960); it is on a posthumous collection of short stories, *Everything That Rises Must Converge*, that her reputation largely rests.

For O'Connor, the habit of art (a phrase of Maritain's she found congenial) began with the habit of looking. It was the particular habit of her genius. And yet, in all the time spent looking, she seemed to see little of beauty, either in nature or in her own kind. Her essay about peacocks, which she raised with devotion and pleasure, speaks of their beauty, but in an unmoved voice. In her letters and essays she reports their activities with the dull eye of a farm wife. One imagines that in her mind the word "beauty" was always preceded by the word "mere." Why, then, did she go on looking? Because it amused her and was her vocation. And why, if the central mystery that shaped her life was, as she said, the Incarnation, the Son of God's taking on human flesh, was her approach to the human: "Anything the human being touches, even Christian truth, he deforms slightly in his own image." She says deforms, not forms: the human contact is always destructive. One is reminded of a similar perception of Gerard Manley Hopkins's in "God's Grandeur":

> *And all is seared with trade; bleared, smeared with toil;*
> *And wears man's smudge and shares man's smell . . .*

But Hopkins's vision shows the presence of God overcoming the corruption of the natural in its own terms:

> *And for all this, nature is never spent;*
> *There lives the dearest freshness deep down things . . .*

Like most contemporary Catholics, O'Connor found that nature didn't matter very much, and that although individual humans could achieve redemption, the race remained, in this world, unredeemed. Whereas the theological center of her life is the mystery of the Incarnation, the emotional one is the doctrine of original sin. Redemptions occur so frequently in her fiction because they are needed so badly. The natural order provides no redemption; it occurs through unlikely means—violence, ugliness—and is always unearned.

It is hard to imagine the possessor of such a vision doing something so ordinary as writing a letter. And indeed, O'Connor's letters are, at first, a bit inhuman. Sure of herself, with an integrity that never wavered, she was sustained from the beginning by her work, her faith, her family, and remained untouched, even in the face of death, by commoner forms of uncertainty.

Her strength was always evident. In 1949, when she was only twenty-four, she wrote the following astonishing words to her agent, in response to a critical letter from her editor at Rinehart:

The criticism is vague and really tells me nothing except that they don't like it. I feel the objections they raise are connected with its virtues, and the thought of working with them specifically to correct these lacks they mention is repulsive to me. The letter is addressed to a slightly dim-witted Camp Fire Girl, and I cannot look with composure on getting a lifetime of others like them.

There are not many twenty-four-year-olds who would be unmoved by the remarks of a professional, one's first editor. But O'Connor, although she often asked for criticism from her friends and was glad to make changes when she thought them improvements, was always quick to contradict sharply any criticism she disagreed with.

Isolated as she was, O'Connor made and kept many friends through her correspondence. There is little chitchat in her letters, and she uses them to discuss important matters with the people she values but does not often get to see. The important matters are always the same: writing and the Church.

It is surprising to discover the writers whom she favors. She reveres Nabokov and says he is her most important contemporary influence. She hotly defends *Lolita*. "All these moralists who condemn Lolita give me the creeps." She admires J. F. Powers, Salinger, Malamud, Iris Murdoch, and her friend John Hawkes; she detests James Jones, Capote, and Carson McCullers, and is critical of Updike and Styron. She is far from a knee-jerk Catholic in her literary responses, equivocal about Green and Waugh and bored by Bernanos.

She is at her most generous when criticizing the manuscripts of her friends. What a superb and practical critic she was, and how helpful: "Don't name any streets Oak and Main. Even if they are that kind of street, cease and desist." "Strangle that word *dreams*." "If there is no possibility for change in a character, we have no interest in him. . . . You could correct this by having the boy not quite so evil, by having him hesitate before each of his evil acts and decide on the evil for a reason which he figures out. Otherwise there is no use to write about him. . . . In fiction everything that has an explanation has to have it and the residue is Mystery with a Capital M."

These letters are particularly valuable in their revelations of O'Connor's intentions about her work, sometimes in specific stories. I have always wondered if the Catholic aspects of her fiction were an overlay contributed by wishful Catholic readers. Aware of this tendency in some readers and critics, she writes to John Hawkes: "I am afraid that one of the great disadvantages of being known as a Catholic writer is that no one thinks you can lift the pen without trying to show somebody redeemed." But clearly her faith informed her life and her fiction. She refers to *The Violent Bear It Away* as "a very minor hymn to the Eucharist." She interprets the Misfit's murder of the grandmother in "A Good Man Is Hard to Find" as "a moment of grace for her . . . but it leads him to shoot her. This moment of grace excites the devil to frenzy." Her more general, theoretical ideas about the relationship of her faith to her work, which she perfects in *Mystery and Manners*, seem to have begun in her letters. I was delighted to see her answer, in a letter to Sister Mariella Gable in 1963, a question that had always puzzled me: Why does she write always about Protestants, never about Catholics?

I can write about Protestant believers better than Catholic believers—because they express their belief in diverse kinds of dramatic action which is obvious enough for me to catch. I can't write about anything subtle. Another thing, the prophet is a man apart. He is not typical of a group. Old Tarwater is not typical of the Southern Baptist or the Southern Methodist. Essentially, he's a crypto-Catholic. When you leave a man alone with his Bible and the Holy Ghost inspires him, he's going to be a Catholic one way or another, even though he knows nothing about the visible Church. His kind of Christianity may not be socially desirable, but it will be real in the sight of God. If I set myself to write about a socially desirable Christianity, all the life would go out of what I do. And if I set myself to write about the essence of Christianity, I would have to quit writing fiction, or become another person.

I wish I did not find this explanation so tortuous—I don't buy the idea of Jimmy Swaggart as a crypto-Catholic—and I wish I found some of her apologetics more accessible. It is far easier to embrace her theories about fiction than her theories about faith. It must be remembered that O'Connor was a strict Catholic who believed all the dogma of the Church and obeyed all its rules, including the one that demanded she ask permission of a priest before she read a book on the Index. Her stand on birth control is a bit chilling.

> The Church's stand on birth control is the most absolutely spiritual of her stands and with all of us being materialists at heart, there is little wonder that it causes unease. I wish various fathers would quit trying to defend it by saying that the world can support 40 billion. I will rejoice when they say, "This is right, whether we all rot on top of each other or not, dear children, as we certainly may. Either practice restraint or be prepared for crowding."

It would be easy, and in some ways a comfort, if one were able to dismiss O'Connor's faith by reducing it to such bristling simplicities. But her faith is complicated. Neither mystical nor social in orientation, she sees the Church as the visible symbol of order; it is, as such, invaluable to her, particularly in the context of modern disorder. Yet she is not deceived about the Church's shortcomings. She sees them, but they do not daunt her. To her friend Cecile Dawkins she writes:

> You judge it [the Church] strictly by its human element, by unimaginative and half-dead Catholics who would be startled to know the nature of what they defend by formula. The miracle is that the Church's doctrine is kept pure both by and from such people. Nature is not prodigal of genius, and the Church makes do with what nature gives her. At the age of 11, you encounter some old priest who calls you a heretic for inquiring about evolution; at about the same time Pierre Teilhard de Chardin, S.J., is in China discovering Peking man.

The Church, for O'Connor, has little to do with its personnel and less to do with their conduct:

I am a Catholic peculiarly possessed of the modern consciousness, that thing Jung describes as unhistorical, solitary, and
guilty. To possess this *within* the Church is to bear a burden,
the necessary burden for the conscious Catholic. It's to feel the
contemporary situation at the ultimate level. I think that the
Church is the only thing that is going to make the terrible
world we are coming to endurable; the only thing that makes
the Church endurable is that it is somehow the body of Christ
and that on this we are fed. It seems to be a fact that you have
to suffer as much from the Church as for it but if you believe
in the divinity of Christ, you have to cherish the world at the
same time that you struggle to endure it.

O'Connor's faith sustained her through a severely circum-
scribed life and the knowledge of a progressively worsening illness
and certain early death. But resignation is not a term one asso-
ciates with her life; her response is altogether grander and more
energetic:

I sent you the other Sewell piece and the one on St. Thomas
& Freud. This letter has the answer in it to what you call my
struggle to submit, which is not a struggle to submit but a
struggle to accept and with passion. I mean, possibly, with
joy. Picture me with my ground teeth stalking joy—fully
armed too as it's a highly dangerous quest. The other day I
ran upon a wonderful quotation: "The dragon is at the side
of the road watching those who pass. Take care lest he devour
you: You are going to the Father of souls, but it is necessary
to pass by the dragon."

The Church, she says, saved her about two thousand years in
learning how to write. Its language and its mode of thinking led
her as well to perceptions like "Part of purgatory must be the
realization of how little it would take to make a vice into a virtue,"
which give her fiction the dimension of transcendence that distin-
guishes it from most contemporary writing.

O'Connor chose to deal with her illness by retiring to rural
Georgia to live on a farm with her mother. Her letters to her
beloved friends are never effusive, barely even emotional. But as

she says to one of them, "I come from a family where the only emotion respectable to show is irritation." Her deep concern for the people she loves expresses itself in practical ways: jokes; concern for health, both physical and spiritual; a willingness to write recommendations and criticize manuscripts; to look for gingerbread mix and funny clippings for friends who were in Europe. Her last letter is to Maryat Lee, and it is full of worry about an anonymous phone call Maryat has received in New York. Flannery writes: "Cowards can be just as vicious as those who declare themselves—more so. Don't take any romantic attitude toward that call." A few days later, Flannery was dead.

Courage is Flannery O'Connor's cardinal virtue, both in her life and in her work. Her fiction compels us because of its daring: it has to do with the people and the events we, most of us, are afraid to consider. The irony and formality of her language make the situations bearable. Her life, too, was full of courage and a sense of irony and formality. There is no hint of self-pity or anguish: her acceptance of her fate was complete. But it was not merely a serene acceptance; she was aware of the irony of her destiny, of how the enforced limitations of her life may have been responsible for the perfection of her work. Flannery O'Connor first went north at twenty-two; perhaps she would have stayed there had she not become ill. What would she have written in Iowa or in Connecticut, living a freer life? As it was, she knew her work and settled down to it, realizing that she would not live long, would not live free of pain.

Her letters are a treasure, or, as Flannery would have said, a grace. Funny, relentless, deeply touching, they reveal the mind of one of our least personal writers. Sally Fitzgerald's introduction to the letters collected in *The Habit of Being* is a model of loving understanding: it illuminates what the letters obscure or distort; it acknowledges the less attractive aspects of O'Connor's character, accepts them, and tries to put them in context. Flannery O'Connor's personal voice is a deep pleasure, if sometimes a harsh one. It is, as Catholics used to say, an edification.

William Trevor's
Fools of Fortune

Few colonizers have attached to the romance of the country they have conquered as the Anglo-Irish have. It may be that no other colonizers have been quite so literary; it may be that the racial closeness of conqueror and conquered has called forth a marriage like that of intense, doomed cousins: irresistible to the romantic imagination, damaging for generations. In creating a myth for themselves and for the Celtic Irish, the Anglo-Irish have seen themselves as victims frozen in a frame of grand heroic isolation. In their great houses, with their famous horses and heraldic dogs, they saw themselves suffering loneliness, misunderstanding. They brooded over the half-beloved natives who could not, in any way that could be trusted, love them back. Blood, poetry, and magic—the coin of the Irish Irish drew them in and yet repelled them. Still, they were, deep in their hearts, *not English*. They belonged nowhere except, passionately, where they were.

As the economics of Ireland turns the great estates into hotels, the old romance cannot survive. Yet it may be impossible to write about Ireland without romance of some sort. The strength of the impulse would seem to be borne out by William Trevor, that highly realistic chronicler of the slow rot of English life, whose reports of England abound in painful details of the corruption of lives shaped by reruns of "Kojak" and "Benny Hill," by Wimpy bars and office affairs and the artifacts of local sex shops.

He has invented his own romance about Ireland, a different one, to be sure, from the one that pervades the literary imagination: it is not lit by the Celtic twilight. Trevor, although Irish Protestant, is middle class, the son of a bank manager. He focuses on the ordinary Irish, caught up in the necessities of Irish history. Trevor is fascinated, in his stories about Ireland, by a pervasive evil that must intrude upon the innocent. His romance, which is a moral one, suggests that the Irish, or some of them—the victims—combine viciousness and innocence in ways inaccessible to the English.

For the Irish, the present constantly butts up against the past in the form of a political reality that is at once utterly present and archaic. Attempts at ordinary decency collide with a tradition of brutality and hatred; myth, despite the will of the living mortal, or beckoned by him, eventually must intrude.

In Trevor's story "The Distant Past," an elderly, eccentric Anglo-Irish brother and sister have made peace with their neighbors in the southern Irish town they've lived in all their lives. The "trouble" in the Twenties—when the butcher held a gun on them, and the shopkeepers imprisoned them in their great house—has been forgotten, has become, for them all, a town joke. But when, in the seventies, another time of the "trouble," their town is ruined economically by the resulting decline in the tourist trade, its citizens turn ugly. Friendships of fifty years erode, and the two old people know that the best they can look forward to is a lonely, isolated death. The story, which begins with the hopeful "In the town and beyond it they were regarded as harmlessly peculiar," ends: "It was worse than being murdered in their beds."

In "Beyond the Pale," an unhappy English tourist meets a young man revisiting the place—now a fancy hotel—where he used to meet his childhood sweetheart. The girl has grown up to become a terrorist, and the young man, appalled by the deaths she has caused, kills her, then returns to the place of their childhood happiness to kill himself. Yet in another time, in another place—in England perhaps—the two might have married, brought children of their own back to the hotel. Distraught, the English tourist asks what causes this perverse necessity: "Has it to do with the streets they came from?" she asks, "Or the history they learnt, he from his Christian Brothers, she from her nuns? History is unfinished in this island; long since it has come to a stop in Surrey."

"The Troubles"—the term itself has a mixture of domesticity

and drama—is an irresistible subject for the Irish writer. The relation of past to present, the sickening sense of historical repetition, the unsure conjunction between individual will and national fate—its very attractiveness contains its literary dangers. The mistake that is usually made—as in, for example, Thomas Flanagan's sprawling *The Year of the French* or Julia O'Faolain's admirable but convoluted *No Country for Old Men*—is for the author to be too inclusive, to trace pattern with too heavy a hand, to fall for the romance of violence himself. These dangers Trevor has avoided both in his stories and in his novel *Fools of Fortune* by his spare, elliptical treatment of political and family history. The temptation for the writer about Ireland is to go epical; Trevor's novel instead has a condensed, lyrical tone.

It is a daring technical move, because his plot is full of complications and action. Massacre, suicide, madness, revenge, illegitimate birth, are all contained in a narrative of 240 pages, a narrative written largely in the form of conversations between a husband and wife who have been forcibly separated for fifty years. The novel's action begins in 1918, when Willie Quinton is a boy, although the past is felt always as a living presence: we no sooner learn about the situation of the current Quintons than we hear about their nineteenth-century ancestor Anna.

She is the first of a series of three English brides who make the journey from Dorset in the course of a hundred years, cutting themselves off from the decent life of the English provincial rectory for the romantic soil of Ireland. With Anna Quinton, who dies of famine fever contracted when she tries to help her miserable neighbors, the family tradition of active concern for the Irish Irish is begun.

Nineteen eighteen is a time of peace and prosperity in Ireland for the Quintons. Kilneagh, the Quinton estate, is presided over by Anna Quinton's grandson, Willie's father. The household has a reputation for taking in strays; in one wing of the house live Aunt Pansy and Aunt Fitzeustace, middle-aged maiden ladies; Philomena, their maid, employed out of charity when the priest she worked for died; and Father Kilgarriff, Willie's tutor, a Roman Catholic priest unjustly defrocked for his kindness to a young girl.

"I wish that somehow you might have shared my childhood," writes Willie to his wife sixty years later. For up to 1918, Willie's childhood is that rare thing, happy, and Trevor succeeds in that even rarer thing, portraying a happy childhood convincingly. The details of Willie's life are rendered lightly, offhandedly: " '*Agricola*,' Father Kilgarriff said on the day I began to learn Latin. 'Now there's a word for you.' " The Quintons live a good and happy life; we read of it with a pleasure that allows for no apprehension of what is to come.

The tragedy begins with the burning of Kilneagh house by the Black and Tans, led by a Sergeant Rudkin, who is seeking revenge because an employee of the Quinton Mill has been hung on the estate by Irish revolutionaries. The murdered man was hired by the decent Quintons, who couldn't refuse employment to a returning soldier. Kilneagh is turned into a ruin; Willie's father and two sisters are killed, and Willie's mother becomes a reclusive alcoholic. She leaves Kilneagh for lodgings in the town of Fermoy, where she is nursed by a devoted Kilneagh servant while Willie miserably attends the town school.

Trevor's rendering of the slippage of this elegant, passionate woman is wonderfully done. Occasionally, for her son's sake, she rallies: for a visit to the lawyer, tea at the local hotel, but the attempts are disastrous and an embarrassment to Willie. She retreats to her bed, where she cryptically admonishes him to avenge his family's history upon Sergeant Rudkin, who is now a greengrocer in Liverpool.

Despite all the horrors he has witnessed, Willie seems to possess the potential for a normal future. Trevor's account of his days in his boarding schools is a skillful comic interlude that, like the accounts of Willie's childhood, make the shock of what follows far more intense. His mother kills herself on the one day in years that her servant has gone home to visit her family. At her funeral, he sees again his cousin Marianne, who becomes the last Englishwoman in the novel to be pulled into the Irish fate. In a combination of sympathy and frustration, she offers herself to Willie, and conceives a child. She runs away from finishing school in Switzerland, writing her parents in Dorset only the short, heartless message "Willie will take care of me," and returns to Kilneagh, to find Willie gone and the rest of the household and town mysteriously silent about his whereabouts. Marianne's desperate search for him, her confusion, her adolescent sense of being the only uninitiate in a world where all the adults know the code, are excruciating. Only gradually does she learn that Willie has murdered Sergeant Rudkin in Liverpool and must spend the rest of his life a fugitive to escape punishment.

Marianne returns with her child, Imelda, to Kilneagh. The fate intended for both of them seems at first benign: the old aunts take them in; Father Kilgarriff presides over the house. But of course the Quintons are "fools of fortune"; ordinary life will always escape them. "There's not much left in anyone's life after murder has been committed," Father Kilgarriff tells Marianne. But Marianne refuses to see Willie's act as murder: for her, it is an affair of honor and of ancient justice. She writes in her diary:

I had never even heard of the Battle of the Yellow Ford until Father Kilgarriff told me. And now he wishes he hadn't. The furious Elizabeth cleverly transformed the defeat of Sir Henry Bagenal into victory, ensuring that her Irish battlefield might continue for as long as it was profitable. Father Kilgarriff had told you too, in the scarlet drawing-room with the school-books laid out between you. Just another Irish story it had seemed to you and perhaps, if ever you think of it, it still does. But the battlefield continuing is part of the pattern I see everywhere around me, as your exile is also. How could we in the end have pretended? How could we have rebuilt Kilneagh and watched our children playing among the shadows of destruction? The battlefield has never quietened.

Marianne, as well as everyone the child Imelda meets, insists on turning Willie into a hero. "Often Imelda tried to imagine him, wondering if he was like the Earls of Tyrone and Tyrconnell. The nuns at the convent spoke of him as a hero, even as somebody from a legend, Finn MacCool or the warrior Cuchulainn."

But when Imelda reads the details of how her father murdered Sergeant Rudkin, she finds it neither beautiful nor heroic. The newspaper account allows for no glamorization: "The head was partially hacked from the neck, the body stabbed in seventeen places." Finding it impossible to reconcile the bloody reality of her father's act with the myth created for it, Imelda becomes insane. After fifty years of wandering, Willie returns home to Kilneagh, to his mad middle-aged daughter and his seventy-year-old bride, never fully known. Willie and Marianne begin a peculiar old age in which they can live peacefully with their history of horror. Together they return to their land and they watch their daughter. "They are aware that there is a miracle in this end. . . . They are grateful for what they have been allowed, and for the mercy of their daughter's quiet world, in which there is no ugliness." Imelda seems, although destroyed, a vessel of beauty and health for others.

> Imelda is gifted, so the local people say, and bring the afflicted to her. A woman has been rid of dementia, a man cured of a cataract. Her happiness is like a shroud miraculously about her, its source mysterious except to her. No one but Imelda knows that in the scarlet drawing-room wood blazes in the fireplace while the man of the brass log-box reaches behind him for the hand of the serving girl. Within globes like onions, lights dimly gleam, and carved on the marble of the mantelpiece the clustered leaves are as delicate as the flicker of the flames. No one knows that she is happiest of all when she stands in the centre of the Chinese carpet, able to see in the same moment the garden and the furniture of the room, and to sense that yet another evening is full of the linnet's wings.

In inventing Imelda's fate, Trevor himself seems to have succumbed to the pull of Irish myth. She embodies the Irish genius: visionary, magical, poetic. The Irish have no talent for action; the triumphs of the active life elude them. When they try to act, they are doomed usually to tragic failures easily avoidable by any other race.

At the end of the novel, the Quintons are at peace, not only with old age but even with insanity. It sounds, almost, like the stuff of melodrama, brimming with high sentiment. Yet Trevor has avoided the melodramatic and the sentimental by a combination of formal rigor and moral tact. Melodrama requires a heavy ladling of suspense; we see, at the beginning, the speed of the train, the innocence of the heroine, the villain's leer. We know from the beginning that all will come together: the train, the heroine, the villain, in a way that cannot admit of other possibilities. We need only wait. But in *Fools of Fortune*, Trevor creates characters who are doomed not by their natures but by the nature of Irish history. Willie is a well-intentioned, ordinary boy. He might have had a good life. He might almost not have avenged his family. Only the suicide of his mother pushes him to an act he really wishes to avoid, an act that both his nature and most of his background make him unwilling and unsuited for.

Marianne might not have become obsessed with the honor of the ancient Irish; Imelda might have grown up, profiting by the kindness of those around her; she might never have had to know the details of the stabbing. And Willie might never have come back to Kilneagh. In a subtle plot maneuver, Willie returns to Ireland, ten years before his final homecoming, to attend the funeral of Josephine, his mother's servant. But although he is assured that it is safe for him to return for good, he prefers the consolations of his roses and his villa in Tuscany. He doesn't come home as the conquering hero who would have had to possess some of the vigor of youth for his return to be a triumph. The end of *Fools of Fortune* is written in the quiet tone that follows shattering violence: nothing can be rebuilt; no life, really, can go on; it can only be lived out.

Trevor the realist turns his tough moral gaze on the romantic situation he has created. Willie is a good boy, but he is a murderer. He has hacked a head from a body he has stabbed in seventeen places. Marianne takes a kind of lustful joy in the vengeance of Irish history; in demanding to be a part of it, she sacrifices her daughter. Yet in the end, something is salvaged. Revenge is over; the cycle of violence will not go on, at least for these people. The cost of the peace they have won, however, is enormous: theirs is the peace of the futureless.

Christa Wolf:
Accident/A Day's News

Christa Wolf has set herself nothing less than the task of exploring what it is to be a conscious human being alive in a moment of history. She has approached the problem differently in each of her five novels. Urgency and seriousness mark her work. There is nothing of the entertainment in anything she writes. Plot exists where it does only as a kind of inevitable vector; two of her novels are reworkings of stories whose endings are predetermined, so that plot is beside the point of authorial planning. *Cassandra* retells the Trojan War from the point of view of the murdered, disbelieved prophetess; *No Place on Earth* is about an imaginary meeting between the suicidal Romantic poets Heinrich von Kleist and Karoline von Günderode.

Wolf was a child when the Nazis took power; she came of age in the middle of a nightmare. *The Quest for Christa T.* and *Patterns of Childhood* try to look squarely at what the effects of such a childhood might be on the growing, perceiving child who must go on to live the rest of her life having been told (but not believing) that the nightmare is over. In her most recent novel, *Accident/A Day's News*, Wolf looks on the Janus face of modern technology. The novel takes place in one day, a day on which the narrator lives through the experiences both of the Chernobyl nuclear disaster and of waiting for the news of her beloved brother's complicated (and ultimately successful) brain operation.

Christa Wolf is East German. Her work is stripped of elements that exist merely to give pleasure, as if she has refused the corrupt blandishments of the bourgeois palate and wants to seek only the most useful, nourishing of foods. The considerable beauty of her novels emanates from their spareness. Even *Cassandra*, the busiest of them, doesn't contain diversions. But her books aren't cold, distant, or judging. She doesn't share Beckett's austere vision. Nature and domestic life are sources of great pleasure: life lived in houses, meals prepared and shared with friends, a view of a lake, the scent of herbs crushed in the palm as one walks up a mountain. The task of integrating a life, the exhausting effort of living fully and justly, shape all of Christa Wolf's fictions. Her books are difficult, like certain kinds of prayer. But finishing them, the reader is covered by a sense of completeness, of having been taken on a journey in the company of a seer who has stared, with attention, mercy, and courage, into the world's heart.

Certainly *Accident/A Day's News* is a difficult book. Even the subject—nuclear disaster and surgery that can ruin, stop, or prolong life—is difficult to contemplate. Wolf's prose is extremely dense; her structure is an intricately connected web of associations. I'm not sure that she has been well served by her translators, who seem to have swallowed large lumps of German syntax whole. There is no action in the novel except that of waiting for news: the news of the extent of radioactive damage and of the results of risky surgery.

The "I" of the narrative is a woman, a writer alone in a house in the country. Before Chernobyl, many of her pleasures were simple, natural ones: tending her garden, cooking herself meals. But waiting for the news of spreading disaster, she must confront the truth that what had once been a source of pleasure and nourishment for her may now be a source of poisoning and death. She explores the nature of disaster and salvation that technology can bring. The world may be unlivable; the doctors may have saved her brother's life. Her task, as waiter-for-the-news, is to try to understand the nature of the news that she will hear, of the men (she makes the point that they are not women) whose activities will cause events to occur, the nature of the world that the events will leave in their wake.

"All of a sudden," she writes, "I found myself wondering whether the perpetrators of those kinds of technology whose hellish danger is part and parcel of their very essence have ever in their lives put into the soil kernels so minute that they stick to the fingertips, later to see them sprout and to watch the plants' growth. . . . I immediately recognized my fallacy, since everybody has heard or read that hardworking scientists and technicians are just the ones who frequently seek relaxation through gardening."

What does it mean to live a life? Christa Wolf keeps asking. To read her, we must accept a language that is aphoristically thick, must believe, for example, that a mother and a daughter have telephone conversations like this one:

"My oldest daughter sounded tired, I still pounced on her with the question: What do you consider our blind spot? Oh, Mother! I asked her whether her answer would include the expression 'living a lie.' Not necessarily, she said, she would talk about that region of our soul, our perception, which remained in the dark because it was too painful for us to face."

What makes Wolf's language and method psychologically satisfying and rescues the novel from lifelessness is that she roots her most abstract notions in concrete life. The telephone conversation with her older daughter is balanced by another with her younger daughter, in which mother and daughter discuss children's behavior. A proud grandmother, the narrator is enchanted by hearing that a one-and-a-half-year-old, her grandson, puts a wing nut on his thumb and prances around the kitchen saying, "Me Punch. Me Punch." Isn't he advanced? the narrator asks her daughter. Certainly most one-and-a-half-year-olds aren't up to that. She tells her daughter that "Shakespeare and Greek tragedy wouldn't do a thing for me now compared with your children's stories. And, by the way, did she know that the radiation level at the time of the aboveground nuclear-weapons tests in the 1960's was said to have been higher than now.

"You sure know how to make a person feel good, said my youngest daughter."

This pattern of traveling from the particular to the universal, from the familial to the political, this refusal to separate realms of thought, characterizes all of *Accident/A Day's News* and allows it both a naturalness and an enormous scope. At one point in the novel, the narrator goes from thinking about the odd details of her brother's surgery—that which determines all personality can be wrapped in foil, tied off, picked at like a piece of metal—to bicycling into the village for her day's errands. She sees a four-leaf clover; it reminds her of the war. She passes her porch, where she waves visitors off, and remembers that the man who once lived in the house was taken off by the Russians because he was a driver for the Gestapo. She is brought back to thinking of her brother, with whom she lived through the war, remembering that in his anesthetized condition, he has not experienced Chernobyl. She thinks of the faces of the victims on television: she will not allow these faces to become abstract to her, removed: "Now we hear that every new technology requires sacrifices at first. I tried to steel myself against the faces of people which might appear—did appear—on television, who would try to force a smile. Whose hair would have fallen out. Whose doctors would use the word 'brave.' "

When Christa Wolf tries to understand the impulses that have led the men who have devoted themselves to feeding the ever-growing monster of nuclear technology, she roots her question in the idea of desire. "Whence this desire for fission, for fire and explosions!" she once asked her brother; their relationship has taken the form of her asking questions in heated terms and his insisting that she cool down, lower the volume of her language. "You forbade me to use the word 'desire' in this connection," the narrator remembers. "Desire, desire . . . you said. That was another one of those exaggerated, partisan expressions. It was much simpler than that. Once someone had begun to invent something. Or to discover something: then he just couldn't stop anymore."

He reminds her that she has been like this in her writing, has known that words can wound and has not stopped the projectile of her wounding words. What, she wonders, is the connection between language and this taste for destruction that seems built into the species? She has read that language, agriculture, and murder became part of the human experience at the same evolutionary time. Devoting her life to language as she has, is she part of the murderous complicity whose end is the China syndrome? How does her desire for purity of speech tie in with the scientist's compulsion to follow whatever lead is offered him, and the brain surgeon's confidence that he can play with those body parts that render us recognizable to ourselves? "Is it worthwhile, brother," she asks, "staking one's life on being able to express oneself ever more precisely, discernibly, unmistakably."

These are exactly the things on which Christa Wolf stakes her life. She uses language as if her life depended upon finding the connections among the conflicting elements that make up the whole of life. *Accident/A Day's News* has the grandeur of a noble labor. The woman, the writer, the sister, the mother, the cook, the gardener, the citizen of the world, must use her whole life to keep back the lie of separateness: the poison of the lie that fission is to be desired, the disease of schizophrenia with which each modern man and woman lives, forgetting that terrible forces shape our lives. Is *Accident/A Day's News* hopeful or despairing? The question is impossible to answer; the terms are wrong. What it offers is a model of passionate engagement: we are where we are, where others—not only ourselves but those who go before and after us—are, have been, will be. It is a precious place. The book ends with a final message from the woman to her brother: "How difficult it would be, brother, to take leave of this earth."

Mary McCarthy:
Occasional Prose

It begins with the deaths of friends. A signal to the reader, a clue to the author's situation, who she is and where she's been. The writer says, in effect, that she is at that point in her life when all her friends are dying. But no voice could be less funereal, less tempted to the warm broth of nostalgia and regret. For this is the voice of Mary McCarthy: combative, adversarial, discriminating, and engaged. It is a voice that we have come to think of as more than a bit symbolic. She is, of course, the *femme de lettres,* and in her case both sides of the phrase have weight. The voice is above all assured, and the assurance is twofold: an intellectual assurance that allows her to range freely around the culture of the West, not literature only, but philosophy, history, politics, music, gardening, art. But the assurance has a second source: it is the assurance of a woman certain always of her power to attract.

No woman, or no man either, starting out now could have it. We feel overmastered by specialists; the generalist has become for us a journalist, pureeing all of culture into an undistinguished slop. Who of my generation would have the confidence to begin an essay in this way: "I want to distinguish at the outset three types of prose narrative." Or feel free to say: "Quite poisonous people, on the whole, are attracted to the visual arts and can become very knowledgeable about them." Or to describe in this way her behavior at a Christmas party at which guests must choose their own gifts: "As usual, that year I picked the most expensive thing on the table.

Those traps of hers held no terror for me. Being a hypocrite about my wants was never one of my faults."

She describes herself at twenty: "I had been telling my friends . . . that in politics I was a royalist—an impractical position, I knew, for an American, since we did not even have a kingly line to restore." If we analyze this sentence, the joke of it lies in its implication that if we *had* a kingly line to restore, the position would not have been so impractical: it might have made sense. But even the joke defines Mary McCarthy, and defines her difference from those of us who came after. It is not impossible to imagine that to declare oneself a royalist in a 1930s Vassar dorm would have been, even temporarily, to cut some kind of swath. But to imagine someone saying it in the same dormitory while the voice of Mick Jagger blared in the background—in that context the position would be merely pathetic: a plain girl trying to be daring by dressing up in garbage clothes. Mary McCarthy's may be the last generation to be comfortable with drawing a firm line between high and popular culture, stepping clearly to one side and declaring itself immune to the other. It is, after all, a question of time and energy: What does one do with a day? We are all of us now capable of admitting that we wouldn't miss an episode of "Hill Street Blues." But it is not possible to think of Mary McCarthy settling down in front of the tube with a bag of Doritos. In the time we spend on aerobics, she is reading *La Princesse de Clèves*.

But in no sense is she an elitist (a word she would hate). She is in love with excellence, but that passion must share its place with her love of justice. She has never fallen back to the exhausted rear flank of the neoconservatives, who are tired of fighting for a just society and have settled instead for a Florida condo patrolled by armed guards. She is political in a way that seems no longer open to us: politics for her is a world of ideas; its roots are philosophy, not sociology or media studies. And so her work is marked by seriousness, but she is never merely mandarin. Style vivifies her, and the humor bred of a highly developed sense of style. She says of her friend F. W. Dupee: "He was never a bohemian; he was too much attracted to style for that." The same is true of her. Yet she admired her friend for "being on the protective picket line for the students at Columbia in 1968, the day he got a new and expensive set of the finest porcelain teeth—example of rueful courage, since he expected to be hit by a night stick." Like her friend, McCarthy has never stepped back from the fray.

If she is not the smug and punitive reactionary, she is even less the dreary "thinker" making her way at night from the stacks of the university library to some dire flat with roaches on the countertop, a mattress on the floor. "Things" matter to her—"good things," as opposed to "nice things," for which she could muster the highest scorn. She would never deny that she is a materialist, but she sees clearly the problems of materialism in a world where all resources, but especially things of beauty, are finite. This is the problem she addresses in her brilliant "Living with Beautiful Things." We have all, more or less since the nineteenth century, acted as if it were true that beauty is truth, truth beauty, and we have, in our largess, extended the equation: beauty is goodness, or at least it leads to it. But to assume that the good beauty leads to is moral in its nature has been, according to McCarthy, the source of our error. The only good that the proximity to beauty seems to bring about is the creation of good taste: a circular movement whose value is limited and that cannot even be counted on to occur. What does occur in the presence of beauty is some mysterious sense of security and order—but even that is not automatic. "The daily service of beautiful things conduces to decorum; it is a rite, a kind of communion, as we notice whenever we wash a fine wine glass as opposed, say, to a jelly jar. . . . And yet museum attendants seem to be immune to contagion from the god." The problem with beautiful objects, as McCarthy explains to us, is that their pleasure is the eye's. And, she tells us, "the eye is a jealous, concupiscent organ, and some idea of ownership or exclusion enters into our relation with visual beauty. The eye is a natural collector, acquisitive, undemocratic, loath to share." Listen to the beauty of that last sentence; there is, of course, rhythmic beauty, but it shimmers, too, with elegance of thought. And whereas most modern thought is quite defeating in its murkiness, McCarthy's ideas shine clear. This is precisely because she is never merely abstract; she traverses easily the avenue between the worlds of ideas and things, crossing from side to side for clarification, refreshment, to have a good time, or to make a point. Consider her description of Joan Didion's narrative line, which she compares to a French seam: "one big stitch forward, one little stitch back, turn over and repeat on the other side of the cloth."

This genius of Mary McCarthy's serves her most superbly in her reminiscence of Hannah Arendt. For McCarthy, as for many of us, Hannah Arendt seemed to incarnate the perfect blend of the *vita activa* and the *vita contemplativa*. She was the representative of the old, ideal Europe—our own now, on the Upper West Side. How easy, then, to reduce her to an icon, to make her *stand for* rather than *be*. From the outset, McCarthy acknowledges her friend's greatness of mind. But she tells us that this kind of homage is not what she's about; she wants to present her friend before us bathed in the intimate light of a friend's mourning. The triumph of the presentation comes from McCarthy's acute selection of details:

> She would press on a visitor assorted nuts, chocolates, candied ginger, tea, coffee, Campari, whiskey, cigarettes, cake, crackers, fruit, cheese, almost all at once, regardless of conventional sequence or, often, of the time of day. It was as if the profusion of edibles, set out, many of them, in little ceremonial-like dishes and containers, were impatient propitiatory offerings to all the queer gods of taste. Someone said that this was the eternal Jewish mother, but it was not that: there was no notion that any of this fodder was good for you; in fact most of it was distinctly bad for you, which she must have known somehow, for she did not insist.

McCarthy speaks of Hannah Arendt's feet: "She liked shoes; in all the years I knew her, I think she only once had a corn." How much this tells us of the ease and caring of two women of genius! It is oddly touching, too, because the corn is an affliction no longer real to my generation. Is it because we spend so much time in boots, sneakers, and sandals? Because at home we walk barefoot? Our good, uncomfortable shoes are only worn for occasions; they are, for us, part-time and discardable. To avoid the fate of the corn plaster, what have we given up?

But Mary McCarthy would have no patience with the kind of romantic backward looking I am tempted to indulge in. The world, she is always telling us, is full of interesting things. It is simply a matter of looking. *Cast a Cold Eye* is the title of one of McCarthy's earlier collections. The eye of *Occasional Prose*, though, is not cold but tender, the reflective vision beautifully matured.

Mary McCarthy:
Cannibals and Missionaries

There are some women writers whose faces appear in the mind's eye whenever one thinks of their books; they are beauties, these women, and we are astonished and heartened at the good fortune and improbability they stand for. George Eliot, we think, had to be a writer, with her long horse face, but in the case of, say, Colette and Virginia Woolf, the choice of writing seems a pure election: other lives were clearly open to them. Mary McCarthy's face is of a different order of beauty from Colette's or Woolf's. One looks at the early photographs, and an American looks back, an Irish girl—for the face is girlish and demanding, the charm quite clearly birthright, not accomplishment. The owner of that face, one is sure, would never *strive* to please.

As Elizabeth Hardwick has noted, Mary McCarthy's place in American literary history and literary life—two quite different spheres—would have been impossible to achieve without a kind of difficult feminine charm. There is an assurance that beauty can bring a woman; properly used, it allows her a freedom from apology, a sense of safety, an assured ingratiation—the soil that cultivates probity and the possibility of the difficult question naturally asked. She is certainly asking difficult questions in *Cannibals and Missionaries*, her first novel in eight years.

McCarthy's voice has always been perfectly reliable; the stirring and disturbing tone of the born truth-teller is hers, whether she is writing essays or fiction. Her perspective is always feminine: Antigone grown up, her absoluteness not diminished as she takes on sex. She has never been easy on herself or her characters, or tried to make anyone look better. This is true whether she is describing her failure to best an anti-Semite ("Artists in Uniform"), her fears about traveling as a reporter in Vietnam ("How It Went"), or her heroine's response to divorce in "Cruel and Barbarous Treatment":

> She knew that being a potential divorcée was deeply pleasurable in somewhat the same way that being an engaged girl had been. In both cases, there was at first a subterranean courtship whose significance it was necessary to conceal from outside observers. . . . But with the extramarital courtship the deception was prolonged where it had been ephemeral, necessary where it had been frivolous, conspiratorial where it had been lonely. . . . That it was accompanied by feelings of guilt, by sharp and genuine revulsions, only complicated and deepened its delights, by abrading the sensibilities, and by imposing a sense of outlawry and consequent mutual dependence upon the lovers. But what this interlude of deception gave her, above all, she recognized, was an opportunity, unparalleled in her experience, for exercising feelings of superiority over others.

This represents the essence of McCarthy's sensibility: the fineness, the formality, the stance that cannot imagine any but a moral perspective. No one born after 1930 could have written any of those sentences. The ease and balance, largely moral, suggest a lost world.

Where are we, then, to place *Cannibals and Missionaries*, which its publishers present as a "thriller," in the context of Mary McCarthy's work? She is not the sort of writer who would toss off a book as a lark or a diverting experiment, so why has she done it?

It is clear to me that this, the most political, the least autobiographical of her novels, would have been impossible without her experience of traveling to Vietnam as a reporter. Many of the details of that experience, particularly those about physical fear and communal bonding, find their way into this novel in the accounts of the passengers' ordeal. *Cannibals and Missionaries* is the story, among other things, of a committee of liberals who are hijacked while traveling to Iran to examine the atrocities of the Shah's regime. It speaks, with McCarthy's habitually unsentimental voice, to the problem of witness and political responsibility among nonprofessional men of goodwill. For McCarthy, terrorism is disturbing in the same way that sexual promiscuity would have been for Emily Brontë: it is political activity without manners, without form; therefore it is incapable of yielding much meaning and is inevitably without hope. In some crucial way, it is not serious: it has no stake in the future.

By a stroke of good fortune for the terrorists in this book, the airplane that they hijack contains not only the liberal committee but also a group of art collectors on an archaeological tour. It takes the terrorists a while to realize their luck, but they come to understand that they will be able to put the West in the most vulnerable and humiliating of positions: it will have to prove its devotion simultaneously to art and to human life. The terrorists bring the passengers to a deserted Dutch polder—a model farming community built on land reclaimed from the sea—and say that they will exchange the collectors for the works they collect: Helen will be flown out after her Vermeer is flown in; Harold can leave when his Cézannes arrive.

It is a fascinating situation, and it gives McCarthy the opportunity to speak of a new and terrible phenomenon: "put a terrorist next to a work of art and you get an infernal new chemistry, as scarifying to 'civilization' as the nuclear arm." And the situation of a hijacking allows the writer delicious opportunity to examine character: it's a kind of Canterbury pilgrimage with machine guns.

One can imagine McCarthy's glee as she made out the passenger list for this ill-starred flight. She introduces us first to Frank Barber, the Episcopal rector of Saint Matthew's, Gracie Square, whom we hate instantly for his attachment to the woolen hats his family's eggs wear as a sign of the number of minutes they have lived under boiling water. This, and his habit of saying "Darn it" at the breakfast table. Next we meet Aileen Simmons, president of Lucy Skinner College, the kind of woman who was once referred to as a "game girl." She is fifty, unmarried, devoted to her students and her Arkansas family, politically responsible, in all her actions moderate, and torture to be in the room with. We encounter Gus Hurlburt, a saintly Missouri bishop, and Senator Jim Carey (who perforce reminds the reader of another silver-haired, poetic Irish senator, a presidential candidate whom we were once exhorted to keep neat and clean for). Then there is Sophie Weil, a New Journalist (her name is unfortunate, and McCarthy, who translated Simone Weil's "The Iliad, or The Poem of Force," might have thought again). And then Victor Lenz, a badly groomed Middle East scholar who insists upon bringing his cat. They seem at first not a riveting bunch, and one is grateful for the arrival of Henk Van Vliet de Jonge, a Dutch member of parliament, poetic as the senator, and handsomer.

We wait impatiently for the hijacking, so we can see these characters tested. Of course, some will behave their worst under the stress of danger and captivity. Aileen's manners and perhaps her morals turn out to be the most shocking. When the hijacking first occurs and it seems that only the committee will be captured, she resents the exclusion of the first-class passengers: "Don't you think you ought to *tell* those people who they are? It's not fair—honestly, is it—for them to be let go while we sit here with a price on our head because some of us, like the Senator, are celebrities. . . . It wouldn't hurt those millionaires a bit to be held for ransom."

Aileen is surely one of the most annoying women in recent fiction, with her rouge, her dyed hair, her sense of place, "as though the conviction she had of her importance were a religious matter." The Reverend Frank is almost as grating. His relentless and simplistic optimism is an offense not only against the facts but against the mysteries of the human heart as well. "We will be bigger people for it, if we will only let ourselves. . . . Through this unforeseen contact with our captors, we can be enlarged."

But there are heroes on the committee, two pure, two motley. The pure are the old bishop and the young journalist. The bishop is perfectly good, an innocent who shares his birthday cake with the hijackers. And Sophie has the passionate engagement that differentiates her from two lesser heroes—Jim and Henk, who view the world with a detached, spectator's irony and who, although they are real forces for good, recognize the limits of their moral natures.

There are heroes, too, among the terrorists: Ahmed, decent, loyal, innocent as the bishop; and the Dutch leader of the group, Jeroen, whose doomed life McCarthy examines with great insight. His temperament is artistic: he began his adulthood wanting to "consecrate himself in poverty to the value people called 'art'; by learning, if possible, to make some of it himself." But he gives up sketching in the Rijksmuseum for trade unionism, and then for the Communist Party, which he then rejects for the purer art of terrorism:

Now art, even the Party kind of making propaganda, lost all interest for him, except in the sense that a deed was a work of art—the only true one, he had become convinced. The deed, unless botched, was totally expressive; ends and means coincided. Unlike the Party's "art as a weapon," it was pure, its own justification. It had no aim outside itself. The purpose served by the capture of the Boeing was simply the continuance or asseveration of the original thrust; ransom money, the release of fellow activists, were not goals in which one came to rest but means of ensuring repetition. Direct action had a perfect circular motion; it aimed at its own autonomous perpetuation and sovereignty. And the circle, as all students of drawing knew, was the most beautiful of forms. Thus in a sense he had returned to where he had started: terrorism was art for art's sake in the political realm.

The most important achievement of *Cannibals and Missionaries* is McCarthy's understanding of the psychology of terrorism, the perception, expressed by Henk, that terrorism is the product of despair, "the ultimate sin against the Holy Ghost." Once again, McCarthy is asking the difficult question, confronting the difficult problem. For surely terrorism threatens us all, not only physically and politically but morally and intellectually as well. It postulates a system of oblique correspondences, a violent disproportion between ends and means, against which we have no recourse. She comes to terms as well with our peculiar but irrefutable tendency to see human beings as replaceable, works of art as unique. For the lover of formal beauty who is also a moralist, it is the most vexed of questions. I'm not sure McCarthy has anything new to say on the subject, but she does not imply that she does.

Often, artists have responded to the prospect of atrocity by creating a well-crafted work of art. One thinks of Milton's "On the Late Massacre of the Piedmontese," a perfect Italian sonnet whose hundredth word is "hundredfold." In response to the truly frightful prospect of anarchic terrorism, Mary McCarthy has written one of the most shapely novels to have come out in recent years: a well-made book. It is delightful to observe her balancing, winnowing, fitting in the pieces of her plot.

The tone of *Cannibals and Missionaries* is a lively pessimism. Its difficult conclusion is that to be a human being at this time is a sad fate: even the revolutionaries have no hope for the future, and virtue is in the hands of the unremarkable, who alone remain unscathed.

Stevie Smith:
Novel on Yellow Paper

Like all genuine eccentrics, Stevie Smith believed herself supremely ordinary. The setting of her life was willed, stubbornly, rebelliously: a choice of genius in the comic mode, of camouflage and self-protection. She lived in the suburbs with her aunt. There was much in her of the hearty, slightly hysterical spinster: sherry at four, hot drinks at ten, and witty drawings hidden underneath the blotter of the sitting room desk. Every word she wrote balanced between terror and hilarity. No writer is more death-struck, and no modern has her knack of finding in the detritus of ordinary life such cause for mirth.

Novel on Yellow Paper shares the preoccupations of all of Stevie Smith: laughter, literature, death. It is a novel of nerves; it jumps, darts, turns, shrieks with laughter, recoils in horror, runs for a book, settles down to weep in quiet at the great blank cruelty of human life. It is the story of Pompey Casmilus, a young woman who lives in the suburbs and works as a secretary for a kindly publisher of women's magazines. Pompey's vision is unfixed and always shifting. Death, madness, grief peer over one shoulder, but behind the other is a sight so risible, a conversation so irresistible in its absurdity, that death and madness, cruelty and grief, must flee. At the end of the novel, Pompey is mourning her lost lover. She had decided that she is not right for marriage; that her rhythm is friendship, with its comings and goings; that her beloved Freddy in his resolute small-mindedness would choke her quite to death.

And I was lying in bed, crying with influenza and exasperation, when into my bedroom came my Aunt the Lion of Hull. There was going to be a church bazaar. Auntie Lion was going to the bazaar dressed as a fan. Now all the ladies of the parish were going to the bazaar as a fan. But Auntie Lion was not at one with her fan. Standing in front of the double mirror in the bedroom she was making lioning faces and noises because of the obstinacy of the fan: Now it is fixed how do I look?

But the genius of Stevie Smith is not a serene one; it does not bring about resolutions, moments of stasis. No sooner has she enjoyed the sight of her aunt dressed as a fan than she is overcome with love for her and fears her loss. And, within a page, she tells us of her mother's painful death:

What can you do? You can do nothing but be there, and go on being there steadily and without a break until the end. There is nothing but that that you can do. My mother was dying, she had heart disease, she could not breathe, already there were the cylinders of oxygen. There was the nurse and the doctor coming day and night. But if you cannot breathe how can you breathe the oxygen? Even, how can the doctors help you. Or? You must suffer and then you must die. And for a week this last suffering leading to death continued. Oh how much better to die quickly. Oh then afterwards they say: Your mother died quickly. She did not suffer. You must re-member to be thankful for that. But all the time you are remembering that she did suffer. Because if you cannot breathe you must suffer. And the last minute when you are dying, that may be a very long time indeed. But of course the doctors and the nurses have their feet very firmly upon the ground, and a minute to them is just sixty seconds' worth of distance run. So now it is all over, it is all over and she is dead. Yes, it is all over it is all over it is.

What a great deal of life we are taken over in three pages. The loss of young love, the hilarity of suburban manners, filial devotion, and suffering, the coldness of the objective vision, the finality of death. The comprehensiveness, the range, of this short passage, its sheer interest, its felicity—all are possible only because the narrative voice is finely and deliberately controlled at every moment. The seemingly throwaway "well"s, "and"s, "now"s, the parody diminutives, the quick, short repetitions, are anything but throwaway, in fact. They create the illusion of the spoken voice; they capture the nervous aural genius of the brilliant talker. It is a voice determined to take itself unseriously yet to speak of all that is most serious in life. It is a social voice, a party voice. Above all, it wishes not to bore; above all, it wishes to be amusing. For the speaker, Pompey, cannot keep out of her mind—even as she tells us about funny clippings she has cut from the women's pages— visions of horror, of cruelty, that have struck her with the terrors of the damned in hell.

She tells us she has seen the devil. Not for her the almost comforting fiend with its iconographic wings, tail, leer. Not, she tells us, "anything at all of the dark mind of Milton soaring up over the dark abyss, very damned and noble. No this was the fiend that is neither like Goethe's Mephistopheles, that almost too impudent spirit of negation . . ."

She sees the devil on the streets of Hythe after she is recovering from the flu:

. . . up on the hills by the canal, there were pieces of paper, and there were cartons that had held ice cream and there were those little cardboard spoons that go with it. And there were newspapers and wrapping papers.

There was every sort of paper there, only the devil was there too, and he was not wrapped up in paper.

It was a dreadful vision that I had there of the heart of this fiend. And very stormisch and sad I was too, and full of the black night of foreboding, and when I came back to the hotel I was very profoundly disturbed. Very horrified and bristling with the breath of the frightful fiend was Pompey.

The vision, in its very formlessness, its emptiness, its ordinariness, is the true heart of darkness. Papers on the street in a holiday town: the devil. The horror is real. And yet Pompey's diction tries to make light of her horror; the jump into self-parody, the use of the swallowed-whole German *Stormisch*, the children's-book in-

version "Very horrified and bristling with the breath of the frightful
fiend was Pompey." Yet the horror remains. Yet it does not remain
forever. There is so much to talk about. There is the list of funny
quotations to bring out. We must be told the story of *Phèdre,* of
The Bacchae. There are wonderful friends we must meet. And the
important decision must be discussed: will she marry Freddy?

The pace of *Novel on Yellow Paper* is slightly frantic; it is marked,
almost, by a determination never to be still. For stillness might
reveal the truth that Pompey fears above all else, the vision she
gets glimpses of: there may be nothing at the center, things may
not be what they seem. She had her first glimpse of this possibility
as a child, in a tuberculosis sanatorium, when a nursemaid took
her on her knee.

> If I was in the mood for it I could play up to her fancy, but
> even while I was doing this I was immensely terrified. Her
> feeling for me, I felt this very keenly but could not for some
> time understand why it so much dismayed me, was in outward
> appearance, so far as being hugged and set on her knee, was
> what in outward appearance my mother . . . ? No, do you see,
> but it was profoundly disturbing, how in essence her feeling
> was so arbitrary, so superficial, so fortuitous. And so this feel-
> ing she had for me, which was not at all a deep feeling, but
> as one might pet, pat and cuddle a puppy, filled me with the
> fear that a child has in the face of cruelty. It was so insecure,
> so without depth or significance. It was so similar in outward
> form, and so asunder and apart, so deceitful and so barbarous
> in significance. It very profoundly disturbed and dismayed and
> terrified me.

It is then, as a child, that she learns to think of death as a friend,
to reckon suicide a blessing and a comfort.

The voice we hear throughout the novel is a voice whose function
is to cover over terror. Pompey is forever terrified; she feels at
every moment her utter vulnerability, as if she were a burn victim,
unhealed. She loves Racine, the Greeks, because they present the
possibility of imperviousness. One is struck, time and again, by
the central moral virtue in all of Stevie Smith's work: courage. For
it is an act of the highest morality to swallow terror whole, to allow

oneself to be distracted by the Lion Aunt, the advice in the Love-lorn Column, the fate of Phèdre and of Pentheus on the mountain. Pompey is self-absorbed, but she is not a narcissist. Against tremendous odds, she goes on loving life.

And so *Novel on Yellow Paper* is a tale of heroism comically told, a heroism deeply modern: the triumph over the terror of the human condition. Stevie Smith has much in common, after all, with Kafka: the horror of the meaningless, the obsession with the ordinary details and routine of modern life. But where he falls into despair, she ends up laughing. The final vision of *Novel on Yellow Paper* is, to be sure, a vision of death. But it is the death of the tigress Flo, affronted by the insult of having been offered artificial respiration by the zookeeper: "She looked, she lurched, and seeing some last, unnameable, not wholly apprehended final outrage, she fell, she whimpered, clawed in vain, and died."

But the tigress Pompey lives on. She cannot die just yet; she has much more to tell us.

Adam Hochschild:
Half the Way Home

The only child of older parents leads an unreal life. From the start he is worshiped like the Christ Child; he has made his parents, by his very birth, prodigious. The mother stands out among her equals, a living river of fecundity that mocks the curse of age. The father can be seen by his coevals as the man they fear they can no longer be. The child is long awaited, or a windfall for which his parents never dared to hope. He is the subject of enormous expectations and fears. He looks with awe at the parents of his friends: less kind perhaps, less patient, certainly less tired. A father coaching Little League, a mother running down a hill, become for him the emblems of a glamorous and easy joy. He sees how his friends need not fear quite as he does for their parents; mortality does not brush quite so near these others, nor does the glaring eye of fate so certainly approach. The pressures exhaust him, and yet only with his parents is he truly happy; try as he may, he is not himself among the commoners. Still, he envies his friends their easy lot, as Isaac must have envied the sons of others, not led up the mountain, not the living symbols of their fathers' worth before the Lord.

All these burdens were Adam Hochschild's, and more. He was the child of a frail and loving mother who bore him at the age of forty-two and of a father, fifty when Adam was born in 1942, who controlled Amax Inc., one of the largest mining companies in the world. But Adam Hochschild did not follow his father into the corporation. Rather he became a reporter for the *San Francisco*

Chronicle and worked for *Ramparts* magazine; in 1974 he co-founded the left-wing magazine *Mother Jones. Half the Way Home* is largely the story of Hochschild's relationship with his father, and if the reader choked with anxiety about mortgage payments and doctor bills thinks this book has nothing to tell him or her, he or she is wrong. For Hochschild illuminates, with a rare tact, the situations of fathers and sons, and he avoids the traps of sentimentality and rancor both.

Harold Hochschild, Adam's father, was a German Jew whose own father arrived in New York in 1886 and made a fortune in metals. The Hochschilds did not mix with their Jewish neighbors, and in marrying Adam's mother, with her perfect WASP connections, Harold realized his dream of being included in the Social Register. He married Mary Marquand when he was forty-eight and she was forty; their son speculates on the unlikeliness of their marriage, which was nevertheless extremely happy. Mary Hochschild sounds like a devoted and imaginative mother. But she could not protect her son from his father; what is more, she didn't even try. She papered over Adam's terror of Harold with a genial repression, and in doing so betrayed her son. For he had to believe the justice of his father's criticisms if the mother who adored him went along with them.

Harold Hochschild tormented his son from the best of motives. He believed that the world was a difficult place and that his son was born to run it. Everything became a form of training; nothing was left to chance. The excursions that were meant to constitute father-and-son outings are chilling to read about. All those places that Harold rightly surmised ought to be pleasant—the Staten Island ferry, the New York piers—were prisons for the paralyzed son, who couldn't wait to get home. Then there were the required thanks, upon which Harold placed an inordinately high premium. "I think he also had the unspoken hope that on one of these trips I would say 'I'm glad we did this' or 'I love you.' I seldom gave him that satisfaction: my taciturn resistance was the one weapon I had against him. When I sometimes slipped in my stubbornness, I knew it registered, for I would hear from my mother, always the eager intermediary, 'Father was so pleased yesterday when you put your arm around him.' "

The reader observes in horror this frozen dance of father and son—and mother on the sidelines: the rapt, encouraging observer. Harold seems to be a man for whom spontaneity was impossible. Watch him at his exercise: "At 6:15 each evening, Father swam across the lake and back. He swam by a never-changing routine, stepping into the water instead of diving, shifting from breaststroke to sidestroke to backstroke to crawl at regular intervals. As a safety precaution, someone followed in an electric-powered boat, cruising noiselessly some yards behind him."

Adam beautifully captures the magic of a mountain lake at dusk and the poignant sorrow of father and son: "It was the time of day when the lake was at its loveliest, its surface a calm, dark mirror for the mountains. Sounds echoed across it: the splash of his hands in the water, a murmur of voices and laughter on shore; the wind had quieted; all was at peace. Father was in the water, so I could not talk to him, but I could still be close to him, fulfilling some obligation and perhaps, after all, some wish."

Some of the strongest moments in the book occur when Adam is evoking Eagle Nest, the family estate in the Adirondacks. The natural pleasures of the setting were enhanced by its becoming, in the summers, a little Russia. Harold's sister, Gertrude, surprised the family by marrying—also late in life—Boris Vasilievich Sergievsky, a White Russian pilot-adventurer whom Harold suspected always but who brought the lame and soulful Gertrude joy. And brought joy and life to Eagle Nest as well, for he contrasted with the Prussian-hearted Harold in a way that could only do a boy's heart good. Unfortunately, the author does not succeed in making Boris real to us: his many lives, his dancing, singing, womanizing, become the exploits of a *character,* whereas the grim, methodical round that is Harold's life rings out in somber truth.

Eagle Nest was lovely, but for the Hochschilds even vacations were no vacation. Harold let no opportunity go unused if it could be a corrective for his son's behavior. He invented an odd ritual called Getting the Beer, in which Adam had to bring in bottled beer on a tray and serve the guests—a gesture symbolic at best in a house where servants numbered in the double digits. It all smacks of those Renaissance manuals for the training of princes: you are to rule the world; to be served, you must know how to serve. Adam's worst sin in his father's eyes was talking too much at table; this could cause him to be summoned to his father's study in the morning and told, in perfectly modulated tones, that he had bored the guests.

Only after his father's death did Adam Hochschild come to understand that much of Harold's behavior stemmed from his discomfort with his Jewishness. In going over his father's papers, the author found a memo, written in 1940, speculating on the possibilities of a great pogrom in America and suggesting that if this were to happen, the shortcomings of Jews themselves would be at fault:

> He talks about Jews who are too "loud," about low ethical standards in Jewish-dominated trades. He declares: "It is an unhappy fact, acknowledged by members of what may be termed the Jewish intelligentsia to each other but not to Gentiles, that a large proportion of the Jews in America are not properly educated to American business and social standards. . . . Jews should lose no opportunity to convert the better-bred and better-educated Gentile minority to a friendlier attitude. . . . If Jews can win the respect or at least the tolerance of such Gentiles, the spread of active anti-Semitism will be impeded."

Adam is saddened by his father's racial self-hatred rather than simply censorious about it. And this tone, of sadness for the obstacles his father threw up for himself, is the triumph of the book. It would have been easier for Hochschild to write a memoir whose message was: Isn't it wonderful that I, son of a multimillionaire, with the world at my feet, saw the light, and instead of being secretary of state have founded *Mother Jones*. But he is exceedingly modest and evenhanded about his political education, which began when, as a teenager, he visited South Africa and observed the results of his father's company's enterprises.

The enterprises that paid for Eagle Nest and first-class hotels and restaurants condemned the black people he saw to lives of inhuman labor. It would indeed have been easy to present himself as the hero of the piece and his father as the villain, but he does not. He grants his father all the complications of his complicated nature: Harold was an ecologist, responsible for some of the most effective environmental legislation in New York State. He was an early opponent of the Vietnam War and a lifelong supporter of Communist China. At the end of his life, through his love for his grandchildren, he was able to relax enough so that his son could approach him. But not too closely. *Half the Way Home* does not end with a dramatic reconciliation scene in which father and son understand all; it ends with a quiet and extremely moving description of a son's vigil at his father's deathbed. Adam puts his head on his father's chest to determine if he is still breathing, and tells the nurse he hears a heartbeat. But no, she tells him, it is not his father's beating heart he hears; it is his own.

Virginia Woolf:
A Room of One's Own

Virginia Woolf foresaw with clarity the responses to *A Room of One's Own*. She wrote in her diary in 1929:

> I forecast, then that I shall get no criticism, except of the evasive jocular kind . . . that the press will be kind & talk of its charm, & sprightliness; also I shall be attacked for a feminist & hinted at for a sapphist. . . . I shall get a good many letters from young women. I am afraid it will not be taken seriously. . . . It is a trifle, I shall say; so it is, but I wrote it with ardour and conviction. . . . You feel the creature arching its back & galloping on, though as usual much is watery & flimsy & pitched in too high a voice.

As usual, Woolf's standards for herself were mercilessly high. A trifle? Hardly. Yet it is easy to see why it was, by some critics, so perceived. Originally given as lectures at Newnham and Girton colleges, *A Room of One's Own* was published in October 1929, at a time when feminist writing was so little in vogue as to be effectively moribund, when the feminist movement, connected as it had come to be almost exclusively with female suffrage, considered its work finished. October 1929. It is astonishing to contemplate that *A Room of One's Own* fell into the hands of the London literary public at the same time that Wall Street investors were leaping from their windows in despair. Understandably, the political attentions of intellectuals were turned not to the problems of women but to economic and world crisis. The name of Mussolini is spoken by Woolf in this essay, but his presence is peripheral; it is eclipsed by his brother the college beadle, chasing women from lawns, forbidding them the library.

A Room of One's Own opened Woolf up to the charges—snobbery, aestheticism—that were by that time habitually laid at the Bloomsbury gate by the generation that came of age in the late twenties. To an extent, the accusations are just; Woolf is concerned with the fate of women of genius, not with that of ordinary women; her plea is that we create a world in which Shakespeare's sister might survive her gift, not one in which a miner's wife can have her rights to property; her passion is for literature, not for universal justice. The thesis of *A Room of One's Own*—women must have money and privacy in order to write—is inevitably connected to questions of class. "Genius like Shakespeare's is not born among labouring, uneducated, servile people." The words are hard; how infuriating they must have been to, say, a D. H. Lawrence. But Woolf is firm. Genius needs freedom; it cannot flower if it is encumbered by fear, or rancor, or dependency, and without money freedom is impossible. And the money cannot be earned; it must come to the writer in the form of a windfall or a legacy, or it will bring with it attachments, obligations.

Woolf's sense of the writer's vocation is religious in its intensity. The clarity of heart and spirit that she attributes to writers like Shakespeare and Jane Austen, who have expressed their genius "whole and entire," demands a radical lack of self that might be required of a saint. Yet the writer cannot, for Woolf, *work* to be rid of the self; the writer must be born into a world that never allows grievances to appear, or must be born of a soul made of stuff that will not bear the impress of resentment.

When the writer's personal grievances intrude, the art is muddied, cracked. It is the fault Woolf finds with Charlotte Brontë:

> The woman who wrote those pages [of *Jane Eyre*] had more genius in her than Jane Austen; but if one reads them over and marks that jerk in them, that indignation, one sees that she will never get her genius expressed whole and entire. . . . She will write in a rage where she should write calmly.

She will write foolishly where she should write wisely. She will write of herself where she should write of her characters.

Serenity, selflessness, freedom from rage: the words recall the mystics' counsels. Yet unlike the mystics, with their dualistic bias, Woolf finds the body good, the senses delightful: they feed, they do not distract, the spirit. "One cannot think well, love well, sleep well, if one has not dined well," she insists. Her joy in sensual satisfaction is magnificently expressed in her description of a lunch at the Oxbridge men's college; it is one of the immortal meals in literature. Of its aftermath, she writes:

No need to hurry. No need to sparkle. No need to be anybody but oneself. We are all going to heaven and Vandyck is of the company . . . how good life seemed, how sweet its rewards, how trivial this grudge or that grievance, how admirable friendship and the society of one's kind, as, lighting a good cigarette, one sunk among the cushions in the window-seat.

Woolf says that we who live after the First World War have lost something beautiful, some necessary grace. We do not hum under our breaths; we are cats without tails; we are encumbered by our anger, our sense of doom; more important, perhaps, by our sexual self-consciousness. The war destroyed illusions, particularly for men. Women have, for Woolf (how unrealistically hopeful *her* illusion), given up their roles as "looking-glasses possessing the magic and delicious power of reflecting the figure of man at twice its natural size." Therefore, men are angry; Woolf sees this anger in everything she reads about women when she begins her quest to discover why women are so poor (their college serves stringy beef, custard, and prunes), why so few women have written.

The first question provides an easy answer: women are poor because, instead of making money, they have had children. The second question is far more complex, and her attempt to answer it leads her to history. She reads the lives of women and concludes that for a woman to have written she would have had to overcome enormous circumstances. Women were betrothed in their cradles; they were married at fifteen; they bore a dozen children, and those children died, and they went on bearing children. Moreover, they were uneducated; they had no privacy; even Jane Austen had to write in the common sitting room and hide her work under blotting paper so as not to be discovered. Yet even when they were freed from the practical impediments imposed upon their sex, they could not write because they had no tradition to follow. No sentence had been shaped, by long labor, to express the experience of women. "It is useless to go to the great men writers for help, however much one may go to them for pleasure. . . . [They] never helped a woman yet, though she may have learnt a few tricks of them and adapted them to her use." Of all women writers, only Jane Austen found a sentence to fit her.

The shapely sentence: it is another necessary legacy, the lack of which makes every woman writer *parvenue*. For Woolf is certain that the experience of men and the experience of women are extremely different, and they need different sentences to contain the shapes of their experience. Women's writing has, in addition, been impoverished by the limited access women have had to life: what could the writing of George Eliot have been like, she wonders, had Miss Evans fought in the Crimea; what would the work of Tolstoy have been had he lived in seclusion in a suburb with a woman not his wife? Yet the hiddenness, the anonymity of women's lives has endowed them with a great beauty, and the challenge Woolf gives to women writers is to capture these lives in all their variety:

All these infinitely obscure lives remain to be recorded, I said . . . and went on in thought through the streets of London feeling in imagination the pressure of dumbness, the accumulation of unrecorded life, whether from the women at the street corners with their arms akimbo . . . or from the violet-sellers and the match-sellers and the old crones stationed under doorways; or from drifting girls whose faces, like waves in sun and cloud, signal the coming of men and women. . . . Above all, you must illumine your own soul with its profundities and its shallows, and its vanities and its generosities, and say what your beauty means to you or your plainness, and what is your relation to the everchanging and turning world of gloves and shoes and stuffs swaying up and down among the faint scents that come through chemists' bottles down arcades of dress material over a floor of pseudo-marble.

This is, indeed, a challenge whose proportions are heroic. The novelist imagined by Woolf, a young woman named Mary Carmichael, who has money and privacy, has not achieved it in her first book, *Life's Adventure*, despite the deeply heartening sentences "Chloe liked Olivia. They shared a laboratory together." Miss Carmichael is a good novelist; she writes with spirit; she has many new and interesting things to say. But she is not a genius. Given her tradition, how can she be but "awkward . . . and without the unconscious bearing of long descent which makes the least turn of the pen of a Thackeray or a Lamb delightful to the ear."

Woolf lays down *Life's Adventure* with disappointment, saying "she will be a poet . . . in another hundred years' time." She turns to the window and sees a man and a woman getting into a taxi. This sight she finds so immensely attractive, so profoundly soothing, that it reminds her how unnatural it is to think of the sexes as separate, how natural to think of them as cooperating with one another. And it leads her to speculate that just as there are two sexes in the natural world, there must be two sexes in the mind, and that it is their union that is responsible for creation. She recalls Coleridge's idea that a great mind is androgynous:

Coleridge certainly did not mean . . . that it is a mind that has any special sympathy with women; a mind that takes up their cause or devotes itself to their interpretation. Perhaps the androgynous mind is less apt to make these distinctions than the single-sexed mind. He meant, perhaps, that the androgynous mind is resonant and porous; that it transmits emotion without impediment; that it is naturally creative, incandescent and undivided.

The androgynous mind must be a pure vessel—we are back, once more, to the important idea of purity—for the transmission of reality, "what remains over when the skin of the day has been cast into the hedge . . . what is left of past time and of our loves and hates." But it is particularly difficult for a modern to transmit reality. Modern women are frustrated and angry, their experience is limited; modern men are obsessed with the letter "I"; their writing is full of self-conscious indecency, self-conscious virility. It is essentially sterile.

Thus, unless men and women can be androgynous in mind, literature itself will be permanently flawed. And this is the reason for Woolf's insistence on £500 a year and rooms of their own for women. It is not that she wants women to write better than men: "All this pitting of sex against sex . . . all this claiming of superiority and imparting of inferiority, belong to the private-school stage of human existence where there are 'sides,' and it is . . . of the utmost importance to walk up to a platform and receive from the hands of the Headmaster himself a highly ornamental pot."

It is to encourage writing of genius, to discourage flawed work, that Woolf is so insistent upon money and privacy for women. And by whom are these works to be created? By Shakespeare's sister, the imaginary woman invented by Woolf who killed herself because of the frustration of unexpressed genius. "If we face the fact . . . that there is no arm to cling to, but that we go alone and that our relation is to the world of reality and not only to the world of men and women, then the . . . dead poet who was Shakespeare's sister will put on the body which she has so often laid down."

Was it the body of Shakespeare's sister that Virginia Woolf laid down when she walked into the river? The tone of *A Room of One's Own* discourages the speculation. It is an exalted tone, an inspired tone; there is nothing petty in it and nothing of the merely personal. Human happiness, the happiness of writers—questions by which we, in our age, seem enthralled—do not enter these pages. What is important, what is essential, is that works of genius be created. In that writers' unhappiness interferes with their creation, one should be concerned with the happiness of writers. The important thing is that they must express reality; they must express their genius, not themselves. They must illuminate their own souls, but they must not allow the souls to get in the way of reality. For pitted against reality, against the great tradition of immortal literature, the self is puny; it is of no interest.

The tone of *A Room of One's Own* is exalted, but it is also conversational. A human voice provides its music, a voice of great charm. It came to be written because Virginia Woolf was asked to lecture at women's colleges on the subject of Women and Fiction.

Her interest in the subject was vital. She had felt cheated in her education and felt the cheat for all those who had gone before her—she was as angry, in some ways, as Charlotte Brontë. But there was another reason for the writing of this book. When one thinks of that reason, one likes to think of Virginia Woolf not, for the moment, as the Olympian virgin of the early portrait, or as the august woman of letters of the late ones, but as the woman in one of the snapshots. Her legs are crossed; there is a dog at her feet. She looks friendly; she may be approachable. It is November 6, 1929. She is writing to her friend G. Lowes Dickinson, explaining the reasons for *A Room of One's Own:* "I wanted to encourage the young women—they seem to get fearfully depressed."

Edna O'Brien:
A Fanatic Heart

"I thought that ours indeed was a land of shame, a land of murder, a land of strange, throttled, sacrificial women," says the narrator of Edna O'Brien's story "A Scandalous Woman." Of Irish murder and Irish shame we have heard much, but the news has been in the mouths of men. Edna O'Brien tells the Irish woman's inside story. She has—as only the finest writers can—created a world; she speaks in a voice identifiably and only hers. No voice could be less androgynous or more rooted in a land. Her great subjects are childhood and sexual love; both themes come to flower in a soil teeming with lively and portentous objects. Clothes, stuffs, foods, medicines, in her hands turn into vessels brimming with meaning and value. And her language itself takes on the texture of a precious thing, precious and yet familiar, held close to the body, kept, always, in the center of the home. Think of the sentence I quoted at the beginning of this paragraph: "shame," "murder," "strange," "sacrificial." All the words are fitting; none of them shocks. But only Miss O'Brien would use the word "throttled." It is the emblem of her genius: the genuinely surprising word, not in itself exotic but conjuring in the reader a response inexorably physical and true.

The narrator of many of the stories in *A Fanatic Heart* is a young Irish girl who lives the life of the overwrought, obsessively observant outsider. The world of adults she perceives is often incomprehensible to her. She watches adults move, as if in a trance, toward their destruction, propelled by a passion she finds beautiful and wishes to share in herself. Sex for these doomed creatures always brings tragedy: this is Ireland, and the love between men and women can only leave women worn out and men jaded, careless, longing to be away, or choked in a helpless romance unable to express itself. Everyone pays, but women pay the highest price.

Miss Amy Connor in "The Connor Girls" falls for a wastrel bank clerk who disappears mysteriously before the wedding; she leaves the town, and it is rumored "that Miss Amy had worked in a beauty parlor in Stephens Green, had drunk heavily, and had joined a golf club." Another bank clerk is the cause of grief to Eily in "A Scandalous Woman." Eily is one of the town beauties: "She had brown hair, a great crop of it, fair skin, and eyes that were as big and as soft and as transparent as ripe gooseberries. She was always a little out of breath and gasped when one approached, then embraced and said, 'Darling.' . . . For one Advent she thought of being a nun, but that fizzled out and her chief interests became clothes and needlework."

This description—the gooseberry eyes, the breathlessness, the temporary religious vocation replaced by interests of a more ordinary girlish sort—is Miss O'Brien at her best. The physical detail burrows into the mind; how clearly one sees Eily—the breathless transparent one, bound for sex trouble. The girl who is the narrator of this story is younger than Eily, honored by her friendship with this beautiful, worldly creature and more than happy to be the go-between for her and her Protestant lover. Of course, Eily becomes pregnant; the town forces her lover to marry her. He is resentful and does his duty reluctantly, moving away from her emotionally until she goes mad. At the end of the story, the narrator, now a pregnant, unhappily married woman, sees Eily chastened, psychiatrically rehabilitated, a ghost of her former self.

Of course, not all Irish women so flagrantly and casually betray the secret of their sex; there are nuns and mothers in whom sex is concealed or pressed into the service of another love. "Sister Imelda" describes the rapt, devoted love of a passionate, intelligent, and lonely young nun and a young girl, equally passionate, intelligent, and lonely. Their love, although partaking in aspects of the sexual, is more or less than that. It is the love of two sensualists caught up in a fantasy of asceticism; it is all about the dream of perfection and perfectibility, about self-denial and the areas of human life unable to be quashed despite good intentions and, indeed, holy vows. By the end of the story, the young girl grows out of her crush on the nun, becomes worldly, wears too much makeup, chases after boys. Always, though, in her mind's eye will be the image of the betrayed, mysterious one she had to leave if she was to have an ordinary life.

Mothers, too, in these stories must be left and left violently if the daughters are to mature into women of any sort. In "My Mother's Mother," a young girl says, "I thought how much I needed to be without her so that I could think of her, dwell on her, and fashion her into the perfect person that she clearly was not. I resolved that for certain I would grow up and one day go away. It was a sweet thought, and it was packed with punishment."

The punishment, of course, is mutual: for the obsessed, starved mother—whose love is a salvation for the child, a threat for the maturing woman—and for the woman herself. "A Rose in the Heart of New York" is a brilliant evocation of the balked tenderness between a mother and a daughter. As a child, the daughter cannot bear to be separated from her mother; to be out of the mother's sight is, for her, a little death. Yet as a woman, trying to mend her estranged relationship with her mother by taking her on vacation, she can only be brutalized by the woman's unhappiness, her attempts to instill guilt, her lust for consolation. Brutalized by her mother's hungers, she must brutalize, until, at the end, the mother's death only marks the final failure of mutual love. After the funeral, the daughter finds, hidden above a mantelpiece, an envelope addressed to her. There are no words for her, only crumpled, many-times-folded money. "In her mind she concocted little tendernesses that her mother might have written—words such as 'Buy yourself a jacket,' or 'Have a night out,' or 'Don't spend this on Masses.' She wanted something, some communiqué. But there was no such thing."

The overwrought, observant girl in these stories grows into a woman who leaves the things she has loved and feared in Ireland. She becomes an exile: unmothered, unbefriended, torn from the land. Of course, she will try to find in the sexual love of men all she has left behind; she will look to romantic love for the placement she had in the home she could not wait to leave. And of course, the romances will be doomed to fail; no human relation could bear so much freight. But in the failure how splendid, and what a rendering of sexual life Miss O'Brien spreads before us in the stories about men and women that account for so large a part of her reputation.

In turning from the stories of childhood to the stories of sexual love, we lose the mocking humor whose source in the Irish stories is the provincial's insistent misapprehension of the larger world. The lovers in Miss O'Brien's stories are, for better or for worse, powerful citizens of the great world. They inhabit the glamorous professions: the women are journalists, poets, television stars; the men are wealthy businessmen dealing in interesting, valuable commodities. For these people, crossing the English Channel, or indeed the Atlantic Ocean, means no more than crossing to the next village meant to the people in the stories about Ireland. Actually, the larger journey is of less significance, for the people who cross the ocean are equally at home in any city they touch down on, whereas for the Irish villagers, to walk a mile down the road is to make a journey to the moon.

The women in these stories give themselves to love as a kind of self-immolation; to open themselves to love is to open themselves to madness, and each time, knowing this fully, they cannot resist. They are lifted up, these women, they are cruelly dropped down, and all their awareness does nothing to prevent them from their fate. Body and soul, they are taken over. The woman in "Baby Blue" "did rash things, went outdoors, but had to be indoors at once, and barely inside was she than suffocation strangled her again, and yet out in the street the concrete slabs were marshy and the spiked railing threatening to brain her."

These love affairs take place in the carefully appointed houses of women whose houses mean a great deal to them but for whom domestic life has no place. The women try to do ordinary tasks—cook an ordinary meal, sew on an ordinary button—but the acts become incandescent. Every gesture, however innocently intended, turns into seduction and must lead the lovers out of the kitchen and into bed. Children, in these stories, are absent: away at school, snatched from their mothers by their punitive fathers, who declare their former wives unfit by virtue of the very passion that drives them to the husband of some other woman, allowed to keep her children and to share her man.

Miss O'Brien, however, does not present us with another tired episode in the ancient history of "the other woman." Glimmering in these stories, like a gimlet in a swamp, is a pervasive ironic morality. The other woman, after all, is not so different from the wife; she is grasping, she is vengeful, she is greedy, and she has the will to hurt. In these stories no one is an innocent, and everyone must suffer. Ireland can be left, but the curse of sex hangs over the head of all the world.

Miss O'Brien combines the romantic's passionate feeling for language and the material world with the classicist's unerring sense of form. Each of her stories is shaped into a complete and satisfying whole; she has the courage and the sureness of vision to derive from the singularity of her characters' experience general truths about the world. It is a painful world, a vale of tears where ghosts jostle the beautiful fleshly living for a place in the fanatic heart.

The Priestly Comedy
of J. F. Powers

The scandal of Chicago's late Cardinal Cody was of the innocent, old-fashioned, irresistible kind. Money, power, sex—the ingredients of first-rate scandal—all were there, but the tone remained provincial. We felt, in our interest, at once familiar and ashamed, as if, eye at the motel room keyhole, we were watching a small-town pharmacist sweating over his girlfriend. It called up all the Eastern clichés of the Middle West. Cody was accused of diverting diocesan funds to Helen Dolan Wilson, his stepcousin. It was rumored that they had had a romantic liaison for many years and that he had bought her an expensive house in Florida.

To an outsider it was rather touching: the old-fashioned Irish name, the distant kin relationship, the real estate. A modern priest would have done it better, had more fun, not got caught. And the money would have been placed, somehow, in money market funds, or a tax-free shelter with an untraceable corporate name.

The whole business cannot be taken fully seriously by an Easterner, but one can feel the energy of local obsession in the outrage of the natives, who hear America singing in the stockyards and the railroads and proclaim that theirs is the real America. The Cody case underscores the difference between the New York and Chicago Churches. Chicago is a thousand miles west of New York, a thousand miles farther from Rome. It opens out onto those large, incomprehensible prairies settled by people without much Irish or Italian blood. Much earlier than Easterners, Midwesterners believed they could be Catholics and real Americans at the same time. Even now, Eastern Catholics have a sense of themselves as part of an immigrant Church—even the Kennedys, with their good teeth and their Harvard degrees, changed things only slightly; people are still surprised when Catholic boys get their own offices in Washington.

The Midwestern Church early on lost its Mediterranean tone. The Irish were in charge, particularly in Chicago—there was Daly in City Hall and Cody in the Chancery—but moving farther west, the Germans grew in power, and the comfort of the ghetto as an imaginative construct was a quickly forgotten temptation. In the middle of the continent, these farmers, businessmen, and their sons held to the faith, but the stuff of their dreams was manufactured in the New World. The self-made man, hearty, well-heeled, at home in first-class trains, in suites at the Palmer House, was the man they wanted their sons to be. They did not dream of these boys taking New York or Washington—to say nothing of Paris or Rome. Chicago was the focus of ambition and mythology. In Chicago, these Catholics could be at the center of the things the Protestants felt too high-minded to want, but moving west, they could never have access to real power.

They never believed it, though; they never accepted their differentness. For dress as they might, play golf, vote Republican, send their children to college, they were still led by men who wore black dresses, stayed unmarried, listened to their secrets in dark boxes, owed allegiance to a foreign power to which they wrote in a foreign tongue. The success of Catholics at assimilating was undeniably connected to the ability of their priests to *pass,* to seem only slightly and interestingly different from Protestant ministers, to be as welcome as they at the annual Jaycees lunch, while secretly praying for the conversion of the Chamber of Commerce and dreaming of Bishop Sheen as a White House adviser.

Vatican II was supposed to have changed all that, but the Cody case revealed only partially buried deep structures. Consider the odd role of Andrew Greeley in the Cody affair. Greeley is a Catholic priest whose credentials make him respectable in the secular academy. He has a post at the University of Arizona and runs a research institute in Chicago. He has a syndicated column. He has published over eighty books. Attractive, presentable, intelligent, he has devoted a large amount of energy to proving that Catholics are not the isolated bigots that people imagine them to be. That they're no different from other people. Jews, say.

How the existence of Cody must have galled him. Authoritarian, hierarchical, rigid, Cody created genuine misery for the liberal elements in his diocese. But he also served as a live, powerful suggestion that Catholics are not like everyone else, never have been, never can be. Greeley is the author of a best-selling novel, *The Cardinal Sins*, that some see as a roman à clef. The cardinal keeps a woman, is kept by a homosexual member of the Italian curia, is in the grips of the Mafia and the neofascists. Another character—a priest, a social scientist, a liberal—saves the day, the diocese, the cardinal. Greeley's second novel, *Thy Brother's Wife*, has another liberal priest-hero, who has always been in love with his sister-in-law. Despite his outspoken attacks on everyone from Pope Paul VI to the right-wing leader of a Spanish cult, this lovable guy is elected cardinal of Chicago. Unlikely are the heads that wear Greeley's hats.

At the height of the agitation over Cody's alleged financial irregularities, a newspaper, the *Chicago Lawyer*, published what it said were transcripts of tapes made by Greeley, which portrayed him as contemplating a scheme to oust Cody and to replace him with the more moderate Joseph Bernardin of Cincinnati. According to the transcript, four years earlier Greeley talked about subjecting Cody to "the worst kind of public scandal by turning an investigative reporter loose on the archdiocese, and tell[ing] him to blow the Chicago thing wide open." Greeley claims that the transcript represents only idle, late-night ramblings of the novelistic imagination. (You know how novelists are.) But the story gave weight to Cody's claim that he was being hounded by malcontents. Until he died, Cody reportedly continued to ignore federal grand jury subpoenas for his financial records; he refused to be questioned by either prosecutors or the press. Even Richard Nixon was more accessible.

There is only one American writer whose work could give the Cody affair quarter: J. F. Powers. Powers is a comic writer of genius, and there is no one like him. In vain one looks for precedents— English scenes of comical clerical life in Sterne or Trollope or Goldsmith do not do; the English tone is sweeter, for those clergymen never have to worry if the community wants someone like them around. In those novels, if the clerics themselves do not represent personal power, they represent an institution whose power is unquestioned. The furtive, hot desire for assimilation is impossible to imagine in the rural towns where those parsons christen, marry, bury. And the high drama circling round the priests of Bernanos or Graham Greene flies nowhere near the carefully barbered, untonsured heads of the Powers clergy. It is America that Powers writes about, and the peculiar situation of its Catholic priests illumines the larger world that they inhabit as the lives of outsiders who remain outside by the fixed nature of their identities must always do.

The isolated world—the pilgrimage, the madhouse, the country house, the colonial outpost—is a natural setting for the kind of comedy whose implications are at once moral and social. Life is denser in such places; personalities conform to types and types to personality; objects tell as they do not where the press of things and people is less close. It is in the close, packed atmosphere of parishes and monasteries that the comedy of Powers grows and flourishes, an odd, rare bloom: satiric, harsh, and yet not condemning, falling with an undisguisable relish upon the clergy's faults yet based on a tough and weary faith in what these clergymen so ineptly represent. Powers's voice is dry, supremely ironic; it is a difficult one for Americans, who like their comedy, it seems, with fewer modulations and do not read him.

Despite winning the National Book Award in 1963 for his novel *Morte D'Urban*, Powers has never had the audience he deserves. His output has been small, one novel and three collections of stories, *Prince of Darkness* (1947), *The Presence of Grace* (1956), *Look How the Fish Live* (1975). And he has one subject: priests; his stories on other topics are far less memorable. His great and unique talent lies in his ability to record the daily lives of priests; he does this with sympathy, yet with close, hilarious attention to the errors of their lives spelled out by their possessions and their diction.

He writes without romance and without rancor, perhaps because he sees the priests he likes as largely powerless. He never expects heroics from them; the irony of their lives that he so clearly sees is that the expectation of heroics is implicit in their vocation. Yet they inhabit the actual world, west of Chicago, and they are unexceptional, average Americans, who must live out the history of apostolic succession in a mode particularly American. Truly American, they cannot really comprehend the European ideal of the Roman Church. Like the millionaire who builds himself a villa in Michigan—installing copies of the Venus de Milo in each of his ten bathrooms—they both misunderstand the ideal and rudely try to force domestication on it. In addition, being priests, they are necessarily alone—unsure tenants, poor relations, dependent upon the charity of strangers, whom they must, if they are true to their vows, serve, impress, and keep as strangers.

"The Forks" concerns a pastor and a curate; it is a story about power and authority, youth and age, idealism and realpolitik, as well as about the uneasy cohabitation of God and Mammon. The pastor, known only as Monsignor, has taken Christ's counsel to the unjust steward. He has made friends for himself with the Mammon of wickedness, so well that he is far more at ease with local businessmen than he is with the Roman Church. Speaking of his bishop, Monsignor says to his curate:

"He reminds me of that bishop a few years back—at least he called himself a bishop, a Protestant—that was advocating companionate marriages. It's not that bad, maybe, but if you listened to some of them, you'd think that Catholicity and capitalism were incompatible!"

"The Holy Father—"

"The Holy Father is in Europe, Father. Mr. Memmers lives in this parish. I'm his priest. What can I tell him?"

"Is it Mr. Memmers of the First National, Monsignor?"

"It is, Father. And there's damned little cheer I can give a man like Memmers. Catholics, priests, and laity alike—yes, and princes of the Church, all talking atheistic communism!"

Monsignor imagines himself a man of culture and his curate a boor. But his notion of European culture is entirely Midwestern; in an outburst of outraged sensibility, he complains that his housekeeper has included green olives in the "tutti-frutti" salad he has asked for; he plans a lady garden in the back of the rectory, calling for a fleur-de-lis, a sundial, a cloister walk "running from the rectory to the garage." Father Eudex, the curate, who tries to help the janitor with the job of digging, sees the project as expensive and, in this country, "Presbyterian."

Yet the center of the story is not truly social comedy but a serious moral-religious issue. The local tractor company, a successful concern with an execrable record toward its employees, solves its excess-profits problem by sending out regular checks as "donations" to the local clergy. Father Eudex, whose sympathies are strongly pro-labor, understands the checks to be the most blatant whitening of the sepulchers, but he doesn't know what he should do with his—send it to the missions, hand it over to the company's workers' strike fund? The pastor advises him to put it toward the new car he has been wanting, a car that will make the right kind of point about his station.

Father Eudex makes his decision after a parishioner comes to him seeking not spiritual but financial advice and accuses him of not being "much of a priest" when he suggests she give some money to the poor. He flushes the tractor company's check down the toilet in a rapture of righteous divestment. But Powers ends the story with Father Eudex's priggish reflection on the superiority of his position to that of his fellow clerics who might have used their checks for good works. The final disembodied line, "And you, Father?" refuses to settle the question whether virtue lies in the pure act, with its wage of pride, or in the muddled gift, which serves the poor by abetting the wicked.

In "Prince of Darkness," Powers introduces us to the inner life of Father Ernest Burner, an entirely mediocre time-server, a glutton, a cynic, adolescent in his desire to be on the opposite side of whatever position is taken by the younger curate. Powers's attitude and tone are complicated, and are the source of the story's comedy. Burner lives in front of a mythic backdrop; even Powers's most secular readers know the image of the devoted pastor burning himself out for his flock. Burner knows he fails, but he does not change. He is a romantic whose sin is sloth, the least romantic of the lot. He fantasizes a heroic life, a martyr's death. Even if we have our doubts, even if we suspect that the *Dies Irae* might find Father Burner hiding under his bed—Powers shows us Burner hitting golf balls into his Roman collar, claiming that he is off to visit the sick when he is taking flying lessons, leaving a used match in the holy-water font—we cannot help seeing the pathos of his adolescent dreams, even his most down-to-earth one: being named a pastor. We don't want him to have to write his mother again, telling her that he has been appointed assistant yet another time and that she will have to wait even longer to fulfill their joint dream of her becoming his housekeeper:

> He thought of himself back in her kitchen, home from the sem for the holidays, a bruiser in a tight black suit, his feet heavy on the oven door. She was fussing at the stove and he was promising her a porcelain one as big as a house after he got his parish. But he let her know, kidding on the square, that he would be running things at the rectory. It would not be the old story of the priest taking orders from his house-keeper, even if she was his mother.

We never see Powers's priests doing any harm to the laity. There are no scenes of tormented penitents being denied consolation. It is impossible, for example, to be genuinely worried about the penitent in this confessional scene:

> "Were you married by a priest?"
> "Yes."
> "How long ago was that?"
> "Four years."
> "Any children?"
> "No."
> "Practice birth control?"
> "Yes, sometimes."
> "Don't you know it's a crime against nature and the Church forbids it?"
> "Yes."
> "Don't you know that France fell because of birth control?"
> "No."
> "Well, it did. Was it your husband's fault?"
> "You mean—the birth control?"
> "Yes."
> "Not wholly."
> "And you've been away from the Church ever since your marriage?"

"Yes."

"Now you see why the Church is against mixed marriages. All right, go on. What else?"

"I don't know. . . ."

"Is that what you came to confess?"

"No. Yes. I'm sorry, I'm afraid that's all."

"Do you have a problem?"

"I think that's all, Father."

"Remember it is your obligation, and not mine, to examine your conscience. The task of instructing persons with regard to these matters—I refer to the connubial relationship—is not an easy one. Nevertheless, since there is a grave obligation imposed by God, it cannot be shirked. If you have a problem—"

"I don't have a *problem*."

The language is perfect, "pure" Powers: the "problem," the "connubial relationship," the logical leap from birth control to the fall of France, and the penitent's understandable confusion. But after all, she doesn't have a "problem"; she'll be all right. In Powers's stories, no one suffers nearly so much as the priests themselves.

In "The Valiant Woman," the priestly suffering occurs at the hands of a truly monstrous housekeeper, the worst possible type of shrewish wife. Father Firman, the pastor, is as trapped as any tormented husband; he can't bear the guilt of getting rid of Mrs. Stoner, and besides, he can't afford to pension her off. Yet she has ruined his life:

She hid his books, kept him from smoking, picked his friends . . . , bawled out people for calling after dark, had no humor, except at cards and then it was grim, very grim, and she sat hatchet-faced every morning at Mass. But she went to Mass, which was all that kept the church from being empty some mornings. She did annoying things all day long. She said annoying things into the night. She said she had given him the best years of her life.

Powers flawlessly brings home the real horror of the woman, hostile, omnipresent, self-satisfied, encyclopedically misinformed.

She smiled pleasantly at Father Nulty. "And what do you think of the atom bomb, Father?"

"Not much," Father Nulty said. . . .

"Did you read about this communist convert, Father?"

"He's been in the Church before . . . and so it's not a conversion, Mrs. Stoner."

"No? Well, I already got him down on my list of Monsignor's converts. . . . And that congresswoman, Father? . . ."

"And Henry Ford's grandson. . . . I got him down. . . ."

"But he's only one by marriage, Father. . . . I always say you got to watch those kind."

In "Lions, Harts, Leaping Does," Powers explores once again the nature of the priesthood, but here his approach is not comic. The story is anomalous in Powers's canon; its tone is meditative, somber; there are dream passages, visionary sections. We meet Father Didymus, a Franciscan friar, in the last days of his life. Didymus is a perfectionist—a *perfectionalist,* one might say—tormented by his failure to live up to the Franciscan ideal, an ideal of poverty, simplicity, sanctity. He is a teacher of geometry and suffers, though he comes late to an awareness of it, from pride in his ability to make nice moral distinctions; the spiritual life becomes for him a geometric problem: which solution is the most elegant, the most seemly, the most formally satisfying? In having lived this way, he has entirely lost charity, the necessary center of the ideal to which he strives to conform.

In the character of Brother Titus, a simpleminded lay brother, the ideal of charity is embodied. Every day he sits and reads to Didymus from Bishop Bale's book of martyrs, "a denunciation of every pope from Peter to Paul IV." Titus is truly interested in only two books, *The Imitation of Christ* and *The Little Flowers of St. Francis*; he knows them by heart and would prefer to read only from them. But in the spirit of genuine brotherhood, he reads what Didymus wants. "Father Didymus, his aged appetite for biography jaded by the orthodox lives, found this work fascinating. . . . It was in sober fact a lie."

One cannot come to a genuine understanding of Powers's work without a careful reading of this story, for it is a story informed by faith. Judiciously spread through the text, coming always from the mouth of Titus, are quotes from spiritual writers that provide the unassailable standard against which all Powers's priests live their flawed lives. "O how joyous and how delectable is it to see religious men devout and fervent in the love of God, well mannered and well taught in ghostly learning." Titus, deficient in intelligence, cannot be ordained to the priesthood, yet he, of all Powers's characters, comes closest to the priestly ideal. Didymus's incisive yet ungenerous intellect keeps him from sanctity. When his brother, also a priest, asks Didymus to visit him on his deathbed, Didymus refuses on the grounds that to go would indicate excessive earthly attachments. At the news of his brother's death, he realizes that the decision not to go to his brother has been a sinful one, a sin of pride and of lack of charity. "Harshly, Didymus told himself he had used his brother for a hair shirt."

When he comes to this realization, he opens himself up to true sanctity, giving up all delusion. He is also struck with an affliction of the eye, which renders the visible world a chaotic jumble to him: "The background of darkness became a field of varicolored factions, warring, and, worse than the landscape, things like worms and comets wriggled and exploded before his closed eyes." It is the final loss to the geometrician, this believer in natural order as a prefiguration of the supernatural.

Powers has not written again in this vein, but "Lions, Harts, Leaping Does" shares some of the concerns of his novel, *Morte D'Urban*. In *Morte D'Urban*, we can see the extended use Powers makes of the priesthood as a kind of metonymic device to explore the themes of community, America, the spiritual/moral life. The book's central character, Father Urban Roche, is a product of the Midwest's most treasured image of itself. His success in the pulpit stems from his mastery of the Midwestern conception of Madison Avenue lingo. His particular linguistic specialty is the recycled dead metaphor. God is "The Good Thief of Time, accosting us wherever we go, along the highways and byways of life." In priests' retreats, Urban refers to parish priests as "those heroic family doctors of the soul," and to himself as "this poor specialist." And yet he is a member of a foreign organization, the Catholic Church, and even more suspicious, within that body he is a member of a religious order, the Clementine Fathers. Urban's reasons for joining the priesthood and the Clementines are revealing; the boy Harvey

Roche became the man Father Urban because he perceived at a young age that the best of America was reserved for Protestants:

> You felt it was their country, handed down to them by the Pilgrims, George Washington, and others, and that they were taking a risk in letting you live in it. . . . He knew, too, that Catholics were mostly Irish and Portuguese, and that their religion, poverty, and appearance . . . were all against them.

The one man Harvey meets who seems to have it made, as the Protestants do, is the visiting Father Placidus, a Clementine father who spurns rectory hospitality to "put up at the Merchant's Hotel, where bootblacks, bellboys, and waiters who'd never seen him before seemed to welcome him back." So Harvey becomes Urban, not because he is called to serve God but because he sees the priesthood as the easiest way to stay in the best hotels, to meet the best people, to live like a Protestant.

But the glamorous Father Placidus is an anomaly within his order. The Clementines are almost to a man third-raters. Urban is their one star, and they resent him even as they take advantage of his talents. He has perfected the skills of the successful executive and adapted them to the service of the Church:

> The usual thing was to drop in on executives at their places of business, but to let them know right away that he didn't want anything, and if nothing developed, he'd soon be on his way. "Just wanted you to know where we are. Drop in on *us* sometime." Later if he ran into somebody he'd met in this fashion, it was like old times. Hello—*hello!* He watched the paper for important funerals, too, and turned up at some of these. Wherever he went, people always seemed glad to see him—and, of course, it was all for the Order.

Urban is exiled to the order's new rural retreat-house-in-the-making in Duesterhaus, Minnesota, and taken off the preaching circuit. He is reduced to scraping floors and stripping wallpaper—work for which he has no talent—under the leadership of Father Wilfrid, who is a fool and, worse, a bad manager.

There had been a priest somewhere in Wilf's family for over a hundred years, but if Wilf's uncle had died four days sooner, or if Wilf had been ordained four days later, the chain would have been broken. Wilf was the only priest in the family at the moment, but two nephews were on the way. That was about what it came down to, Wilf's life story, that and the time Wilf had spent a week on retreat with the late Father Flanagan of Boys Town, that and attending a funeral at which Al Capone had been among the mourners, that and bringing in a Greyhound bus whose driver had taken ill on one of those hairpin curves in the Ozarks. "I guess I've always been something of a 'take charge' guy, Brother."

It is understood, but never stated, that Urban is sent to Duesterhaus to increase his humility, or, put another way, to insure against taking undue pride in his success as a preacher. But he is ineradicably the American entrepreneur; even in exile, he arranges local speaking engagements, which are hugely successful:

A number of couples came up to him afterward and thanked him for coming, one woman asking if there was any way of obtaining a copy of his talk, and one man saying that, though he was not a Catholic himself, he had always regarded Catholicism as one of the world's top religions and had never felt closer to it than he had that evening. The toastmaster (not a Catholic himself) expressed regret that Father Urban had been questioned so closely along certain lines. "Not a-tall, not a-tall," said Father Urban, and accepted an invitation to have a nightcap with the toastmaster and his wife at their home.

A world unfolds to us, of toastmasters and nightcaps and of priests as good at pleasing as the businessmen they preach to. Here is Powers's comedy at work: self-satisfaction oozes from the well-oiled pores of his characters as it does from Malvolio or Tartuffe. Yet no great evil is done by these fat bankers aching to be nonsectarian. They swim in a warm, prosperous ocean of bonhomie and a belief in their own broad-mindedness, which they mistake for culture. Powers records them, sticking them, like fat, shining beetles, on a pin.

Urban's most important function is the procuring of rich benefactors for the order. Like the Monsignor in "The Forks," he sees his vocation as the making of friends with the Mammon of wickedness. In a revealing passage, Powers allows us to glimpse Urban's thoughts on that most difficult of Gospel parables:

> Our Lord, in Father Urban's opinion, had been dealing with some pretty rough customers out there in the Middle East, the kind of people who wouldn't have been at all distressed by the steward's conduct—either that or people had been a whole lot brighter in biblical times, able to grasp a distinction then. It had even entered Father Urban's mind that Our Lord, who, after all, knew what people were like, may have been a little tired on the day he spoke this parable. Sometimes, too, when you were trying to get through to a cold congregation, it was a case of any port in a storm. You'd say things that wouldn't stand up very well in print.

Urban cannot tolerate mystery, paradox, irony—the ingredients of Christ's lesson; therefore he is no match against the real evil that intrudes, in the persons of the very benefactors whom he courts. There is Mrs. Thwaites, an unspeakable octogenarian, who keeps two TV sets going at all times and has an elevator for the sole purpose of taking her to her fallout shelter in case of atomic attack. She has stolen back all her Irish nurse's wages by beating her—and probably cheating—at dominoes.

Billy Cosgrove, a shady businessman and a paradigm of arrogant vulgarity, is impressed with Father Urban's "urbanity," gives the Clementines a lease on a fancy building—and then takes it away when Urban finally censures his behavior. The incident that occasions this censure is the center of a chilling scene. Piqued at having had a bad day's fishing, Billy tries to drown a swimming deer. When Urban stops him, finally realizing that Billy has gone too far, Billy literally throws him out of the boat and leaves him stranded, forced to swim home.

This scene marks the turning point in the novel; it is the beginning of both Urban's worldly failure and his spiritual awareness. *Morte D'Urban*'s great distinction is that it is a conversion story told in comic terms. Urban's peripeteia takes place in the context of a virtuoso display of Powers's talent for recording American kitsch. His encounter with Billy happens at a fishing lodge named Henn's Haven, where "the stuffed birds and fur-bearing animals on the walls wore cellophane slipcovers" and where the proprietor draws Father Urban's attention to a sign that says: WE DON'T KNOW WHERE MOTHER IS, BUT WE HAVE POP ON ICE! Instead of being knocked off his horse on the road to Damascus, he is knocked out by a bishop's golf ball.

Shaken by his failure with Billy and Mrs. Thwaites, and by a successfully resisted carnal temptation offered by Mrs. Thwaites's daughter, physically damaged by his encounter with a golf ball, Urban begins to have mysterious headaches, which his barber's son, a neurosurgeon, diagnoses as psychosomatic. At this point, Urban is elected to be the order's provincial. Now chief executive, he loses his executive ability, his love of the rich, his desire to see the Church "the best-run company . . . second only to Standard Oil." He loses his energy as well; he makes unpopular decisions. He finds his soul but, in so doing, presides over the collapse of his order.

Perhaps Father Greeley should read J. F. Powers; it might remind him of the comic possibilities inherent in American religion, which Americans nearly always forget. Because we tend to see religion as unsusceptible to humor, we have outlandish expectations of it, expectations that only a demagogue can pretend to fulfill. In the face of the most recent events in American religion, and its stars— Cody, Greeley, Jerry Falwell, even—Powers's vision, clear, ironic, and secure, continues to refresh and nourish. The recent republication in paper of *Prince of Darkness* and *Morte D'Urban* makes the books once more available.

Ingeborg Bachmann: Children Were Only Allowed to Whisper

"When you could think of nothing more to do with your life, then you spoke entirely truthfully, but only then," says the narrator in Ingeborg Bachmann's story "Undine Goes." What statement could be more extreme? To be at the point where one can think of nothing to do with one's life is to be at the point where will, desire, and imagination fail.

Reading Ingeborg Bachmann necessarily entails abandoning the terms of one's own comfort, following in her enterprise of seeing everything, covering over nothing that might terrify or make the ordinary life impossible to live. Her relentlessness of vision demands that the reader allow himself or herself to be hypnotized, taken over by her repetitive cadences and burning images of grief and loss. Miss Bachmann's vision is structured by a series of mutually annihilating pairs: thought and action, life and truth, female and male. She burns up the ordinary, muffling possibilities, the compromises, the dialectics of accommodation and survival. And yet, in the beauty of her images, in her belief in a merciful natural order—from which the moral, thinking human is almost entirely cut off—there is tremendous affirmation of the world. The human faculty of sensuous apprehension, which in language expresses itself in the creation of images, provides the only solace to the lacerating demands of consciousness.

Ingeborg Bachmann was a writer of genius. Nevertheless, although her stories were published once in 1964, she has been, until the recent publication of *The Thirtieth Year*—a reissue of Michael Bullock's excellent translation—long out of print in English. Why have we been deprived of her? It is a commonplace that the smaller, lyrically distilled work is less important than the larger, more expansive one. And Ingeborg Bachmann's femaleness has complicated her reception in the German-speaking world. It is nearly impossible for a woman artist to have any sort of intense personal life without its becoming an issue connected to the public perception of the nature of her work. Bachmann became a kind of cult figure, famously neurotic, famously suffering. (The introduction to the new volume, by Karen Achberger, compares her image to that of other doomed women—the German terrorist Ulrike Meinhof and Marilyn Monroe!) This imagemaking suggested to literary circles that she should not be taken with the highest seriousness. Her death created further problems of response: she died after setting herself on fire in 1973; it's unclear whether this was accidental. But she has been acknowledged as a great poet and novelist in the German-speaking world; there is a museum devoted to her in Austria, and her work has been adapted into operatic and dramatic forms.

Bachmann was born in 1926; her childhood was lived out under Nazism. After the war, sitting in the rubble with her friends Günter Grass and Heinrich Böll, exchanging manuscripts, she tried to create a new language, a pure speech: speech without desire, imagination, will. Speech beyond power. What would the nature of such speech be? And why is Bachmann's tone often so oddly joyous? In her words we hear the joy that grows up in the quiet after the disaster—the joy that comes when one looks at the ruined city and sees in the space created by collapse the brave, frail hope.

The story "Youth in an Austrian Town" begins with a description of a tree "so ablaze with autumn, such an immense patch of gold, that it looks like a torch dropped by an angel." But the enlivening vision is followed hard upon by the consciousness of decay and loss. "Who, faced with this tree, is going to talk to me about falling leaves and the white death? Who will prevent me from holding it with my eyes and believing that it will always glow before me as it does at this moment and that it is not subject to the laws of the world?" But this is a story, not about perception, but about war. Taking exactly the opposite route from Günter Grass, Bachmann compresses into less than ten pages the history of Germanic consciousness, its cruelty, its killing spirit, and the aftermath of destruction and war. Cruelty is woven into the fabric of upbringing in this Austrian town. The children "are only allowed to whisper and for the rest of their lives they will never lose the habit of whispering. At school the teachers say to them: 'You should be beaten until you open your mouths. Beaten' . . . Between the reproach for talking too loud and the reproach for talking too softly, they settle down in silence."

When the war breaks out, the brutality imposed on children in private finds in the public world a magnifying mirror.

> The time of veiled hints is past. People speak in their presence of shooting in the back of the neck, of hanging, liquidating, blowing up, and what they don't hear and see they smell, as they smell the dead of St. Ruprecht, who cannot be dug out because they have been buried under the movie theatre into which they slipped surreptitiously to see *Romance in a Minor Key*. Juveniles were not admitted, but then they were admitted to the great dying and murdering which took place a few days later and every day after that.

The children's experience is shaped by their language, language that is dangerous and creative and generative of itself. The children's horrors and isolation, their passionate secret lives, mirror themselves in their words:

> The children are in love but do not know with what. They talk in gibberish, muse themselves into an indefinable pallor, and when they are completely at a loss they invent a language that maddens them. My fish. My hook. My fox. My snare. My fire. You my water. You my current. My earth. You my if. And you my but. Either. Or. My everything . . . my everything. . . . They push one another, go for each other with their fists and scuffle over a counter-word that doesn't exist.

The mutually reflective horrors of the public and private worlds are bearable only because of the image of the flowering tree, which Bachmann recalls for the story's end. The sorrow created by language and consciousness can be relieved only by the potency of the physical world. In the title story, the young hero is saved from suicidal self-consciousness only by a near-fatal accident that leaves him bruised and his companion dead. Simple life—regained after he seems to have lost everything—restores to him the idea of life's value. The story's final words have the ring of New Testament promise: "I say unto thee: Rise up and walk! None of your bones is broken."

But in the story "Everything," a father's horror at the inevitable imprint of experience on his son's consciousness causes him spiritually to abandon his child and the child's mother. The literal death of the child is seen to be the outcome of the father's will that he should be effaced. "I didn't want this child anymore. I hated him because he understood too well, because I already saw him treading in everyone's footsteps." The matter of the story is highly abstract, but Bachmann pins it down with her searing images. The father explains his awestruck feelings upon observing his wife's pregnancy by saying that the world "seemed to me to be waxing. Like the moon before which one is supposed to bow three times when it is new and stands tender and breath-coloured at the start of its course." To begin in such promise and end in self-inflicted nullity— how real Bachmann makes this sorrow!

The relations of men and women call up at once Bachmann's profoundest dualizing pessimism and her most visionary hopes. In her astonishing "A Step Towards Gomorrah," she explores the nature of relations between women—and by necessity those between women and men. Charlotte is a musician who is courted after a night's drinking by Mara, an unhappy girl in a red skirt. Charlotte sees in Mara's exaggerated femaleness a type of her own, in Mara's posture an exaggeration of her own position in relation to her husband. The recognition calls up in her a sadistic desire to dominate the girl. In the end she rejects all possibilities available in favor of a dream of "my kingdom," "the millennium" when she could take over the world, name her companions, establish rights and duties, invalidate the old pictures and design the first new ones. "For it was the world of pictures that remained when everything had been swept away that had been condemned by the sexes and said of the sexes. . . . The picture of the huntress, the great mother and the great whore, the good Samaritan, the decoy-bird, the will o' the wisp and the woman placed under the stars." Charlotte lies down beside Mara, but only, finally, to rest and dream, "to hope for the kingdom. Not the kingdom of men and not that of women. Not this, not that."

This, then, is the kingdom presided over by Ingeborg Bachmann's vision: not this, not that, but the strenuous, exhausting search for the new truthful language, the new set of saving images.

David Plante:
A World of
Baffled Love

The world of David Plante's Francoeur family is male and foreign. It is a world of silences, of baffled and balked love, of pain borne stoically, of Indian cruelties and natural ties, of French Catholic pieties and the bleak light of failed New England cities. David Plante began the story of the Francoeurs—a French-Canadian working-class family living in Providence, Rhode Island—in his brilliant novel *The Family*, which was nominated for a National Book Award in 1978. He continues their history in his equally superb *The Country*, which opens with the return from England of Daniel, the expatriate writer among the seven Francoeur sons. He returns to find his proud, beloved father in decay, his mother—susceptible, as always, to madness—disappearing now into the thick penumbra of her own delusion. By the end of the novel, Daniel will bury his aged father, cleanse and clothe the ancient body of his widowed mother, and journey into the woods in hope of understanding the lost language of his Indian forebears.

The father of this family, Arcase Francoeur, called Jim, the grandson of a French fur trader and a Blackfoot Indian woman, is a worker in love with the romance of work, in love with his tools, his hours, his slow climb, his production. Staunchly and proudly anti-union, he suffered the great crisis in his life when he was fired in middle age from his machinist's job, the delayed revenge of union leaders whom Jim had fought to keep out of the plant for years. All his adult life, Jim Francoeur was a Republican, believing in the myth of benevolent paternalism, confident that his labor and honesty would win him the modest and peaceful life he desired for his family—a life in which ease and pleasure are not even thought of as prizes worthy of being wished for. But the stark relentlessness, the joylessness, of the husband has driven his wife mad, and the madness of the one Francoeur woman is the crack in the dark rock that is the foundation of the family. Madness, like language, laughter, hope, is associated in this novel with the female, and the relentless attempts of the family men to push these elements out of their lives lead, in the view of Daniel, the narrator, only to insanity and sorrow.

Shortly before his death, the father sits in silence and in sorrow, covered by a sense of failure. "I've been a bad man," he tells Daniel. "I have done no good in the world. . . . I was never good with your mother. She was never happy with me." "You have worked so hard," his son says. "For no good," replies the anguished father. His dream of a solid, just reward has been dissipated in the effervescent, oddly energetic gas of his wife's insanity. While he sits and weeps, she rambles, hits the backs of chairs with her fists, invents fantasies of lands where people walk backward and shake hands behind their backs.

David Plante brilliantly renders the exhausting scattershot that is the language of the mad: "What I always say, well, open arms, you hold them, your sons, with open arms, who was it? I can't remember, said that?, that's what I say, open arms, they come, they go, and I, well, I left my parents, didn't I?, hold them with open arms, you know what that means, don't you?" Her husband is tied to her, will not leave the house because she will not, although she complains of being kept a prisoner in her husband's house. All his devotion is useless; it makes her no happier, no better. At his death, she is buoyant, cheerful; she dresses for his funeral for the first time in months—swearing till the last moment she will not go. She has brought danger into the house, and laughter. Daniel's love of language and story is hers. She tells him—and he knows she is right—that he is *her* son, not his father's.

The ghost of Stephen Dedalus, that professional writer-son, broods over *The Country*, for the novel is, among other things, the

portrait of the artist as a young man. Yet if Stephen Dedalus is
here, he is a kinder Stephen, and more merciful. Regret for the
gulf between son and father, brother and brother, mother and son,
provides the dark color of David Plante's prose, but the regret is
entirely untinged by contempt. That his family will never understand what he writes makes Daniel wonder at the value of his
writing, not rail against the stupidity of his kind. The father tries
to understand what it is, exactly, that his son does, this writing that
he calls work but is so unlike any work the father has done in his
long life as a worker. "Is it difficult to write a book?" the father
asks, hoping to learn something, as he might from his other son,
the engineer. Daniel tells his father that the hardest thing is "to
write, not about what I feel and think, but what someone else
does." The father tries to understand, but it has been years since
he has read a book. Yet he respects his son. The distance between
them, the light shed on his life by his son's, does not disturb him.
"Work hard. . . . And be a good boy," he says to Daniel, as he
might to any of his sons, saying goodbye.

Daniel's vocation, to understand his family through language, is
fulfilled only after his father's death. Throughout the novel, Daniel
is obsessed with the lost language, the lost *languages*—Indian,
French, French-Canadian—of the family. Before his father's death,
Daniel has a vision while watching him stand alone: "His lips were
moving. I saw, standing in the woods behind him, his mother, large
and dark, and deeper in, a larger, darker woman, and then another
and another . . . going back and back, to a great dark mother, to
whom my father could pray in a language I did not know."

At the end of the novel, Daniel returns to the island where,
years before, the sons, in a doomed gesture of filial love, bought
their parents a house they never enjoyed. Daniel journeys to the
island, past his father's death. Only his father's death teaches him
the language of the large, dark Indian women; only through his
father's death can he walk through the woods to the dark mother.
It is a journey *of* language, *through* language; a journey and a last
lament:

My father was born, as I was, among the ghosts of a small
community of people of strange blood. They were people who
saw that they were born in darkness and would die in darkness,

and who accepted that. They spoke, in their old French, in whispers, in the churchyard, among the gravestones, in the snow, and with them, silent, were squaws with papooses on their backs, and the woods began beyond the last row of gravestones. . . . Their religion was my religion, the religion of a God who spoke an old parochial French . . . a religion, not of recourse, but of stark truth: death is what we live for, and as terrible as it is, to die is better than to live. Those of the religion were honest, and they were noble, and my heart bled for them.

But the world of the father is gone, the world of his Indian grandmother hopelessly corrupted. The novel began with Daniel on the train, meeting an Indian boy, a juvenile delinquent who says that what he likes are dumps with old cars in them. Later, Daniel tries to contact the boy, but the boy is not at home when he calls, and Daniel understands that he must go back to England, to his real life.

"Only in the realm of praising may Lament go / Jubilance knows, and Longing acquiesces— / only Lament is learning still," writes Rilke, in the voice of Orpheus, the poet. *The Country* is a haunting lament, a controlled cry of loss and knowledge won through language, sorrow, memory, impossible and comprehending love, love learned through childhood in the body of the family, the country.

Ford Madox Ford:
A Man Who
Loved Women,
a Womanly Man

It may not be creditable; it may even be thought, by some, ignoble; it is nevertheless true: we do not read as angels, without sex.

I am the sex less dominant in the area of letters; fewer women have written books than men, and fewer, probably, have read them. And so I am often conscious of a sense of exclusion—more or less pronounced when, reading as I do with the history of my womanhood at my elbow, I read certain books. Most books, let us admit it, were written by men for men. To read a book at all—that is, a serious book—is for a woman a slightly rebellious act. Should she not be doing something else? Something practical, something to serve someone, something to appease that monster Mrs. Woolf has named forever and set out for us, the Angel in the House. No, you will say, that is as it used to be; even Virginia Woolf has been dead for fifty years. But I say although the Angel in the House has been named, and although we now have weapons to combat her, she still hovers; she still makes reading a different occupation for women than for men. And she has allies in some writers. Some, clearly, want women kept out. When I read Milton, Melville, Conrad, I feel I am, quite daringly, having to impersonate a man; I must enter the Men's Club in drag, for clearly, as I am, I am not wanted. Some writers are more tactful. Blake and Fielding greet me with the message: "Well, I hadn't thought of you, of course, but now you're here, come in, come in. Why not?" Flaubert and Joyce say: "If you must you must; I guess you're up to it." Dickens, in distress, half mutters: "Really you needn't bother your pretty head." Colette would prefer it if I were a young man, quite self-educated, careless of his dress.

No one makes a woman so welcome as Ford Madox Ford. I feel, when I sit down to read him, that he has arranged for me what he imagined was the ideal situation for the reader. The reader, and the writer too: the writer must have an audience. When Dowell, the narrator of *The Good Soldier*, describes the ideal conditions for the telling and the hearing of his story, he says:

> I shall just imagine myself for a fortnight or so at one side of the fireplace of a country cottage, with a sympathetic soul opposite me. And I shall go on talking, in a low voice while the sea sounds in the distance and overhead the great black flood of wind polishes the bright stars. From time to time we shall get up and go to the door and look out over the great moon and say: "Why it is nearly as bright as in Provence!" And then we shall come back to the fireside with just the touch of a sigh because we are not in that Provence where even the saddest stories are gay.

It is clear to me that Dowell's ideal listener can only be a woman, a woman with whom he is on intimate terms. But, you will say, that is not Ford speaking, that is Dowell; how stupid you have been, mistaking the voice of the narrator for the voice of the author. And of course, who could be more unlike Dowell, the poor, impotent, deluded sad schlemiel, who never gets the girl until it's time to nurse her? No one could be less like Dowell than Ford. Ah, yes, but there is the code word: Provence. For Dowell, as for Ford, Provence is the correct place to live a life; it is the home of the noblest poetry, the most superb cuisine. It has the ideal climate. And besides, whether the invitation to listen comes from Dowell, or from Ford, or from both, the point is this: how rare it is to see, anywhere in fiction, an invitation that suggests to a woman: "This is for you." No need to pretend, the invitation goes on; no need to feel inferior: it is exactly for your womanhood I want you. This is for you.

I have been trying, then, to understand what it is about Ford Madox Ford, the writer and the man, that draws me so. Of course, his style is peerless and his vision of the human heart unmatched. But there are other writers whom I admire as much as I do Ford, and my feelings for them are not the same. It is not that I think of Ford as master, teacher: he is one of those singular writers, like Sterne, like Dostoevsky, from whom other writers cannot learn much. No, my feelings for Ford are odder and more complex. I feel that Ford courts me as a woman reader. He courts me in two ways: by his immense sympathy with the world of, the perspective of, the condition of women, and by his masterful portrayal of them. Ford has created two of the wickedest, most destructive women in literature; he has also created the only true feminist heroine in the history of the novel.

Perhaps Ford's wartime history made him sure of himself as a male; whatever the reason, he is charmingly ready to portray himself busy with the occupations traditionally reserved for women. Has any great writer spent so much time describing himself as a cook? Has any other writer made the decision about whether he will go on with his career as a writer based upon the fate of a shallot in a stew? For this, Ford says in *It Was the Nightingale*, was the omen upon which his future as a writer depended:

In Red Ford, whilst the crock boiled over the sinking fire the cottage was filled with a horde of minor malices and doubts. The stairs creaked; the rafters stirred; in the chimney the starlings, distressed by my fire, kept up a continuous rustling. The rest of that empty house I had only dimly seen by the light of one candle. It was unknown ground. I had a sense that the shadows were alive with winged malices and maladies and that the dark, gleaming panes of the windows hid other, whispering beings, that jeered behind my back, hanging from the rose stems in the outer night. And the crock went on boiling out destiny. If the skins came off the shallots I was to make a further effort. If not I was to let go.

Even the landscapes Ford most loves are feminine, domestic in their proportions. Gringoire, clearly Ford's alter ego in *No Enemy*, dreams, in the midst of battle, of the perfect situation:

> There came upon me an intense longing . . . for the green country, the mists, the secure nook at the end of a little valley, the small cottage whose chimneys just showed over the fruit trees—for the feelings and the circumstances of a sanctuary in which one could cross one's second over one's index finger and in the face of destiny cry: "Feignits."

Ford is not one of those domesticated males who dream of sanctuary with the woman of their choice cast securely in the role of servant while they do the grand work of art or politics. He sees the work of domestic economy as utterly critical for the happiness, indeed the very future, of the race; and he sees it as a matter for men as well as women to be concerned with. He even sees the essential humor in the man's intruding himself into women's traditional sphere. We learn of Gringoire that:

> Above all [he] loved to talk about cooking for he boasted that he was not only the best but the most economical cook in the world. How that may be your Compiler hesitates to say. To eat a meal prepared by Gringoire was certainly an adventure and when you felt adventurous had its titillations. But only Mme. Selysette who had accompanied him into his English wilds from the distant South could have told you whether Gringoire was as economical in his cuisine as he professed to be. For he swore that the savior of society would be the good but excellently economical cook.
>
> But Mme. Selysette, dark, alert, and with exquisitely pencilled brows and as loyal as she was goodhumoured, never got beyond saying that in his culinary furies Gringoire needed at least three persons—whom I took to be herself, the diminutive maid and the almost diminutive stable boy—to clear up after he had boiled an egg.

If all this were not enough to make rapturous the woman who longs—and I assume any literary woman of good sense and full heart is always longing—for some indication that there are, some-where, men who write the most beautiful sentences imaginable and still like women, there is more. Ford was ardent on the subject of woman suffrage. He even went so far as to write a pamphlet for the Women's Freedom League, a pamphlet entitled "This Monstrous Regiment of Women." The core of his argument is as simple as it is quixotic: women should be given the vote because it is obvious that they are not men's inferiors, certainly not in administrative ability. The proof for this is that England has never prospered so much as it has with women on the throne: the ages of Elizabeth and Victoria were high points in the history of the island. How wonderful it would be to have Ford on one's side when one is told by a fool that *he,* personally, won't support the ERA because it can only lead to unisex toilets. If only one had Ford at one's side, to say something like this:

> The other day . . . I was talking to a distinguished personage who was loudly contending against the claims of women to have any administrative faculties. And I mentioned that during these two great periods of British expansion and British prosperity, women sat upon the throne of England. My argumentative friend said:
>
> "Oh! as for Victoria, she was a nasty old woman, and Queen Elizabeth ought to have been a man."
>
> This is the sort of argument that has to be met by those of us who support the claims of women to political equality with bootblacks and uncertified imbeciles.

If only one had the Ford of *A Man Could Stand Up* at one's side to tell one, in the most beautiful sentences imaginable, why men need women and women need men! To tell us, for example:

> That was what a young woman was for. You seduced a young woman in order to be able to finish your talks with her. You could not do that without living with her. You could not live with her without seducing her; but that was the by-product. The point is that you can't otherwise talk. You can't finish talks at street corners; in museums; even in drawing rooms. You mayn't be in the mood when she is in the mood—for the

intimate conversation that means the final communion of your souls. You have to wait together—for a week, for a year, for a lifetime, before the final intimate conversation may be attained . . . and exhausted. So that . . . That in effect was love.

You seduced a young woman in order to be able to finish your talks with her. This implies, of course, that young women are immensely worth talking to. Never is it suggested by Ford that a proper woman *only* talks, or only listens. A proper woman lives with the man she loves. A proper woman desires and is desired. Ford is one of the few writers I can think of who does not punish his women characters for being sexual. The wicked women—Leonora Ashburnham and Sylvia Tietjens—are wicked not because they have sexual natures but because something in their sexual natures has been balked. Their wickedness is connected to their sexuality; with Ford, the sexual is a symptom of a much larger way of looking at the world, of placing oneself in it. But their wickedness does not begin with sex, and their sexual transgressions are far from the most important of their sins. And, essentially, both Leonora and Sylvia—both convent bred—are in love with chastity. Their ruling goddess is Diana; both are superb on horseback and in the light of the moon.

Sylvia Tietjens and Leonora Ashburnham are tormentors and destroyers. It is possible to say that, certainly, but that is not enough to say, that is not all of it, particularly in the case of Leonora. Ford endows Leonora with a childhood. We see her among her sisters, in the straitened, gallant, even dangerous circumstances that her family live in in Ireland—the great house only a hairsbreadth from ruin, the tenants taking potshots in the hedges. And we cannot but sympathize with this lovely "clean run" girl who hasn't a ghost of an idea of the relations between the sexes. The intrusion of her father's advice—appropriate perhaps to an Irish landlord whose people hate him, but utterly wrong in the England where the landlord plays the loving father or the feudal lord to grateful, skilled, and loyal tenants—is the cause of all the Ashburnhams' misery. It is the collision of the practical, the economical, with the ideal in Leonora's nature that calls up all the unmerciful, unyielding aspects of a chaste nature reared in the kind of convent that exists precisely to be the walled garden of Catholic girls of the upper class. Let us not forget it: Leonora was betrayed by her husband. But what galls her is not only the sexual infidelity—which she sees as a necessary and entirely comprehensible trifle; what she cannot bear is the economic ruin that stalks her and her husband everywhere. And she is not wrong: they were near bankruptcy; she did rescue them from that. Only, in rescuing her husband from bankruptcy, she broke him, because she did not understand the Good Soldier's first duty: he must be generous to his inferiors. It is, it must be, the purpose and the shape of his life to shelter all the weak creatures, so vulnerable and everywhere around him. His job is to temper the wind to the shorn lamb; should he fail at this, he is merely a moral fraud, cadging an easy living from the labor of strangers.

Leonora destroyed her husband; it must be admitted. And in the end, only she, of all the novel's characters, has prospered. But it is the genius of *The Good Soldier* that the intricacies of Dowell's narration reveal the utter impossibility of the whole situation for everyone, and not the least Leonora. Her conduct toward Edward and Nancy is monstrous. But the situation itself is monstrous; Edward had absolutely no business declaring his love to Nancy. It was the betrayal of everything both he and Leonora stood for. The Good Soldier does not make love to his ward. And when Leonora pushes Edward to the exhausted confession that all he really wants is that Nancy, far from him in India, should continue to love him, Leonora is right in calling that desire monstrous. For how could it not ruin Nancy's life, to be forever in love with a man she will never again be permitted to lay eyes on?

Morally, certainly, Leonora has her justifications. But the vision of *The Good Soldier* is, finally, not moral; everything about it points to the necessity of a highly developed moral consciousness and its utter insufficiency for helping anyone to live a life. *The Good Soldier* is a romance; the good are too beautiful for this world; they die or go mad. Leonora is "the woman who is needed by society. She desired children, decorum, and establishment; she desired to avoid waste; she desired to keep up appearances." This tendency to prosper in the world as it is is the very antithesis of the qualities that go to making up a romantic heroine. Leonora destroys and prospers; she cannot be a heroine. But how well we understand her; how much of her we are allowed to see!

If Leonora Ashburnham had a spotless childhood, Sylvia Tietjens of *Parade's End* did not. She was born a "wrong'un"; everyone knows it: her mother, her confessor, the old retainer on the family estate. As a child she tried to put walnut shells on the paws of a kitten; as a young woman she nearly beats to death a white bull-dog—who reminds her of her husband—for the offense of being in pain. She is a killer: obsessed, obsessive, mad in her torments and determined to torment. Yet she is, in her way, magnificent, and Ford gives her full marks for her appeal: "Brilliant mixture as she was, of the perfectly straight, perfectly fearless, perfectly reck-less, of the generous, the kind even—and the atrociously cruel."

Perhaps the only flaw in Ford's rendering of Sylvia is that he is unconvincingly generous to her. Are we really to believe that all Sylvia's magnificent hatred could have been drenched by the love of a good man and a brood of kiddies? When Mark Tietjens on his deathbed says, "Poor bitch! The riding had done it," can we possibly believe him? In her last scruple, her refusal to endanger the child in Valentine's womb—the primal decency of woman to woman—Ford saves Sylvia from the verdict of utter treachery. But there is nothing in Sylvia's past to account for her sudden scruple; would the woman who claimed to be dying of cancer in order to prevent her husband from taking up with another woman, and then took to her bed for months to make them appear heartless, stop at the final, most vicious blow to the man who has not ceased to obsess her: the ruination of his child? Sylvia is a killer; her creator has stopped her hand.

Sylvia is a killer. "If you wanted something killed you'd go to Sylvia Tietjens in the sure faith that she would kill it: emotion: hope: ideal: kill it quick and sure. If you wanted something kept alive you'd go to Valentine." To Valentine Wannop: suffragist, athlete, Latinist, former tweeny maid, lover and beloved. To Val-entine, undoubtedly a hero. Heroically, she worked as a tweeny maid to keep her mother alive—her mother, who wrote the only novel worth reading since the eighteenth century—and to send her brother to school. She is fearless; she is passionate; she breathes the breath of life into her man, who would die without her, and without whom she would die. Ford has described the raptures of an ardent woman with a prose that rises and falls, that rages and becalms: the objective correlative of the female experience of desire. There is, for me, no sexier scene in any novel than the one in which, in his empty apartment, Christopher holds Valentine by the wrist while they speak to her mother on the telephone.

Valentine and Christopher set up house in one of Ford's beloved domestic landscapes, English but southern, fertile and undemanding to the eye. They nurse Mark Tietjens and throw in their lot with his wife, Marie Léonie, alias Charlotte, his mistress of twenty-five years. They are kitchen gardeners; they make a living selling old furniture. They are in everything together. Together they go to auctions; Christopher finds Valentine better at driving a bargain than himself. They are about to have a baby. Valentine worries that what Marie Léonie says is right: that she will lose her man because of the state of her underclothing and because she does not cover herself in clouds of Houbigant. But we know, and she knows, that really she will never lose her man. They have the happiest marriage in all of literature; even Sylvia Tietjens cannot destroy it.

There is, there must be, something risible about the image of Ford as lover. The fishy eye, the Colonel Blimp physique, the tallowy hair, the dead-white fattish hands: hardly the ingredients of the romantic hero. Yet he was irresistible to women, and he was susceptible to them, to almost everybody's sorrow. How this piqued Joyce, who was inspired to write this poem about it:

> O Father O'Ford, you've a masterful way with you
> Maid, wife and widow are wild to make hay with you
> Blondes and brunettes turn-about run away with you
> You've such a way with you, Father O'Ford.
>
> That instant they see the sun shine from your eye
> Their hearts flitter flutter, they think and they sigh:
> We kiss ground before thee, we madly adore thee,
> And crave and implore thee to take us, O Lord.

Well, Joyce couldn't know; he didn't have it in him to understand. But women must have loved Ford for his courtliness, the generosity of his thoughts about them, and the elegance of his sentences. And because it must have been so obvious, the kind of man he was: a man who loved women, a womanly man.

II

THE WORLD,
THE CHURCH,
THE LIVES
OF WOMEN

More Than Just a Shrine: Paying Homage to the Ghosts of Ellis Island

I once sat in a hotel in Bloomsbury trying to have breakfast alone. A Russian with a habit of compulsively licking his lips asked if he could join me. I was afraid to say no; I thought it might be bad for détente. He explained to me that he was a linguist and that he always liked to talk to Americans to see if he could make any connection between their speech and their ethnic background. When I told him about my mixed ancestry—my mother is Irish and Italian, my father was a Lithuanian Jew—he began jumping up and down in his seat, rubbing his hands together and licking his lips even more frantically.

"Ah," he said, "so you are really somebody who comes from what is called the boiling pot of America." Yes, I told him; yes, I was; but I quickly rose to leave. I thought it would be too hard to explain to him the relation of the boiling potters to the main course, and I wanted to get to the British Museum. I told him that the only thing I could think of that united people whose backgrounds, histories, and points of view were utterly diverse was that their people had landed at a place called Ellis Island.

I didn't tell him that Ellis Island was the only American landmark I'd ever visited. How could I describe to him the estrangement I'd always felt from the kind of traveler who visits shrines to America's past greatness, those rebuilt forts with muskets behind glass and sabers mounted on the walls and gift shops selling maple sugar candy in the shape of Indian headdresses, those reconstructed villages with tables set for fifty and the Paul Revere silver gleaming? All that Americana—Plymouth Rock, Gettysburg, Mount Vernon, Valley Forge—it all inhabits for me a zone of blurred abstraction with far less hold on my imagination than the Bastille or Hampton Court. I suppose I've always known that my uninterest in it contains a large component of the willed: I am American, and those places purport to be my history. But they are not mine.

Ellis Island is, though; it's the one place I can be sure my people are connected to. And so I made a journey there to find my history, like any Rotarian traveling in his Winnebago to Antietam to find his. I had become part of that humbling democracy of people looking in some site for a past that has grown unreal. The monument I traveled to was not, however, a tribute to some old glory. The minute I set foot upon the island I could feel all that it stood for: insecurity, obedience, anxiety, dehumanization, the terrified and careful deference of the displaced. I hadn't traveled to the Battery and boarded a ferry across from the Statue of Liberty to raise flags or breathe a richer, more triumphant air. I wanted to do homage to the ghosts.

I felt them everywhere, from the moment I disembarked and saw the building with its high-minded brick, its hopeful little lawn, its ornamental cornices. The place was derelict when I arrived; it had not functioned for more than thirty years—almost as long as the time it had operated at full capacity as a major immigration center. I was surprised to learn what a small part of history Ellis Island had occupied. The main building was constructed in 1892, then rebuilt between 1898 and 1900 after a fire. Most of the immigrants who arrived during the latter half of the nineteenth century, mainly northern and western Europeans, landed not at Ellis Island but on the western tip of the Battery, at Castle Garden, which had opened as a receiving center for immigrants in 1855.

By the 1880s, the facilities at Castle Garden had grown scandalously inadequate. Officials looked for an island on which to build a new immigration center, because they thought that on an island immigrants could be more easily protected from swindlers and quickly transported to railroad terminals in New Jersey. Bedloe's Island was considered, but New Yorkers were aghast at the idea of a "Babel" ruining their beautiful new treasure, "Liberty Enlightening the World." The statue's sculptor, Frédéric-Auguste Bartholdi, reacted to the prospect of immigrants landing near his masterpiece in horror; he called it a "monstrous plan." So much for Emma Lazarus.

Ellis Island was finally chosen because the citizens of New Jersey petitioned the federal government to remove from the island an old naval powder magazine that they thought dangerously close to the Jersey shore. The explosives were removed; no one wanted the island for anything. It was the perfect place to build an immigration center.

I thought about the island's history as I walked into the building and made my way to the room that was the center in my imagination of the Ellis Island experience: the Great Hall. It had been made real for me in the stark, accusing photographs of Louis Hine and others, who took those pictures to make a point. It was in the Great Hall that everyone had waited—waiting, always, the great vocation of the dispossessed. The room was empty, except for me and a handful of other visitors and the park ranger who showed us around. I felt myself grow insignificant in that room, with its huge semicircular windows, its air, even in dereliction, of solid and official probity.

I walked in the deathlike expansiveness of the room's disuse and tried to think of what it might have been like, filled and swarming. More than sixteen million immigrants came through that room; approximately 250,000 were rejected. Not really a large proportion, but the implications for the rejected were dreadful. For some, there was nothing to go back to, or there was certain death; for others, who left as adventurers, to return would be to adopt in local memory the fool's role, and the failure's. No wonder that the island's history includes reports of three thousand suicides.

Sometimes immigrants could pass through Ellis Island in mere hours, though for some the process took days. The particulars of the experience in the Great Hall were often influenced by the political events and attitudes on the mainland. In the 1890s and the first years of the new century, when cheap labor was needed, the newly built receiving center took in its immigrants with comparatively little question. But as the century progressed, the economy worsened, eugenics became both scientifically respectable and popular, and World War I made American xenophobia seem rooted in fact.

Immigration acts were passed; newcomers had to prove, besides moral correctness and financial solvency, their ability to read. Quota laws came into effect, limiting the number of immigrants from southern and eastern Europe to less than 14 percent of the total quota. Intelligence tests were biased against all non-English-speaking persons, and medical examinations became increasingly strict, until the machinery of immigration nearly collapsed under its own weight. The Second Quota Law of 1924 provided that all immigrants be inspected and issued visas at American consular offices in Europe, rendering the center almost obsolete.

On the day of my visit, my mind fastened upon the medical inspections, which had always seemed to me most emblematic of the ignominy and terror the immigrants endured. The medical inspectors, sometimes dressed in uniforms like soldiers, were particularly obsessed with a disease of the eyes called trachoma, which they checked for by flipping back the immigrants' top eyelids with a hook used for buttoning gloves—a method that sometimes resulted in the transmission of the disease to healthy people. Mothers feared that if their children cried too much, their red eyes would be mistaken for a symptom of the disease and the whole family would be sent home. Those immigrants suspected of some physical disability had initials chalked on their coats. I remembered the photographs I'd seen of people standing, dumbstruck and innocent as cattle, with their manifest numbers hung around their necks and initials marked in chalk upon their coats: "E" for eye trouble, "K" for hernia, "L" for lameness, "X" for mental defects, "H" for heart disease.

I thought of my grandparents as I stood in the room: my seventeen-year-old grandmother, coming alone from Ireland in 1896, vouched for by a stranger who had found her a place as a domestic servant to some Irish who had done well. I tried to imagine the assault it all must have been for her; I've been to her hometown, a collection of farms with a main street—smaller than the athletic field of my local public school. She must have watched the New York skyline as the first- and second-class passengers were whisked off the gangplank with the most cursory of inspections while she was made to board a ferry to the new immigration center.

What could she have made of it—this buff-painted wooden structure with its towers and its blue slate roof, a place *Harper's Weekly* described as "a latter-day watering place hotel"? It would have been the first time she had heard people speaking something other than English. She would have mingled with people carrying baskets on their heads and eating foods unlike any she had ever seen—dark-eyed people, like the Sicilian she would marry ten years later, who came over with his family at thirteen, the man of the family, responsible even then for his mother and sister. I don't know what they thought, my grandparents, for they were not expansive people, nor romantic; they didn't like to think of what they called "the hard times," and their trip across the ocean was the single adventurous act of lives devoted after landing to security, respectability, and fitting in.

What is the potency of Ellis Island for someone like me—an American, obviously, but one who has always felt that the country really belonged to the early settlers, that, as J. F. Powers wrote in *Morte D'Urban,* it had been "handed down to them by the Pilgrims, George Washington and others, and that they were taking a risk in letting you live in it." I have never been the victim of overt discrimination; nothing I have wanted has been denied me because of the accidents of blood. But I suppose it is part of being an American to be engaged in a somewhat tiresome but always self-absorbing process of national definition. And in this process, I have found in traveling to Ellis Island an important piece of evidence that could remind me I was right to feel my differentness. Something had happened to my people on that island, a result of the eternal wrongheadedness of American protectionism and the predictabilities of simple greed. I came to the island, too, so I could tell the ghosts that I was one of them, and that I honored them—their stoicism, and their innocence, the fear that turned them inward, and their pride. I wanted to tell them that I liked them better than I did the Americans who made them pass through the Great Hall and stole their names and chalked their weaknesses in public on their clothing. And to tell the ghosts what I have always thought: that American history was a very classy party that was not much fun until they arrived, brought the good food, turned up the music, and taught everyone to dance.

Abortion: How Do
We Think About It?

Abortion is, of all moral issues, peculiarly conducive to displays of bad taste. Anti-abortionists write autobiographies of week-old fetuses for *Readers' Digest* and show slides of queerly inhuman creatures in sacs like spaceships. But their pro-abortion counterparts are little better: they wear T-shirts with coat hangers printed on top of the word NO! and carry photos of botched abortionees, naked in motel rooms. The very language of both sides suggests the unease of the campaigners. Almost no one mentions the word "abortion"; one is pro-life or pro-choice. And this jargon is effective, as all jargon is meant to be, in obscuring the issue, in bringing to one side or another the shy, befuddled partisan, unhappy with words that make the issue clear. Life and choice are, after all, not concepts anyone is likely to be *anti*.

These features, the excessively concrete image, the excessively abstract word, are both the result of abortion's peculiar nature: it is a specifically physical issue that calls into question the most general moral issues. And so both physical and moral terms fall short in speaking to the questions. Is the fetus a human person or a bunch of cells with no particular significance? Is the act of abortion an act of self-determination or a crime? The terms are impossible because we have no way of thinking that describes the issue well.

The physicality of the fetus is perplexing because it is hidden; the unborn are invisible. One philosopher, Roger Wertheimer, wonders what would happen to people's positions on abortion if a mutation or technology made it possible for them to see a developing fetus in the womb, even perhaps to observe and to fondle it. The idea creates the sort of unease we feel when a beggar threatens to unwrap his ulcerated leg, and the discomfort points to the uniqueness of the issue. In what other context must one decide upon the very existence of a victim one cannot see, upon whose nature one can only speculate, whose value may be calculated only as potential.

Invisibility is not the only odd aspect of the abortion issue; there is, in addition, the question of time. In what other moral issue is time so crucial? The period of gestation is short, from beginning to end less than three hundred days. And the period in which a woman can get a safe abortion is even shorter. The decision to abort is made under doomsday pressure; there is a certain point after which it will simply be too late. Moreover, many moralists judge the seriousness of the crime by the advancement of the pregnancy; it is considered by some to be more heinous to have an abortion after the first trimester of pregnancy, most unspeakable of all to have one after the fetus is "viable." The concept of "viability" or "quickening" has always been an important issue in the discussion of abortion. "Quickening" is the point at which the mother feels the fetus moving, and it usually occurs in the fourth or fifth month of pregnancy. For some thinkers, it is only after this point that the fetus is human. For them, abortion is murder after quickening, a therapeutic procedure before.

Time is an issue because we are talking about an organism in a state of rapid development; for some moralists the *nature* of the organism can change entirely at one quickly approached, irreversible point. One cannot think of any other putative crime in which time plays such an odd role: a theft is no more or less a theft in August than in May, nor is a lie, nor is kidnapping. The only possible exception is torture; it is clearly worse to torture someone for five months than for two. But you can see the extremes of thinking to which one is led when looking for analogies, extremes that anyone who speaks about abortion in moral terms has difficulty avoiding.

Yet whatever moralists have said or lawyers have decreed, women have always aborted simply because they have always had unwanted pregnancies. And the reason for that is largely connected to another odd physical fact: sex makes babies. There are few other causal relationships so oblique: an act of physical passion occurs and nearly a year later a child may be born. The connection is, at best, extremely tentative. What genius discovered it first? How did he make anyone believe him? Anthropologists have reported the difficulty of convincing modern primitives of the link between intercourse and birth, but the causal relationship is so peculiar that even sophisticated women with ready access to contraception forget it. Linda Francke, author of *The Ambivalence of Abortion*, a *Newsweek* editor and a graduate of Miss Porter's, had an abortion as a result of a pregnancy she incurred by failing to use any birth control at all. And the testimony of the women who speak in her book indicates that her case is far from rare.

Once again, abortion is unique among moral situations. One stabs a man and he dies; the surprise is not great. One lights the dynamite fuse and the building blows up; the astonishment would occur if the sequence did *not* follow. But in fact most people do not have sex because they want a baby; they have sex for pleasure. "It is the future generation that presses into being by means of these exuberant feelings and supersensible soapbubbles of ours," says the pessimist Schopenhauer, indicating the badness of the arrangement.

The invisibility of the fetus, the odd relationship of time and cause that make the nature of pregnancy and abortion so puzzling, create difficulties when one tries to make comparisons with other moral issues. Part of the difficulty lies in the terms of the discussion. "Life"; "Human"—they are so impossible to define that the only definitions that seem secure are the crudest ones: life begins at conception, a human being is a human being from that moment; therefore, to do away with this human life is a simple murder. But we do not habitually think of life as only biological existence; the problem for supporters of abortion is that the criterion of biological existence is so inexorable that it makes others (quality of life, rights of the individual) seem only vague by comparison. And anti-abortionists stress the vagueness of their opponents' ideas, digging in their entrenching tools of syllogism and empirical data with the energy of the marginally secure.

But it is the comparison of abortion to other acts that is unsatisfactory, and it is because of the physical circumstances that the

comparisons do not work. Most commonly, abortion is compared
to murder; but one has no doubt that the victim of a murder is an
independent person, and it is hard to believe that one created a
murder victim in one's own body when one thought one was doing
something entirely different. And it is probably never true that the
victim of a murder could not survive unless he were fed by the
blood and protected by the body of the murderer, or that it would
be precisely the refusal of this protection that would constitute the
murderous act. To compare abortion to murder is at best naive.
And yet there is no other human act to which it comes closer.

If one wants to think clearly about abortion as a crime, one must
understand that it has been practiced and continues to be practiced
by women who are in no other aspect of their lives criminal. It is
estimated that over 1.2 million abortions are performed annually
in the United States. The number of murders in the United States
in 1976 was only a little over 17,000. Although it is not a good
rule to judge the morality of an act by the number of people who
commit it, the wide disparity between the number of abortions
and the number of murders indicates, among other things, that at
least in the minds of most people the acts are qualitatively different.

Anti-abortionists say that permissive abortion laws will lead to
a devaluation of human life. But as Daniel Callahan points out, in
Abortion: Law, Choice and Morality, this is almost impossible to
demonstrate, since "there is no evidence that societies which have
liberal or permissive abortion laws are societies in which the meaning and value of life in general are demonstrably more threatened
than in societies which do not have such laws." And there is another
complication if one is examining the problem of abortion from the
point of view of society as a whole. It is, after all, quite possible
to argue that abortion is beneficial for society. It is difficult to
imagine that the world would be a better place if the forty million
to fifty million fetuses legally aborted each year grew up to repro-
duce themselves at the frightening rate that adult humans seem
to do.

After the dizzying and finally unsatisfactory experience of trying
to pin down the nature of abortion on moral grounds, it is steadying
to encounter James C. Mohr's *Abortion in America* and Linda Bird
Francke's *The Ambivalence of Abortion.* Mohr's approach is historical,
Francke's anecdotal, and both approaches seem more instructive

than trying to determine how far along a pregnant woman has to be before she must be forbidden to dance on the head of a pin.

Mohr's book begins with the surprising revelation that

In 1880 no jurisdiction in the United States had enacted any statutes whatsoever on the subject of abortion; most forms of abortion were not illegal and those American women who wished to practice abortion did so. Yet by 1900 virtually every jurisdiction in the United States had laws upon its books that proscribed the practice sharply and declared most abortions to be criminal offenses.

Mohr's explanation for the ability of women to practice abortion without sanction in the early part of the century is that most people accepted the idea that a fetus was not a human being until it quickened, and therefore it was not wrong to abort until the fourth or fifth month. In fact, the prevalence of abortifacients indicates that attempts at early abortion were quite common.

At the beginning of the nineteenth century, it was difficult for anyone to determine whether a woman was pregnant or simply suffering menstrual irregularity until the woman herself had felt the child stir within her. Women often took advantage of this ambiguity to induce abortion early in their pregnancies. But increasing medical sophistication made it possible for doctors to determine pregnancy earlier and more surely. It was this same increase in medical sophistication that led to a quickly growing sense of professionalism among doctors and a strong desire that their professionalism be acknowledged by the public.

This desire for public acknowledgment of physicians' professional status is, Mohr feels, the most important reason for the growth of anti-abortion legislation since the 1840s. It was doctors who were behind such legislation from the beginning. Among their major enemies, in the competition both for professional status and for patients, were abortionists, who advertised competitively in newspapers with a brazen lack of professional decorum. Mohr contends that abortionists' greed and competitive free-market tactics contributed to their downfall. By making themselves so conspicuous in the popular press, abortionists made themselves an easy target. But they also got themselves a good deal of business, and in part their success stimulated doctors' interest in stopping their activity.

Among the most fascinating sections of Mohr's book are the abortionists' advertisements that he reproduces. Perhaps the most successful abortionist of the period was one "Madame Restell," an English immigrant whose real name was Ann Lohman. Madame Restell's empire spent sixty thousand dollars a year on advertising both abortifacients and actual operations; Mohr links the success of her million-dollar-a-year business to her ability to adapt modern business techniques—mail order and advertising in particular. Her advertisement in the *Boston Daily Times* of January 1, 1845, is a model of proto–Madison Avenue tact:

> Madame Restell's experience and knowledge in the treatment of cases of female irregularity is such as to require but a few days to effect a perfect cure. Ladies desiring proper medical attendance will be accommodated during such time with private and respectable board.

One of Restell's competitors, Madame Drunette, advertised "French Lunar Pills." Also on the market during the week of January 4, 1845, were "Dr. Peter's French Renovating Pills"—"a blessing to mothers . . . and although very mild and prompt in their operations, pregnant females should not use them, as they inevitably produce a miscarriage." Dr. Melveau's "Portuguese Female Pills" were likewise "certain to produce miscarriage."

How innocent it seems at a hundred years' remove: the diction— who could prosecute anyone who would use the term "fluoral bas" to describe menstrual problems?—the archaic print Mohr reproduces, the almost touching invocation of foreign authority and glamour. By comparison, the twentieth-century abortionists who advertise in the yellow pages seem much more disreputable and certainly lacking in art. Yet, of course, illegal abortion has always been an unattractive business. Madame Restell committed suicide in 1878 after she was arrested, following the discovery of a naked woman, dead as a result of a bad abortion, in a trunk in a railway station. The suicide sparked a fervid anti-abortion campaign.

The anti-abortion fever, which was largely initiated by doctors, was encouraged by the growth of Nativism. By the end of the Civil

War, the medical community believed that the majority of women having abortions in the United States were married, upper-middle-class Protestants. Thus, opponents of abortion tried to convince the legislators that allowing abortion to flourish would encourage the obliteration of the white, native-born American strain by the ever-growing foreign one. It was an effective technique; by the 1840s, the steadily climbing native population rate of the early 1800s had reversed itself, and the downward spiral of native births was beginning to cause alarm. At the same time, the presence of immigrants in large numbers was first being felt, particularly in the great cities.

As well as playing on the legislators' and the public's Nativist tendencies, opponents of abortion tried to link the rise in abortion (estimated at 500 percent between 1800 and 1870) to the rise of feminism. Dr. Montrose Pallen noted in 1868 that feminism was creating "insidious new ideas of women's duties," such as the notion "that her ministrations in the formation of character as a mother should be abandoned for the sterner rights of voting and law making . . . until public conscience becomes blunted, and duties . . . are shirked, neglected, or criminally prevented."

The feminist response was, surprisingly enough, to join with antifeminist physicians in condemning abortion. "For most feminists," says Mohr, "the answer to unwanted pregnancies was abstinence." *The Woman's Advocate,* a feminist newspaper published in Dayton, Ohio, attributed the tragic (but understandable) necessity of abortion to husbands' failure to "check their sensualism." This response lends some weight to the twentieth-century feminist idea that those who oppose abortion are really opposed to female sexuality.

The liaison that one would have predicted, between physicians and clergymen, was nonexistent throughout most of the nineteenth-century abortion controversy. Until 1865 there was complete silence in the religious press, both Protestant and Catholic, on the issue of abortion. Mohr gives three reasons for this: clerical disbelief that religious women were practicing abortion; a sense that any sexual matter was inappropriate to a religious publication; and a genuine belief that abortion before quickening was an innocent act. Once again, anti-abortion legislature advocates used prejudice as an effective tactic; they taunted the tardy Protestant clergy with the Vatican's early position against abortion at any point during pregnancy and suggested that Catholics had power to demand and to exact obedience that Protestants did not. Again, the anti-abortionists were effective; by the middle 1870s, the clerical establishment was solidly behind its medical brethren.

By 1900, abortions were illegal everywhere in America. Mohr's book unfolds the story of the ability of relatively small groups to change radically the legislative, and consequently the social and demographic, complexion of America. He shows us a curious parade of fashionable ladies, disreputable practitioners with fake foreign names, doctors uneasy about their status, feminists uneasy about their sex. This study helps us to understand that abortion in America has had a history of uncertainty and manipulation; it is helpful to know that what is presented as an eternal verity—the criminality of abortion—has been with us for less than a hundred years. Mohr presents his facts clearly and lucidly. (Could he be persuaded not to refer to some of the more poisonous abortifacients consumed by women in their desperation as cocktails?) *Abortion in America* allows us to examine a perplexing question from an angle new to the issue, the historical, with its oddly calming light.

Linda Bird Francke's *The Ambivalence of Abortion* falls into a category of book that is distinctly contemporary: the collection of interviews that assumes that there is something special to be learned in hearing people talk about their particular experience. The appeal of such books is, of course, that of gossip, or eavesdropping. As with both those modes of education, what is learned from anonymous interviews can also be extremely instructive. And, in the case of abortion, the technique is appropriate and helpful. For people learn, particularly in those realms in which we are most fallible, least rational, largely through imitation and identification. Reading this book, in one sense, is like being on a train where the strangers sitting next to you tell you everything. Only, in this case the topic is carefully limited: everyone is talking about abortion.

Francke's intention in writing this book is to help people understand how complicated having an abortion is. She hopes that her book will serve as a corrective to those who insist that abortion is a snap as well as to those who suggest that only a doomed life will follow. She decided to write the book after her anonymous contribution to the op-ed page of *The New York Times,* which described the difficulty of her own abortion, elicited an almost unprecedented number of letters.

Francke has interviewed hundreds of American women in abortion clinics, in airports, at the dinner table. She has, in addition—and this is one of the most valuable aspects of the book—interviewed men who wait in abortion clinics with nothing to do but drink countless cups of coffee and smoke countless cigarettes. Everywhere she went, Francke talked to people about abortion until "it seemed as though every woman I met had had at least one."

Paradoxically, the availability of legal abortion places a new kind of strain on women. Francke, for example, chose not to go on with her pregnancy because she had three children already and was just beginning to be able to work at the job that interested her. At the same time, her husband was newly able to contemplate changing the job that frustrated him; they would be able, perhaps, to go on vacation, finally. Are these sufficient reasons to terminate a pregnancy? How can one answer that question? Having gone through with the abortion, Francke found herself haunted by a "little ghost."

What comes through in these almost addictive interviews is the very peculiar responses women have, not only to abortion, but to pregnancy as well. One woman got pregnant because she thought diaphragms were bad karma, and another was happy to find out she was pregnant because "a lot of times on TV if you ever notice nobody can have children easily." One young woman told Francke that if her parents were dead she'd have the baby. One woman was made pregnant in the 1930s by a Hungarian diplomat and found out on vacation with her father in England that her nightmare abortion had not been successful. After having an abortion, some women get dressed and go to Burger King and some want to die. Many women think they will be punished by never being able to have children, and others plan to have a child the next year. Some women are proud of their courage in taking their lives into their own hands; some mothers cannot admit that their daughters, yards away from them in a treatment room, have had sex. Francke has a good eye for detail, as when she notes that the teenager who pops gum and does not cry is wearing a T-shirt with poodles embroidered on the front.

Francke tells us, finally, that there is every conceivable response to abortion, but that nearly all of them are neither clear nor simple, that the women she talked to who had abortions, even multiple abortions, are neither monsters nor fools, and that one out of three abortions in the United States is obtained by a teenager. We also learn that one out of four pregnancies in the United States is now terminated.

It is to Francke's special credit that she does not pretend that abortion is an easy issue. She hopes for greater advances in birth control but knows that even perfect technology will not do away with human uncertainty and the ambivalence surrounding the creation of new life. She suggests that more extensive "counseling" would be beneficial but is realistic about its limits. This is a book that was written to be helpful, but unlike most helpful books, it does not suggest salvation. It does offer, to both men and women, some sense of the universality of a predicament that many of us find distressing if not impossible to comprehend.

Abortion:
How Do We Really
Choose?

I am having lunch with six women. What is unusual is that four of them are in their seventies, two of them widowed, the other two living with husbands beside whom they've lived for decades. All of them have had children, and if I have one quarrel with the way they've lived their lives (and it's a minor one, for they are heroes to me, models of how to live fully and generously), it's that they devoted too much of their intellectual and organizational energy to their families. Had they been men, they would have published books and hung their paintings on the walls of important galleries. But they are women of a certain generation, and their lives were shaped around their families and personal relations. They are women you go to for help and support. We begin talking about the latest legislative act that makes abortion more difficult for poor women to obtain. An extraordinary thing happens. Each of them talks about the illegal abortions she had during her young womanhood. Not one of them was spared the experience. Any of them could have died on the table of whatever person (in none of their cases, a doctor) they were forced to approach, in secrecy and in terror, to deal with a pregnancy that they felt would blight their lives.

I mention this incident for two reasons. First as a reminder that all kinds of women have always had abortions. Second because it is essential that we remember that an abortion occurs to a living woman who has a life of which a terminated pregnancy is only a small part. Morally speaking, the decision to have an abortion doesn't take place in a vacuum. It is connected to other choices that a woman makes in the course of an adult life.

Anti-choice propagandists paint pictures of women who choose to have abortions as types of moral callousness, selfishness, or irresponsibility. The woman choosing to abort is the dressed-for-success yuppie who gets rid of her baby so she won't miss her Caribbean vacation or her chance for promotion. Or she is the feckless, promiscuous ghetto teenager who couldn't bring herself to just say no to sex. A third, purportedly kinder, gentler scenario has recently begun to surface. The woman in the abortion clinic is there because she is misinformed about the nature of the world. She is having an abortion because society does not provide for mothers and their children, and she mistakenly thinks that another mouth to feed will be the ruin of her family, not understanding that the temporary truth of family unhappiness doesn't stack up beside the eternal verity that abortion is murder. Or she is the dupe of her husband or boyfriend, who talks her into having an abortion because a child will be a drag on his life-style. None of these pictures created by the anti-choice movement assumes that the decision to have an abortion is made responsibly in the context of a morally lived life by a free and responsible moral agent.

How would a woman who habitually makes choices in moral terms come to the decision to have an abortion? The moral discussion of abortion centers around the issue of whether or not abortion is an act of murder. At first glance, it would seem that the answer should follow directly upon two questions: Is the fetus human? and Is it alive? It would be absurd to deny that a fetus is alive or that it is human. What would our other options be: to say that it is inanimate or belonging to another species? But we habitually use the terms "life" and "human" to refer to parts of our body—"human hair," for example, "live red-blood cells"—and we are clear in our understanding that the nature of these objects does not rank equally with an entire personal existence. It then seems important to consider whether the fetus, this alive human thing, is a *person*, to whom the term "murder" could be sensibly applied. How would anyone come to a decision about something so impalpable as personhood? Philosophers have struggled with the issue of personhood, but in language that is so abstract that it is not helpful to ordinary people making decisions in the course of a lived life. It might be more productive to begin thinking about the status of the fetus by examining the language and customs that surround it. This approach will encourage us to focus on the choosing, *acting woman* rather than the *act* of abortion—as if the act were performed by abstract forces without bodies, histories, attachments.

This focus on the acting woman is useful because a pregnant woman has an identifiable, consistent ontology, and a fetus takes on different ontological identities over time. But common sense, experience, and linguistic usage point clearly to our habit of considering, for example, that a seven-week-old fetus is different from a seven-month-old one. We can tell this by the way we respond to the involuntary loss of one as against the other. We have different language for the experience of the involuntary expulsion of the fetus from the womb depending upon the point of gestation at which the experience occurs. If it occurs early in the pregnancy we call it a "miscarriage"; if late, we call it a "stillbirth." We would have a very extreme reaction to the reversal of these terms.

If a woman referred to a seven-week-old miscarriage as a stillbirth we would be alarmed. It would shock our sense of propriety; it would make us uneasy; we would find it disturbing, misplaced—as we do when a bag lady sits down at a restaurant and starts shouting or an octogenarian arrives at our door in a sailor suit. In short, we would suspect that the speaker was mad. Similarly, if a doctor or nurse referred to the loss of a seven-month-old fetus as a "miscarriage," we would be shocked by that person's insensitivity: could she or he not understand that a fetus that age was not what it had been months before?

Our ritual and religious practices underscore the fact that we make distinctions among fetuses. If a woman took the bloody matter—indistinguishable from a heavy period—of an early miscarriage and insisted upon putting it in a tiny coffin and marking its grave, we would have serious concerns about her mental health. By the same token, we would feel squeamish about flushing a seven-month-fetus down the toilet, something we would quite normally do with an early miscarriage. There are no prayers for the matter of a miscarriage, nor do we feel there should be. Even a

Catholic priest would not baptize the issue of an early miscarriage. When someone sent me a bereavement card after my miscarriage, I was embarrassed for and angry at the person; she had wrongly described my experience, and in doing so had failed to do it, and me, justice.

The difficulties stem, of course, from the odd situation of a fetus's ontology: a complex differentiated and nuanced response is required when we are dealing with an entity that changes over time. Yet we are in the habit of making distinctions like this. At one point, we know, a child is no longer a child but an adult—that this question is vexed and problematic is clear in our difficulty in determining who is a "juvenile" offender and who is an adult criminal and at what age sexual intercourse ceases to be known as statutory rape. We wouldn't want to have every child given adult punishment, nor would we want every ten-year-old girl who has reached puberty declared an adult, capable of informed consent. As a responsible society we understand the necessity to act differently with humans at different stages of development. So at what point, if any, do we on the pro-choice side say the developing fetus is a person with rights equal to its mother's?

The anti-choice people have one advantage over us, because their monolithic position gives them unity on this question and we on the pro-choice side tolerate differences of opinion. I am made personally uneasy by third-trimester abortions, abortions that take place when the fetus could live outside the mother's body, but I also know that these abortions are extremely rare and often occur to very young girls who have had difficulty comprehending the realities of pregnancy. It seems to me that late abortions should be decided on a case-by-case basis, and that fixation on this issue is a deflection from what is most important: keeping early abortions, which are by far the majority, safe and legal. I am also politically realistic enough to understand that bills restricting late abortions are not good-faith attempts to make distinctions about the nature of fetal life. They are, rather, the cynical embodiments of the hope of anti-choice partisans that technology will be on their side and medical science's ability to create situations in which younger fetuses are viable outside the mother's body will increase dramatically in the next few years. Ironically, medical science will probably make the issue of abortion a minor one in the near future.

The RU-486 pill, which can induce abortion early on, exists, and whether or not it is legally available, women will begin to obtain it. If abortion can occur through chemical rather than physical means, in the privacy of one's own home, most people not directly involved will lose interest in it. Once again, it is the perception of the experience that is at work: the image of a woman alone, bleeding into her toilet, does not seem criminal to people in the same way as does a woman lying in a hospital gown, being attended to by a physician in white. Yet the experience for the fetus is the same, and the moral issue is identical. But as the pill becomes more widespread, abortion will cease to be public and will lose its political charge. Terry Randall and his followers will not be able to chain themselves to every bathroom door in America, nor will they be able to harass every woman leaving a drugstore. As abortion switches from a public to a private issue, it will cease to be perceived as political; it will be called personal instead.

But because abortion will always deal with what it is to create and sustain life, it will always be a moral issue. And whether we like it or not, much of our moral thinking about abortion is rooted in the shifting soil of perception. In an age in which much of our perception is controlled by media that specialize in the sound bite and the photo op, the anti-choice partisans have a twofold advantage over us on the pro-choice side. The pro-choice moral position is more complex, and the experience we defend is physically repellent to contemplate. None of us in the pro-choice movement would suggest that abortion is not a regrettable occurrence. Anti-choice proponents can offer pastel photographs of babies in buntings, their eyes peaceful in the camera's gaze. In answer, we can't offer the material of an early abortion, bloody, amorphous in a paper cup, to prove that what has just been removed from the woman's body is not a child, not in the same category of being as the adorable bundle in the adoptive mother's arms. It is not a pleasure to *look* at the physical evidence of abortion, and most of us don't get the opportunity to do so.

The theologian Daniel Maguire, uneasy with the fact that most theological arguments about the nature of abortion are made by men who have never been anywhere near an abortion clinic, decided to visit one and observe abortions being performed. He didn't find the experience easy, but he knew that before he could in good conscience make a moral judgment on abortion, he needed to experience through his senses what an aborted fetus is like: he needed to look at and to touch the controversial entity. He held in his hand the bloody fetal stuff; the eight-week-old fetus was the size of his thumb, and it certainly bore no resemblance to either of the two children he had held moments after their birth. He knew at that point what women who have experienced early abortions and miscarriages know: that some event occurred, possibly even a dramatic one, but it was not the death of a child. (Obviously, we are in difficult territory when we are trying to talk about the physical nature of something to which most of us are denied physical or tactile access. People who present images like those in the film *The Silent Scream* exploit these difficulties, by manipulating the image through technology: speeding up and slowing down the film, adding music. The whole issue of the imaging of a fetus via sonogram is too difficult to discuss here: our relation to an image projected on a screen, our feeling that what happens on television is more real than real life, make the experience semiotically extremely complex. A physician who works with cardiac patients has reported to me that, according to these patients, seeing their hearts projected on a screen during catheterization was more disturbing to them than the actual surgery. On a personal note, when I saw the seven-week-old embryo that was to be my son, I was disturbed at how inhuman it looked; I couldn't believe that this thing would become my child.)

Because issues of pregnancy and birth are both physical and metaphorical, we must constantly be stepping back and forth between ways of perceiving the world. And because, when we speak of gestation, we are talking, often, in terms of potential, we are speaking about events and objects to which we attach our hopes, fears, dreams, and ideals. A mother can speak to the fetus in her uterus and name it; she and her mate may decorate a nursery according to their vision of the good life; they may choose a college for an embryo, a profession, a dwelling. But it is important for those of us who are trying to think morally about pregnancy and birth to remember that these feelings are our own projections onto what is, in reality, an inappropriate object. However charmed we may be by an expectant father buying a little football for something inside his wife's belly, we shouldn't make public policy based on it, nor should we force others to live their lives in conformance with our fantasies.

As a society, we are making decisions that pit the complicated future of a complex adult against the fate of a mass of cells lacking cortical development. The moral pressure should be on distinguishing the true from the false, the real suffering inflicted on living persons as opposed to our individual and often idiosyncratic dreams and fears. We must make decisions on abortion understanding how people really do live. We must be able to say, with confidence, that poverty is worse than not being poor, that having dignified and meaningful work is better than working in conditions of degradation, that raising a child one loves and has desired is better than raising a child in resentment and rage, that it is better for a twelve-year-old not to endure the trauma of having a child when she is herself a child.

When we put these ideas against the ideas of "child" or "baby," we seem to be making a horrifying choice of "life-style" over "life." But in fact, we are telling the truth of what it means to bear a child, and what the experience of abortion really is. This is extremely difficult in the case of abortion, where the object of the discussion is hidden, changing, potential. We make our decisions on the basis of approximate and inadequate language, often on the basis of fantasies and fears. It will always be crucial to try to separate genuine moral concern from phobia, punitiveness, superstition, anxiety, a desperate search for certainty in an uncertain world.

One of the certainties that is removed if we accept the consequences of the pro-choice position is the belief that the birth of a child is an unequivocal good. In real life, we act knowing that the birth of a child is not always a good thing: people are depressed, angry, rejecting, sometimes, at the birth of a child. But this is a difficult truth to tell; we don't like to say it, and one of the fears preyed on by anti-choice proponents is that if we cannot look at the birth of a child as an unequivocal good, then there is nothing to look toward. The desire for security of the imagination, for typological fixity, particularly in the area of "the good," is an understandable desire. It must seem to some anti-choice people that not only are we on the pro-choice side murdering innocent children; we are also murdering hope. Those of us who have experienced the birth of a desired child and felt the joy of that moment can be tempted into believing that it was the physical experience of the birth itself that was the joy. But it is crucial to remember that the birth of a child itself is a neutral occurrence emotionally: the charge it takes on is invested in it by the people experiencing or observing it.

These uncertainties can lead to another set of fears, not only about abortion itself but about the implications of abortion. Many anti-choice people fear that to support abortion is to cast one's lot with the cold and technological rather than with the warm and natural, to head down the slippery slope toward a Brave New World where handicapped children are left on mountains to starve and the old are put out in the snow. But if we look at the history of abortion, we don't see the embodiment of what the anti-choice proponents fear. On the contrary, there seems to be a real link between repressive anti-abortion stances and repressive and in-humane governments. Abortion is illegal in South Africa and Chile, countries where torture is regularly practiced. It is paid for by the governments of Denmark, England, and the Netherlands, which have national health and welfare systems that encourage the health and well-being of mothers, children, the old, and the handicapped. Abortion was made illegal in Fascist Italy in 1927; Hitler was fanatically anti-abortion, as his words indicate with unmistakable clarity: "Women inflamed by Marxist propaganda claim the rights to bear children only when they desire, first furs, radio, new fur-niture, then perhaps a child. . . . Nazi ideals demand that the practice of abortion shall be exterminated with a strong hand."

It is interesting to note the common thread that runs through the statements of the Nazis and the anti-choice spokespeople: women who want to choose when to have their children are self-indulgent materialists. In fact, this accusation of self-indulgence masks a discomfort with female sexuality, sexual pleasure, and sexual autonomy. It is only possible for a woman to have a sexual life unriddled by fear if she can be confident that she need not pay by a failure of technology or judgment (and who among us has never once been swept away in the heat of the sexual moment), taking upon herself the crushing burden of unchosen motherhood.

It is no accident, therefore, that measures to restrict maternal conduct during pregnancy—and new focus on the physical auton-omy of the pregnant woman—come into public discourse at pre-cisely the time when women are achieving unprecedented levels of economic and political autonomy. What has surprised me is that some of this new anti-autonomy talk comes to us from the left. An example of this new discourse was Christopher Hitchens's article in the April 29, 1989, *Nation,* in which he asserts his discomfort with abortion. Hitchens's tone is impeccably British: arch, light, man-of-the-left. "Anyone who has ever seen a sonogram or has spent even an hour with a textbook on embryology knows that the emotions are not the deciding factor. In order to terminate a pregnancy, you still have to still a heartbeat, switch off a developing brain, and whatever the method, break some bones and rupture some organs. As to whether this involves pain on the 'Silent Scream' scale, I have no idea. The 'right to life' leadership, again, has cheapened everything it touches." But what he's saying isn't at all unlike what Hitler said in 1938. "It is a pity," Hitchens asserts, "that . . . the majority of feminists and their allies have stuck to the dead ground of 'Me Decade' possessive individualism, an idealogy that has more in common than it admits with the prehistoric right, which it claims to oppose but has, in fact, encouraged."

Hitchens proposes, as an alternative, a program of social reform that will make contraception free and support a National Adoption Service. For him, it would seem, women have abortions for only two reasons: because they are selfish or because they are poor. If the state will take care of the economic problems and the bureaucratic messiness around adoption, it remains only for the possessive individualists to get their act together and walk with their babies into the communal utopia of the future. Hitchens would allow victims of rape or incest to have free abortions on the grounds that since a woman didn't choose to have sex, she should not be forced to have the baby. This would seem to be putting the issue of volition in a wrong and telling place. For Hitchens, it would appear, if a woman chooses to have sex, she can't choose whether or not to have a baby. The implications of this are clear. If a woman is consciously and volitionally sexual, she should be prepared to take her medicine. And what medicine must the consciously sexual male take? Does Mr. Hitchens really believe, or want us to believe, that every male who has unintentionally impregnated a woman will be involved in the lifelong responsibility for the upbringing of the engendered child? Can he honestly say that he has observed this behavior—or indeed would want to see it observed—in the world in which he lives?

It is essential for a moral decision about abortion to be made in an atmosphere of open criticalness. We on the pro-choice side must accept that there are indeed anti-choice activists who take their position in good faith. I believe they are people, however, for whom childbirth is an emotionally overladen topic, people who are susceptible to unclear thinking because of their unrealistic hopes and fears. It is important for us in the pro-choice movement to be open in discussing those areas involving abortion that are nebulous and unclear. But we must not forget that there are some things that we know to be undeniably true. There are some undeniable bad consequences to a woman's being forced to bear a child against her will. First is the trauma of going through a pregnancy and giving birth to a child who is not desired, a trauma more long-lasting than that experienced by some (and only some) women who experience an early abortion. The grief of giving up a child at its birth—and at nine months it is a child whom one has felt move inside one's body—is underestimated by both anti-choice proponents and by those for whom access to adoptable children is important. This grief should not be *forced* on any woman, or indeed encouraged by public policy.

We must be realistic about the impact on society of millions of unwanted children in an overpopulated world. Most of the time, human beings do not have sex because they want to make babies. Yet sex has, throughout history, resulted in unwanted pregnancies. And women have always aborted. One thing that is neither hidden, mysterious, nor debatable is that the illegality of abortions will result in the deaths of women, as it has always done. Is our historical memory so short that none of us remember aunts, sisters, friends, or mothers who were killed or rendered sterile by septic abortions? Does no one in the anti-choice movement remember stories or actual experiences of midnight drives to filthy rooms where the aborted woman is sent out, bleeding, to her fate? Can anyone genuinely say that it would be a moral good for us, as a society, to return to these conditions?

Thinking about abortion, then, forces us to take moral positions as adults who understand the complexities of the world and the realities of human suffering, to make decisions based on how people actually live and choose, and not on our fears, prejudices, and anxieties about sex and society, life and death.

-The Parable of the Cave; or, In Praise of Watercolors

===================

Once, I was told a story by a famous writer. "I will tell you what women writers are like," he said. The year was 1971. The women's movement had made men nervous; it had made a lot of women write. "Women writers are like a female bear who goes into a cave to hibernate. The male bear shoves a pine cone up her ass, because he knows if she shits all winter, she'll stink up the cave. In the spring, the pressure of all that built-up shit makes her expel the pine cone, and she shits a winter's worth all over the walls of the cave."

That's what women writers are like, said the famous writer.

He told the story with such geniality; he looked as if he were giving me a wonderful gift. I felt I ought to smile; everyone knows there's no bore like a feminist with no sense of humor. I did not write for two months after that. It was the only time in my life I have suffered from writer's block. I should not have smiled. But he was a famous writer and spoke with geniality. And in truth, I did not have the courage for clear rage. There is no seduction like that of being thought a good girl.

Theodore Roethke said that women poets were "stamping a tiny foot against God." I have been told by male but not by female critics that my work was "exquisite," "lovely," "like a watercolor." They, of course, were painting in oils. They were doing the important work. Watercolors are cheap and plentiful; oils are costly: their base—oil—must be bought. And the idea is that oil paintings will endure. But what will they endure against? Fire? Flood? Bombs? Earthquake? Their endurance is another illusion: one more foolish bet against nature, or against natural vulnerabilities; one more scheme, like fallout shelters; one more gesture of illusory safety.

There are people in the world who derive no small pleasure from the game of "major" and "minor." They think that no major work can be painted in watercolors. They think, too, that Hemingway writing about boys in the woods is major; Mansfield writing about girls in the house is minor. Exquisite, they will hasten to insist, but minor. These people join up with other bad specters, and I have to work to banish them. Let us pretend these specters are two men, two famous poets, saying, "Your experience is an embarrassment; your experience is insignificant."

I wanted to be a good girl, so I tried to find out whose experience was not embarrassing. The prototype for a writer who was not embarrassing was Henry James. And you see, the two specters said, proffering hope, he wrote about social relationships, but his distance gave them grandeur.

Distance, then, was what I was to strive for. Distance from the body, from the heart, but most of all, distance from the self as writer. I could never understand exactly what they meant or how to do it; it was like trying to follow the directions on a home permanent in 1959.

If Henry James had the refined experience, Conrad had the significant one. The important moral issues were his: men pitted against nature in moments of extremity. There are no important women in Conrad's novels, except for *Victory,* which, the critics tell us, is a romance and an exception. Despite the example of Conrad, it was all right for the young men I knew, according to my specters, to write about the hymens they had broken, the diner waitresses they had seduced. Those experiences were significant. But we were not to write about our broken hearts, about the married men we loved disastrously, about our mothers or our children. Men could write about their fears of dying by exposure in the forest; we could not write about our fears of being suffocated in the kitchen. Our desire to write about these experiences only revealed our shallowness; it was suggested we would, in time, get over it. And write about what? Perhaps we would stop writing.

And so, the specters whispered to me, if you want to write well, if you want us to take you seriously, you must be distant, you must be extreme.

I suppose the specters were not entirely wrong. Some of the literature that has been written since the inception of the women's movement is lacking in style and moral proportion. But so is the work of Mailer, Miller, Burroughs, Ginsberg. Their lack of style and proportion may be called offensive, but not embarrassing. They may be referred to as off the mark, but they will not be called trivial.

And above all I did not wish to be *trivial;* I did not wish to be embarrassing. But I did not want to write like Conrad, and I did not want to write like Henry James. The writers I wanted to imitate were all women: Charlotte Brontë, Woolf, Mansfield, Bowen, Lessing, Olsen. I discovered that what I loved in writing was not distance but radical closeness; not the violence of the bizarre but the complexity of the quotidian.

I lost my fear of being trivial, but not my fear of being an embarrassment. And so I wrote my first novel in the third person. No one would publish it. Then a famous woman writer asked why I had written a first-person novel in the third person. She is a woman of abiding common sense, and so I blushed to tell her: "I wanted to sound serious. I didn't want to be embarrassing."

Only her wisdom made me write the novel I meant to. I can say it now: I will probably never read Conrad again; what he writes about simply does not interest me. Henry James I will love always, but it is not for his distance that I love him. The notion that style and detachment are necessary blood brothers is crude and bigoted. It is an intellectual embarrassment.

And I can say it now: I would rather own a Mary Cassatt watercolor than a Velázquez oil.

Here is the good side of being a woman writer: the company of other women writers, dead and living. My writer friends, all women, help me banish the dark specters. So does Katherine Mansfield; so does Christina Rossetti. I feel their closeness to the heart of things; I feel their aptness and their bravery.

I think it is lonelier to be a man writer than a woman writer now, because I do not think that men are as good at being friends to one another as women are. Perhaps, since they have not thought they needed each other's protection, as women have known we have needed each other's, they have not learned the knack of helpful, rich concern that centers on a friend's work. They may be worried, since they see themselves as hewers of wood and slayers of animals, about production, about the kind of achievement that sees its success only in terms of another's failure. They may not be as kind to one another; they may not know how. These are the specters that men now must banish. Our specters may be easier to chase. For the moment. They were not always so.

To this tale there should be an appendix, an explanation. Why was I so susceptible to the bad advice of men? What made me so ready to listen? Where did I acquire my genius for obedience?

I had a charming father. In many crucial ways, he was innocent of sexism, although he may have substituted narcissism in its place. He wanted me to be like him. He was a writer, an unsuccessful writer, and my mother worked as a secretary to support us. Nevertheless, he was a writer; he could think of himself as nothing else. He wanted me to be a writer too. I may have been born to be one, which made things easier. He died when I was seven. But even in those years we had together I learned well that I was his child, not my mother's. His mind was exalted, my mother's common. That she could earn the money to support us was only proof of the ordinariness of her nature, an ordinariness to which I was in no way heir. So I was taught to read at three, taught French at six, and taught to despise the world of women, the domestic. I was a docile child. I brought my father great joy, and I learned the pleasures of being a good girl.

And I earned, as a good girl, no mean rewards. Our egos are born delicate. Bestowing pleasure upon a beloved father is much easier than discovering the joys of solitary achievements. It was easy for me to please my father; and this ease bred in me a desire to please men—a desire for the rewards of a good girl. They are by no means inconsiderable: safety and approval, the warm, incomparable atmosphere created when one pleases a man who has vowed, in his turn, to keep the wolf from the door.

But who is the wolf?

He is strangers. He is the risk of one's own judgments, one's own work.

I have learned in time that I am at least as much my mother's daughter as my father's. Had I been only my mother's daughter, it is very possible that I would never have written: I may not have had the confidence required to embark upon a career so valueless in the eyes of the commonsense world. I did what my father wanted; I became a writer. I grew used to giving him the credit. But now I see that I am the *kind* of writer I am because I am my mother's daughter. My father's tastes ran to the metaphysical. My mother taught me to listen to conversations at the dinner table; she taught me to remember jokes.

My subject as a writer has far more to do with family happiness than with the music of the spheres. I don't know what the nature of the universe is, but I have a good ear. What it hears best are daily rhythms, for that is what I value, what I would wish, as a writer, to preserve.

My father would have thought this a stubborn predilection for the minor. My mother knows better.

Offenses of the Pope

The Holocaust almost by necessity calls up distortions of memory and interpretation; yet it is only through a radical refusal of such distortions that the rupture it made in the fabric of history can begin to be healed. There is no incorporation of the Holocaust into the rest of life: there never should be. The best one can hope to do is to remove oneself from participation in untruth.

This would seem to be a minimal and obvious moral statement, and one to which the Pope as spiritual and moral leader should be vigilantly and passionately committed. But the behavior of John Paul II has shown that he is involved in the heinous process of distortion that has been so much a part of the world's response to the Holocaust. In the cases of both his beatification of the Jewish convert Edith Stein and his receiving Kurt Waldheim in the Vatican, John Paul II seems to be embarked on an odd course of rewriting history, one that his particular experience in wartime Poland may have shaped. He seems, as well, to want to desingularize the Holocaust experience of the Jews, asserting that other people, particularly Catholics, suffered at the hands of the Nazis and emphasizing the heroism of those Catholics, particularly clergy and prelates, who spoke out against the treatment of the Jews.

Put in a correct historical and moral context, these aims would not be unworthy. But such a placement would require first of all that the Pope acknowledge the difference between the situations of Catholics and Jews at that time. Jews were subject to a deliberate and systematic annihilation. This in no way applied to Catholics, who generally suffered because of misidentification, citizenship, or political activity—not religion. Second, the Church would have to acknowledge its guilt in having failed to speak out against the Holocaust. And it would have to admit that those few Catholics who did speak out were a distinct minority, that their voices were drowned out by the complicitous silence or the explicit anti-Semitism of the majority of the members of the Church. The Pope has taken none of these courses. Rather he receives a man many consider a war criminal, Kurt Waldheim, into his chambers and addresses him as a man of peace.

Let us examine the cases of Edith Stein and Kurt Waldheim separately. I find the situation of Edith Stein problematical. On one level, she should be the saint of any intellectual woman's dreams. A prize student of phenomenologist Edmund Husserl, with an acknowledged first-rate mind, a forceful and dynamic writer, she is the first modern intellectual to be beatified. But I should admit, before going any further, my bias. I am the daughter of a man who converted to Catholicism for many of the same reasons as Edith Stein. I am, therefore, drawn both to examine closely and to be suspicious of the motives of any Jew who converts. The germ of Jewish self-hatred, implanted by a hostile world, is so endemic to the psychic experience of every Jew that I suspect that no decision to convert can be made free of it. To convert from a minority and despised religion to a majority and revered one is an easier process, to say the least, than the opposite course. Withdrawal from the world has never been encouraged in Jewish thought or practice, and one can understand that for a temperament like Stein's, attracted to such withdrawal, recourse to the contemplative life of Carmel would have obvious appeal. I am not here attempting to go into the relative merits of the *vita activa* versus the *vita contemplativa*. Except in one special sense. It seems to me that there are moments of history that create such extraordinary pressures for public action that the recourse into privatism becomes a very different act from what it would be ordinarily. But there is something much more serious. Stein suggests in her letters that the Holocaust was God's punishment for the Jews' role in the death of Christ. Even a hint of this should be grounds for exclusion from beatification.

The Pope has called Edith Stein a martyr for the faith. But Edith Stein was not killed because she was a Catholic; she was killed because she was a Jew. The gestapo did not systematically search out and kill Aryan members of Carmel. To suggest that she was martyred for any reason other than her Jewishness is an unpardonable insult to Holocaust victims. If she is a martyr, there are six million others. Are they to be beatified as well?

If the Pope were genuinely concerned about harmony between Catholics and Jews, would he have chosen to beatify Edith Stein? And if good relations with Jews—to say nothing of the honor due to victims and survivors of the Holocaust—counted with him, would he agree to see Kurt Waldheim? Many leaders of nations, including our own, have refused. John Paul could easily have done this.

It has been argued that the Pope is not an ordinary head of state and that in receiving Waldheim he has acted in the spirit of Christ the Healer, the Reconciler, who dined, after all, with publicans and sinners. This is a gross misunderstanding of the theology of reconciliation, of biblical history, and of political morality. A sinner cannot be reconciled until he or she has acknowledged the sin and begun to repent of it. Waldheim has denied any wrongdoing; he has been involved in decades of cover-ups, which have added to the gravity of his original crime. The Pope did not receive Waldheim neutrally: he praised him as a man of peace. When Jesus sat down with publicans and sinners, he didn't then call them philanthropists. It has been suggested that the Pope may have censured Waldheim privately. Even if this was the case, it wouldn't be enough. This is a public issue; and he has given his public support.

It is interesting to me which publicans and sinners the Pope will *not* dine with. He will appear on a balcony with Pinochet (although, admittedly, he was critical of Pinochet's policies) but not with Castro. And if the Pope is so concerned with reconciling differences, let's see him invite the head of Planned Parenthood International to lunch. Just as Pope Pius XII could have condemned Hitler and chose not to, his successor chooses to be involved in the cover-up of Nazi crimes and the rewriting of history so that a collaborator becomes a hero.

As a Catholic, I have no patience with my fellow Catholics, such as John Cardinal O'Connor, who assert that the important thing now is for Jews not to lose their commitment to interfaith dialogue. Grave offenses have been committed against the Jews by the Catholic Church. There is no reason for Jews to trust or forgive the Church until it has acknowledged the depths of its offenses.

Mary Cassatt

When Mary Cassatt's father was told of her decision to become a painter, he said: "I would rather see you dead." When Edgar Degas saw a show of Cassatt's etchings, his response was: "I am not willing to admit that a woman can draw that well." When she returned to Philadelphia after twenty-eight years abroad, having achieved renown as an Impressionist painter and the esteem of Degas, Huysmans, Pissarro, and Berthe Morisot, the *Philadelphia Ledger* reported: "Mary Cassatt, sister of Mr. Cassatt, president of the Pennsylvania Railroad, returned from Europe yesterday. She has been studying painting in France and owns the smallest Pekingese dog in the world."

Mary Cassatt exemplified the paradoxes of the woman artist. Cut off from the experiences that are considered the entitlement of her male counterpart, she has access to a private world a man can only guess at. She has, therefore, a kind of information he is necessarily deprived of. If she has almost impossible good fortune—means, self-confidence, heroic energy and dedication, the instinct to avoid the seductions of ordinary domestic life, which so easily become a substitute for creative work—she may pull off a miracle: she will combine the skill and surety that she has stolen from the world of men with the vision she brings from the world of women.

Mary Cassatt pulled off such a miracle. But if her story is particularly female, it is also American. She typifies one kind of independent American spinster who keeps reappearing in our history in forms as various as Margaret Fuller and Katharine Hepburn. There is an astringency in such women, a fierce discipline, a fearlessness, a love of work. But they are not inhuman. At home in the world, they embrace it with a kind of aristocratic greed that knows nothing of excess. Balance, proportion, an instinct for the distant and the formal, an exuberance, a vividness, a clarity of line: the genius of Mary Cassatt includes all these elements. The details of the combination are best put down to grace; the outlines may have been her birthright.

She was one of those wealthy Americans whose parents took the children abroad for their education and medical care. The James family comes to mind and, given her father's attitude toward her career, it is remarkable that Cassatt didn't share the fate of Alice James. But she had a remarkable mother, intelligent, encouraging of her children. When her daughter wanted to study in Paris, and her husband disapproved, Mrs. Cassatt arranged to accompany Mary as her chaperone.

From her beginnings as an art student, Cassatt was determined to follow the highest standards of craftsmanship. She went first to Paris, then to Italy, where she studied in Parma with Raimondi and spent many hours climbing up scaffolding (to the surprise of the natives) to study the work of Correggio and Parmigianino. Next, she was curious to visit Spain to look at the Spanish masters and to make use of the picturesque landscape and models. Finally, she returned to Paris, where she was to make her home, and worked with Degas, her sometime friend and difficult mentor. There has always been speculation as to whether or not they were lovers; her burning their correspondence gave the rumor credence. But I believe that they were not; she was, I think, too protective of her talent to make herself so vulnerable to Degas as a lover would have to be. But I suppose I don't believe it because I cherish, instead, the notion that a man and a woman can be colleagues and friends without causing an excuse for raised eyebrows. Most important, I want to believe they were not lovers because if they were, the trustworthiness of his extreme praise grows dilute.

She lived her life until late middle age among her family. Her beloved sister, Lydia, one of her most cherished models, had always lived as a semi-invalid and died early, in Mary's flat, of Bright's disease. Mary was closely involved with her brothers and their children. Her bond with her mother was profound: when Mrs. Cassatt died, in 1895, Mary's work began to decline. At the severing of her last close familial tie, when her surviving brother died as a result of an illness he contracted when traveling with her to Egypt, she broke down entirely. "How we try for happiness, poor things, and how we don't find it. The best cure is hard work—if only one has the health for it," she said, and lived that way.

Not surprisingly, perhaps, Cassatt's reputation has suffered because of the prejudice against her subject matter. Mothers and children: what could be of lower prestige, more vulnerable to the charge of sentimentality. Yet if one looks at the work of Mary Cassatt, one sees how triumphantly she avoids the pitfalls of sentimentality because of the astringent rigor of her eye and craft. The Cassatt iconography dashes in an instant the notion of the comfortable, easily natural fit of the maternal embrace. Again and again in her work, the child's posture embodies the ambivalence of his or her dependence. In *The Family*, the mother and child exist in positions of unease; the strong diagonals created by their postures of opposition give the pictures their tense strength, a strength that renders sentimental sweetness impossible. In *Ellen Mary Cassatt in a White Coat* and *Girl in the Blue Arm Chair*, the children seem imprisoned and dwarfed by the trappings of respectable life. The lines of Ellen's coat, which create such a powerful framing device, entrap the round and living child. The sulky little girl in the armchair seems about to be swallowed up by the massive cylinders of drawing room furniture and the strong curves of emptiness that are the floor. In *The Bath*, the little girl has all the unformed charming awkwardness of a young child: the straight limbs, the loose stomach. But these are not the stuff of Gerber babies—even of the children of Millais. In this picture, the center of interest is not the relationship between the mother and the child but the strong vertical and diagonal stripes of the mother's dress, whose opposition shape the picture with an insistence that is almost abstract.

Cassatt changed the iconography of the depiction of mothers and children. Hers do not look out into and meet the viewer's eye; neither supplicating nor seductive, they are absorbed in their own inner thoughts. Minds are at work here, a concentration unbroken by an awareness of themselves as objects to be gazed at by the world.

The brilliance of Cassatt's colors, the clarity and solidity of her forms, are the result of her love and knowledge of the masters of European painting. She had a second career as adviser to great collectors: she believed passionately that America must, for the sake of its artists, possess masterpieces, and she paid no attention to the outrage of her European friends, who felt their treasures were being sacked by barbarians. A young man visiting her in her old age noted her closed mind regarding the movement of the moderns. She thought American painters should stay home and not become "café loafers in Paris. Why should they come to Europe?" she demanded. "When I was young it was different. . . . Our Museums had not great paintings for the students to study. Now that has been corrected and something must be done to save our young over here."

One can hear the voice of the old, irascible, still splendid aunt in that comment and see the gesture of her stick toward the Left Bank. Cassatt was blinded by cataracts; the last years of her life were spent in a fog. She became ardent on the subjects of suffragism, socialism, and spiritualism; the horror of the First World War made her passionate in her conviction that mankind itself must change. She died at her country estate near Grasse, honored by the French, recipient of the Légion d'honneur, but unappreciated in America, rescued only recently from misunderstanding, really, by feminist art critics. They allowed us to begin to see her for what she is: a master of line and color whose great achievement was to take the "feminine" themes of mothers, children, women with their thoughts alone, to endow them with grandeur without withholding from them the tenderness that fits so easily alongside the rigor of her art.

Getting Here from There: A Writer's Reflections on a Religious Past

===

To begin speaking about the words "spiritual quest" in relation to myself fills me simultaneously with amusement and alarm. Amusement because the words "spiritual" and "quest" conjure up the imagery of the knight consecrate, Galahad after the Holy Grail, dying picturesquely at the very moment he fulfills his goal. I can't see myself in the part. And alarm because the very word "spiritual" suggests to me the twin dangers of the religious life: dualism and abstraction.

Abstraction I define as the error that results from refusing to admit that one has a body and is an inhabitant of the physical world. Dualism, its first cousin, admits that there is a physical world but calls it evil and commands that it be shunned. I'd venture to say that these two "sins"—dualism and abstraction—are the cause of at least as much human misery as pride, covetousness, lust, envy, hatred, gluttony, and sloth. Those names come very easily to my mind—names learned in childhood, memorized in childhood. They form one of those lists, those catalogues, that made the blood race with the buildup. So many catalogues there were in the church I grew up in, so many lists: seven capital sins, three theological virtues and four moral ones, seven sacraments, seven gifts of the

Holy Ghost. A kind of poetry of accumulation, gaining power like an avalanche from its own momentum—perhaps a small influence, but an important one that I grew up hearing every day of my life, for my childhood days were shaped and marked by the religious devotions of my parents, by the rhythmic, repetitive cadences of formal prayer. It bred in me a love for strongly rhythmic prose.

I can never talk about the spiritual or the religious life without talking about early memory, which is anything but disembodied. Whatever religious instincts I have bring their messages to me through the senses—the images of my religious life, its sounds, its odors, the kind of kinesthetic sense I have of prayerfulness. These are much more real to me than anything that takes place in the life of the mind. I want to say that I've never been drawn to any kind of systematic theology except as a kind of curiosity, though as soon as I say this I want to qualify it, because what makes me even more nervous than the word "spiritual" are the words "evangelical" or "charismatic." The religious impulse unmediated by reason terrifies me, and it seems to me that we are always having to mediate between the emotions, the body, the reason. So even though I can't be moved forward in any way by systematic theology, I like it to be there, in the same way that I like modern architecture to be there, even though I don't want to live in it.

And the body must not be left out. I was born into a church shaped and ruled by celibate males who had a history of hatred and fear of the body, which they lived out in their lives and in the rituals they invented. They excluded women from the center of their official and their personal lives. When I tried to think of any rituals that acknowledged the body, except for rituals involving death and in a very oblique way birth, the only one I could think of was what used to be called "the churching of women," which is a blessing for the mother, a kind of purification after the mess of birth. It's a remembrance of the purification of the Virgin Mary; she would have been actually submerged in water, not merely symbolically cleansed, for the reentry into the legitimate world, where body life could once again be hidden.

I keep having to backtrack; every time I say something I instantly think that I haven't quite told the truth, because I have to confess and acknowledge my own dualism. Much of what is beautiful to me in my religious experience is its bodylessness. I remember the early-morning Masses of my childhood. In my memory the atmosphere is always gray, a kind of false dawn, air without heat or light. I'm walking with one of my parents, never both, because these memories are the tête-à-têtes of the anointed "only child," the child of parents who preferred her to each other. The women in my memories are wearing coats of muted colors, kerchiefs, round-toed nunlike shoes. The nuns themselves are disappearing in their habits, faceless. They are only forms. The church is coldish. It is silent. In the sacristy you can hear the mysterious, inexplicable, untraceable noises of the priest and the altar boy—the cruet's tinkle, the vestments' rustle. There are whispered words.

And then there is the Mass. What an excellent training ground the regular attendance at Mass was for an aspiring novelist! First, there's the form of the Mass itself, which popularly has been compared to drama, but the likenesses with the novel are also not at all unapt. The central event of the Mass occurs—interestingly for the novelist, I think—way past its middle. It's the consecration, the turning of bread and wine into the body and blood of Christ. I have to say a word about this, because for orthodox Catholics this is an actual transformation of substance. (The doctrine is called transubstantiation.) That is to say, for an orthodox Catholic the bread and wine are no longer believed to be bread and wine; they have changed in their essence, in what the scholastic philosophers called their substance, so that they are no longer bread and wine but have been actually transformed into the body and blood of Christ. Somewhere there's a conversation I like between Mary McCarthy and Flannery O'Connor in which McCarthy tries to get O'Connor to admit that she really believes that transubstantiation is only a symbolic act. And Flannery O'Connor is reported to have said, "If I thought it were just a symbol I'd say the hell with it."

For the novelist, then, there is a central dramatic event. But interestingly, there is also a regular alternation of levels of language and types of literature within the Mass itself. There's scriptural invocation, reflective prayer, the poetry of the Psalms, the Old Testament and Gospel narratives, and the repetitions: the Sanctus, the Agnus Dei, the *Domini non sum dignus,* repeated three times, the first and last time to the accompaniment of bells. Different types of Masses offer to the sensitive ear examples of different kinds of formality and embellishment, from the simple daily Low

Mass to the more formal Sunday Low Mass to the High Mass, complete with choirs, chants, and all the liturgical stops pulled out.

I'm not saying that as a child I consciously understood this. Obviously, I didn't. But I absorbed it unconsciously, this elaborate and varied and supple use of language. From a very early age I had it woven into my bones. Once again, Flannery O'Connor says that the writer learns everything important to him or her before the age of six. So every day, for however often I was taken to daily Mass, I was learning lessons in rhetoric.

And I was also learning a lot of other things. If we accept the truism that all writers are voyeurs, then we can say that an hour a day in a confined space like a church, where one has the leisure or the boredom to observe others of one's kind when they imagine themselves to be in private communion with their deepest souls, is as useful for a prospective novelist as a wiretap. Daily Mass was the home ground of the marginal, the underemployed; you always wondered why they weren't at work or getting ready for work. A child at daily Mass got to observe at close range the habits of old women, of housewives at eight-thirty already tired out for the day, of men down on their luck praying for a reversal of their bad fortunes.

You also got wonderful lessons in structure. The structure of the Mass, like that of the parish, composed itself around the figure of the priest, the center of all our earthly attentions, the center of parish life, at an observable distance on the altar for an hour of our time. The erotically charged yet unreachable figure of the priest! And around him, theoretically invisible and yet of course the pulse of parish life, the women: jockeying, serving (except on the altar, where they were forbidden to be), dreaming, losing and gaining lives against the backdrop of history. And the single figure of the priest, who could contain in himself the whole world. The priest was theoretically available to all and yet was available to no one, just as the Church was in theory open to all and in theory welcoming of all, but operated in fact on principles of initiation and exclusion. For all that, it has always contained a membership that includes representatives from all of Europe and all the places where the Europeans set down their iron-shod feet.

So to be a Catholic, or even to have been one, is to feel a certain access to a world wider than the vision allowed by the lens of one's own birth. You grew up believing that the parish is the world, and that anyone in the world could be a member of the parish. But of course the parish was a fiercely limited terrain: the perfect size and conformation for the study of the future novelist. Anachronistically limited, its hierarchies clear, its loyalties assumed and stated and then in practice always undermined, it has at its center issues of money. You learned from the parish how the watermarks of class and privilege work. You could see how the impressive personality, the personality of the clergy, can change life.

A novelist builds a fence enclosing a certain area of the world and then calls it his or her subject. To be a Catholic, particularly in Protestant America, made one an expert at building the limiting, excluding fence. Inside the paddock there were shared assumptions about everything from the appropriate postures for kneeling to the nature of human consciousness. But there was always a right way and a wrong way, and you always knew which was which.

One could be, at least in the time when I was growing up, a Catholic in New York and deal only in the most superficial of ways with anyone non-Catholic. Until I went to college I had no genuine contact with anyone who wasn't Catholic. The tailor and the man who ran the candy store were Jews, and the women who worked in the public library were Protestants, but you allowed them only the pleasantries. Real life, the friendships, the feuds, the passions of proximate existence, took place in the sectarian compound, a compound, like any other, with its secrets—a secret language, secret customs, rites, which I now understand must have been very menacing at worst or at the best puzzling to the outside world.

But we never knew that, because we never understood that the rest of the world was looking. We weren't interested in the rest of the world. If some of us did assume that the rest of the world was looking, our response was to be all the more zealous in keeping the secrets secret. One of the greatest treasures a novelist can have is a secret world, which he or she can open up to his or her reader. When I turned from poetry to fiction in my mid-twenties, I had a natural subject—the secrets of the Catholic world. And since the door had not been very widely opened before I got there, I was a natural. I think that accounts to a great extent for the popularity of *Final Payments*.

Now we're going to descend into autobiography. I don't know

how successful I can be in conveying the extent to which my family life was shaped by Catholicism. My parents' whole marriage was based on it; it was literally the only thing they had in common. My father was an intellectual Jew, who had had a very wild life. And simply to give you the outlines of it will give you a sense of its wildness. He was born in Lorain, Ohio. He also lied a lot, so it's extremely hard to trace what's the truth. I think this is the truth; at least I'm not consciously passing on lies. But it could also perhaps *not* be the truth. So I possibly have a great-grandfather who was a rabbi, but my father also said that his mother was a concert pianist, and who knows? He told me, for example, that his father ran a saloon; in fact, he ran a dry goods store.

In any case, my father went to Harvard in 1917. At that time there was a rigid quota system for Jews, and I think it must have caused him tremendous pain. Because what I think is that at Harvard he determined to "pass" at any cost. And my father, who was endlessly inventive, figured out that the best way for a Jew to pass was to be right-wing. My father became righter-wing than anybody, with a couple of interesting pit stops. For example, he went to Paris and England for a while in the twenties. And one persona that he created for some reason was to pass himself off as a Middle West Presbyterian. He looked a lot like me—I don't know why anybody believed him. Maybe they thought all Americans look alike. He wrote a series of articles in English journals, passing himself off as a Midwest Protestant who understands that Europe is really a superior culture to his own.

His other pit stop was also in the late twenties. He published a girlie magazine called *Hot Dog*. I remember being twelve, and my father had died when I was seven, and I came upon this magazine while looking through his pictures. By today's standards it was exceedingly mild. But I was an exceedingly prudish twelve-year-old, and I took a look at this thing and I saw that my father had been the editor, and I was appalled and I ripped it to shreds and threw it away. So I have no record of it. But I'm pretty sure I didn't make it up.

In any case, my father became a Francoist in the thirties. You rarely meet somebody who can say that sentence—everybody else's father was in the Lincoln Brigade. Not mine. And in the course of several later adventures he met my mother. They met through a priest. My mother is the daughter of very simple Irish and Italian Catholics. I think she embodied for my father a kind of peasant Catholicism that he romanticized. But both of them could say with truthfulness that their faith was the most important thing in the world to them.

From an early age I had to take the measure of myself against their devotedness, and I always found myself wanting. Throughout my childhood I prayed to be spared martyrdom. But then I always felt guilty for the prayer. I was no little Teresa of Ávila setting out in the desert hoping to convert the Moors; the priests in China having bamboo shoved under their fingernails and Cardinal Mindszenty imprisoned in his upper room terrified me. I didn't want that for my fate, but I was told that it was the highest fate. So as a child I had always to be consciously choosing an inferior fate. It was a real burden.

But I do remember that, although I didn't want to be a martyr, I did want to be a nun. I remember being taken by my parents to the Convent of Mary Reparatrix on Twenty-ninth Street in New York. It's a semicloistered convent—the nuns weren't allowed out, but people could talk to them. And I remember going into the chapel with my parents and a very old nun. I saw a young nun kneeling in a pool of light. I saw her from the back only. The habits of the Sisters of Mary Reparatrix were sky blue. I've never seen a color like that in a nun's habit, and I'm quite sure I didn't invent it. But if I had wanted to invent it, it would have been perfect, because it was a color dreamed up for movie stars. It was the color of Sleeping Beauty's ball gown, and that was what I wanted for myself. I wanted to be beautifully kneeling in light, my young, straight back clothed in the magic garment of the anointed. I knew that was what I wanted, but I knew I didn't want to drink filthy water or walk barefoot in the snow. A few times, though, I did try some local free-lance missionary work.

Once, for instance, I had just finished reading the life of Saint Dominic Savio, who was a Neapolitan orphan. I was six or seven. Saint Dominic walked into a playground and heard his rough playmates—nobody uses the phrase "rough playmates" anymore—using blasphemous language. And he didn't skip a beat. He held up a crucifix, and he said to those boys, "Say it in front of Him." And the boys fell silent. Inspired, I tried the same thing in my neighborhood. I walked into the crowd of boys with my crucifix aloft, and I said, "Say it in front of Him." And they were glad to.

The comedy of Catholic life. It comes, of course, like all other comedy, from the gap between the ideal and the real. In my case the ideal was so high and the real was so real that the collision was bound to be risible. I tried walking with thorns in my shoes for penance, but then I found out that it hurt. So I walked around on the heels of my shoes and put the thorns in the toes, so I could have them in my shoes but not feel them. My heroisms were always compromised and always unsuccessful. I tried to talk the man in our gas station into taking the nude calendar off his wall. He told me never to come into the office again. I tried to make the candy store man, whom I genuinely liked, stop selling dirty magazines. He stopped giving me free egg creams, and our friendship ended. But he went right on selling dirty magazines.

I always tried. The serious part of the ideals that shaped my early life was that they did teach me that life was serious. I think all children believe that. I think parents cheat children by refusing to understand that everything is serious to them and that it is the modulations of the adult world that cause them such confused grief. At a very early age I was taught that happiness was not important; what was important was to save my soul. I was not supposed to be only a good girl or even a lady, although I was supposed to begin there. I was not supposed to even strive to be popular, successful, beloved, or valued by the world. I was supposed to be a saint. The cautionary and inspirational tales of my youth were the lives of the saints.

The lives of the saints. I recently took down a saints' lives book that was mine as a child. I sometimes read it to my children today. To my children, these people—Saint Barnabas who juggled, Saint Nicholas who found children pickled in the basement of an inn and brought them back to life—are fairy-tale characters. They're characters like Ali Baba or Rapunzel. My daughter likes the picture of the boy Saint Hugh kicking the devil downstairs. She asks me if the devil is real. And I tell her, "No, no, he's not real; he's like the banshee or the Loch Ness monster." And as I tell her that, I realize that for me the devil *was* real. And he was feared. My mother cured me of early narcissism by telling me that if I kept looking in the mirror the devil would pop out behind me and that when I was looking at my face it would turn into the face of the devil. I stopped immediately. I was thinking about eternal life, and so was she, and we couldn't afford to take the risk.

There's a sentence in the incomparable story "In Dreams Begin Responsibilities," by Delmore Schwartz, in which the boy says, "Everything you do matters too much." Did everything matter too much for me? I'm not sure. But at least it mattered. What you learned with a background like mine was that everything mattered terribly and that you could never do enough.

I remember a friend of mine, a Jew, telling me years later that he felt sorry for Christians because if you took seriously the words of Christ "Greater love hath no man than this, that a man lay down his life for his friends," then as long as you were alive you hadn't done enough. But this is not such a bad thing for an artist. For the life of the working artist is a perpetual reminder that everything you do matters. Nothing is enough.

Speaking of the lives of the saints makes me try to differentiate among the kinds of narratives that a pious Catholic child encountered. There were the Old Testament narratives, which always seemed to me forbidding and harsh and frightening—exciting as war movies were exciting and dangerous, but of no comfort. Abraham and Isaac, Moses left in the bulrushes, Joseph thrown down the well by his brothers, the boy David all alone with a slingshot: you had the vision of children for whom the adult world offered no protection. There were the failing parents and the implacable voice of God. I always felt as if the narratives of the Old Testament were accompanied by a kind of rumble. The colors were dark and vibrant. I was drawn to them, but I wanted to get away. To Jesus and the children.

I remember a jigsaw puzzle I had of Jesus and the children: the warm, inviting lap, the face of infinite acceptance. And there were the other images—the prodigal son forgiven, the daughter of Gyrus raised, the blind man given his sight, the lame man his nimbleness, the good thief ushered into paradise. But there was also a disturbing underside of New Testament violence. It was disturbing in a way that Old Testament violence was not, because in the old narratives the violence all seemed of a piece with the rest of the vision of the world, whereas in the Gospels it was always a surprise and something of a cheat. It was the terrible massacre of the innocents, the beheading of John the Baptist, the sufferings and death of Christ himself—somehow the triumph always paid for by some ancillary, unwilled or only partially willed carnage. Easter paid for by Lent. How fully I lived my childhood Holy Weeks, the most solemn time of the year, religiously then as now my favorite! The black vestments, the stripped altar, the shocked silence of the congregation, and then the midnight fire and the morning promise of Easter. In my memory Easter was always warm; you could always wear your spring coat and your straw hat, although in my adulthood more than half the Easters have been covered in snow.

The third kind of narrative, the lives of the saints, were magical in ways that the Bible of both Testaments was too austere to permit. Saint Francis talked to birds and wolves. Saint Elizabeth of Hungary, a queen, carried bread to the poor and the plague-ridden, although her husband the king had forbidden it. She hid the bread in her apron to keep it from the eyes of her husband and the palace guards. Her husband the king found out; he confronted her with his soldiers at the castle gate, demanding that she show him what was inside her apron. She opened her apron, and where there had been bread there were roses. He fell on his knees before his wife.

It occurs to me that one good fortune in being brought up a Catholic and a woman was that you did have images of heroic women. And that's not so frequently the case in other religious traditions. In the tradition of Catholicism you have a poem spoken by the Virgin Mary that points out her place in the divine order. And she speaks with pride. She says, "My soul doth magnify the Lord and my spirit hath rejoiced in God, my savior. Because He has regarded the loneliness of His handmaid, and behold from henceforth all generations shall call me blessed, for He that is mighty hath done great things to me and holy is His name." That's an example of a woman's speech and a woman acknowledging her importance in the hierarchy, which at least in some subliminal way a girl got to hold on to.

In the lives of the saints you had a lot of examples of women who defined themselves not in terms of men but in terms of each other. You had the founders of orders. You had women who defied the Pope, defied the bishops, to go off and do things that women were not supposed to do. You had "doctors of the church"—women saints who were given that title. Did I know at age five what that meant—"doctor of the church"? Not exactly. But there was something there. You had an image of an alternative female world that often had to trick the male world in the same way that Saint Elizabeth had to trick her husband the king. A lot of women have survived through trickery. It was not entirely a bad life, but I hope it's one we can soon forget. Still, it wasn't a bad arrow to have in your quiver.

The saints came in various personality types. There was the meek Little Flower and the fierce Spanish Teresa. There was Saint Jerome in the desert with his blood-red eyes and the Curé of Ars, the friend of everybody in his little village. There were monks and scholars, widows and virgins, popes and ferrymen. I've stopped doing missionary work among the candy store owners of the world, but I do try to remind people of wonderful women writers who are undernoticed and often out of print. Louise Bogan, I think, is an exquisite poet—as good as anybody who has written in this century. Except for one small collection, her work is out of print. I offer you a poem of hers called "Saint Christopher," since we're talking about saints' lives. I think it will give you something of the flavor of those lives, which were so wonderful for a child to hear, getting from them a sense of narrative.

> A raw-boned and an ignorant man
> Keeps ferry, but a man of nerve,
> His freight a Child and a Child's toy.
> (Which is our globe, you will observe.)
>
> But what a look of intent love!
> This is the look we do not see
> In manners or in mimicry.
> Strength's a derivative thereof.
>
> The middle class is what we are.
> Poised as a brigand or a barber
> The tough young saint, Saint Christopher,
> Brings the Child into the safe harbor.

Among all these saints, among all the types that were represented and honored, there are no artists, unless you count Saint Francis de Sales, who is the patron saint of writers, and he was hardly what we would call a creative writer; he was a composer of meditations. From the way I've described the riches of the Catholic background, you may think it would be almost inevitable that any pious child would grow up to be an artist. But as a group, Catholics—particularly Catholics in America and even ex-Catholics—are <u>scandalously underrepresented in the arts</u>. I'm always surprised by this, but I shouldn't be. The orthodox have no need of consolation, and a closed world has no need of descriptions of itself. For a Catholic who took the teachings of the Church seriously, art for art's sake is as foreign as the idea of a Moslem heaven. Even knowledge was encouraged not for its own sake but in the service of God. I've just gone through an old prayer book of my mother's, which I used to read a lot as a child. And I came across these prayers, which illustrate the notion that the life of the mind was never for itself but always in the service of God.

This first prayer is to Saint Catherine of Siena, who was a doctor of the church. It goes:

O glorious Saint Catherine, wise and prudent virgin, Thou who didst set the knowledge of Jesus Christ above all other knowledge. Obtain for us the grace to remain inviolably attached to the Catholic faith and to seek in our studies and in our teaching only the extension of the kingdom of Jesus Christ our Lord and of His holy church, both in our selves and in the souls of others. Amen.

The second prayer is to the Virgin Mary, which is supposed to be said by students:

Under thy patronage, Dear Mother, and invoking the mystery of thine immaculate conception, I desire to pursue my studies and my literary labors. I hereby solemnly declare that I am devoting myself to these studies chiefly to the following end: That I may the better contribute to the glory of God and to the spread of thy veneration among men. I pray thee, therefore, most loving mother, who art the seat of wisdom, to bless my labors in thy loving kindness. Moreover, I promise with true affection and a waking spirit, as it is right that I should do, to ascribe all the good that shall accrue to me therefrom wholly to thine intercession for me in God's holy presence. Amen.

Nobody walking fully under the banner represented by those prayers could create a modern work of art. The artistic ego, a product of the Renaissance, coincided with the loosening of the grip of the Church over the hearts and minds of women and men. The enclosed garden of my childhood was enclosed by a system that said all acts found their meaning in the reiteration of the Truth. Capital T. Whereas that might have been a vessel of inspiration for the author of *The Divine Comedy* or the *Pange Lingua*, it could be of no help to a modern artist, particularly a novelist whose origins are in the secular mind of the eighteenth century.

When you're talking about the Catholic Church you always have to go back and forth between the levels of the spiritual, the private, the ideal, and the real. Because the Catholic Church, for better and for worse, is a worldwide church that encompasses races and classes of all sorts. And I think that the silence of American Catholics in relation to the arts is an accident of class, ethnicity, and history as much as it is of spiritual overidealism. I think we have to remember that the Catholic Church in America is the Irish Church. And the Irish Church is a church that is obsessed and committed to the idea of keeping silence. There's a famous Irish expression: "An Irish person will tell you something and then will say, 'Mind you, I've said nothing.' "

In working on my novel *The Other Side,* I had the funny experience of listening to researchers who have done oral histories of the Irish. And I could tell they weren't Irish themselves. They went into nursing homes, where the old people had nothing to do—they're a captive audience—and interviewers ask questions and ask questions and these old people answer with tremendous politeness and a great flurry of language and convey absolutely no information.

People always say, "Well, the Irish are so garrulous. They love to talk." They love to talk, but they don't like to tell you anything. So if you're happy to have a good time and listen to the shape of the language itself, you'll have a wonderful time talking to an Irishman. If you want to know anything about his or her life, forget it. People say, "Well, he'll get drunk and . . ." Nothing. That has nothing to do with it. You will not get at the truth. The Irish are obsessed with concealing the inner life.

I think this is another reason why there has been such a silence, such an absence of the Catholic voice, in America. There's a lot of talk about the Irish Renaissance in Ireland. But those are not Catholic writers; you're talking about English Protestants who happened to set down roots and then get romantic about the auld sod. Nothing made Joyce more crazy than to hear Yeats carrying on about the Celtic twilight. And Yeats, of course, couldn't stand the Irish that he came in contact with. He wanted to fantasize about them heroically, but if he happened to meet one of his workmen in front of the tower, he'd just as soon send him to jail as invite him in to dinner. So when you're talking about the Catholicism in America and the presence of the arts, you have to talk about the presence of the Irish, which adds a lot of complications.

Well, how did I get from there to here? An easy answer would be that I substituted art for faith, so that I found my new priesthood. That would be an easy answer, but it's not true. I don't believe in the religion of art, although I do believe in the vocation of the artist—altogether a more slogging enterprise. I don't believe that the aesthetic and the religious are one. To my mind, an experience to be properly religious must include three things: an ethical component, the possibility of full participation by the entire human community, and acknowledgment of the existence of a life beyond the human. Art need do none of these things, although it may. Most art does not suggest a life beyond the human, unless you want to say that all inspiration is beyond the human and therefore art acknowledges this tacitly. I think that's fudging the question. There can be all sorts of sources of inspiration. They need not be personal; they need not be suprahuman or extrahuman.

And even the greatest art, even the greatest art when it is the simplest art, requires a certain prior cluing in, a kind of training, however informal, in the rudiments of the art. Great art need have nothing in it of the ethical, although the greatness of some great literature is enhanced by ethical components. But some is not. And certainly it would be absurd to make those claims for painting or music. This is why I say that the aesthetic and the religious are not necessarily one.

So how did I get there from here? How did I get here from

there? You may notice that when I speak of religious influences I speak of the memories of childhood. I was fourteen when the Second Vatican Council began. Virginia Woolf tells us that on or about December 1910 the world changed. Well, the great changes in the Church coincided—unfortunately perhaps—with the great changes in my body. I became at puberty properly irreligious, and I say "properly" with great advisement. I think one should beware of the religious adolescent; he may be planning your assassination in the night. I was fourteen when one of the greatest events in the Church's history took place. I'm reminded again—a bit irrelevantly but not unpleasantly, I hope—of a poem, by Stevie Smith, called "The Conventionalist":

> *Fourteen-year-old, why must you giggle and dote?*
> *Fourteen-year-old, why are you such a goat?*
> *I'm fourteen years old, that is the reason.*
> *I giggle and dote in season.*

I'm afraid I was giggling and doting when Pope John was opening the windows of the Church. And the outside world beckoned me with much more force than the confused and angry Church of the early and mid sixties. It's always amusing to me to talk to non-Catholics about their fantasy of what the Second Vatican Council did. They all imagine that we were clapping and singing and shouting "Hallelujah!" Most people were furious. Most people were confused and angry and outraged. They felt that the rug had been taken out from under them, particularly if they grew up, as I did, in a working-class neighborhood. There was no great sense of jubilation. It was a lucky thing for Pope John that he died; he got to look good, like John Kennedy.

It was at that point that I began to think of myself as a poet, as an artist. I had no more interest in being a saint. And a good thing too—I stopped trying to get people to not sell magazines, and I stopped putting thorns in my shoes. When I looked back over my shoulder to see what they were doing in the open-windowed Church, the part of me that was learning about great art could only run away. People were playing guitars at Mass now and rewriting Peter, Paul and Mary tunes to express Church dogma.

> *Take this bread*
> *And take this wine*
> *And take our hearts*
> *And take our minds*
> *At this Eucharistic feast*
> *We are all priests.*

I was fourteen. What could I do?

Well, it's fun to make fun of these excesses. I like doing it very much. But I don't think the answer is to turn the clock back. I don't want it turned back, because the people who are plumping for the reintroduction of Gregorian chant into the liturgy are also funding the contras in Nicaragua, and they're doing it for the same reason. But I am grieved every time I enter a parish church and hear an unlovely liturgy, and I often have to leave for my own protection. I'm in a queer position: the Church of my childhood, which was so important for my formation as an artist, is now gone. As Gertrude Stein said of Oakland, "There is no there there."

But there *is* something there, something that formed me and that touches me still: the example of the nuns killed in El Salvador, of liberation theologians standing up to the Pope, of the nuns—the "Vatican 24"—who signed the statement asserting that it was possible for Catholics to have different positions on abortion and still be Catholics. These sisters, many of them in their sixties and seventies, faced the loss of everything—their sisterhood, their community, their lives, and things we wouldn't think of, like their medical insurance. They had no Social Security; they had no pension plans; they faced literally being thrown out on the street. They are extraordinary women.

These people whom I am moved by and whom I admire are nevertheless people who are very different from me. And what I admire in them is at a very great remove from the world of literature and art. Nevertheless, I can't quite give up what they stand for. I don't want to give it up because I don't want to give it over to John Cardinal O'Connor and his kind.

So what do I do? I write my fictions. And my relation to the "there" that is not there I make up each day, and it changes each day as I go along.

More Catholic than the Pope

While standing in the lobby of the administration building of a moderately sized Catholic college, I saw a recruitment poster for an order of nuns that said, in those light, slanty letters that are supposed to indicate modern spirituality: ARE YOU LOOKING FOR AN ALTERNATE LIFE-STYLE? Kind of like looking for Mr. Goodbar. Out of the closet and over the wall. It is not the Church of my childhood, that repository of language never to be used again, words white-flat and crafted: "monstrance," "chasuble"; words shaped to fit into each other like spoons, words that overlap and do not overlap, words that mark a way of life that has a word for every mode, a category for each situation: "gifts of the Holy Ghost," "corporal works of mercy," "capital sins," "cardinal virtues."

Surely there is no romance like the romance of a lost order, no desire like the desire for distinguished exile. It is not American, this image of exclusion and trial by fire. America deals with its dissidents like a rich and clever mother: she insists upon the embrace, either bought by the careful gift or yearned for on the part of the child who can no longer bear neglect from such a worldly bosom, from a mother so absorbed in her own activity that she forgets her banished young. The American exile must cross the ocean for distinction; he will probably come back. The European exile sits on the doorstep of his next-door neighbor, sullen, hyp-notized by plots and theories of conspiracy.

Marcel Lefebvre has the face of the born exile. He looks out at us from the newspapers, exhausted, finely made. He is not Irish; he is not Italian; neither Bing Crosby nor John XXIII. He looks even sadder than Paul VI, and thinner, and more exhausted. He is a gentleman, a quality one is not supposed to yearn for in suc-cessors to the Apostles. There is a story about one of the Cecils who came home sporting a beard, to the outrage of his father, who told him that gentlemen never wore beards. "But," his son ob-jected, "Our Lord wore a beard." "Our Lord," his father said, "was not a gentleman." Archbishop Lefebvre *is,* and a French gentleman. There are those of us who fear we would have fared badly in the company of Peter but know we would have been a smash with one of the Medici popes. Lefebvre suggests *la vieille Europe*: château silver, ancient and perfect servants, a chapel near the tennis courts, where one could confess to one's impeccable chaplain one's latest indiscretion with the young gardener and be told that sins of the flesh are not central to the spiritual life; where it would be sug-gested that among people of consequence these things are bound to occur.

Lefebvre's publicity has come to him chiefly because he has insisted upon saying Mass in Latin, against the orders of the Second Vatican Council. At first glance, it seems a monstrous punishment: typical of the rigidity of the Church of Rome. Why should Lefebvre be disciplined for saying Mass in Latin, according to the old rite, the rite established by the Council of Trent in the sixteenth cen-tury? Anyone who has gone anywhere near Catholics in the past several years knows that dissatisfaction with the liturgy is enor-mous. The new Mass is piecemeal, tentative, on the whole a botched job. Lefebvre seems to be standing for a kind of purity, aesthetic and spiritual, that was lost to the Church in the sixties in its lust to make up for lost time, to become—that word we love to hate—relevant, to join the twentieth century in all its least satisfying aspects.

But when one looks into Lefebvre's case, it quickly becomes obvious that the Latin Mass is the merest symbol of what the archbishop objects to. He is against his age. His rhetoric is des-perate, and it has the excitement of desperation. It has the excitement, too, of an archaism revivified: it is the language of a conflict, but a conflict that seems ancient, and consequently grand. His metaphors are sexual and pestilential. He speaks of "the cancer of liberalism." He refers to his detractors as "mercenaries, wolves, and thieves." He describes ecumenism as "confusion through bastardization." But he does not stop there: he makes his metaphor an elaborate conceit. "You cannot marry truth and error," he said in a sermon delivered in Lille in 1976, "because that is like adultery, and the child will be a bastard—a bastard rite for Mass, bastard sacraments, and bastard priests."

Bastard. *Bâtard.* How exciting, from the mouth of an archbishop. The world is serious; the truth is obvious; the lines are clear. The words suggest the kind of wrongheaded heroism that makes conservatives attractive when they seem to be directing the finest possible display of arms toward a target that is so remote from the real business of the world that even their hitting the target is no danger. The archbishop, for example, is a bug on Freemasonry. "They celebrate Black Masses and are in league with the devil." With the devil? Those square guys with their rings and pins that go to conventions and have scholarship funds? It is a French hobbyhorse, and it has the charm of a foreign obsession.

Another of Lefebvre's targets is what he calls "modernism." To most of us, it is as puzzling an enemy as Freemasonry. Who uses the word but literary scholars, speaking of Pound and Joyce? Modernism is one of those threats to the health of the Church that people stopped talking about in the late fifties. It used to mean, to the hierarchy of the clergy who were our particular guardians against it, liberalism, atheism, socialism, democracy. It led to communism; it enshrined the human reason. It said that truth was not absolute, was not objective. It believed in change, in progress, in metamorphosis through historical development. Modernism is not an identifiable movement: it is a term invented by the enemy, and so it has a shifting meaning. Pius X, pope from 1903 to 1914, wrote the definitive attack on modernism in his encyclical *Pascendi Dominici Gregis: On the Doctrine of the Modernists* (1907). But he did not name names. Lefebvre's society, the Society of St. Pius X, is named after this pope, who is also known as the "Scourge of Modernism."

If Pius X is Lefebvre's hero, his villains are Luther and, especially,

Descartes, Voltaire, and Rousseau. His view of history is centered on the French Revolution. The world, for Lefebvre, has steadily declined since 1789. He sees as evidence of the decadence of the recent papacy the last two popes' having spoken of the Declaration of the Rights of Man as a victory for humanity. I am struck by Lefebvre's insistence that it is the French Revolution that destroyed the world. It is not a position that has even occurred to me; it is not something I have ever heard anyone say. I am struck as well by the *Frenchness* of Lefebvre's position. In February 1977, when French followers of Lefebvre took over the church of Saint Nicholas du Chardonnet, they were led by priests crying, "Catholic and French forever."

Politically, Lefebvre is a monarchist. That position has, again, the charm of the impossible. What American can be threatened by the idea of a king? Kings are for cartoons, or caricature. Artists put crowns on Nixon to show his absurdity, to take away his sting. In conjuring Lefebvre, we begin to glimpse a man who loves tradition, and order, and certainty, and authority. He is a man who loves the pleasure of the hierarchy. And so his relationship with the Pope and the hierarchy of the Church is puzzling. For who, if not the Pope, represents authority? And in what body does hierarchy survive with greater health in our age than in the body of the Church?

Lefebvre's troubles with Church authorities began in 1974. In 1970, he was given official sanction to begin the Society of St. Pius X, a fraternity of priests whose bent was traditionalist. The Society was centered in Ecône, Switzerland. Soon a seminary was opened. Its style was strictly preconciliar. The Second Vatican Council emphasized the importance of the Church's coming to terms with the modern world by being open to it. The curriculum of Lefebvre's seminary, mostly in Latin, stressed Scholasticism, the system of Thomas Aquinas. The study of "modern thought" was forbidden. "Modern philosophies," the archbishop declared, "prepare the cult of man, and this is irreconcilable with Christianity." He asserted that a Catholic's concern must be with the world beyond.

Lefebvre's seminary was astonishingly successful. At a time when seminaries all over the world were closing for lack of candidates, Lefebvre had to turn people away. The news of the seminary's success reached Rome, and in November 1974, two ecclesiastics, one a former rector of Louvain University, were sent by the Vatican to investigate. Stories of that visit vary; some say that the former rector challenged important dogmas, such as the Resurrection of Christ; others hint that Lefebvre was told that, if he simply celebrated one Mass in the new rite while the emissaries were at the seminary, he would be left alone. In any case, the archbishop refused to say Mass the new way, and the clerics left in a huff, incensed at the archbishop's arrogance. Shortly after their departure, Lefebvre issued a strongly worded statement that stressed the seminary's loyalty to the Church while protesting against "neo-Modernist" and "neo-Protestant" tendencies that had become part of the Church since the Council.

In 1975, Pope Paul VI wrote Lefebvre two personal letters asking him to conform to the decisions of the Vatican Council regarding both the liturgical changes in the Mass (not only the change from Latin to the vernacular but important changes of diction whose implications were doctrinal, such as "This blood will be shed for you and for all men," formerly "This blood will be shed for you and for many") and the Church's new position on religious liberty and the necessity of separating Church and State.

Lefebvre did not even respond to the Pope's second letter. This was probably a tactical error, for the Vatican soon canceled its canonical endorsement of the seminary. However, although the Pope can forbid a bishop to ordain priests, as he has done in Lefebvre's case, he cannot make the ordinations invalid. Even the Pope cannot take a bishop's rank from him; the Pope, as the Bishop of Rome, is really only a "brother bishop." So although Lefebvre was suspended *a divinis*—that is, forbidden to exercise his priestly and episcopal function—the priests he ordains in defiance of the Church's order are considered by the Church true priests. In June 1976, Lefebvre ordained thirteen priests and thirteen subdeacons. It is estimated that these priests serve a congregation of sixty thousand: fifty thousand in Europe and ten thousand here.

The Vatican response to the ordination was dramatic. Pope Paul was harsh in his public condemnation of Lefebvre—far harsher, in fact, than he was to those who challenged the Church from the left. No bishop in this century has been censured as Lefebvre has been. Two paradoxes, then, emerge. One is that the Roman Catholic Church, traditional bastion of the right, seems far more comfortable with the left in this decade than it does with extreme conservatives. The other is that the only real schism to afflict the Church, despite the upheaval generated by the Second Vatican Council, comes not from the left, not from Dutch theologians with their Marxist sympathies and their relativist stand on morals and scriptural interpretation, but from a traditionalist French bishop who obeys too literally the dicta of the past popes. (The late Reverend Leonard Feeney started a similar right-wing schism in the fifties by upholding literal interpretation of the doctrine "Outside the Church there is no salvation.") Connected with this is the anomaly that a leader of the rebellion is one whose worldview indicates that he values obedience to authority and connection to tradition so highly that when he sees the Church breaking with tradition he breaks with the Church.

And so *l'incident Lefebvre* engages my imagination. It inspires in me an embarrassing richness of nostalgic fantasy: sung Gregorian Masses, priests in gold, the silence of Benediction, my own sense of sanctity as an eight-year-old carrying a lily among a hundred other eight-year-olds on Holy Thursday. The Society sparks the romance of a lost cause, perhaps the least dangerous romance of all. I imagine Lefebvre a gallant, clerical Charles Boyer, bathed in a clarifying bitterness. When I learn that he has dedicated a chapel in Oyster Bay, Long Island, I am interested. I imagine a new brand of American conservative priest. God knows there has been no dearth of conservative Catholic priests, but they have all been of the beefy John Wayne or the florid Bob Hope variety, hysterical about sex and communism, with a lousy sense of pulpit oratory. I imagine I will find in Oyster Bay a group of priests superbly educated on the French model—Latinists, Scholastics, with perhaps an expert on Palestrina in the group. But there is more: I grew up on Long Island among radically conservative Catholics, and there is a particular aptness for me in the coincidence of a movement that embodies what I have left and lost being placed in the physical world of my childhood. I feel I must write about these people; I so nearly could have been one of them.

I tell my friends I am going out there. My friends are worried. They kiss me on the forehead before I leave, as if they are afraid they will not see me again, as if they are seeing me off on a voyage

of indeterminate length and destination in a vessel whose seawor-
thiness they seriously doubt.

II

Oyster Bay is about half an hour from my mother's home in the
town where I grew up. My mother drives me to the train. She,
too, is nervous. "Don't get in over your head," she says, a piece
of advice she has continued to give me over the years, with an
astonishing lack of despair. My mother has railed against the
changes in the Mass every Sunday since 1964, but she wouldn't
dream of disobeying the Pope. "Who the hell do they think they
are?" is her comment on the Lefebvrists. My mother, who, like
the devil, can quote Scripture to her own ends—although, being
a Catholic, she does it rarely—draws herself up as she does for
such an occasion and says, " 'Behold thou art Peter and upon this
rock I shall build my church,' " and then, snorting as she does when
she is particularly sure of herself, says, "Who do they think they're
kidding?"

I get off the train at Oyster Bay and look around for a taxi. The
taxis are parked behind a trailer. I knock on the car door and tell
the man where I want to go. He is one of those Paul Robeson
types of black men by whom I feel entirely protected. He says,
"Isn't that one of those new churches people are always starting
up?" He tells me that the headquarters of the Society is on the
old Woodward estate. The Society of St. Pius X bought the estate
in 1977 for $250,000, anticipating that it would serve a regular
congregation of six hundred. Zoning regulations, however, prevent
the Society from offering public Mass there on Sunday; residents
feared problems with parking and traffic.

William Woodward, one of the Woolworth heirs, was shot on
his property in 1955 by his wife, who mistook him for a burglar.
The plot thickens like a custard; the romance clusters coalesce. I
imagine Simone Signoret pacing the grounds in a state of drunken
mourning. I am worried for the taxi driver. I imagine the place
surrounded by uniformed guards who will insult him. At the same
time, I have a wild desire to ask him to wait for me; I'm afraid I'll
never come out again.

At the door, I have my first disappointment. Just below the

threshold, there is a piece of yellow-orange indoor-outdoor carpeting. It is not the fabric of my fantasies, but I wipe my feet on it anyway, determined to ingratiate myself. The door is answered by a beautiful black woman, who does not meet my eye and tells me I am early. I do not think I am early, but I do not want to argue. I am probably congenitally incapable of arguing with anyone who might be a nun, and this woman is wearing a long black dress. Her hair is invisible under a blue scarf. She tells me to wait in the parlor, that she will get "Father." Women who work with priests tend to refer to the priest simply as "Father," the way nurses refer to physicians as "Doctor," as in "Doctor will be right with you."

Alone in the parlor, I feel instantly guilty, and yet determined, from the depths of my wickedness, to find some hidden clue before I speak to the priest. When he comes to the door, I am scanning the bookshelves for significant titles. It is not a good beginning.

I am shocked that this is the man they have elected to talk to me. He is no more than a boy, with that impossible, untouched, virginal complexion I expect on no one over sixteen. He is boyish, but it is a civilized boyishness. He offers to show me around. A measure of my alienation from the Church is that I have never spoken to a priest who was younger than I.

He takes me first, as propriety would demand, to the chapel. The stained-glass window is nineteenth-century and unremarkable, but there is a fine piece, a papal seat, which the priest tells me is fourteenth-century. The rug going up to the altar is a fake Oriental. I make a mental note to talk seriously to them about carpeting.

Father takes me down to the huge indoor tennis court, which he tells me they are using for storage. They have bought out a lot of religious-supply houses that, he says, were wiped out by the Second Vatican Council. When I see what they have bought out, I am nearly ill with disappointment: the tennis court is full of those mass-produced, entirely undistinguished, entirely undifferentiable statues that adorned every church built in America before 1955. Virgins on globes stand with serpents between their toes. Christ fingers his bleeding heart. It was precisely this kind of mediocrity that gave anyone with an eye second thoughts about the Church. He shows me stacks of missals they bought, missals that became useless when the Mass was said in English. He tells me they bought out the company that made St. Joseph Missals. I had one: I remember the glossy photographs beside appropriate feast days, the work of an artist who probably spent his secular life drawing for Ivory Snow. Before I know what I am saying I exclaim, "But St. Joseph Missals were the tackiest of any of them." "Tacky?" he says, looking puzzled. I am again disappointed; I cannot take seriously the spiritual life of anyone for whom "the tacky" is not a lively concept. "It's not the sort of thing we worry about," he says, walking up the stairs in front of me. "We are interested in building devotion in the hearts of the people." We return to the living room. We take out my tape recorder. It is clearly a procedure he is used to.

I ask about his childhood. Disappointingly, it sounds like the Catholic version of Andy Hardy's. He is from Detroit; his father is an accountant, his mother a housewife. Both parents went to Catholic colleges, his father to Notre Dame, his mother to a place called Marygrove. Marygrove: it sounds as if it had Jane Wyatt as a valedictorian. He always wanted to be a priest, he said, except for a vague flirtation with being a fireman. He says his home environment was very cultured. I perk up. His mother, he says, listened to the Metropolitan Opera on Saturdays. I slump back down in my seat. I ask him to describe his early experiences of spirituality. He is not particularly good on spirituality, but then I've never met a priest who was. There is an interesting aspect to the involvement of a man of twenty-six in such a movement as Lefebvre's; the Second Vatican Council began before this young man was in his teens. He was never even an adolescent in the old Church. Only a child.

In discussing the makeup of the Society, Father tells me there are few intellectuals in the American branch, although they make up a significant proportion of the European membership. And he talks about the beauty of the universality of the Church, how its appeal transcends class differences. He speaks of how one of his classmates in the seminary, an Oxford graduate who teaches the Spiritual Exercises of Saint Ignatius in several languages, embraced "the common," in the Church, for its vitality. It is an image that appeals to me strongly: Chaucer and his Miller in the same pew. It is a particularly European image, for in America the best and the brightest have left the Church early or used it only as a metaphor. And I am pulled in by the priest's discussion of "the Catholic spirit." Every Catholic, he says, receives a Catholic sense at Baptism, which enables him to distinguish what is Catholic from what is not. It is this sense, he says, that has brought many people into the Society. In worship, the Catholic sense is the sublime sense of rendering honor and glory to God using all the beauty of the ages. The Catholic sense is an understanding of human nature, or "nature baptized." Because God is a god of nature. He wants us to use natural things as a path to salvation. Since Adam and Eve sinned through material creation, he says, it is through material creation that we must get back to God. And this, he says, is something that Protestants do not understand.

I think of the difference between a modest Romanesque chapel in Italy and a New England Congregationalist church. I think of the temperance movement. And I am ready to agree with him, because it is a game I was taught to excel in: that trick of sheep and goats. Even today, I think of certain things as being quintessentially Protestant: Fig Newtons, trust funds, slipper socks. It is with some sense of personal shame that I let him go on.

The Catholic spirit, he says, is plugged into the Spirit of the Universe because it is based on the Natural Law. I recognize the Thomistic phrase. The Catholic spirit is a redeemed human spirit that recognizes the value of natural things and blesses them. It is a spirit best expressed in the Latin countries, he says, with their love of dance and the good things of life. Again, it is an agreeable fantasy: the world as a wedding, the family dance. He says it is the Providence of God that the Italians have been chosen to run the Church. Imagine if the French were in charge, he says. There would be a drama every minute. Or the Germans; they would never have got started. I like him for his cosmopolitan ethnocentrism; I have always felt that the hasty generalization is one of the real pleasures of civilized discourse.

Afraid of being lulled by dreams of Napoli by moonlight, I decide to press him on the hard issues. On sex he is not bad at all, or at least he is not simplistic. He says that the focus of the Church has always been on the sanctity of sex, on acknowledging sexuality but insisting that sexual energy be used in a more "sublime" way. So delighted am I to hear someone using the word "sublime" that the argument seems valid to me. A celibate, he says, concentrates that sexual energy on his personal love of God. He speaks of the erotic imagery of the medieval mystics and how it could make many an Irish pastor blush. I am impressed now; he's a long way from the chaplain of my high school, who referred to French kissing, that King Charles' Head among Catholic adolescents, as "swapping spit."

We move from sex to politics. He says that although the arch-bishop is a monarchist, he, the young priest, feels comfortable with the American system of "enlightened capitalism." I ask if he is interested in placing members of the Society in positions of political power. He says no, because the danger of corruption is too great. "Our position as regards politics," he says, "is trying to establish the Kingship of Our Lord Jesus Christ on earth. Archbishop Le-febvre says that this is the major issue that separates him from the Vatican . . . [who] feel that it is out of date now, not a practical goal, and the thing that you've got to work for is a better mankind. . . . We believe that laws should reflect the Natural Law and that the Church should be given a privileged place in the nation. And that's why Archbishop Lefebvre has spoken favorably about people like Franco and a couple of dictators in South America, either from the point of view of their establishing law and order or, in regards to Franco, in terms of their preserving some modicum of Catholic life in the nation as such."

Our honeymoon is clearly over, and while I am out of love, we move quickly to the question of religious liberty. Lefebvre feels that the Council's proclaiming the doctrine of religious liberty was a clear case of heresy. "We do not believe that anyone has the absolute right in God's eyes to be wrong. . . . Error has no rights," the priest says. I ask how one determines error. "It's a question of faith," he says. "What our Catholic faith tells us, we believe to be right." I suggest the paradox of that position in light of the Society's defiance of the authority of the Church. "But," he says, "they're not the Church." I hint that his reasoning is ever so slightly circular. Not circular but linear, he says: If the Church has uni-formly taught one thing throughout history and then suddenly changes its mind, then it is the change that is the aberration. It is such a perfectly simplistic view of history that I do not ask him to pursue it. For essentially the basis of Lefebvre's position is his view of history, a highly fanciful conviction that the world before the Enlightenment was an orderly, harmonious family of colorful but always essentially docile children over which Holy Mother Church ruled, firmly but benignly. This vision is as much an article of faith to the Lefebvrists as their belief in the Assumption of the Blessed Virgin; that they do not *call* it dogma is entirely beside the point.

I ask Father what he would do with people who would not conform to the teachings of the Catholic Church: what, for example, would he do with Jews? He assures me that he would protect them, as many of the medieval popes did. What about Protestants? I ask him. Protestants are different, he says; they are heretics. And what, I ask him, should be done with heretics? "The way of dealing with them in the Middle Ages I think was good. They were more or less removed from the scene." "How?" I ask. "By being executed," he replies, with perfect equanimity. "If you are to consider the immense harm, the eternal harm that we believe can be done by the spreading of heresy, then to kill someone for the crime of heresy is perfectly acceptable." I cough uneasily into my microphone; some of my best friends are heretics. He notes my unease and goes on to say, "Today, however, without changing the basic principle, we wouldn't go about it in the same way, simply because we have too many heretics today. . . . So we certainly maintain the same principle, that that's the way it should be done, but nonetheless, as a simple point of prudence, adapting ourselves to the time where we are today, for us to actually mount a campaign to establish the Church as the one true Church and to burn heretics would be absurd today."

I am somewhat relieved. But not very.

In a moment, I have my first vision of the nice boy from Detroit struggling with his identity as the protégé of a French extremist. He says he has some trouble with French criticism of the American system, their calling our Constitution "Masonic," for example. The Church, he asserts, has done far better in America, at least in temporal terms, than anywhere else in the world, far better than in France, with its history of anticlericalism and confiscation of Church property. Is there some dissatisfaction with the foreign masters? Four times in our conversation he has criticized the French: they are dirty, they are Jansenistic, they love drama excessively, they cavil over philosophical points at dinner. Does this boy really feel at ease with a system that says he should want to execute nice Mrs. Jones next door—who gave him oatmeal cookies and angel food cake—simply because she is a Presbyterian? He notes the contradiction before I do and tries to defend it by pointing to the prosperity of the American Church. He does not convince me. I wonder if he is convinced. But I do not like to press him; he is such a nice boy; he has said too much already; he makes me feel as if I'm smoking three cigarettes at once; he makes me feel like Tallulah Bankhead.

We go over the old faith-reason argument. I shamelessly drag in Galileo; he shamelessly defends the position of the Church. He asserts that the "little people" want to be told what to do in Confession, that they want to be judged, they do not wish to make judgments for themselves. I think of Dostoevsky's Grand Inquisitor, who asserts that Christ has only made people unhappy by giving them freedom when what they want is miracle, mystery, and authority. Father goes on talking about the little people. We have ceased to surprise each other. My questions are beginning to lose energy. I ask him one that I think is a gift, a throwaway so he can end on a good note. Already fumbling with the lock on my briefcase, I ask him if the preservation of the great artistic and cultural heritage of the Church is an important priority to his Society. I am sure of his answer. But in a moment, I am jolted out of my careless lethargy. "No, it's not," he says, in his considered, good boy's tone. "In fact, Archbishop Lefebvre looks a little askance at the art of the Renaissance. He finds that to be the expression of a pagan mentality that's entering here, not the Christian spirit of the Middle Ages, but a pagan spirit. Especially the ceiling of the Sistine Chapel."

I am glad it is my last question. The answer gives me a headache. Its logic is so perfectly loony, and yet, in its looniness, so consistent, that I find difficulty in formulating a response. He ushers in the laymen.

I can hardly bring myself to ask questions of the first woman they send me. One of the penalties of upward mobility is a sense of guilty indebtedness to the old neighborhood. And this woman could have lived on my block; she could have been a friend of my mother's. Her hairstyle means she still uses rollers, and I see her in rollers as I speak to her, in a supermarket, or cooking frozen peas and minute steaks. I see her going quietly, not without considerable kindness, through her life, and it seems utterly wrong that she should have made some sort of decision that would place her like this before me, a smart aleck with a microphone, saying, "Tell me about your life."

But I want to know what made her do it, leave the Church, for women like this have traditionally looked to the parish church as the center of the community. It is a leaving that requires courage, not only social but spiritual, for this woman has been brought up believing that to leave the Church is to give up salvation. "Tell me how you came to be here," I ask, the least pointed and perhaps most inadequate question of my day.

She doesn't want to tell me her name—"in case I say something stupid." She incapacitates me as an interviewer; I want to make up answers for her; I want her to look good.

She says it was not her idea to come to St. Pius at first; it was her husband's. Her husband brought her son, because he was dissatisfied with the education, particularly the religious education, the child was getting at the local parish school. He was no longer taught the Baltimore Catechism, and when he was about to make his First Communion, the parents were told that the children would not have to go to Confession because it frightened them and anyway children were not capable of sin. The woman believes neither that children are frightened by Confession nor that they are incapable of sin. Her son's First Communion made concrete many of the woman's dissatisfactions with the new Church. The sisters who were preparing the child for First Communion asked him to draw a picture of what he believed the table looked like at the Last Supper. The child included a bowl of fruit. "Now, to me, that's not the Last Supper," says the woman. It bothered her significantly. She was even more disturbed that in her older son's religion class the students were asked to listen to the song "The Sounds of Silence." "I happen to know that comes from the movie *The Graduate*. That's no movie for a religion class."

I ask her if she misses her old parish, and she says no, that she's very involved here, cooking for the priests, helping out in the school. I ask her if she's lost friends as a result of her decision, and she says, "Not really." It's just, she tells me, that they don't see the people they used to see as much, because "it's bound to come up." She offers to get me more coffee. I carry the tray into the kitchen for her. It's all I can do not to help with the dishes.

The second layman is a man, who looks, thank God, less vulnerable. He is an engineer. The trouble with all these people is that they all remind me of somebody I grew up with: he is all my cousins who went into the army after high school and put themselves through college at night. He doesn't understand how anyone could fail to believe the Bible is literally true: "There's so much evidence, all the archaeology." He doesn't understand how the girls in his office, "nice girls, smart girls, well-educated girls," can believe in abortion. It's common sense, he says; a baby is a baby. He is not worried about the birth control issue, because the Japanese have invented a new thermometer that can pinpoint ovulation to the second. He says he came to the Society because the new Church didn't breed any respect, because he wanted a place where his children could learn morals and the Catholic Church was becoming too wishy-washy. I ask him what he wants for his children. He says, "I'd like them to have their heads on straight." When I ask him what that means, he says, "Common sense." I ask if he would be in the Society if he didn't have children, and he says he doesn't know. I ask him if it was emotionally painful for him to leave the established Catholic Church, and he says, "Not really." I speak to his son, who is ten. They have both come to the headquarters for the day to help out with some of the repairs. They are crazy about each other, this father and son, namesakes, tool-carriers. He is a nice man, with his irrational belief in common sense, with his upside-down devotion to science. He offers to give me a ride to the train.

I understand these two laypersons' decision to come to the Society. They are frightened by change, they want a life for their children that they, as parents, can comprehend, a life that has something to do with their own childhood. They were raised in a tradition that told them they must distrust human reason and their own powers of decision, a tradition that provided them with answers before they thought of the questions, with a ritual full of mystery that promised never to change. The Grand Inquisitor was right about them: freedom did make them unhappy. They believe it will make their children unhappy. They want solidity; they want the deep richness of a past that is not theirs only. They want to be told what to do. They have come to the right place. What's more, they have found community. They spend their weekends with each other, cooking, fixing the wiring, working in the book-store. They all seem very happy.

I have more difficulty placing the black woman who answered the door. I walk into the kitchen and ask if I can speak to her. She bustles about, covering a canned ham with foil, putting a light under the frozen carrots. I ask why she is here. She says, "It's like falling in love, isn't it? You can't explain it. It just happens."

Her face is, of all the faces I have seen that day, the most compelling. She is a woman in her thirties; she has never married; she was a practical nurse; she was in the army. We talk inconse-quentially; my tape runs out. We both laugh and agree not to put in another. She tells me that I do not look as if I am at peace and that she will pray for me. She asks me to call her and have lunch sometime. I say I would like that. She is the only person I have spoken to who seems to attach any emotion to her religious life, and she has met in me for that reason a singular hunger. Or perhaps it is simply that as a type she is less familiar to me, and I grant her a grace I deny to those I grew up amongst. At the door we embrace. There are tears in my eyes, but she does not meet my eyes, and I am glad. I do not want her to see me.

III

The next day, my mother drives me to the Mass that one of the St. Pius priests will say at the VFW Hall in Hicksville, where there are less prohibitive zoning laws and no neighbors worrying about the traffic. I ask my mother if she wants to go inside with me to hear the Mass in Latin, which is one of the things she keeps saying she wants to do before she dies. "No, thank you," she says. "I'm interested in saving my soul, if you don't mind."

On the table outside the room where the Mass will be held there are religious articles—gunmetal plastic rosaries, medals, statues—and scores of religious booklets and hardcover books. Many of the publications are by or about Archbishop Lefebvre and the Society, but I am surprised to see some remnants of an old genre I had thought extinct: titles like "Clean Love in Courtship" and "Why Squander Illness?" I am riveted by the section on the stigmata: "The Stigmata and Modern Science," "Padre Pio" (an Italian stig-matist who lost some clout for predicting that the world would end in 1952). And "Theresa Neumann." Theresa Neumann is one of those in jokes that Catholics recognize each other by: a German stigmatist whose career of illness and suffering made Job look like a malingerer. I read about her early life while waiting for the Mass to begin:

> Though there is no record of her having made a vow of virginity, there is proof that she had firm unshakable determination to remain a virgin dating back to her childhood. She never attended a dance and never allowed any young man the slightest familiarity. Once when working on the hayloft over the barn, she made a perilous jump of about twelve feet down to the threshing floor rather than allow a young man to touch her. It is quite possible that the trouble that manifested itself in the spine later on was due in part to this jump. . . . Her intention of entering a convent dates at least back to her fifteenth year. When, in spite of her declared intention of doing so, young men still persisted in pressing their suit for her hand in marriage she determined to end it once and for all, and the example of St. Thomas can be quoted in defense of the measures she took: she gave one of these suitors such a castigation with the goad she used on the oxen in the plough that she was never troubled again.

I daresay.

Watching the other people praying, I try to get some sense of them as a crowd. They could be any working-class group, a collection of bowlers or steelworkers and their wives. No one is wearing anything strikingly fashionable. I am surprised to see only two cripples in the congregation; I had imagined that people whose bodies had betrayed them would cling to some form of ritual continuity. All the women are wearing hats or kerchiefs or that bizarre Catholic fashion of the fifties, the chapel veil, a narrow circlet of black or white lace that covered the minimum amount of female head canonically acceptable. Ages vary, but I would say that if there is one group more represented than any other it is the fifty-to-sixty-year-olds. There are a few children, but not so many as I expected. A disproportionate number of them have red hair.

The priest begins the Mass, his back to us. I had forgotten one of the features of the old Mass: its inaudibility. I pick up some phrases, but the altar boys spend most of their time, it seems, with their foreheads to the floor, which does nothing for the acoustics. I am not bathed in a broth of bittersweet nostalgia; rather I feel vaguely frightened. And I remember feeling vaguely frightened during the Masses of my childhood. Perhaps it was the sense of exclusion, or the sense that something monumental was about to take place. Or perhaps the combination bred terror. The green silk back of this young priest stirs poignant memories, but I am deprived of the pleasure of remembered words because he speaks too low for me to hear him. I remember now that most priests did.

It is the Sunday before Lent, and the priest, a different one from yesterday's but equally boyish, speaks about the need for penance. He reminds the congregation that they are responsible for the sins that crucified Christ. It is the Protestants, he tells them, who do not believe in penance; it is the Protestants who have always tried to underplay Lent. There is no sense of penance in the modern Catholic Church, he says; the idea that making penance voluntary would make it more meritorious was another one of their modern ideas that backfired, because now no one does penance. He reminds the congregation that *they* are required under pain of sin to keep the preconciliar fast.

Again, it is an appealing idea: lean Lent, the pleasure of austerity. But no one looks very austere; and I suspect that their Lenten meals will be largely made up of fish sticks and Velveeta; not *omelettes aux fines herbes* but deviled eggs. I reproach myself for what any spiritual adviser before or after the Reformation would have called a false sense of spiritual values. But this Mass seems no more serious to me than the new Masses, where the mystery of Transubstantiation is sung to the tune of "Five Hundred Miles." My desire for flippancy is as strong here as there. If the modern mode is a studied casualness, the offhandedness of this Mass is no less bleak. It is not solemn, and I am not drawn in.

I have made arrangements to drive into the city with yet another priest. This one is older; I am relieved to see that he had a bad shave. At least he needed one. But he is, of the three of them, the least cheerful, the most suspicious of me. He has written a book called *Conspiracy Against God and Man*. I bought it, along with the pamphlets on the stigmatists. It is published by the Western Islands Press, the publishers of the *John Birch Society Blue Book.* The thesis of this priest's book is that the Communist conspiracy is only the latest in a series of conspiracies whose major motive is to destroy the Church. The conspiracy flowered brilliantly in the seventeenth and eighteenth centuries among a Bavarian sect called the Illuminati, who were an important influence on the Freemasons, particularly the French Freemasons. And we all know what the Freemasons caused: the downfall of history, the French Revolution, which has led to the shambles of modern life:

It is all too apparent that we are engaged in a deadly war for the very survival of civilization itself. For the spread of collectivism is not merely the result of a natural tendency of decay, but it is purposefully fostered in a concerted attempt to wipe out all opposition by reducing men to helpless wards of the State, thereby undermining the very natural law which is "written in their hearts." While the "new morality," which is amorality, is pictured as a great advance for modern man, true morality is subtly scorned when it is not openly attacked. And this is being done not merely in institutions run by a pagan Establishment, but also in seminaries—both Catholic and Protestant. Error is held up as truth; truth is mocked as narrowness; logic is scorned as coldness and insensibility; contradictions are peddled as mysteries. Family life is undermined and property rights increasingly denied. When not mocked, patriotism is often used against the good of the people, who are duped into believing that it means loyalty to a man, an Administration or a party, rather than loyalty to the principles that are embodied in our Constitution. Naturalism, the religion of pantheism is fed to us in the name of modern theology, while degrading ideologies are given to us as philosophy.

It is an energetic diction, and the book is a strange mix of old Birch hobbyhorses and strangely foreign obsessions. Most American conservatives would not devote more than half a book to an attack on Freemasonry. The author even apologizes for the attack: "We do not wish to offend anti-Communist Masons, many of whom are among 'our staunchest patriots.' " And when trying to make the point that most of the discontent among the poor that is used as a justification for social change is simply whipped up by the left, he uses the example, not of Vietnam, but of Algeria.

The priest asks me if I mind sitting in the back of the car. It's half an hour before I realize why: it is because I am a woman. I also realize that I am probably the only person writing an article of this nature who would get into the back seat of a car without asking why, simply because I was told to do so by a priest. *"Numquam solus cum sola."* It is an old rule: a priest must never be alone with a woman. Priests were not supposed, in the old days, to sit in the front seat of the car with a woman, but it was always a rule to be obeyed at the discretion of the particular priest. Some ignored the rule; some put even their mothers in the back seat.

Our conversation covers most of the same ground as the talk with yesterday's priest. There are no new responses; there is no real energy in his voice until we get to the Midtown Tunnel and he discovers he has left his wallet home. He turns and looks at me for the first time. "Do you have any money?" he asks, a Brooklyn boy, someone I might have gone out with, but only once. The kind of boy who wears white socks and black shoes and forgets his wallet. I hand him the toll like Rosalind Russell, as if it is nothing. He prefers that I do not go into the dark of the parking garage with him. I wait for him on the sidewalk. When he comes out of the darkness, he asks me—is that a threat in his voice?—why I don't come back to the True Church. I tell him I'm thinking about it. Over the weeks, I think of little else.

IV

I do not get time to visit the school the Society has started until nearly three weeks later. The school is housed in a building rented from the Lutheran Church: a concrete irony. The principal, whom I met at Mass, shows me around. When we enter classrooms, children leap to their feet and say, "Good morning, Miss Gordon." It makes me quite nervous, all this leaping and recognition. When I mention this to one of the priests, he says, "You soon learn to get used to it."

The principal's quick eye catches a boy in the corner. "Mr. Finnegan, do you know you're not wearing your uniform tie?" Mr.

Finnegan knows. He is covered with a confusion that is dangerously familiar to me: it brings back the terror of the time I did not wear my uniform shoes and had to spend the day in the principal's office, of the time I could not win the statue of Saint Joseph, even though I had the highest average in the class, because I had forgotten to have my report card signed. Am I endowing the principal's voice with a brutality not its own?

We go into the ninth-grade English class, and I am impressed by the teacher, who speaks to her students of Dickens with the passion of someone who has taught less than two years. At the end of class, she initials everyone's assignment sheet to make sure they have copied down the homework. In the teachers' room we talk about the excitement of teaching literature, about Shakespeare, about Jan Kott. She is a lovely woman, but I am sure she worries about her legs. She is twenty-four and lives with her parents. She is very proud of her father, a New York cop. I confuse her literary comprehension with liberalism, and I confess my unease about a curriculum determined by a bunch of John Birchers. She stiffens. "The John Birch Society has been very much maligned," she says. She tells me about a book that points out that the whole country is run by groups we don't even know the name of. I nod. The bell rings. She leaves for her next class.

Three tenth-grade girls want to interview me for the school paper. They are wearing uniforms almost identical to the one I wore in tenth grade. They ask me questions about being a writer. I ask them why they came to St. Pius School. The three of them concur: It was because their parents wanted them to. All of their parents formerly attended a Latin Mass at a church in Westbury run by the Reverend Gommar DePauw. There is quite a bit of bad blood between Father DePauw and the Lefebvrists. DePauw puts out a periodical called *The Sounds of Truth and Tradition,* whose logo is "TNT." The one issue I read contained a virulent attack on Lefebvre and his movement. Apparently these girls' parents were drummed out of Father DePauw's church and came to St. Pius. The girls say they are happy to be in this school because in the public schools where they went there was no discipline; one girls tells me students smoked marijuana in the middle of class and the teachers did nothing. One of the girls admits that she missed her old high school at first, missed the variety of students there.

But now, she says, she feels very much at home: all the students are good friends; they spend a lot of time with each other; they find they don't have much in common with the students they used to go to school with. I ask them if they were lonely in their neighborhoods. They say no; they have each other.

I ask them what they want to be when they grow up. One girl doesn't want to go to college; she says she'd be happy working as her sister does, in an insurance company. But one girl wants to be a writer, and I commit against her one of the worst acts of child abuse: I see myself in her. I tell her she must go to a good college; I tell her that she must work hard at writing, that she must look at things carefully. I am really saying that I want her to be like me, not like her English teacher, not like the principal. But she is not unhappy; she is probably no worse educated than she would be in a public school. I do not tell her to keep in touch with me. I do not know if she would like to. As I leave the classrooms, I touch the paper cutouts of the Crucifixion, of the Stations of the Cross, and I wonder of these children: What will become of them?

They are not what I was looking for, these people on Long Island. I was looking for miracle, mystery, and authority; I was interested in style, in spirituality, in a movement that combined the classical ideal of the Gregorian Mass with the romantic image of the foreign life, suggesting illegitimacy. I had imagined a group of thoughtful, saddened communicants led by priests devoted to a vision of sanctity made fecund by the grandeur of the past, anguished pastors reluctantly accepting their place outside the arms of Holy Mother. But it is difficult to coordinate the drama of the French archbishop with the reality of his American flock, reading their St. Joseph Missals and their pamphlets about stigmatists, sending their children to a school whose curriculum is determined by a man who teaches industrial arts in a public high school, where the children will be chivied about uniform ties. I can only make the connection in terms that are quintessentially American. I see now that what these people, deeply American in their longings, really want, both priests and laity, is not the Middle Ages but the 1950s, not Thomas Aquinas but Bishop Sheen, not Philip the Good but Joe McCarthy. Lefebvre's vision is distinctly European, but the fruits of it in this country are a puzzling mixture, a populist expression of an aristocratic ideal, a colonial adaptation of an Old World mode, as unsettling as those photographs one sees of Indians wearing top hats.

America reacts to invaders by ingesting them; perhaps the most predictable course for the Society will be a hectic florescence followed by a sullen homogenization. Perhaps not. The Society provides for its people community and orthodoxy, the distinction of marginality, the allure of a foreign rule. And it promises to precisely the people most frightened by change that they need not change again, that they have found a home, the house they were born in, the Church of their childhood.

But it is not the Church of my childhood, and it is certainly not the Church of any adult to whom I bear even a distant similitude. If one, through a combination of instinct and training, hungers for the past, for the texture and substance of an age perhaps less slapdash than our own, then one is tempted by an order that suggests that the present is not all we have. But the pleasure of a world pared down is an equivocal one; there is, at the end, too much left out in deference to simplicity, consistency; even, perhaps, peace of mind.

Finally, it will not do, the image of a prelate who cannot love his age, supported by priests in love with theories of conspiracy, priests who could have been my brothers, followed by a congregation in love with virgin martyrs and rote devotion. And finally, it is a relief to be on the train, knowing I will not have to see them again. But there is loss as well, or more properly disappointment, as if I had got off the *métro* looking for Balmain's and found myself in Kresge's.

-"I Can't Stand Your Books": A Writer Goes Home

A friend of mine who is intensely interested in the fulfillment of immigrant fantasies recently asked me if my family was proud of me. I was able to say with perfect frankness that they were not, that except for my mother, one cousin, and one aunt, they considered me an embarrassment or a lost soul. This led me to wonder about the connections among my family's reaction to me, the place of the writer in the Irish-American community, and the faintness of the Irish-American voice in the world of letters.

Let me begin with my uncle's funeral. My uncle was a lovable man, heroic even, in a way particularly Irish Catholic. He was the most nearly silent man I've ever known and perhaps the kindest. Like many Irishmen, he married late; he devoted his young manhood to family responsibilities. When he was forty, he met a young, beautiful, intelligent woman—a semiprofessional tennis player, a Wellesley graduate who shared his passion for sports. In the early 1950s, she had done the daring thing of touring Europe alone on a motorcycle; she did the equally daring thing of wearing pants to our family gatherings. When my uncle announced to his mother that he was to marry this woman, my grandmother took to her bed for a week. Only with his wife's encouragement, my uncle finished his teaching degree and, at forty-five, got his first full-time job. But the real focus of his life was supporting her in her career as a

tennis player; he coached her, accompanied her all over the country
to tennis tournaments. They were perhaps the most happily married couple I have ever known, but I never saw them touch or
even stand near each other, or address to each other an intimate
word. My aunt became, in time, an ardent feminist, and my uncle
accompanied her to ERA rallies. This shy, silent man stood in
groups of women and carried signs saying ERA TODAY. When I
went to his house the day after the funeral, attached to his refrig-
erator with a magnet was a list of members of Congress who needed
to be written to in order to enlist their support for the ERA.

I loved my uncle very much; so did everyone else who stood
before his coffin. We all wept. I held my baby son in my arms and
wept, leaning my cheek against his for comfort. Who could imagine
a situation in which an attack was less expected, less appropriate?
Yet one of my uncles chose this time to say to me: "I just want
to tell you I can't stand your books. None of us can. I tried the
first one; I couldn't even get past the first chapter. The second one
I couldn't even get into; I didn't even want to open it up. I didn't
even buy it; I wouldn't waste the money."

Well, it would have been easy to laugh, but I didn't laugh; or
easy to say, "A prophet is always without honor in his own family."
But who is with honor in my family? Not my cousin the doctor.
Not my cousin the businessman, with his million-dollar house. The
honored person in the family is my cousin the nun. She walked
into the funeral parlor; if the family could have carried her on their
shoulders, they would have. She came up to me, after a while, and
took my hand. "Mary," she said, "I just feel I need to tell you that
I think your books are dreadful. I know that many people find
them good, but I don't. They're just too worldly for me. Of course,
I do understand that a lot of hard work went into them." Later,
she said to one of my aunts, "She didn't really want to put all that
sex in those books. The publishers made her."

They all thought my books were dirty. This brings out an aspect
central and important to the Irish character: sexual puritanism. It
is different in its flavor from Anglo-Saxon puritanism, and also
from the French Jansenism that is its historical source. There is
nothing thin-blooded about it and nothing of the merely finicky.
Because it exists alongside a general sense of the enjoyableness of
life, a love of liquor and horses, a sense of the importance of

hospitality and of the beauty of the earth. And it lives side by side with a robust and lively wit. It would be easy to say that the source of it is the Roman Catholic Church; for certainly the folklore of the Celts abounds with heroes, male and female, who shy away from nothing in the body's life. Yet it is not only Catholicism that explains it. The Italians are Catholic, and the French, and the Spanish: these races are emblems in the popular mind for warm-bloodedness, for sexiness, and for romance. Of all Catholic countries, only Ireland came up with men who believed what the Church told them about sex. Only in Ireland are the churches filled with a near-even mix of male and female. Only in Ireland would a man married at thirty be thought of as marrying young.

I think that what is at the root of Irish puritanism is a profound fear of exposure, shared by both men and women in an oddly equal degree. "Silence, exile and cunning," said Stephen Dedalus, is the only route to survival. Cunning, of course, is understandable: it is the coin of exchange of any oppressed group. The wily slave, the tricky peasant, is a staple of every folklore in the world. Silence, too, is another form of protective coloration not unknown by the oppressed. But exile, the ultimate, most deeply willed concealment of identity, is the most singular part of Joyce's formula. To be an exile, to choose exile, is to put oneself among a group of people who will always have to struggle to understand one, is to put oneself in a situation where one's gestures are not readily legible, where one is not given away by a word, a look, a tone of voice. To be permanently in exile is to be permanently in disguise; it is an extreme form of self-protection. And self-protection is an Irish obsession.

Irish sexual puritanism is only a metaphor, as it is really in all of us, for an entire ontology. I am convinced that this desire to hide for self-protection is at the core of a great deal of Irish behavior—behavior that was shipped successfully from Ireland to America. This is, of course, another reason why the Irish, a people so imbued with the power of the Word, do not value writers in their midst. A writer speaks out loud; a writer reveals. And to reveal, for the Irish, is to put oneself and the people one loves in danger.

In *That Most Distressful Nation*, Andrew Greeley says of the Irish-American terror of standing out that "if brilliance and flair are counterproductive, the slightest risk-taking beyond the limits of approved career and personal behavior is unthinkable. Art, music, literature, poetry, theater, to some extent even academia, politics of any variety other than the traditional, are all too risky to be considered. The two most devastating things that can be said to the young . . . Irishman who attempts to move beyond these rigid norms are 'Who do you think you are?' and 'What will people say?' "

The second of these two questions, "What will people say?" is used by nearly all but the most courageous parents from every ethnic group. But the first question is, I think, a rarer one. It is, after all, *the* ontological question. "Who do you think you are?" The implied answer, or the implied right answer for the American Irish, is "I'm not much." This answer contains the Augustinian worldview that so permeates the Irish; it isn't mere immigrant inferiority. "I'm not much" doesn't mean "I'm not much, but the WASPs are a lot." It means that the human condition isn't much, and anyone who thinks it is is merely a fool. And better, far better, to be invisible than to be a fool. And the proper response to the fool is ridicule.

Irish ridicule is different, for example, from its black counterpart. "Black ridicule," Andrew Greeley says, "is an exercise in verbal skill, designed to display virtuosity in the ability to be outrageous. Irish ridicule is intended to hurt, to give as much pain as is necessary to keep each other at a distance." I agree with Father Greeley that Irish ridicule is intended to hurt, but it is also a balked expression of love. It is also a desire to protect, or at least to urge self-protection upon the victim. It is the stick to beat in front of the stray member of the herd, to urge him or her back to his or her proper place, the place of hiding. It is a language whose purpose is two levels of concealment. It conceals the speaker's concern or his overt hostility, and it urges the victim to conceal himself or herself. The Irish are masters at the language of concealment.

Why this obsession with concealment? It is not simply the manifestation of the fear of an oppressed group. Certainly Jews have been at least as oppressed as the Irish, to say nothing of the blacks. Yet neither American Jews nor American blacks have shown the Irish reluctance for self-expression. One understands the factors that have enabled the Jews to turn their pain into literature. I spoke with Richard Fein, the Yiddish scholar and translator, who suggested some reasons for the extraordinary articulateness of the Jews. The Jews, he said, are a people brought up on critical commentary upon a text; it is natural that this process would transform itself to fiction. The high literacy rate among immigrant Jews, the Yiddish press's policy of translating and serializing the best of European fiction, the presence of intellectuals—all factors the Irish miss in their experience—can account for the audibility of the Jewish-American experience, the silence of the Irish. But blacks had none of the advantages of Jewish immigrants, and their advantages were far fewer than those of the Irish. Their literacy rate was much lower than among the Irish; they were even more cut off from ancient poetic traditions than the Irish, and intellectuals were certainly much rarer among them. Yet from the time of slavery onward, blacks have expressed their sense of pain and injustice in language: the poetry of spirituals, of the blues, nowhere has its counterpart in anything Irish. There is no Irish Langston Hughes, no Irish Jean Toomer, no Irish Richard Wright, no Irish James Baldwin, no Irish Toni Morrison. The great linguistic facility of the Irish restricted itself in this country to two forms: popular journalism and political speeches.

I have been for some time puzzled, unable to explain why the country of the bards, the country of Goldsmith and Swift, of Maria Edgeworth and Oscar Wilde and George Bernard Shaw, above all the country of Yeats and Joyce, the country of O'Casey and Synge, of O'Connor and O'Faolain, produced so little in its American literary branch. It would make good sense to teach a course in the American Jewish Literary Experience, or in American Black Literature. But a course in American Irish Literature would take up barely half a semester. You could begin, if you were a loose constructionist, with O'Neill and Fitzgerald; but the majority of their work would have to be excluded. You could go then to James T. Farrell, whose *Studs Lonigan* recorded—with vigor but, to my mind, with sloppiness that borders on the dime novel—the experience of the Chicago Irish in the 1920s and 30s. You would have to jump, then, to J. F. Powers's brilliant tales of fifties priests. Then you could go on to William Alfred's *Hogan's Goat*, to Elizabeth Cullinan, to Maureen Howard and William Kennedy. After that, there would be nowhere to go.

What happened to make the Irish so comparatively silent? In part, it is the lack of an audience. Whereas American Jews and American blacks seem patently exotic, American Irish, seemingly more familiar, are less interesting to the book-buying American public—largely WASPs and Jews. And, I think, the silence of the American Irish is connected to the singular relationship the Irish have to the English language, a relationship heightened by the experience of immigration. The Irish have been, for hundreds of years, a colonized people. But they were colonized by a people who did not look so physically different from themselves. And the colonizers conquered the land, subjected the people, and imposed their own language without succeeding in eroding national identity. What an odd set of circumstances this is! As a working language, Irish was lost to the Irish by the nineteenth century. It ceased quickly to be the language of commerce and the language of government, but it ceased as well to be the family tongue. And so Irish poetry was lost to the majority of the Irish. But the memory of the figures embodied in the poetry was not.

The English could not conquer the racial identity of the Irish for the added reason of the strength of their Catholic faith. But in terms of language, the very strength of Catholicism in Ireland created another kind of colonization. For the sacred language, the language of ritual, was not Irish or even English: it was Latin. And by the time of the late Middle Ages, the Irish character of the liturgy was lost to the Irish; they had become successfully Romanized.

Despite this double linguistic colonization, the Irish maintained a lively oral tradition, of tales involving fantastical creatures, heroes and saints. All that was there for Yeats and the other Celtic twilighters to draw upon. But it was not what Joyce drew upon; it interested him no more than the price of potatoes and considerably less than the aesthetic theories of Flaubert. No one appreciates local color like a colonizer; to fix the colonized in a highly ornamental carapace of the past is to keep them from genuine contemporary power. So it is not surprising that the Irish-Americans, once they gained the necessary literacy, did not follow the path of Yeats. But why did none of them follow the path of Joyce—the Joyce, at least, of *Dubliners*—and draw upon the verbal facility so much a part of their culture to create a realistic picture of the contemporary urban life they and their kind were living?

The American Irish are a people who were doubly colonized linguistically and who arrived in America already knowing the language. Yet this knowledge of the language didn't spare them from the hatred and contempt of the natives. Sharing a tongue, and even physical characteristics, made no difference to the Yankees. And what did it do to the immigrants themselves? Did it make them resentful of their fellow immigrants, with whom they had to share menial, degrading jobs, even though they possessed the advantage of speaking the English language? Did it, perhaps, create in them the illusion that if they behaved, didn't make waves, didn't stand out, they might be accepted? The similarity of language between the Irish and the Yankees made problems of identity more complicated and less clear, a situation that echoed the earlier experience of oppression by the English. And the Irish-American solution once again was to keep out of the world of the dominant group, to create a parallel world in which success could be defined and measured, to ignore, insofar as possible, the inferior position in which they were placed.

All these factors—linguistic colonization occurring at the same time as a preservation of national identity, a self defined in highly local terms, the creation of parallel worlds—are some reasons why there have been so few Irish-American writers. To think of oneself as a writer of literature rather than a journalist or a popular writer, one must think of oneself as a citizen of a larger world. By this I do not mean that one necessarily defines oneself as outside the smaller community—my own prejudice is that to lose the identification with the small community is to lose irreplaceable riches. But if one is going to think of oneself as a writer-artist, one must think of oneself as in the company of other great artists. Artists who will not come from one's own community, who have lived in different ages, spoken different languages, written about people who exist only because these writers have preserved their lives. And if one is a writer whose early years were formed in a small, closed community, one must have the courage to understand that it is outside the community that one may very likely find the people who will be the audience for one's work.

I want to say, of course, that not everything about the Irish Catholics is harmful to a writer. For one thing, the Irish are always interesting. There is the wit and the refinement of language that the sense of the necessity for constant ridicule engenders. And the very hiddenness of the lives of Irish-Americans makes them an irresistible subject for fiction. One has the sense of breaking into a private treasure, kept from the eyes of most, and therefore a real piece of news.

I once wrote that "Irish Catholics are always defending something—probably something indefensible: the CIA, the virginity of Mary—which is why their parties always end in fights." The problem is that the Irish-Americans are nearly always defending the wrong thing; nevertheless, most people find nothing worth defending, and the posture of the mistaken defender is compelling to the spirit, whether its bent is classical or romantic. The Irish have always in the back of their eye the vision of the ideal. Therefore, they must always be failures. For it is impossible to live up to the ideal; but to be attracted to it, to keep it in the back of one's eye, to know that one's endeavors are, however successful, inevitably failures, is to see the human condition in its clearest, most undiluted colors, to feel its starkest music in the bone.

There is the starkness of the Irish temperament; there is also its kindness. I go back to my uncle. The Irish-American experience has fed me because my uncle could have thriven in no soil but the Irish-American. And someone needs to tell about him. I have said it once; he was the kindest man I ever knew. He was capable of the deepest disappointment in people. He went to Communion every week of his life; his wife was an atheist. Although he never said a personal word to me, he had the capacity to make me feel immensely beloved and perfectly safe.

I had thought he was proud of my success. At his funeral, I talked about this to my favorite aunt, his sister. She, alone, defended me at my uncle's funeral. She didn't quite have the courage to confront the uncle who insulted me, but at least she directed her comments to the air around his head. "Imagine saying such a terrible thing at a funeral," she said, looking up at the ceiling.

My aunt and I were walking out of the funeral parlor to go to the cemetery. "They are awful, aren't they?" she said of the family who had insulted me. Well, I told her, they were awful, but they were so awful and so foolish that they couldn't hurt me. What mattered was that I knew my uncle who had just died was proud of me.

"Oh, he was proud of you," she said. "He always loved you very much. But he thought your books were very dirty. He couldn't read them, you know."

I walked with my infant son to the car that would drive us to the cemetery, and I thought how perfectly the experience of Irish-American Catholicism had been captured in my uncle's death and burial. And I wondered how much of it I would want to pass on to my children. That was a question to which I had no answer. But I knew one thing for certain: there was no doubt that I would write about it.

NYTBR
(1988)

III

PARTS OF A
JOURNAL

Notes from California

I

M. takes me to the grave of Marilyn Monroe. The roses on the grave are held together with pink ribbons. On the ribbons are messages in gold paper letters. The letters say:

> Sweet Angel Marilyn
> With God in Heaven Forever
> In Heaven Your Home
> Pray for me Here
> I Love you only forever.

On another grave are the words:

> Leesa de Bois
> December 25, 1977
> What Shall We Do With Our Lives?

II

In the evening, in the room where I work, not in the historic room where I can see the tower, in the blank room, here, I read this in a book by Kierkegaard: "I knew a person who on one occasion could have saved my life, if he had been magnanimous. He said, 'I see well enough what I could do but I do not dare to. I am afraid that later I might lack strength and that I might regret it.' He was not magnanimous, but who for this cause would not continue to love him?"

I cannot think what this could possibly mean.

III

A local artist has created an installation of *retablos* and ex-votos, images of saints, expressions of gratitude for favors granted. But his *retablos* commemorate unanswered prayers. Among the flowers and the images of saints, such things as this are written:

> Because my mother who cared so much for us and who we really loved felt depressed to see us without home or money, she killed my little sister Summer and my little brother Brian while they were asleep and then she killed me in spite of my screams, and then she committed suicide. I ask Saint Dominic Savio, protector of the poor, Why did she do this to us? And I will ask him for all eternity.

IV

A man I sat next to at dinner tells me this:

"I was traveling from Denmark to Germany. It was 1959. I took a ferry into Germany, and after that a train. From the train you could still see the devastations from the war. I don't read German or Danish. The papers, the immigration papers, were in German and Danish. I made a mistake on the immigration form. I wrote in the place of entry for the place of exit and vice versa. I knew I'd made a mistake, but I didn't feel like changing it. When I got to Berlin, they told me there was trouble with my papers, and they put me in a detention cell. I was guarded by a Russian soldier. I didn't feel in danger. I lit up a cigarette. The Russian soldier knocked it out of my mouth. But I knew he was only pretending to be angry. I knew he only wanted to communicate. I gave him a cigarette. He looked around to see that no one was watching him. He lit the cigarette. He put his gun down. He smiled at me. Then he said: 'Jack London.'

"I smiled back and said: 'Tolstoy.'

"He said: 'Mark Twain.'

"I said: 'Dostoevsky.'

" 'OK,' he said.

" 'Spasibo,' I said. 'Da.'

"I knew that he could have killed me but that he was not going to kill me."

V

I am waiting to get my hair cut, reading a crumpled copy of *Life* magazine. There is a picture of an old Greek woman standing behind a church. She is wearing the traditional old woman's garments: black kerchief, black shoes, long black dress. She is toothless, grinning. She is holding in her hand a grinning skull. In the back of the church there is a graveyard. Against the walls of the church there are piles of bones, sorted by type: skulls in one pile, leg bones in another. The old woman asked the photographer to take her picture holding this skull. She could tell, she said, that it was the skull of one of her old rivals. She did not say how she could tell. But she wanted her picture taken, she said to the photographer. "Because she is dead and I am not dead. You can see me here, alive. I want everyone to see me here, alive."

VI

Everywhere I have been I have thought at least once a day of my dead father. He has been dead for over thirty years. In a book he inscribed for me are these words, in his handwriting, a translation of a line of Virgil: "Among the dead there are so many thousands of the beautiful."

VII

At the cemetery where Marilyn Monroe is buried, some of the gravestones have inscribed on them the likeness of a mountain and a lake. Two people, a husband and a wife, have inscribed their signatures in bronze. A dentist has his name and D.D.S. A famous drummer has below his name "One Of A Kind." Flowers grow in pots on the flat gravestone of a famous murdered girl.

People are buried with their nicknames: Fannie, Muzzie, Poppy.

People are buried with testimonials. "She left the greatest legacy of all. She left us love."

The famous dead of movies, and the dentist, and Leesa de Bois, December 25, 1977, Christmas, no other date inscribed.

Did she die on the day of her birth?

"What shall we do with our lives?"

The famous dead of movies lie in the shadows of green buildings that seem made of bottle glass.

An art collector has constructed for his death a mausoleum bigger than a house.

Having a Baby,
Finishing a Book

WAITING, NEAR CHRISTMAS

I am waiting for a child to be born. Heaviness takes on new meaning; the word itself has weight. It is a day in cold December. I am in a New York apartment, where I usually do not live. My heaviness, the fact that I was awakened ten times in the night by my three-year-old daughter's sickness, and the steaminess of the windows of this overheated room make the air potent with unreality. Each gesture weighs, weighs down. And in the corner, weighing unimaginably more than any flesh, is the manuscript of my novel, which I had planned to finish before this baby was born. I have been here nearly a month. The doctor thought the baby would be early; he is late. He: we know it is a he; we are one of those modern families. So, of course, I brought the manuscript with me; of course, I believed I would work.

I have not even looked at it, partly because any action is physically difficult for me; I could excuse myself this way. But the truth is, it is impossible for me to believe that anything I write could have a fraction of the importance of the child growing inside me, or of the child who lies now, her head on my belly, with the sweet yet offhand stoicism of a sick child. Her doctor said she can put nothing, not even water, in her stomach. I give her sips of water; she keeps them in her mouth a moment and then spits them into a metal bowl. She puts her head again on my belly and drifts in and out of sleep.

The clock ticks; the apartment, it seems, is heating up even more. I lean my head back, close my eyes. My daughter is deeply asleep now. I could lift her to the couch; I could begin to write. I could do this easily, if I believed in its importance.

WAR

I am the mother of a son now. In twenty years, if there is a war, he will be called to it. Will I let him go? If he is twenty, will I be able to stop him? Yet if none of the mothers let their sons go, wouldn't that stop things, wouldn't it always have? This is sentimental. Mother of a warrior is historically, and in literature, the most honorific title a mother can have. Second, perhaps, to mother of a king. I do not understand this. I would prefer my son to have a hidden life. No honor is worth his danger. All night I cannot sleep, for I am worrying about the war. The war in twenty years, which I will not be able to stop. I will hide my son if he wants it. But if he wants to fight, what will I do? If he wanted to fight the Nazis, I would have sent him with pride. But the loss of him would be the end of my life.

The most courageous people in the world are the people who go on after their children have died. The woman in *Mrs. Dalloway* whom of all women Clarissa most admires: "Lady Bexborough who opened a bazaar, they said, with the telegram in her hand, John, her favorite, killed." My first prayer since I have become a mother is: Let me die before my children. Yet I would not have them die alone. Only to spare their dying alone would I willingly live after them.

Which is better, the dishonorable war, so that one can do what one really wants—hide the son in the cellar—or the honorable one and then the honorific fate as the mother of a hero? Literature is, as in so many other questions pertaining to motherhood, no help.

THE JOURNALS OF KATHERINE MANSFIELD

Will you touch me with the child in my arms? is no mere pleasantry. . . . If I had a child, I would play with it now and lose myself in it and kiss it and make it laugh. And I'd use a child as a guard against my deepest feeling.

When I felt: "No I'll think no more of this: it's intolerable and unbearable," I'd dance the baby.

That's true, I think, of all women. And it accounts for the curious look of security that you see in young mothers: they are safe from any ultimate state of feeling because of the child in their arms.

They are safe also from the need to perform or even to think about any *ultimate* moral act. At night, waking from sleep, when the children are not near me, I worry about the membrane that my obsession with them creates between me and the outside world. This is why a certain kind of childless woman rightly fears what having children would do to her moral life. There is nothing more absorbing than a baby, nothing more intoxicating, and, if things are going badly, nothing more drowning. The outside world pales before it; there is no outside world.

The egotism of the infant is well known; less well known the egotism of the mother. Because it is an egotism that reaches out, takes up another creature, makes it no less egotistical. So to decide to have children, especially in this world, is perhaps not the highest moral choice. At some points refusal is the highest morality, but it is not, has never been, the kind of morality that most interests me.

Really, though, I have misread Katherine Mansfield. She is talking about acuity and depth of feeling rather than morality. Or about acuity as morality. This morality, or this definition of it, is open only to a childless woman. Often childless women write the most interesting things about mothers and children. I can no longer imagine what it is to be a childless woman. When I write about childless women now, it is the *other* life I write about—the life outside.

MY CURTAINS: SNOWBOUND

I am working in my bedroom, which I have never before done. Writing a poem, which I rarely do. Both the place where I write and what I am writing are a way of getting back slowly.

As I work in this room, it takes on for me the feeling of sanctuary. I like to sit down at the window and look at my pretty curtains,

light blue and white—the blue a faded dream color, the flowers
fleurs-de-lis or mulberries, the border blue-gray chrysanthemums.
The street shines with rain. I look out at the house across the
street—a red ranch, low, emblematic of 1950s happiness. I like
the family that lives there. The father and I talk about dogs.

Now it has gone nearly dark; it is nearly seven o'clock. In ten
minutes I will have to go downstairs. Back to the life of the family,
which flares below, flame-colored. While here, in this room—made
secret by these curtains, by the very fact that it is where I am
working—the light is matte. I haven't enough time left to do what
I wanted to do today, but it's my own fault; instead of writing when
I could have looked out as the rain became snow, grew heavy, then
blue from its own weight, I spoke on the phone. I should not have
answered the phone. And now that light is lost forever. I will not
be able to describe it as I might have had I looked at it and written
as I looked. I ought to be longing for spring, but it is winter light
I find the most congenial.

It has snowed so much this hour that I know we are snowbound
for this night. It is a feeling I like, the snow at once isolating and
enclosing. I like it because this is the weather most like motherhood.

MY DAUGHTER POSES FOR A SCULPTURE

A friend of mine is sculpting my daughter. We go to her studio,
and my daughter takes off her clothes and plays with clay. One of
the sculptor's hands is larger than the other because of her work.
On her walls are pictures of the skeletons of animals, so she can
know them. She cannot know my daughter in this way. How can
she know her? In a way I cannot. My daughter is for her the object.
She will make something of her. No mother can make something
of her child. Even if she uses the child as the basis for a work of
art, it is not her child she is making something of.

I say to my friend, about my daughter: her chin is narrow, the
eyes farther apart. My friend tells me my daughter and I have the
same bone structure. So when I tell her about my daughter's face,
am I telling her about my own? My friend says, "No one knows
a child's face the way a mother does." There are no faces I know
as well as my children's. Yet anyone else could probably describe

them better. Anyone else might make of them a better work of art. Even if I thought I were writing about them, it would not be my children I was writing about. Something would happen to them, something that would make them not my children. Or else I would have to worry about them, alone on the page, in the world, so vulnerable. And I would never be able to describe what it is I really feel for them without the animal sounds and gestures that are so much the truth of it: grunts, snorts, licking, kisses, swoons of terror and delight.

THE DEATHS OF CHILDREN IN LITERATURE

I hate Ben Jonson because of his poem on the death of his son. The most hateful line in literature is: "Here doth lie/Ben Jonson his best piece of poetry." I could not even write about the death of a child.

I discuss with another writer what is the saddest part of *King Lear*. For me it is the death of Cordelia. For him it is Lear on the heath. This says everything about the difference between us as writers.

For Hardy, children augment hopelessness. The child's suicide note, "Done because we are too menny," is unbearable to read. If I ever read *Jude the Obscure* again, I will skip over it.

The greatest differences between modern life and the life of other times are those brought about by contraception and the drop in infant mortality. Looking at sex differently, and its issue, we have changed our lives. Some historians say that the maternal bond is a modern invention. I do not believe this. Read the Psalms. On the other hand, read the story of Isaac. The cruelest story in any language. It could not have been written by a woman.

If I were a Victorian, I would have cried at the death of Little Nell. I cry when I hear a Dolly Parton song about a child who dies. On this subject, I am not to be trusted. My training, my professional history—all those books, those years in graduate school—mean nothing. I respond merely to the event described. Unless I suspect the writer of using it as a pretext. Then I hate the writer.

A BABY IN THE SUMMER

It is the first hot day of the year. A drugged and meager light sifts through the haze; almost as in a dream I see the chestnut tree through the window, its flowers set within its leaves like little candelabras. I can see the chestnut from the bed where I lie with my baby, skin to skin. The pleasure of this is like the pleasure of a drug; it prevents activity. Only I *am* active. I am feeding. Perfectly still, almost without volition, I nourish. A film of moisture covers my flesh and my son's. Both of us drift in and out of sleep. I could be any woman lying here; there is nothing original about me. I am ancient, repetitive. In a life devoted to originality, I adore the animal's predictability. The pleasures of instinct are more real than I would ever have known.

The joy of this moment is that there is nowhere else for us to be. Summer will come, the early yellow-green of the leaves at the window will deepen into purest green, then take on blue in the light of some summer afternoons. Henry James says "summer afternoon" is the most beautiful phrase in the language. Only now that summer is here can I admit I longed for it. I never remember longing for summer, for heat. Is this a sign of age? But that question is an affectation. I am young; I am the mother of a baby; it is the first hot day.

Now it is over, the inactive time, the pleasure in the haze. It is time to go to my novel. My novel, which has sat in the corner all winter, all spring. The thought of going back to work on it makes me feel physically ill. Infinitely more enjoyable to lie here in the haze in silence with a baby.

THE QUESTIONABLE

Finally, I answer a month-old letter from my English editor. Till now, I haven't felt I've had the right to. But now I can, now that I've got back to work. Only as a practicing writer do I feel I earn his regard. If I were not a writer with the kind of success that earns one an English publisher, I would never have known anyone like him. He is of a very good family. He was brought up in India when it was still colonial. I tell him, only partly joking, that only through him can I understand the British class system, and it was all worth it, all those poor people dying, suffering, all the chilblains and inferiorities, all of it was worth it to produce him.

He looks at me with my children and says, sadly, as if he has missed something, "Your relationship with your children is as different as possible from mine with my mother. I was brought up by servants. At eight, I was sent to England to school, thousands of miles away. I saw my mother only a few weeks in the year."

I think: This is a terrible story. How terrible for both of them. But he is one of the most splendid men I know—kind, cultivated, accomplished, capable of enjoying pleasures of a very great variety.

Everything I think about my children could be wrong.

I write him a letter. "Now I have begun to write, I greet you." The sentence echoes in my head; I am remembering some rhythm. Then it occurs to me, what I am hearing. It is the gladiators' greeting to the emperor: "We who are about to die salute you."

GIVING IT UP

I have given it in now, given it away. I have just come from making the last changes with the editor.

New York is lit for Christmas; luxury is everywhere, and promise, and I feel luxurious. Luxurious to walk alone here, without children. It is my favorite kind of weather. People in furs, but hatless, walk through the lively air. They are all going to wonderful parties; every gift they carry in their bags is beautiful.

I stop at a place that is trying to imitate a Parisian *charcuterie*. I order bread and goat cheese, a glass of red wine. And pay three times what it is worth. With pleasure, I overpay; with pleasure tip cabdrivers much more than they've earned.

And then, preparing to go home, I feel quite empty. I miss the children. The book is gone now; it is no longer mine. I will not have any more babies. So what will follow will be, simply, my life. Caring for my children. Thinking of the next book. Which, in my mind now, as I leave the bejeweled city, I can never love so much as the book I have just come from giving up.

Some Things I Saw

THE CASE OF BERTHE MORISOT

Losing My Temper in the National Gallery, and Types of Feminist Shame

It is the first one-woman show of hers in America. The National Gallery, a place where I have been happy. Official nineteenth-century America built these marble halls, these splashing pools so you can hear the sound of water while you're looking at the pictures, the pictures of the great collectors, making their money God knows how. I have never seen many of Morisot's paintings, and the ones I saw I found rather disappointing, a secret I don't tell anyone, but they seem pale to me, with nothing of Cassatt's drafts-manship or bold coloration—although it may be unfair to compare them simply because they were contemporaries and friends. And of course, female. Renoir said female painters were like a five-legged calf, a version of Dr. Johnson's dancing dog (I wonder if he knew it). But Morisot was important because there is no doubt that she is a serious and highly accomplished painter, and unless one is comparing her to the greatest geniuses—Manet and Monet and Degas (I am not easy saying Cassatt, although I mean it)—as good as the best of her age. I'd rather look at most Morisots than at most Renoirs and Sisleys and Pissarros; the faults I find in her I find in them, and I find her subject matter more interesting.

But before I am allowed to look at the work of Morisot, I am forced to look at her image. "Forced" sounds like a highly un-grateful language for the privilege of being allowed to look at a very beautiful painting: Manet's *Le Repos.* The curves of the sofa and the female figure (Morisot), the creaminess of the white dress— it is a beautiful picture of a beautiful woman. But it is a portrait *of* Berthe Morisot, not *by* Berthe Morisot. I feel angry for her, insulted, as if a virtuoso had been invited to her first recital and stole the audience's attention by perfectly playing a solo before she got on stage. I enjoy the Morisots, particularly the pictures of her daughter, and I am compelled by a self-portrait she does in late middle age: the face is serious, heavy, matronly, the eyes are deep-set, the hair is severely pulled back. But I keep thinking about *Le Repos.* Nothing Morisot has painted is as beautiful as this portrait of her. I have to keep thinking about her as a female body, as the object of an erotically charged vision greater than her own. I didn't want to have to think about her that way. Just for one afternoon, I wanted to think of her as a painter, dislodged from her biography, from her physical beauty—separated from the admiring and powerful male gaze.

I keep thinking of another painter who was a famous object of male artistic vision: Georgia O'Keeffe. I had an odd reaction to seeing Steiglitz's photographs of her, a reaction unshared by anyone I knew. I resented Steiglitz for presenting her to me as so much the object of his desire. I resented her for *posing.* I didn't understand why she did it. It must have taken up a lot of her time. And to *pose,* to make oneself immobile, fixed, seemed to me an act of obedience, a loss of autonomy I couldn't forgive. In those photographs, the immediacy of the camera's eye means that the subject of the photograph, particularly when she is photographed incessantly, has something of the aspect of pornography. I was ashamed of these feelings. But I didn't want O'Keeffe lolling around on sheets for Steiglitz, her hair loose, her breasts unflatteringly droopy. I wanted her up, girt, on her feet, her hair pulled back, her eye not resting on the camera's but on something in the world she could make the object of her own vision: the heart of a flower, red stones in the desert, a window frame of a Lake George house. Of course, Steiglitz's photographs of O'Keeffe helped make her famous; they made her 1924 show a cause célèbre: no one could separate the paintings from the body of the painter. Did she use that, consciously? Was it a strategy, an opening up of a private erotic contract to the art-buying world?

I see those photographs and I'm angry. K. suggests that this may be because of a severe puritanism about female exhibitionism; I suspect she's right. She says that in *Chanson de Roland*, which she's now teaching, there's passage after passage about male military posing. And no one judges *that* harshly. H. thinks O'Keeffe is a lousy painter: too full of self-love. I find her great. H. likes the photographs better than the paintings. For me, it is no contest, so I can forget about them, dislodge the object of male vision from the painter when I see her work. But I cannot dislodge the memory of her face: so arresting it appeared in *Vogue* as often as a model's. Is it possible to separate the image of the beautiful woman's face and body from her work? The question is more difficult for a visual artist. We know, for example, that Virginia Woolf was a beautiful woman, but because the visual aspects of her art are privately apprehended and symbolically rendered by black signs on a white page, we can forget that a physical woman held a pen in her fleshly hand to make these impressions. The writer is always more ghostly than the painter; there is a possible modesty in the hiddenness, the abstraction, of our re-creation of the world.

I try to think if all this could ever be an issue for a male artist. I cannot think of a male artist whose appearance is so much connected to his work that we would have to look at it differently if he looked different. I try to think of a male artist who existed with equal importance as the object of artistic vision and the creator of art. I cannot think of one possible example, nor can I easily imagine it for the future. The primacy of the female body as the locus of erotic charge seems immutable as long as the male heterosexual's is the dominant vision.

The truth is that for me—and I feel ashamed of it—Berthe Morisot's biography, as well as her physical beauty, is inseparable for me from her art. Perhaps this wouldn't be true if I loved the art more purely, as I do Cassatt's and O'Keeffe's. And the fact is that what is important for me is not Morisot's beauty, or her happy erotic and marital life, but her maternity. Morisot introduces into the artistic language the daughter as object of the mother's adoring gaze. Julie is painted in all her stages of babyhood and young womanhood. Was that sensuous mouth an anxiety to the mother, even as the painter rejoiced in it? Mothers desire their daughters' flesh, we desire it to be near our own with an ardor we are afraid to speak of—largely for the daughters' sakes. We have been told over and over again that mothers are jealous of their daughters' youth, and this is perhaps the truth in many cases. But we also rejoice in our daughters' growing and their beauty, and there is an extraordinary poignance to me in Morisot's depicting herself as a sober matron at the same time that she paints her daughter at the dreamy brink of her sexual ascent. I love the drawing of Julie looking over Morisot's shoulder as she sketches, interested in her mother's work but also luxuriating in her usually forbidden nearness to the body of the working mother. This combination of art and life makes me much more emotionally engaged with Morisot's paintings than I am with what I know to be a greater work, Manet's *Le Repos*. Trained in the modern tradition, I react by feeling uneasy, immature. I am supposed to know better. But it shakes up, as well, the notion of modernist purity, because like it or not, what I know about Morisot's life has deepened my experience of her work.

A final admission: nothing of her work moves me as deeply as her final letter to her daughter. Morisot died young, at fifty-four. Julie was only seventeen.

My little Julie, I love you as I die; I shall love you even when I am dead; I beg you not to cry, this parting was inevitable. I hoped to live until you were married. . . . Work and be good, as you have always been; you have not caused me one sorrow in your little life. You have beauty, money; make good use of them. I think it would be best for you to live with your cousins . . . but I do not wish to force you to do anything. . . . Do not cry; I love you more than I can tell you. . . .

So that in the end, both the physical beauty and the depth and tenderness of the connection between mother and daughter were cut down by death. Inevitable, yes, but still unbearable, and worse because we have such palpable evidence of intensely lived physical and affective life.

ABEL GANCE'S NAPOLEON

In the minds of middle-class young men life is associated with a career, and in early youth that career is Napoleon's. They do not, of course, necessarily dream of becoming Emperor, because it is possible to remain like Napoleon while remaining far, far below him. Similarly, the most intense life is summarized in the most rudimentary of sounds, that of a sea-wave, which from the moment it is born until it expires is in a state of continual change. I too like Napoleon and like the wave could at any rate look forward to a recurring state of birth and dissolution.

Italo Svevo
The Confessions of Zeno

That was exactly the problem. I was neither middle class nor male. Nor European. Napoleon was to me a figure of boredom or a joke. Then there is the shame—to be bored or amused by a figure so important to so many great minds and lives (Stendhal, Tolstoy), dreamed over by so many passionate girls of the nineteenth century. And to me—what? Someone famous for tucking his hand inside his jacket pocket, a sausage in fake Roman curls, a conqueror, the prototype for Hitler, rampaging through Europe, cutting countries up like lunch. Jane Austen is meant to be small-minded because she didn't include him.

Shame drives me to see this film, shame and its relations, snobbery and cultural avarice: I can't miss this thing that is not to be missed. And I may have been lying for years about having seen it—the way I lie about having read *The Charterhouse of Parma*, which I have never been able to finish. I go with M. to Radio City, a locus of pure happiness. I came here with my father. It's a place I can *know* we visited; I know I didn't make it up. I can pin down the memory. I remember standing in freezing lines with him for the Christmas show, sitting in silence with him for the Easter show, where the Rockettes, dressed as nuns, formed themselves into a Cross. And our last movie together: Grace Kelly and Alec Guinness in *The Swan*. My father adored the idea of this movie. Two Catholic stars. And this was no Bing Crosby playing Father O'Malley. This was about Europe: the real thing. Somehow it had to do with what he had in mind for me. Thinking me royal, did he imagine some deposed prince of the blood would recognize what he did—my royalty—and take me to reign in absentia with him, in Spain perhaps, in an obscure castle? Waited on by devoted servants proud to work for nothing? A private chapel, with our own saintly live-in priest?

On the night that I was brought into the hospital, in grave danger of losing the baby I was five months pregnant with, *The Swan* was showing on television. I took it as a sign. The television in my room was broken, and I made a fuss, demanding to be moved. I watched the movie, and it wasn't very good. Ten days later, I lost the baby and with it my belief that my father was looking down on me, watching out for me, communicating with me in amiable humane ways conducive to my comfort. I lost the habit at that time of years of a primitive faith. I have not been happier for the loss.

In 1958, I saw *Gigi* in Radio City with my mother. After my father's death. It's the only time she took me into the city. She must have wanted to see the movie badly. It was our only linkage as a family: our love of Hollywood Romance.

At that time, she didn't need a cane for walking, only her built-up shoes. Still, I remember walking up the great staircase with her anxiously. It was difficult, but she was able to do it. I remember being as happy there with her as I had been with him, and feeling a bit bad about it. I had let *her* into *our* place, where I knew *he* wouldn't have wanted her to be.

Everyone is happy in Radio City. It's the size, the thrill that something so monumental should be devoted to the most familiar and accessible of pleasures—movies. The Art Deco opulence has a built-in touch of self-parody, so no one feels left out. This time I notice a statue, a classical huntress formed of cast iron, made not with the usual chaste, noble, self-effacing breasts but with big modern boobs, their large nipples pointing straight out. The girlie magazine elevated to the status of the eternal. "Well, he knew what he liked," M. says, and the statue is a comfort. For all its grandeur, there's no serious pretentiousness about Radio City, which is why it's the perfect place for me to see *Napoleon,* the "classic" I have so pretentiously come to see.

There's a real orchestra in the pit, conducted by Francis Ford Coppola's father, Carmine. Coppola produced this version of Gance's *Napoleon.* I like that familial touch. It's sentimental, but I think of all silent film as partaking of the sentimental, the overdone. The music is overrich, overheroic, but I am charmed by it, as I was charmed by the absurd music of the huge Radio City Wurlitzer that ushered us in.

The first scene is a snowball fight at Brienne, the school Napoleon attended as a boy. Almost immediately we see the face of Rudenko, who plays the child Napoleon. At once I stop simulating interest; the extraordinary face of the child peering above the snowbank arrests me entirely. I am no longer here to be able to say, in the world outside the theater, that I have been here. This is the world I inhabit now, the world of the intense visions of childhood, the world of dream.

The face of Rudenko. Delicate, androgynous, proud, horrified at being stared at. It is almost an affront to look at this child. He should be left alone, but he was born to be looked at. Who could protect him? What relation could he have to a mother, a father? You would have to stand back from such a child, if you were a parent, and let him go, into the world, into his sorrow.

He is leading his fellow students in a snowball fight. At first, he looks out of place, as if he should be home practicing his piano. But then he stoops to an almost absurd posture: he is on one knee in the snow, his back to the boy troops. And we see that he is born to do this, to give orders and then to separate himself from his followers. In real life, children were made ill by the constant repetition of the snowball scene during the filming. Rudenko, the son of poor Russian Jews, had a difficult life. He never wanted to talk about having played Napoleon.

The lighting of *Napoleon* is the lighting of the unconscious, of the unclear world of dreams. Some of the scenes are shot through a blue lens, some through a sepia-colored lens, as if Gance was making us experience our fantasy of what pastness is, of what it means to be walking in Hades, among the dead. Of being voyeurs of the lives of the dead. The half-light: as if we were traveling in a tunnel between two things: waking and sleeping, consciousness and unconsciousness; as if we were at a doorway, having already died, waiting for what is to come after, looking behind at history, looking forward into shadows.

The crowd scenes have the menace of a nightmare. It has always been a fear of mine to be killed, namelessly, by a nameless crowd.

The citizen who is hung outside Napoleon's window could be anybody, guilty or not, someone who just happened to be at the wrong place at the wrong time. Even Napoleon cannot stop his death from happening. He considers trying; he reaches for the gun on his desk but decides against it. My childhood glimpses of the French Revolution were all from the point of view of the murdered aristocrats: *A Tale of Two Cities*, *The Scarlet Pimpernel*. Probably because, even in the fifties, the Church, source of my historical information, thought the Revolution was a drastic and disastrous mistake.

Why am I so afraid of mobs? I've never really experienced one. But I think of the idea of Mardi Gras, of carnival, as monstrous. Horrifying. At the end of it, of course, you could be dead. Statistics say that there are a disproportionate number of births nine months after Mardi Gras or carnival in places where they are celebrated. Anonymous death, anonymous coupling.

The distressing, yet pretty, scene of the *Bal des Victimes*. The sub-title reads: "To be admitted to the Victims Ball, it was necessary to have been imprisoned, or to prove the death of a father, a brother, or a husband." It is 1792. The terror still reigns. But the fashionable have an unprecedented number of parties. Beautifully dressed ladies vie for attention and have rose petals showered upon them as they make their entrances. In the midst of this staccato gaiety Napoleon stands, fixed, puritanical. He looks unhealthy— pigeon-breasted, stoop-shouldered, with the hint of a potbelly de-spite his thinness—the obvious fate of the finicky boy who walked through the school pillow fight, fastidiously shod, with the turned-out toes of the careful child, who later will not allow his con-sciousness to lapse at the ball. Disorder reigns. As a joke, a man wears a balloon at the top of his collar, where his head should be, and pops it: the practical joker as the near-victim of the guillotine. Women are passed from hand to hand; a virile man takes off his jacket and is bare-chested. Josephine appears. Napoleon courts her by beating her suitor in a game of chess. In the midst of increasingly manic activity, two men fight over a woman by means of the stillest of games. Josephine uses her past hardship as an instrument of flirtation: "It was here, M. Bonaparte, that I was summoned to the scaffold." The actress playing Josephine is not exceptionally beautiful, but she has style; she's what in the twenties would have been called a "fascinator." (It is interesting how styles of sexuality in mouths mark a period. For the twenties, lips were bowed. Aggressive teeth with a decided overbite signified the sexually experienced woman—the less obvious, more intelligent choice.) Puritanically, Napoleon walks around the ball casting baleful looks, making censorious comments. "With imbeciles and layabouts like you, France is heading for the abyss." But his puritanism is the preserver of dignity. It is dignity in degradation. His puritanism is a form of stillness, infinitely desirable in the mayhem. Over and over, Napoleon is the center of our attention, the source of our comfort because of his stillness. The evocative power of the film, perhaps all early film, comes from the quality of the movement the camera gives us: jerky; and the light: unclear. The shift from frenetic unsmooth movement to iconic stillness. The stillness becomes the state ardently longed for, a spiritual condition, the peace of contemplation, the end point of the search for what is above us, not subject to us, to change and therefore loss. Napoleon's stillness seems eternal; it is the visual source of our belief in his heroism.

The visual source of all that is not heroic, all that is human and vulnerable, is Napoleon's hair. For a large part of the movie, I can't understand it. Where is the famous Napoleonic curly cap? Hair is important for Gance. The most dreadful bully at the school has wild, evil hair. Danton's is a thick mop, Robespierre's is a hyperrational Enlightenment flip. Napoleon's hair was a deliberate decision on Gance's part. He rejected one wig for Dieudonné (who plays Napoleon) on the ground that it made him look like an old woman. Napoleon's lank, unheroic hair is there purposely to fracture the icon, to force us to look at Napoleon as if for the first time. I later come to realize that the hair is as it is, long and lank, to remind us of Jesus. Sentimental, gentle Jesus. Meek and mild. In the Hollywood posters for *Napoleon* (the film was, finally, never distributed in America), his hair is short and curly.

Why does this film of Napoleon, about whom I know very little, about whom I have hardly thought at all, seem to be the travel folder of the territory of my dreams, the photo album of my unconscious? J. suggests that it's because we see dreams and the past—

which we can't control—as existing in murky light. Emblem of our confusion. Can it be that our first visions after birth were half seen, or seen as half illuminated, and the charge—depressive or elated— that we feel at twilight or at dawn reminds us of that first sight? Or do we know, somehow, that the last things we'll see will be in the same way unclear, elusive, almost out of sight?

WHO'S NOT SINGING IN THE SINGING DETECTIVE?

The dreaming boy alone in the lush tree. The crooner by himself before the microphone. The walking detective (hard-boiled dick) solitary, gun in hand, his heels clicking along the rainy pavement. Is he by himself because he wants to be? Is the role of the isolate, in proximate relation to things longer than they are wide, the role he chose first for himself or is it the austere and wise second choice of the man who knows too much?

Dennis Potter's television movie *The Singing Detective* is all about the stuff male dreams are made of: obviously, deliberately, self-consciously, this is the case of the work. The brilliant technique is there to interweave dream and wakefulness, real (nineteenth-century) reality and primitive fantasy, the numbing, nullifying pressures of present life and the simple voluptuousness of the old songs and the older stories. I watched, at first, transfixed by the verbal and visual facility, but as the hours drew on, I found myself more and more alienated from what I was seeing, more uneasy, until finally I had to force myself to watch. The techniques of *The Singing Detective* are new, but the message certainly is not. Dennis Potter is merely saying something we have heard for a very long time: at the center of the boy's dream is the treacherous, transgressing cunt.

The point of *The Singing Detective* is that it functions simultaneously on many levels. There is the level of the present: Philip Marlow, a washed-up writer of third-rate detective fictions, lies in his bed in a hospital ward. He is the victim of arthritic psoriasis, which renders him loathsome to look at (his skin has turned to horrifying scales) and makes most movements of his limbs and head excruciatingly painful. Around him, the flotsam and jetsam of English society suffer, decay, and die. (Men make far less attractive patients than women. Perhaps it's all those catheters, all those grizzled faces, degenerate-looking because unshaved.) They reveal themselves to be, like the rest of Marlow's humankind, small-minded, mischief-making, lewd, self-deceiving, foolish, devoted to others' harm. The occasional ray of decency pierces the pervading fog: an Indian man, who has the good sense to understand that Marlow's racial slurs are *only a joke,* offers Marlow a sweet and then dies.

But sweetness and light come to the ward in the presence of a pretty nurse, who is not only cheerful and understanding but covers every inch (*every* inch) of Marlow's damaged body with cold cream. This is an important part of his therapy, and Marlow tries to be good, but what would you do, male viewer, if a pretty girl were greasing your penis with cold cream? You might try, like the noble Marlow, thinking of the most boring possible things (the Arts Council, the *Guardian* women's page, your own work, even), but against your will you would succumb. Against your will. The only other time we see Marlow as a sexual performer, he is calling his partner (a whore) filthy names at the climactic moment. But at Nurse Mills's hands, there is no need for nasty language. Marlow's orgasm is entirely unvolitional. It occurs through the ministrations of a woman who asks nothing of him, not even money. She doesn't require so much as a touch. Contact is limited to his penis and her greasy plastic gloves. How could he possibly fail her? Wiping away the semen with Kleenex, she only half blames. She is the perfect woman. "You're the girl in all the songs," Marlow says, and he's right, not just because she's pretty and nice but because she offers sexual satisfaction while eliminating entirely the risk of sexual failure. Marlow loathes himself; of course he would expect that women would loathe him. How could sex with anything like mutuality be anything but terrifying for him? What reason would he have to *feel good about it,* that mandate that we have been given from the sixties on? Why would he trust women, when his early experience of them shows them to be betrayers and tormentors? How could he be other than he is?

Of course, the *self* of Marlow is enormously complicated: that is the point of *The Singing Detective* and particularly its technique. He is his present and his past, his psychoanalysis and his characters, his mordant, nasty, witty language and the soothing words of the songs: "Banality with a beat," he calls them. In the experience of the past that the suffering Marlow remembers, popular songs are an important backdrop. In fact, they solidify the tone of childhood wishes: simplicity and harmony, delicious temporary yearning with no sense that finally it cannot be fulfilled. In Marlow's memory of his childhood, his mother is hysterical, and frustrated, but she *moves*. She is imprisoned in her husband's family house with her appalling father-in-law, who projects missiles of phlegm onto the fire in the middle of dinner, and her mother-in-law, who keeps reminding her that it is not her house. It is not surprising that she takes a lover. We are not surprised at this turn of events, but we are mournful. For whom is she betraying? Her kind, stoical, anxious-to-please husband, his eyes always close to tears, his ears vulnerable below his too short haircut. And the husband sings. The loving, joyous words of the songs come from his mouth, as he leads a singsong in the pub. Impotent in life, he is potent in his singing. He owns the important language: the language of the songs. In *being the singer,* he is able to be self-expressive, to express the deepest desires of the community and therefore to be its point of cohesion. And what is mummy doing all the while? Accompanying him on the piano. She is the silent handmaiden. Only when she is deprived of language and it becomes the property of the man in a way that excludes her are there moments of family happiness.

It is interesting to note who sings in *The Singing Detective*. The only solo female voice that is accompanied by a specific female face is that of Dietrich singing "Lili Marlene." This is the voice of the foreigner, the one who could not be mother. "A tart," Phil's maternal grandfather calls her, "tart" being synonymous for him with non-English. The foreign spy, who is killed by the enemy, is a special locus of desire for Philip as he takes on the skin of his third self, the character of the Singing Detective he has created in his novel. The spy who sings "Lili Marlene" is given the face of Philip's real-life mother. In Philip's detective-novel life, she is shot dead. The other important female characters—Philip's tormenting teacher and his complicated wife—are not allowed into the dream world of the songs.

There are important reasons for this, and they are connected with the ultimate failure of *The Singing Detective* to achieve cohesion or a satisfying end. When *The Singing Detective* works, it works because it embodies and indeed canonizes extremely pervasive and seductive elements of adolescent male fantasy. The Philip Marlow/

Sam Spade character makes sacred, honorable, and noble the male fear of intimacy with the female. The detective is always the moral center of the fiction. He is poor and unsuccessful because his standards are incorruptible. For the same reason, he is alone: he is purer than the rocks on which he sits. Occasionally he is tempted, by a need for either love or sex, to join himself with a female, but it is always to his peril. The beautiful face is always the face of the betrayer and the murderer. Only his secretary understands him, and she is willing to love him in agonizing silence, making him coffee, bailing him out, helping him with his hangover, and being told that she's a great girl and he's sorry he's too ruined to be the man she really deserves. The fiction embodied by the thirties and forties songs embodies as well a world of female undangerousness. One yearns and is yearned for; one loves and is loved, but the high point of erotic imagination is the kiss, not the fuck. Obviously we (contemporary men and women) are supposed to know better than all this, we are supposed to want the loving partnership of equals. But in fact, the loving partnership of equals has very little myth-ological furniture to make habitable its bare rooms. The stories and the songs that all of us grew up on are based on relationships of unequal and skewed power. There is simply nothing that has been embedded in popular culture long enough to render luscious the model of two adults struggling in the modern world. Tracy and Hepburn, Russell and Grant, exist in the realm of comedy, whose touch by its very nature is light, too light to make the deep impress of melodrama on the molten wax of yearning. Too light and too far from death. We see Ingrid Bergman leaving Humphrey Bogart at the airport, and there is music in the background; there is no equivalent to "As Time Goes By" running through our brains as we see Russell and Grant in the newsroom or Tracy and Hepburn on the golf course or in court. There is no theme song for mutuality, just as there is no embodied romance for the female isolate. Hum-phrey Bogart can walk off alone or with Claude Rains, but Hepburn and Russell have to have a man. It is possible to say that we can't believe in the female isolate because of our conviction of female bodily weakness. Even Amelia Earhart went up in flames. Shane rides off into the sunset alone; the female on the frontier must be accompanied.

The romances of popular culture make no place for the solitary female. She can't look death in the face; she has to be saved from it. A stronger presence (male) has to intervene between her and death. She is the conduit of death, but she can do nothing to keep it back. If she can never be alone, how can we ever know who she is? And if she is only death or betrayal, how can there be a truthful end that includes her in any of the traditional delicious genres?

At the end of *The Singing Detective*, Marlow walks out of the hospital with his wife. Why isn't this woman singing? There is a perfect opportunity for her to do it. Near the end, in the process of Marlow's cure, the Ink Spots are singing "You Always Hurt the One You Love." The voice we hear next is Ella Fitzgerald's. But do we see Marlow's wife's face? No; the voice is disembodied.

In real life, change does not amputate the child's life, or the dreamer's; it moves it along. In the context of the film's shaping myth, the force bringing about change would be not the psychiatrist or the sexy soubrette wife but the pretty nurse, who cures by her unselfish love. In the last encounter with her, Marlow tells the nurse she is the nicest and most beautiful person he's met in a long time. He mentions how wonderfully her head sits on her neck. Then he quits, becomes a grownup. We are meant to believe that the boy in the tree will stay there; he will come back, but he will not be powerful enough to defeat the good (adult) man and the good woman, walking down the hospital corridor into the modern world. In the context of everything that went before it, this is unbelievable, the stuff of posttherapeutic "ought." The "ought" is always feebler than the wish, that heady concoction of nonlinguistic, culturally enshrined desire.

Potter's techniques—this ability to harness television's fragmentariness and quick shifts—are new, but the story is a very old one. You can't put old wine in new bottles, and the final product lacks bouquet; the sediment settles at the bottom: the stuff of undigested dreams.

ANDY WARHOL

I am trying to understand why he disturbs me—no, hurts me—yes, that's it: causes me to be in pain. Did he mean to? Or mean nothing? The mockery in the face, always, under the fright wig (was he really frightened?): what a fool you are. Or perhaps, even

less inflected than that: how uncool you are. That is the central
mystery. What was he saying: where was the accusation—foolish-
ness, which would imply some obverse enduring value, or un-
coolness, which would be about constantly shifting trends? Was
he saying something? No, that's not it: you know he was saying
something; you just don't like what he had to say. The central
question was this: What did he care about? Or was he all about
not caring for one thing more than another, perhaps the most
frightening posture of all. Because if he's right, and there's no point
in caring for one thing more than another (except if it's pretty or
cool), there is no point to your life or the life of people you admire
and look to for guidance, meaning, standards—and certainly no
point to their deaths. What is his relation to death?

S. and I take Anna and Emily to see the Warhol show, thinking
they'll be amused by the Brillo boxes and the Campbell soup cans.
A laugh for the children. But it doesn't mean anything to them.
They're bored. If only I could be bored. Or amused. I look first
at the fashionable, well-drawn shoes. The enjoyable reproductions
of ads for corn plasters. The tabloids. The disasters. The sexy boys
who liked to kill. The empty electric chairs where they ended up.
The gawkers at the accidents, the wrecked cars, the mangled
bodies. Infinitely far away. Hundreds of Marilyns, their mouths
messy, violated. Or post-violation. The fashionable women. Edith
Scull with her still, rich hair. Elvis. James Dean. Sullen mouths
available to everyone. Not giving in. Julia Warhol. I see anger in
his messing up her face. It is a violent reaction toward a mother.
He is in every way the opposite of Vuillard, whom I look to for
solace. Vuillard's muted palette, his interior lives not sentimen-
talized—lurking women, mother, sisters, about to spring—but
nevertheless endowed with tenderness, and of course art. He can
draw well, paint well. Good drawing, good painting, matters to
him. I own a pencil drawing of his mother. She is serene, eternal:
like Félicie in Flaubert's *Un Coeur Simple*. That nineteenth-century
French stoicism of the domestic. A place of rest. R. says I like it
because I hope my son will think of me that way when I'm old.

Warhol lived with his mother for most of his life. They lived in
the same house until quite near her death. Closer than my mother
and I. She was an alcoholic, an embarrassment, crazy perhaps, a
pack rat, a torment. But he kept her around. Until she became

senile. Then he put her in a nursing home and didn't get in touch with her. Didn't go to her funeral. Lied to people after she was dead when they asked how she was. "Fine," he told them. What did lying mean to him? What did it mean to him to lie?

I start talking to everyone about him. N. tells me he went to church all the time. This makes me angry at first, then scared. Warhol and me. Postwar, immigrant Catholics. If he is one, then what am I? I am everything not him: female, susceptible, engaged. Yet he went to church more than I do. It makes me furious, because of course it fits right in with a tradition that was highly romantic for people like my father: the decadent tradition, Huysmans, sinning but devout. Devout. What can that possibly mean in a life like Warhol's. A life of watching while people fuck, shoot up, jerk off, kill themselves. Watching. Wishing they'd do it for the camera. I am a camera. The I. The "eye." The unsusceptible I / eye. Is this evil? To refuse to be engaged. To encourage the destruction of others so that you can observe the spectacle. When he found out that Edie Sedgwick had tried to kill herself, he said, "I wish she'd done it in front of the camera." If the Church is about anything, it's about engagement. Yet for a certain stripe of priest, it's a real kick, having the unrepentant sinner, the flagrant sinner, kneeling in front of you every week. A proof of the sweep of the cloak of Holy Mother Church. Much more interesting than the 99 who are not lost. They got the idea from Jesus, after all. The Good Shepherd. I know mine, and mine know me. But I keep wanting to know what it could have meant to him, kneeling there. Did he relish the perverseness of the posture? Was he covering his bets, just in case the most orthodox things his mother believed in were true? What does it mean to say of Warhol: What did it mean? What did meaning mean? Was being in church a goof for him? A laugh? Did he pray? What was the face on the other side of prayer for him?

I am of his time, not Vuillard's. This was his genius: he understood what people really liked to look at. The sickly boy (faggot-in-training), wheezing while his mother buys him movie magazines to cut the pictures of stars from. Rita Hayworth. Sonja Henie. Lush. Cute. All that was not his mother. In the pictures of him at art school, the pictures of him from high school, you can see the unattractive boy trying to be well groomed. The young sissy trying to be careful. How did he get from there to where he was? Where was he? A genius. Knowing what people were really like, what they were interested in. He tells us that the nineteenth century is over. Nature, contemplation. Over. Now people love what they can consume. And what can be has been reproduced. "The day of the unique image, the unique object, is over." When Walter Benjamin says it, it doesn't scare me, because for Benjamin there is some belief in value, some hopefulness. For Warhol there is consumption. Which is death.

I start talking about him obsessively. I bore everyone, talking about the end of the nineteenth century. Which I've just discovered in March 1989. I fall into depression, a depression that makes me want to stop writing. Literally contemplate taking my novel back from the publisher. I am ashamed of everything I've done. It is not of my time. It's a lie, a pathetic one, because I didn't realize I was lying. I thought I was telling the truth, but it's not the truth about the way we live, even about the way we pretend to live. In the nineteenth century, businessmen had to pretend to care about poetry, nature, music. To pass as *hautes bourgeoises,* they had to pretend to like these things. So maybe a few of their children did, by accident. But the arts were supported, and at least people had to pretend to believe. Was that better? Is the truth better? The truth about what people really like to look at, like to see?

The difference between Warhol and Joseph Cornell. Cornell took all the camp images that people love to look at and said, They are part of a wonderful dream, a dream of emptiness, eternal. And because they are boxed, separated, they have the uniqueness, the unreproduceability of a dream. In a photograph I have of Cornell, his thumbnail is frighteningly long. Like a bird's claw. What does it mean about your life if you let your thumbnail grow that long? Cornell had a retarded brother. Some people think his work is about doing something that would make his brother happy, that his brother could understand. At the end of his life, Cornell had a friendship with a waitress, who was murdered. When I read about it for the first time, I wondered if he could have murdered her. You wouldn't wonder that about Warhol. He might have watched somebody killing but not himself have killed. Cornell would have hidden the body. Perhaps in a beautiful box he had made. A box of dreams to accompany her to the emptiness after death. Warhol would have photographed the body, then abandoned it for something newer, perhaps more freshly dead.

The white face under the white hair, Warhol's, says to everything I could possibly say: Bullshit. But he wouldn't say that; it wouldn't be pretty or cool to say that; what he says is worse, much worse. What he says is it doesn't matter. It could be anything. Anything could be anything. One thing or another. Everything passes in front of you. You let the camera run. You take it in. But no, not in, because you are impermeable. The desirable state: to be susceptible to nothing, vulnerable to nothing. Fascinated with people sucking death into themselves while you watch. Terrified of death? But why? What is life, that it should be so valuable? Perhaps only the Something as opposed to the Nothing. The *only thing* that matters, then; the only thing desirable: that the camera should always have something new to fix on. Should not stop.

The Gospel
According to
Saint Mark

To write of this subject in this way is to acknowledge my place among the noninnocent.

It was not something you wrote about, or even something you read: it was what you heard. To come to it this way is strange, even false-seeming. The Bible as Literature. The Gospel as Narrative. Christ the character. Exposition. Denouement. These are words from a later time, a time in which experience is less sensually apprehended, less natural. The first encounter with it was before memory; it was a story that had nothing to do with history or print. We did not read the Bible; we were Catholics. In our house there was, of course, a Bible—the translation: Douay Rheims. We did not record in it the memorable events: birthdays, marriages, deaths. We rarely looked at it. We didn't need to; we were encouraged not to. We heard the truth, and the truth would set us free. The truth was not for reading.

Inevitable, like the seasons, were certain narrative events: the Passion, of course, and Christmas, the Ascension, Pentecost; but the stories took on the flavor of certain weathers. The narrative imprinted itself on household objects: toys. I had a puzzle of Jesus and the children; for my Bible stamp book, I licked the Multiplication of the Loaves and Fishes, Lazarus in his tomb. Above the examining table in my doctor's office, Jesus gave the blind sight.

The narrative was part of bodily life; like food or shelter. You were never apart from it.

Did I draw distinctions among the four evangelists? At the beginning of the Gospel, the priest always said who the story was according to. I never listened to that. Did I have any sense that certain stories were retold in different ways, that one writer included events that another left out, that some embellished on a simple incident and some condensed? Of course not. I stood; and heard. There was no notion of a text. We were not the people of the book; we were the people of the priestly utterance, the restricted information, interpreted, rendered safe only when spoken through the consecrated lips.

I cannot write about the Gospel in a form that suggests a coherent experience of it as a written whole; this would be untrue to what it was for me. The Gospel appeared to me as scenes. Not moving: static. Unconnected to each other, with a separateness that seemed sacred in itself, each scene with me like the color of my eyes.

And yet it would be retreating into a kind of false innocence to pretend that my contact with the Gospels ended when I heard them as a child—or as an orthodox believer. In college, fearing I touched the profane, I studied the New Testament. Hearing people talk about translations from the Greek, versions from different manuscripts, shocked and titillated me. They were talking about it as they would talk about an ordinary work: the epic of Gilgamesh, which we also read that term. I have read the Gospels as an adult, read them silently, alone, not leaving aside the literary sophistication that is part of me as well. But it is reading like no other reading: never disengaged; hooked to memory, belief, loss of belief, the knowledge that it has been a source of pain (in the impossibility of its standards) and growth (perhaps for the same reason). How, then, do I write about it? Perhaps without the illusion of cohesion. But not innocently. No.

I
SHE IS NOT DEAD BUT SLEEPING

The daughter of Jairus. The daughter of somebody important, someone with the confidence (would my father have had it? yes;

the other fathers in the neighborhood would not) to push through the crowd and get Jesus' attention.

The daughter of privilege. The apple of her father's eye. Servants tend her, but they are helpless. How beautiful she is; eyes closed, immobile. On her pallet. The word is exotic; it means the climate is temperate enough for one not to need a bed. So temperate one does not need the lightest covers. In the warm evenings, the breeze is caressive to the skin.

When Jesus gets to the house, He is told she is already dead. He doesn't listen. "She is not dead but sleeping."

If He can say it to her, He can say it to anyone. Perhaps death is always only a perceptual error.

I read: *Talitha cum*—in the middle of the English a foreign word. Immediately we are told what it means. Little girl, I say to thee: arise.

She gets up and walks. She is twelve years old.

For years, I measure my age against hers. I am younger than she at first. Then one year we are the same age: I could be rescued from death. By the time I realize that I am older than she, I no longer believe in the possibility of my own resurrection.

He tells them not to speak of it and to give her something to eat. I imagine Him leaving the house, leaving the others to what is always for me the food in the Gospel: bread and fish.

Reading it now, I discover that Jesus is interrupted on his way to Jairus' house. He is interrupted by a hemorrhaging woman. She doesn't even try to get his attention; she only wants to touch his cloak. Now I realize that this in itself was a daring act; perpetually menstruating, she was in a state of perpetual defilement. And Jesus, having cured her almost against his will (it is her contact with his clothing that dries up her hemorrhages), recoils for a moment, in the grip of a taboo: "aware that the power had gone out of him." The King James renders it "immediately knowing in himself that virtue had gone out of him": the old confusion in words, virtue— *virtu*—and power. In any case, strength and/or virtue is destroyed by contact with the defiled woman.

Jesus is not frozen in a state of primitive recoil. He does not call the woman unclean; He doesn't even refer to her former uncleanness. Jesus changes: something we were never taught to think of, something we were taught to think of as unimaginable. Impressed with the woman's faith, her self-forgetfulness, He overcomes his own initial primitive response. There is room in the kingdom even for the menstruating woman. She need not be set apart.

I have never heard anyone speak of this.

Only after this contact with the hemorraging woman does He go to Jairus' house, to be told that He is too late, the girl is dead. She is not dead but sleeping. She is twelve years old. Is it that she is dead to childhood? Jesus escorts her into womanhood; He permits her maturity. He allows her to move from the recumbent position of the privileged girl child to the ambulatory state of adulthood. He urges the others to bring her food. And then He leaves her.

I am reading the New English Bible. It doesn't say: "She is not dead but sleeping." It says: "The child is not dead, she is asleep." I feel that something has been stolen from me. I require the exact words. I look in the King James: "The damsel is not dead, but sleepeth." Worse. Pure literature. No good to me at all.

I don't have a copy of the Douay Rheims. I ask my mother. She says she thinks she lost it when she moved.

II
THE FIG TREE

Jesus curses the fig tree for conforming to natural law. Why is this incident exciting? It induces a kind of masochistic thrill; to observe sympathetically someone whose demands are, literally, supernatural, requiring not just heroism but betrayal of causality. Simone Weil took the parable terribly to heart: she identified with the fig tree. We are all less fruitful than we might be; we are all in the grip of nature. We would like to blossom, out of season, at a word.

The petulant, irritable Jesus. He appears often in Mark. Mark's tone is harsh. It wasn't something we were listening for in church: *tone.* But the idea of gentle Jesus meek and mild is certainly extratextual. Just after he curses the fig tree, He drives the money changers from the temple, another thrilling episode. No one could possibly identify with the money changers. Their shock, their venal faces registering mercantile outrage, the upraised arm of Jesus, brandishing the rope He uses as a whip, the doves, loosed from their cages, disoriented in the temple courtyard. It is violent: male.

He is often impatient with the pressing demands of the crowd; He is in conflict between the demands of the eternally growing multitude and his mystical nature, which requires solitude. There are always more blind, deaf, possessed. He keeps wanting to escape from them. We never noticed it. But even as He broke out of the frozen attitude of recoil from the menstrual taboo, He breaks out of the attitude of wearied impatience with the needs and the stupidity of the crowd. He says to the father with a possessed child: "What an unbelieving and perverse generation! How long shall I be with you? How long must I endure you?" This because the father insists upon Jesus actually laying on hands; he doesn't believe in the power of his own faith. Finally, though, Jesus responds to the father's less than fully mature needs and says: "Bring him to me."

III
BREAD TO THE DOGS

A Gentile woman comes to beg Jesus to drive the evil spirit out of her daughter. He says to her: "Let the children be satisfied first; it is not fair to take the children's bread and throw it to the dogs." The interpretation of this cruelty from the altar was that Jesus was testing her to show the greatness of her faith. But it also could be simple xenophobia: He thought, originally, that He was preaching to Jews. She beats Him on his own linguistic grounds. "Sir, even the dogs under the table eat the children's scraps." She bests Him using the technique He uses against the Pharisees: turning his own words against Him. But what a time for wordplay: who would say this to a mother, distraught over her child's possession?

She seems, however, to be one of the importunate women from whom Jesus learns. He sends her home; her daughter is cured. He has taken his first step in allowing the world outside the law of Moses into the kingdom.

We were never allowed to think of Jesus as someone who learned or grew or developed. Particularly in relation to a woman.

IV
THE DEVILS

"He would not let the devils speak because they knew who he was."

The possessed man, whose voice is the voice of his possessing spirit, also recognizes Jesus. "What do you want with me, Jesus, son of the Most High God? In God's name do not torment me." For Jesus was already saying to him, "Out, unclean spirit, come out of this man."

To personify evil as something existing outside the self, therefore capable of being removed from the self without impairing the self's integrity. As if evil were detachable, a growth, but one that moved and spoke. And yet the devils seem willing to cooperate with Jesus in his healing. It is their idea to enter into the pigs. *Their* idea or *his* idea: the identity of the devil in relation to the identity of the possessed man is confused. This is evident from the confusion of number: "*My* name is Legion, *he* said, there are so many of *us.*" The notion that the spirit seeks embodiment in the created world. Better to be embodied in a pig than to be bodiless.

The ability of evil to recognize God. To name Jesus, even against his will to be named. To conspire in breaking the messianic secret.

To frame evil in these terms is consoling. It implies the possibility of exorcism. Eighteen years ago, when the film *The Exorcist* came out, it became fashionable to consider hiring those priests who were qualified exorcists to try and cure the mentally ill. How long did the fashion last? What stopped it?

It would be helpful to someone who loved a mad person or a criminal to be able to conceptualize evil this way, as something apart from the person, randomly visited upon him, and perhaps as randomly removable. It lessens the crushing pressure of self-blame: a kind of healing in itself.

The stark visual drama of pigs hurtling over a mountaintop. The animal world responds to the authority of God, so it takes on a kind of animal force. Mark mentions the number of pigs: two thousand. We believe anyone who knows numbers. Any good storyteller, or liar, knows this.

V
THE BLIND MAN AND THE TREES

"The people brought a blind man to Jesus and begged Him to touch him. He took the blind man by the hand and led him away out of the village. Then He spat on his eyes, laid His hands upon him, and asked whether he could see anything. The man's sight began to come back and he said, 'I see men, they look like trees, but they are walking about.' Jesus laid His hands on his eyes again; he looked hard and now he was cured so he saw everything clearly."

The pleasure of partial vision. Did Jesus allow the man only as much vision as he could tolerate? Was the fullness of the visible world too much of a shock all at once? I keep thinking how pleasant it would have been, that partial state: no sharp differentiations, yet an awareness of a life, moving: proof that there are others outside the self.

What does it say, really, about Jesus as healer? There's something almost comic about the situation: I see men as trees walking—back to the drawing board. But there is something wonderfully non-coercive about Jesus' role, a sort of patience as healer and an eagerness to hear the man's version of his own experience. Jesus takes him out of the town. Respectful or reclusive? Or was it cruelty to take the man out of his pleasant distortion? Would it have been merciful to leave the man in the vagueness of perceptual half-truth. Was Jesus tempted to do that first, and then, respecting the man's right to painful sight, did He reject the temptation? Why does it seem like a loss of innocence? As if Mr. Micawber were given a compulsory course in economics. Illusion is not enough; more is demanded. Vision. Testimony. Distinctions made.

VI
JESUS AND THE CHILDREN

How we have fixed on this scene! Or *did* we fix on it before the Victorians fell in love with childhood? It's not, after all, a staple of Renaissance iconography, where the only interesting children were angelic or divine.

He was interested in children in a way that was really original. I look in the Biblical Concordance for references to children in the Old Testament: "in sorrow bring forth children . . . give me children or I die . . . the father's children shall bow down . . . Seled died without children . . . the children rebelled against me . . . as arrows in the hand, so are children . . . do not have mercy on her children . . . the children's teeth are set on edge . . ." Job pleads for the sake of the children, but Elisha sends a bear after the boys who made fun of him. Nowhere, though, is there concern for the education, the upbringing of children, the inner lives of children, the idea that they exist not as possessions, as markers, as earthly immortality, but in themselves. Jesus' concern for them is practical: How do we treat children to help them grow? How do we help children achieve salvation? He thinks seriously of their souls.

Jesus seems genuinely to want the physical presence of children, their company. We often hear Him trying to keep people away, or see Him trying to get away from them, but He rebukes the disciples for shooing the children away. He is described in an affectionate state. Surely, He is the only affectionate hero in literature. Who can imagine an affectionate Odysseus, Aeneas? Even the novel would be queasy, dwelling too long on a scene like this. Affection—a step, many steps below passion, usually connected to women. He is both maternal and paternal with the children. "He put his arms round them, laid his hands upon them, and blessed them."

And yet it is exactly this scene, this event, that generates His most harsh dualism. It is in relation to protecting children that He urges his followers to mutilate themselves in the face of temptation that might prove too strong. He puts his hands on the children and then urges his followers to cut off their own hands. He embraces the children and in the next breath tells the rich man that if he will not give up everything he cannot enter the kingdom of God. He blesses the children and then says, "there is no one who has given up home, brothers or sisters, mother, father or children . . . who will not receive in this age a hundred times as much— houses, brothers and sisters, mothers and children, and land—and persecutions besides; and in the age to come eternal life."

But of course it is exactly this extremism that makes Jesus not Victorian and therefore not sentimental. Is it possible to have a vision that is at once sentimental and eschatological? This may be the one new contribution of the TV evangelists: the angel with the flaming sword is guarding home and hearth. And, of course, the TV. Usually, though, it is the eschatological that prevents the sentimental, and for that reason, if for no other, it is desirable.

Jesus is a complicated character. Character in both senses of the word: literary and colloquial (as in: "He's a real character," implying the capacity for surprising behavior). Though we didn't know it, were not permitted to articulate it, the very complexity of Jesus' character, the self-contradictions, the progressions forward and backward, were what made Him so compelling, so that even after belief had ceased, we brooded on the figure.

In Jesus, the rejection, always, of the middle ground.

VII
THE ABOMINATION OF DESOLATION

The end of the world. This Gospel occurred at the beginning of autumn, the last Sunday in Pentecost. But the words "the abomination of desolation" seared and still cause reverberations. The days were beginning to be short, night would fall suddenly, without transition: darkness took over the face of the earth. You went inside the house, feeling vaguely guilty, anxious. There wouldn't be enough time. For what? Homework? Salvation? Simply, time was the devourer, seeking what it might devour.

In the fifties, it was mixed up with fear of the bomb, mixed up with the mornings of air raid drills spent hunched under desks or in the basement by the furnace, where the focus of my fear was not my own burning flesh but how I would find my mother. I knew it would be chaotic. My mother worked. Suppose she was on her way home, caught, ordered somewhere else while I roamed looking for her.

And then there were the false messiahs. Sermons concentrated upon those. The false messiahs of modern life, offering pleasure, prosperity. I knew myself susceptible to their lure. "If anyone says to you, 'Look, here is the Messiah,' or 'Look, there he is,' do not believe it." But whom would you believe? How would you tell the false messiah from the true? I had no faith in my powers of discernment; I knew myself persuadable. To go off with the false messiah, without my mother and without Jesus—the possibility terrified me and seemed, of all the possibilities, the most likely, for I knew my weaknesses and faults.

"Alas for women with child in those days, and for those who have children at the breast!" I knew I wanted children; I felt that those words were for me. Now I think: How many men would take into consideration the hardships of pregnancy and nursing?

"Learn a lesson from the fig tree. When its tender shoots appear and are breaking into leaf, you know that summer is near." He uses for his own narrative purpose the natural behavior of the fig tree, which He formerly cursed. Is He making amends?

The abomination of desolation. I have never heard another phrase that so fully captures the horror of annihilation. Desolation. We think of it as a species or adjunct of loneliness. But older meanings are more concerned with physical devastation. In the midst of devastation, there must be a terrible sense of loneliness; in the confusion and destruction, the quiet horror: I am alone.

"But in those days, after that distress, the sun will be darkened, the moon will not give her light; the stars will come falling from the sky, the celestial powers will be shaken. Then they will see the Son of Man coming in the clouds with great power and glory. Heaven and earth will pass away; my words will not pass away."

The end of anxiety and chaos: glory. Light-filled but silent, or perhaps only the sound of wind, rushing. When I thought of the word that would not pass away, did I think of the *Logos*? Of course not, but there must have been something comforting about the *word*, removed as it was from all the assaultiveness of apocalyptic imagery, which gave solace.

So by the time I left church, I was calmed down.

VIII
THE ANOINTING BY MARY

The figure of Mary was confused and conflated in my imagination. She was Mary the sister of Lazarus, who chose the better part (my ally, my hope in my rejection of the domestic for the intellectual); she was also the sinful woman, the prostitute. In my archetypal imagination, then, it was possible to be a contemplative and a prostitute but not a contemplative and domestic, and not a prostitute and domestic. It was this Mary whom I saw anointing Jesus.

It is Luke, not Mark, who suggests that the woman who anoints is a prostitute, and also that she wipes Jesus' feet with her hair. The story in Mark is much less erotically charged, but as Elizabeth Schussler-Fiorenza points out, it is politically more important. Schussler-Fiorenza thinks that Mark's version—an anointing of the head rather than the feet—is more likely, since a foot-washing would have been more commonplace and less worthy of note: "Since the prophet in the Old Testament anointed the head of the Jewish king, the anointing of Jesus' head must have been understood immediately as the prophetic recognition of Jesus, the Anointed, the Messiah, the Christ. According to the tradition it was a woman who named Jesus by and through her prophetic sign-action. It was politically a dangerous story."

It's the only story I've ever referred to in fiction. I describe it as justifying the sins of fat Renaissance bankers. In fact, it is the triumph of the aesthetic over the moral. It is Judas, the betrayer, who urges attention to the poor. Yet what is the Gospel all about, if not attention to the poor?

IX
THE MAN IN THE SHEET

An inexplicable passage. We are with Jesus in the Garden. Judas has just betrayed Him; one of the disciples has cut off the High Priest's servant's ear. (In Mark, Jesus does not replace the ear.) Jesus says, " 'Do you take me for a bandit, that I was within your reach as I taught in the temple, and you did not lay hands on me. But let the scriptures be fulfilled.' Then the disciples all deserted Him and ran away."

Among those following was a young man with nothing on but a linen cloth. They tried to seize him; but he slipped out of the linen cloth and ran away naked.

This is an image not susceptible to language. Silently, the identityless young man slips out of his linen cloth. They can't catch him. Where does he go, naked? We imagine him, running silently— but where? We have seen him to the side in early paintings. He is Mystery. Is he an angel? Lazarus? The embodied erotic other? He is entirely without context. He has nothing to do with context. At a point of almost unbearable tension, when Jesus has shown himself most truly vulnerable in human terms: the distraction of the running body. Unseizable. Without history or future. Faceless. Unknowable: the blank screen, the object of desire.

X
THE MEN HE WANTED

"He then went up to the hill country and called the men He wanted."

When I listened to the names they meant nothing to me; it was a signal for me to think my own thoughts. Now I understand that included in Jesus' group were a tax collector and a zealot. That is to say, an employee of the hated Roman Empire and a member of the party politically committed to overthrowing it. "And Judas Iscariot, the man who betrayed him." There was a place made even for the betrayer, only he unplaced himself.

This is perhaps the most important model that the Gospel offers us: the model of inclusiveness—of nonexclusiveness. The Church that later specialized in excommunication didn't learn it from Jesus' example in choosing a group of followers. The modern world, with its explosion of information, gives us more information, perhaps, than we can use about people's differentness from ourselves. We are forced to know that most of the world is unlike us, whoever we are. The crucial need, then, for the accommodation of difference. Can this be done without the genius leader, followed to the point of death? The history of the twentieth century has taught us the dangers of that kind of enterprise. What we have never had is the glimpse of a genius leader committed to embracing differences. It is not possible to imagine any longer: we have to posit a different kind of human being, to whom differentness meant something we can no longer recognize.

XI
THE EMPTY TOMB

After the black shock of the passion, the lightness of Easter. Lighter in tone—a different palate, but also insubstantial, incorporeal after the relentless physicality of Good Friday. But Mark, the harshest, the most spare of the Gospel writers, gives us an unhopeful Easter.

Many scholars believe that the manuscript actually ended with a failure of nerve. The women, seeing the angel at the empty tomb, are terrified. The angel tells them to bring the message of Christ's resurrection to the disciples, but they don't. It is believed that the original manuscript ended with this verse: "Then they went out and ran away from the tomb, beside themselves with terror. They said nothing to anybody but they were afraid."

How extraordinary, to end a heroic narrative with the words "they were afraid." Frank Kermode points out that Mark's ending really should read "they were scared, you see"—an abnormality more striking even than ending an English book with the word "Yes," as Joyce did in *Ulysses*.

To a modern, of course, the inconclusiveness, the pessimism, is satisfying, and more in keeping with the dour Mark, who found the disciples wanting, blind and uncourageous at every turn. The Gospel as we have it ends with Jesus' exhortation of the apostles to evangelize; it moves to his ascension and ends, with an unsatisfactorily dense, abstracted condensation: "Afterwards Jesus himself sent out by them from east to west the sacred and imperishable message of eternal salvation."

What would the history of the Church have been had one of the Gospels ended, not with the promise of victory, but with the proof of defeat?

FOR THE BEST IN PAPERBACKS, LOOK FOR THE

In every corner of the world, on every subject under the sun, Penguin represents quality and variety—the very best in publishing today.

For complete information about books available from Penguin—including Pelicans, Puffins, Peregrines, and Penguin Classics—and how to order them, write to us at the appropriate address below. Please note that for copyright reasons the selection of books varies from country to country.

In the United Kingdom: For a complete list of books available from Penguin in the U.K., please write to *Dept E.P., Penguin Books Ltd, Harmondsworth, Middlesex, UB7 0DA.*

In the United States: For a complete list of books available from Penguin in the U.S., please write to *Dept BA, Penguin*, Box 120, Bergenfield, New Jersey 07621-0120.

In Canada: For a complete list of books available from Penguin in Canada, please write to *Penguin Books Canada Ltd, 10 Alcorn Avenue, Suite 300, Toronto, Ontario, Canada M4V 3B2.*

In Australia: For a complete list of books available from Penguin in Australia, please write to the *Marketing Department, Penguin Books Ltd, P.O. Box 257, Ringwood, Victoria 3134.*

In New Zealand: For a complete list of books available from Penguin in New Zealand, please write to the *Marketing Department, Penguin Books (NZ) Ltd, Private Bag, Takapuna, Auckland 9.*

In India: For a complete list of books available from Penguin, please write to *Penguin Overseas Ltd, 706 Eros Apartments, 56 Nehru Place, New Delhi, 110019.*

In Holland: For a complete list of books available from Penguin in Holland, please write to *Penguin Books Nederland B.V., Postbus 195, NL-1380AD Weesp, Netherlands.*

In Germany: For a complete list of books available from Penguin, please write to *Penguin Books Ltd, Friedrichstrasse 10-12, D-6000 Frankfurt Main I, Federal Republic of Germany.*

In Spain: For a complete list of books available from Penguin in Spain, please write to *Longman, Penguin España, Calle San Nicolas 15, E-28013 Madrid, Spain.*

In Japan: For a complete list of books available from Penguin in Japan, please write to *Longman Penguin Japan Co Ltd, Yamaguchi Building, 2-12-9 Kanda Jimbocho, Chiyoda-Ku, Tokyo 101, Japan.*

FOR THE BEST IN LITERARY CRITICISM, LOOK FOR THE

☐ **THE MORONIC INFERNO**
And Other Visits to America
Martin Amis

With mixed feelings of wonder and trepidation, British writer Martin Amis examines America in an insightful, thoroughly stimulating collection of pieces.

"As surefooted in its march across cultural boundaries as it is enviably, infuriatingly fluent"—*The Boston Globe*

208 pages   ISBN: 0-14-009647-7

☐ **THE WRITER'S QUOTATION BOOK** (Revised Edition)
A Literary Companion
Edited by James Charlton

Updated to include more than 400 witticisms, confessions, opinions, and observations, this charming compendium covers every aspect of books and the writing life.

"Full of sparkle and wit"—*Cleveland Plain Dealer*

108 pages   ISBN: 0-14-008970-5

☐ **WRITERS AT WORK**
The *Paris Review* Interviews: Seventh Series
Edited by George Plimpton

As John Updike writes in the introduction to this volume, these interviews of Milan Kundera, John Barth, Eugene Ionesco, and ten others, are "testimonials to the intrinsic worth and beauty of the writers' activity."

"Even 300 years from now these conversations will be invaluable to students of 20th-century literature."—*Time*

332 pages   ISBN: 0-14-008500-9

You can find all these books at your local bookstore, or use this handy coupon for ordering:

Penguin Books By Mail
Dept. BA Box 999
Bergenfield, NJ 07621-0999

Please send me the above title(s). I am enclosing _____
(please add sales tax if appropriate and $1.50 to cover postage and handling). Send check or money order—no CODs. Please allow four weeks for shipping. We cannot ship to post office boxes or addresses outside the USA. *Prices subject to change without notice.*

Ms./Mrs./Mr. _____

Address _____

City/State _____ Zip _____

☐ **WRITERS AT WORK**
The *Paris Review* Interviews: Eighth Series
Edited by George Plimpton

These thirteen interviews of Elie Wiesel, John Irving, E. B. White, and translator Robert Fitzgerald, among others, reveal definitively that all writers are, in fact, creative writers.

"Long may this splendid series thrive."—*People*
446 pages   ISBN: 0-14-010761-4

☐ **THE SECRET MUSEUM**
Pornography in Modern Culture
Walter Kendrick

From the secret museums where the obscene frescoes of Pompeii were kept to the Meese Commission's report, Walter Kendrick drolly explores society's changing conceptions of pornography.

"Highly illuminating . . . Kendrick writes crisply and amusingly."
—*The New York Times*
288 pages   ISBN: 0-14-010947-1

☐ **THE FLOWER AND THE LEAF**
A Contemporary Record of American Writing Since 1941
Malcolm Cowley

Since the early 1920s, Malcolm Cowley has been reading, writing, and reflecting on literature; this collection of his work presents a fascinating portrait of our times and our literature.

"The creative logic of his connections make him a writer's writer and a reader's critic."—*Saturday Review*   390 pages   ISBN: 0-14-007733-2

☐ **THE WAY OF THE STORYTELLER**
Ruth Sawyer

In this unique volume, a great storyteller reveals the secrets of her art—then goes on to tell eleven of her best stories.

"As invigorating as a wind blowing over the Spring meadows"
—*The New York Times Book Review*
356 pages   ISBN: 0-14-004436-1

FOR THE BEST IN BIOGRAPHY, LOOK FOR THE

☐ **LIFE AND DEATH IN SHANGHAI**
Nien Cheng

Nien Cheng's background—she was a London-educated employee of Shell Oil, and the widow of an official of the Chiang Kai-shek regime—made her a target for fanatics of China's Cultural Revolution. Her refusal to confess to being an enemy of the state landed her in prison for six years. *Life and Death in Shanghai* tells the powerful, true story of Nien Cheng's imprisonment, resistance, and quest for justice. *548 pages   ISBN: 0-14-010870-X*

☐ **THE FLAME TREES OF THIKA**
Elspeth Huxley

With extraordinary detail and humor, Elspeth Huxley recalls her childhood on a small farm in Kenya at the turn of the century—in a world that was as harsh as it was beautiful. *282 pages   ISBN: 0-14-001715-1*

☐ **CHARACTER PARTS**
John Mortimer

From Boy George and Racquel Welch to the Bishop of Durham and Billy Graham, John Mortimer's interviews make compulsive reading, providing humorous and illuminating insights into some of the most outstanding characters of our time. *216 pages   ISBN: 0-14-008959-4*

☐ **GOING SOLO**
Roald Dahl

In this, the acclaimed memoir of his adult years, Roald Dahl creates a world as bizarre and unnerving as any you will find in his fiction.
"A nonstop demonstration of expert raconteurship" —*The New York Times Book Review*   *210 pages   ISBN: 0-14-010306-6*

You can find all these books at your local bookstore, or use this handy coupon for ordering:

Penguin Books By Mail
Dept. BA Box 999
Bergenfield, NJ 07621-0999

Please send me the above title(s). I am enclosing _____
(please add sales tax if appropriate and $1.50 to cover postage and handling). Send check or money order—no CODs. Please allow four weeks for shipping. We cannot ship to post office boxes or addresses outside the USA. *Prices subject to change without notice.*

Ms./Mrs./Mr. _____

Address _____

City/State _____ Zip _____

FOR THE BEST IN BIOGRAPHY, LOOK FOR THE

☐ **BROTHERS AND KEEPERS**
  John Edgar Wideman

One brother became a college professor and a prize-winning novelist—the other was sentenced to life imprisonment.
  "Powerful and disturbing . . . guaranteed to shock and sadden" —*The Washington Post*   *244 pages*   *ISBN: 0-14-008267-0*

☐ **THE BASKETBALL DIARIES**
  Jim Carroll

This is the witty, rebellious, intense book that made Jim Carroll's enormous underground reputation. Chronicling his coming-of-age on the mean streets of New York City in the early 1970s, *The Basketball Diaries* continues to be the distillation of the Carroll charisma.
                       210 pages   *ISBN: 0-14-010018-0*

☐ **LADY SINGS THE BLUES**
  Billie Holiday with William Dufty

In a memoir that is as poignant, lyrical, and dramatic as her legendary performances, Billie Holiday tells her own story.
  "Skillful, shocking, and brutal"   —*The New York Times*
                       200 pages   *ISBN: 0-14-006762-0*